STOLEN VIRUS

GARY F. JONES

BQB

Virginia

Published in the United States by BQB Publishing
(Boutique of Quality Books Publishing Company)
www.bqbpublishing.com

ISBN: 978-1-939371-92-8 (p)
ISBN: 978-1-939371-93-5 (e)

Library of Congress Control Number: 2016932239

Cover and book design by Robin Krauss, www.bookformatters.com

Other Books by Gary F. Jones
Doc's Codicil

To my wife Cheryl,
whose patience made the book possible;
to the many people whose critiques
improved and shaped the book;
and to my editor, Alex Padalka.

TABLE OF CONTENTS

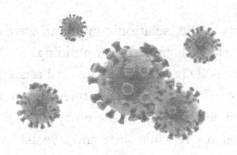

CHAPTER 1

University of Minnesota, St. Paul Campus
Evening, March 11, 2004

In the fading light, Jason drove between the leafless maple trees lining Gortner Avenue. He passed the entrance to the brick Veterinary Diagnostic Lab on his right and turned left into a parking lot. He and Joe, his fellow graduate classmate, left the car and headed to the edge of the lot where a chain-link fence surrounded the university's veterinary isolation facility. They stopped at the entrance gate, their breath turning to mist. It was seven o'clock and the temperature had dropped to eighteen degrees.

Jason took off his gloves and fumbled to get the key into the ice-cold padlock. Finally, he unlocked the gate and held it open for Joe, then closed and locked it behind him. Joe, recently arrived from China, hadn't worn a hat, and his bare hands were shoved deep into the pockets of a thin windbreaker. Jason shook his head and reminded himself to talk to Joe about wearing warmer clothes when they were finished tonight. Raised and educated in Michigan, he was continually surprised when students from tropical and sub-tropical regions tried to get by without buying winter clothing.

They took the sidewalk the fifty feet from Building A to Building

B. The only lights in the isolation compound were the single bulbs over the entrance to each cinderblock building.

Jason passed his ID badge under the card reader, listened for the lock to click, opened the door, and entered the men's locker room. He searched for a pen and signed the entry logbook as Joe stripped. Tall and lanky, Jason swept his shirt and sweatshirt over his unruly auburn hair and down his arms in a single motion. He hung them in a locker and turned to Joe. Shorter and stockier, Joe, in only his briefs and socks, was shivering and rubbing his arms with his hands.

It's at least seventy degrees in here, Jason thought. "Do you feel okay, Joe?" he asked.

Joe didn't feel well. "I'm okay. Still tired, still jet-lagged," he said, and hoped he was right. He hadn't felt well when he boarded his flight to the States four days ago, but he'd passed it off as nerves and claimed to be well when asked the standard questions at the airport. Approval to study in the States had taken a year of dodging bureaucratic pitfalls and he wasn't about to jeopardize the opportunity at the last minute.

Joe showered and stepped through to the sterile passageway on the other side, where clean towels and clothing were waiting. Jason followed.

"What was the temperature when you left Hong Kong?" Jason asked as they pulled sterile white coveralls over their scrubs.

"About eighteen degrees Centigrade. Hong Kong rarely gets below fifteen degrees in March, even at night."

Jason pointed toward a rack of tall rubber boots. "Find your size. It's printed on the bottom. Sterile boot covers are in the cabinet to your right." He thought a moment, converting Centigrade to Fahrenheit. "So Hong Kong is roughly sixty to sixty-five degrees Fahrenheit at this time of year?"

"Yes. Safety glasses?"

"They're in a box on the next shelf up, next to the latex gloves and face masks. Might as well grab those, too. Did anyone tell you about Minnesota weather?"

Joe paused; he didn't want to sound like a fool. "The graduate school sent brochures, but paperwork, packing—I haven't read them yet."

Their plastic boot covers scuffled on the floor as they walked down the brightly lit central hallway. The corridor was spotless; its glistening cream-colored concrete floor and walls smelled faintly of disinfectant. Dubbed the "clean hallway," nothing that might be contaminated was allowed to enter it.

They stopped in front of the first small window and watched the five black-and-white, two-day-old calves in the room. All had been inoculated with bovine coronavirus, or BCV. Three of the calves were indignantly bawling to be fed. The other two were lethargic, their tails coated with feces by diarrhea caused by the virus.

"There's an extra sweatshirt and coat in my car," Jason said. "You can wear them after we finish work. I'll take you shopping for warmer clothing tomorrow."

Joe thanked him and volunteered to feed and examine the calves. Jason noticed sweat on Joe's forehead but shrugged it off. The disposable coveralls were hot; the fabric didn't breathe.

Jason entered the next room and put nipple bottles full of warm milk out for the calves. These calves hadn't been inoculated with BCV, and all of them greedily set to work on the nipples, their fuzzy little tails twitching back and forth with pleasure. He completed his work and recorded his observations in a three-ring binder labeled "BCV Study No. 3." That done, he removed his coveralls, gloves, and boot covers, put them in a medical waste barrel, and exited the calf room to the "dirty" hallway.

The dirty hallway was identical to the clean hallway except for flat pans filled with bright yellow disinfectant sitting on the floor next to each door. Jason stepped into the nearest pan, scrubbed his boots with a long-handled brush, and waited for Joe to exit the first room.

Several minutes passed with no sign of Joe. Jason peered through the small window in the door but couldn't see Joe. Concerned, Jason showered, dressed as before, and took the clean hallway to the first calf room. The shower, change of clothing, and return to the clean hallway were required to control contamination between rooms. For the same reason, entry into rooms from the dirty hallway was never permitted.

Joe was standing in the center of the calf pen, hosing diarrhea into the large drain in the floor. He fiddled with the zipper of his coveralls with one gloved hand.

"You don't have to do that tonight," Jason said. "We only clean pen floors during the day."

Joe kept his head down and continued working. "No problem. Almost done." He finished hosing the brown liquid feces down the drain.

As the spray from the hose hit the floor, minute droplets carrying microscopic particles were blasted into the air throughout the room. The droplets were too large to be inhaled deep into the lungs, but they settled on the calves where they would be licked off during grooming.

The men exited through the dirty hallway, showered, dressed, and left the building. To the west, the campus was dark except for a few streetlights and a light over the entrance to the Diagnostic Lab. In the other direction lay the inky darkness of the empty State Fairgrounds and its vast parking lots. Jason found the extra clothes in his car for Joe and gave him a ride back to his apartment. It was only a ten-minute drive to the apartment complex on Lexington, but Joe asked midway to stop to use a bathroom.

Jason sat in the car at the gas station and looked around at the mud, dead grass, and leafless trees as he waited for Joe. *God, March is a dismal month in Minnesota, and the lakes and ponds just beyond the trees will be a damned heaven for mosquitos in summer,* he thought. He wondered if the graduate school had warned Joe about that.

It was eight o'clock when Jason got back to his apartment and crawled into bed. He'd begun his day at six that morning, trying to catch up on lab work from the previous calf study. Teaching, preparation of lab reagents, a literature search, and working with the calves had kept him busy the rest of the day and into the evening. Although Jason was exhausted, sleep remained elusive. In the dream world between waking and sleeping, his mind repeatedly played the scene of Joe hosing down the floor in the animal room. Something had been wrong, very wrong, but he couldn't identify it.

The next morning, Jason woke up to his alarm with a pit in his stomach. His apprehension increased when he arrived at Joe's to give him a ride, but Joe wasn't waiting outside his building. Impatient, Jason honked his horn a couple of times and waited several minutes. He swore, parked his car, and went to the intercom box. He pushed the button marked "Zedong Xue" repeatedly. There was no response. Jason stood by the door and waited until a blonde in a hurry exited the building. He caught the door before it closed, dashed up two flights of stairs, and trotted down the hallway to Joe's door. Joe didn't respond when Jason knocked, nor when he pounded on the door.

Jason called his graduate advisor, Professor Paul Schmidt, and was rolled into voicemail. He left a message to see if Joe had gotten another ride and got back in his car. He was going to be late getting to the lab.

Jason had to wait his turn on the metered ramp for the four-lane bumper-to-bumper crawl on Highway 36 to Snelling Avenue. Snelling wasn't as crowded, but he hit a red at every stoplight and nervously checked his watch as he turned into the empty State Fairgrounds. He remembered to slow down for the speed trap by the fair's grandstand and made it to the parking lot next to the campus without getting yet another ticket. Anxiously checking his watch, he swore and jogged the block to the dark brick Veterinary Sciences building. He stopped briefly at Paul's office.

Breathing hard from his run, Jason asked, "Were you able to reach Joe?"

Paul, his head bent over his desk revealing his thinning gray hair, was holding a phone to his ear. He looked up and covered the mouthpiece with his hand. "I have him on the phone now. He's coughing and sounds delirious—babbling in Mandarin or Cantonese."

"I'm teaching the lab this morning and I'm already late. I'll check in with you after class."

Paul dismissed Jason with a nod and tried talking to Joe again. "Joe, unlock . . . unlock your door and go to bed. I'm calling an ambulance for you."

Paul hung up and immediately called the University Hospital. "This is Professor Paul Schmidt on the St. Paul campus. A graduate student from Hong Kong is sick. He was coughing and his breathing sounded labored when I talked to him on the phone just now. He seemed to be delirious. Can I have an ambulance pick him up at his apartment?"

"Hong Kong! This kid is from Hong Kong?"

"Yes. He's a recent arrival."

There was a prolonged pause before Paul was given an answer. "I'll transfer you to an infectious disease specialist."

Waiting on hold, Paul tried to remember how often Jason and other students had been exposed to Joe. Few were aware of it, but a tourist from Hong Kong had introduced SARS to Canada last year. There'd been a twenty-percent case mortality rate. Paul searched for a bottle of antacids he kept in a desk drawer.

"This is Dr. Hatfield. You have a graduate student from Hong Kong with respiratory signs?" a man asked.

"Yes, and he had diarrhea last night. He flew in from Hong Kong five days ago. I thought—"

"Five days? From Hong Kong?"

"Yes. I—"

"Holy shit! What imbecile cleared his visa?"

"I thought I'd better give you a heads-up on this before you send an ambulance."

"Thanks. I appreciate the warning."

Paul heard muffled orders barked. He gave the doctor Joe's address and told him he would meet him there.

"We'll bring an extra hazmat suit for you. Don't even think of getting near him until my people arrive," the doctor responded.

Two days later, Paul stood outside the lecture hall, waiting for Jason to arrive. He spotted Jason's red hair in the crowd and beckoned him to step out of the flow of students. "Ready to give your first lecture?" Jason shrugged and tried to hide his apprehension. "Guess I'll find out soon."

Paul steered Jason to a space behind the last row of seats. "You shouldn't have any trouble, but don't mention your calf study, Joe, or SARS in this lecture. Understood?"

"Okay, but why?"

"The dean called this morning." Paul glanced at the students filing into the hall. "We'll talk about it later. Too many ears here."

No problem avoiding those topics, Jason thought. Most students slept through the bovine medicine lectures anyway. He walked to the front of the lecture hall and stepped up to the podium. A bell rang, and the clatter and chatter of the junior veterinary class died down.

Jason turned on the microphone. "Good morning. Many of you

know me from lab classes. For those who haven't met me, I'm Jason Mitchell, a veterinarian and a graduate student in virology. Professor Schmidt asked me to give today's lecture on bovine coronavirus, or BCV. I can also answer questions you have about next week's exam."

The students sat in groups depending on the type of medicine they expected to practice. The twelve budding cow doctors were in the first three rows of the center section, pens ready. Behind them and on the edges of the auditorium were eight students interested in swine medicine and four others who needed a good grade in something to pull up their grade point averages. They were paying attention but didn't seem eager about it. Scattered around the rest of the hall were thirty-five students who had made it clear they never expected to look at a farm animal again. They were reading the paper, doing crossword puzzles, or Sudoku.

Jason pulled up his first slide and tried to keep his eyes on the students who were paying attention. Watching the others ignore him was too rough on his ego. "Bovine coronavirus, or BCV, is the most common virus infecting cattle. Few animals reach six months of age without being infected. All of you are familiar with the sometimes fatal diarrhea BCV causes in neonatal calves," Jason said. He noticed two students sleeping in the back row. "Or at least you should be," he added.

He talked for thirty-five minutes about BCV and the diarrheal diseases it caused in older cattle, ending with one of Paul's favorite aphorisms: "In your future careers, remember that bovine coronavirus is a quasi-species, meaning it has a remarkably high rate of mutation. A highly mutable virus could give us a nasty surprise some day."

He turned the projector off and asked if there were any questions.

A student sitting in the front asked, "Does BCV cause respiratory disease in cattle?"

"One published study suggested BCV can cause pneumonia. Attempts to replicate those results have failed. Dr. Ann Hartman and

I . . ." Jason caught himself before he wandered into the forbidden topic. "Respiratory disease attributed to BCV will not be on the exam."

A student sitting in the back put down her crossword puzzle and looked at Jason for the first time during the lecture. "Dr. Mitchell, was yours the study that put the Chinese graduate student in the hospital? How is he doing?"

Jason almost choked. "Joe, ah . . . was hospitalized with pneumonia. There's no evidence his illness is related to the calf study."

A student in the front row asked, "Wasn't the sick student a recent arrival from China?"

Jason nodded. "Yes, he—"

"Is the SARS epidemic still going on there?" another student shouted. "Isn't that a coronavirus too?"

Paul should have told these students what topics were out of bounds, Jason thought. "SARS is caused by a coronavirus, but I believe the epidemic is over."

"What does SARS stand for?" someone asked.

"SARS stands for Sudden Acute Respiratory Syndrome," Jason said, "but this class only covers coronaviruses of veterinary interest, not human disease. Can we get back to questions about today's—"

"If the student just arrived from China, do you think he might have SARS? I heard there were sixty-seven cases of SARS and thirteen fatalities in Canada last year."

Jason swallowed hard and wondered what the dean would say about these questions. "Anything I say would be speculation."

A blonde in a tight sweater in the front row raised her hand. She was sitting with the students who planned to go into bovine practice, and Jason had seen her a few times in the cattle barn. *She's safe,* Jason thought, and asked her if she had a question related to BCV in cattle.

"Based on sequencing of the viral genes, the North American strain of BCV is the closest known relative of the SARS virus. Isn't it possible that a hybrid of BCV and the SARS virus could be produced if the student had SARS and was exposed to the BCV you gave to your calves?"

Sharp girl! Jason thought. *That was probably the question Paul and the dean wanted to avoid.* Perspiration on his forehead formed into large beads. He shuffled his notes and took a deep breath. "The two viruses are genetically similar, but this is not a lecture on SARS. The exam next week will be one-third of your final grade for this class. Are there any questions about the test?"

There were no more questions. A bell rang, and the class was over. Jason grabbed his notes and bolted for the exit. He took a hallway that slanted downward toward the Veterinary Teaching Hospital, and beyond that, the Vet Sciences building.

Three women from the class fell into step with him. A tall blonde woman on his left asked, "You didn't answer the question about a hybrid virus, but isn't that a possibility? It would explain the pneumonia we've heard your calves had."

"Yeah," a well-built brunette on his right said. "That's the way they think HIV originated. A chimp that ate monkeys was infected by two RNA monkey viruses. The viruses combined and HIV was born."

Jason looked past the brunette and saw salvation. "I don't want to speculate. Excuse me," he said, and dodged into a men's room.

As Jason stood at a urinal, the door swung open and a lanky Pakistani student came in. He put his book bag by the sink.

"Harith, were there three students—women—standing outside in the hallway?" Jason asked. "They might look like they're waiting for someone."

"I didn't notice any, but I'll take a look. Did you want me to ask one of them to come in and shake it for you?" Harith grinned.

Jason glared at him. "Very funny. Please, just check for me, will you? I got sucked into saying things I shouldn't have when I answered questions after my lecture. The three followed me down the hall, grilling me."

Harith chuckled and poked his head out the door. "You are in luck. The hallway is empty."

Harith bellied up to a urinal as Jason washed his hands. "Jason, my friend, how do you get into situations like this?" he asked, his eyes twinkling. "At home in Pakistan, no one ever stumbled into the troubles you do. We couldn't even imagine them. If I can't get a job in academia, I can support myself as a stand-up comic, just telling stories about you."

Jason leaned his head against the wall between the paper towel dispensers. "Give me a break, Harith. This isn't funny."

"Your first lecture must have gone well. I heard students chattering about it."

"They were interested in all the wrong things." Jason cracked open the door and peeked into the hallway. It was still empty. "Thanks, Harith. Catch you later," he said, heading for his office.

Jason unlocked the door to his tiny office and barely had time to sit at his desk before his pudgy officemate Mark walked in and told him Paul wanted to see him.

"You must have given a hell of a lecture," Mark said. "I walked by a group of students who were talking about it. Even the dean seemed interested."

"The dean? Aw, fuck!" Elbows on his desk, Jason held his head in his hands.

"Yeah. The dean was walking by when I passed a group of vet students hanging around a vending machine. He stopped when one of them said something about SARS. He was looking at a bulletin board, but I think he was eavesdropping."

"I'll be lucky if I'm not tossed out of school."

"Why? Most of us can't keep half the class awake for lectures on bovine medicine, but you had them talking about it in the hallways."

"Paul told me not to discuss my last study, Joe, or SARS in my lecture. Those were the only things the class wanted to talk about."

"Oh, they are talking," Mark said. "And for once the chatter is about biology instead of sports."

Jason shoved his chair away from his desk. "I better talk to Paul now or I'll be talking to the dean later."

He paused at the door and turned to Mark. "Don't tell anybody what I said about Paul's instructions, okay?"

"Got it. I won't say a word."

Halfway down the hall, Jason smacked himself in the forehead. The last time he'd asked Mark to keep something quiet, every graduate student in the department knew about it by lunch.

Paul's office was in a second-floor corner of the Vet Sciences building. The office, with ten-foot ceilings and windows on two walls, was large compared to most. Rank and years of tenure had their rewards. The office door was open and Paul was sitting at his desk. He waved Jason in. "Close the door behind you, please."

Jason cringed inwardly. He stepped into the office, shut the door behind him, and took a chair across the desk from Paul.

Paul looked over his reading glasses at Jason. "What in heaven's name did you say about SARS and your study? A couple of students stopped me in the hall to ask if it's true that Joe died of SARS, and whether you think he gave it to the calves. The dean called me to say he'd heard stories about a mutant super virus."

Jason turned pale. "I tried not to mention Joe or SARS, but Christ, that's all the class wanted to talk about. I didn't make any statements other than to say we do not know."

Paul nodded. The one constant in the life of a graduate advisor was that graduate students screwed up, each in their own way. Spreading rumors and gossip wasn't Jason's style. Jason was much more creative; his weakness—and his strength—was a tendency to generate reasonable sounding hypotheses based on skimpy data. That, and repair bills for expensive equipment.

"I thought it was something like that," Paul said. "Don't worry about it. I'll tell the dean what happened."

"How is Joe doing?"

"He's still in isolation. The hospital wouldn't give me any information, and Joe isn't in any shape to take phone calls. Scuttlebutt has it that investigators from the Center for Disease Control will visit us tomorrow."

"The CDC? What should we expect from them?"

"I'm not sure. We've never had anything like this happen before." Paul shifted in his chair. "Answer their questions, but for God's sake, do not speculate." He tapped a pencil on his desk for emphasis. "Stick to the facts. The people who should be nervous are the ones who allowed a sick kid to enter the United States from Hong Kong shortly after a SARS epidemic—an epidemic that started in Hong Kong."

"Do you think they've heard about our study results?" Jason asked.

"If not, I'm sure they'll ask. It was the CDC that identified BCV as a close relative of SARS." Paul leaned back in his chair. "There is no evidence Joe's illness was related to your study." Paul paused a moment. "Unless there's something you haven't mentioned."

"Joe had chills, I think he had diarrhea, and he was sweating the night we did the chores for the calves."

Paul looked at Jason warily. "And?"

"I left the isolation room Joe was working in for a few minutes. There were dark brown fluid feces on the floor near the drain when I returned."

Paul sat up in his chair with a jerk. "Not yellow? You're sure they were brown?"

"Right. The feces weren't from any milk-fed calves. It would have taken Joe several minutes to get out of his contaminated clothing and get to a toilet from that room. I think he took an emergency dump in the calf pen. That's what I would have done if I'd been in his shoes."

Paul began to speak slowly as realization dawned upon him. "If Joe had diarrhea in the calf pen, then the calves were exposed to whatever he has, and he was exposed to BCV." Paul's brow furrowed and he rubbed his chin. "That complicates things."

"Yeah. We finally produced a pneumonia in calves with BCV, but if Joe has SARS, we could have had a BCV-SARS hybrid virus in the study. That would explain the respiratory disease the calves have."

Paul cradled his chin in one hand. "God, I hope not. If Joe was infected with a hybrid virus, the CDC will see it as a potential biological weapon and bring in the FBI." He took off his glasses and rubbed his eyes. "You wouldn't believe how complex our lives will get if that happens. You'd better put sequencing the virus from the calves at the top of your priorities. Order whatever molecular kits you need to speed up the work."

Jason was surprised. Paul had lectured him about thrift yesterday, which usually meant that Paul had gone over budget and was in the red. This was embarrassingly common in the department. It seemed as though professors engrossed in their work were unable to do the simplest budgeting tasks. Whatever the reason, the kits that simplified lab work were fiendishly expensive. "Will our budget cover that?"

"Money isn't an issue. The dean will find whatever funds we need. If this virus can cause a fatal pneumonia in people like it did in those calves, BioSafety Level 3 precautions are mandatory. Everything exposed to the samples must be autoclaved, incinerated, or disinfected by an approved protocol."

"That could delay things. I'd better get busy."

As Jason stood to leave, Paul said, "The dean wants an inventory of samples from the study and new padlocks on all the freezers you and Ann use to store your samples. I asked Ann to take care of it this morning. Check with her. She may need help."

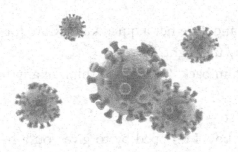

CHAPTER 2

St. Paul
Evening, March 14

Jason, wearing jeans, a T-shirt, and oven mitts, reached into his oven and pulled out a pizza. He turned, kicked the oven door shut with his heel, slid the pizza onto a cardboard circle, pulled off the mitts, and rubbed his hands in anticipation. There was a knock at the door as he picked up his pizza cutter.

His shoulders sagged. "What the hell?" He put the pizza cutter down and headed to the door, kicking a couple of empty pizza boxes lying on the floor out of his way. Jason's housekeeping schedule depended on whether he expected Ann to visit. He'd been dating her exclusively since their senior year in vet school.

Sexual exclusivity would have seemed sacrificial to him in his undergrad years, but a furious co-ed with a nose for traces of strange perfume taught him his choices were either monogamy or laundering his sheets regularly. It hadn't been a tough choice. In equal measure, he was devoted to Ann and to ignoring his laundry.

His irritation melted as he opened the door and saw a big smile on the face that had captivated him since they'd met in vet school at Michigan State. "Ann, come in." He embraced the willowy brunette in front of him and gave her a quick kiss. "Care for some pizza? Did you come to stay the night?"

She kissed him back. "Don't you think of anything but food and sex?"

"But you're so—"

"Can it, big boy. I dropped by to give you a heads up on some odd lab results." She brushed past him and walked into his kitchen. "Mmm . . . smells good. Pepperoni and sausage?"

Jason came up behind her, put his arms around her waist and nuzzled her neck. "And peppers and mushrooms. Is that the only reason you came over?"

Ann snuggled against him. "With everything that's going on, I couldn't face the night alone." She turned and kissed him.

Jason was conflicted. His two favorite things in the world, Ann and food, demanded his attention. "Care for salad and pizza? The pizza is done."

Ann looked at the table. "Where's the salad?"

"I'll slice the tomatoes if you clean and chop the lettuce. Deal?"

"Deal, but put on a clean shirt." She tapped an index finger on the largest of a collection of tomato sauce and ketchup stains on Jason's T-shirt, avoiding other blotches of less certain provenance. "This shirt gives 'grungy' a bad name."

Jason went to his bedroom to change and Ann found the lettuce in his refrigerator. She rinsed it and searched under and around the clutter and dirty dishes on the counter for a clean bowl. She wondered if Jason ever cleaned his kitchen. Lifting a coffee cup, she grimaced at the brown crust around the lip. "Yuck! How do you . . ." She stalked into the bedroom. "Damn it, Jason. I hope you've been washing your sheets more often than you clean your kitchen."

"Unhh," Jason mumbled. A quick calculation and he decided honesty was an extravagance his budget didn't cover. "Of course."

Ann chose to believe him rather than spend the night alone in her apartment. She returned to the kitchen and began clearing the table. "I heard about your lecture this morning. Actually, I heard several versions of your comments on SARS, Joe, the super virus, and the coming pandemic."

"What?" Jason scrambled out of the bedroom, a long-sleeved shirt partially buttoned, his jeans unsnapped, and his fly open.

"I was in the break room at noon." Ann looked up from cleaning the table and waggled her eyebrows. "Were you planning on entertaining me with a show this evening?"

"Uh, no." Jason finished dressing. "What were the stories you heard?"

"Some of the grad students were comparing stories about your lecture. I think there were a few vet students there, too. Paul and Bill were brown-bagging it, and Paul looked like he choked on his sandwich when he overheard the conversation at the next table. He stood up, got everyone's attention, and said we sounded like a group of gossiping old ladies. 'As professionals, you'd better learn to squelch gossip instead of spreading it or the dean will do something to make the lesson stick,' he said. He really looked pissed."

"Christ!" Jason leaned against the kitchen counter. "It all started when students asked a bunch of questions about Joe and our study after the lecture. When I dodged the questions, they made up their own theories. Some hit damned close to what I think occurred. I explained what happened to Paul before lunch, and I'd hoped that was the end of it."

Jason looked so forlorn that Ann stopped cleaning and gave him a friendly hug. "Don't worry. I don't think he's blaming you."

She gave him a kiss. "I tested fecal samples from the calves today. The results were weird. The samples should have been strongly positive for BCV, but they were only weakly positive or suspect."

Jason put his hands on the back of a chair, leaned forward, and stared absently at his table as he thought through the possibilities.

The table—a red wobbly 1960s Formica and chrome eyesore with two God-awful matching chairs—was a paean to Jason's thrift.

He explained to Ann the theory of the hybrid virus he'd discussed with Paul. "A new virus would have spread like wildfire in those calves."

Besides the physical attraction, what drew him to Ann was their mutual interest in biology. He could talk to her about virology and molecular biology without boring her or wondering if she understood. Ann's practical approach to science and medicine kept his tendency to concentrate on the theoretical in check. They were a team, as well as lovers.

Ann pursed her lips slightly and considered Jason's hypothesis while he continued. "The test you used would have been screwed up if the mutation was in the gene for the BCV spike protein, because that's the protein the test identifies. It's also the protein that determines what cell type the virus can infect. That would explain why the virus infected cells in the lungs instead of the gut."

"Okay," Ann said. "So a hybrid of BCV and SARS would explain the calf pneumonia and my odd test results today. You'll have to sequence the gene for the spike protein from the virus we get from the calves to prove that."

"Right. I'll ask Paul tomorrow who can help us with the extra work. We're both already swamped."

Ann put her elbows on the table and rested her head in her hands. "Bill told me the dean doesn't want anyone else exposed to our samples. We'll have to do all the work ourselves." She shook her head and looked at Jason. "It will take us forever to finish this."

"Shit!" Jason took a deep breath. "Has the dean heard about everybody working with BCV and the calves getting diarrhea?"

Ann shrugged. "That was with a different group of calves, before Joe joined our group, and everyone recovered in forty-eight hours.

It couldn't have anything to do with the respiratory disease of this group of calves."

Jason smiled and raised an eyebrow. "True, but it might have saved our butts. We were exposed to BCV, recovered, and were immune to it before the virus mutated. That may have given us a partial immunity to a hybrid virus." He glanced at the pizza. "The pizza is getting cold. Let's talk about this later. I have an idea to reduce our work, too."

"So, what's your idea?" Ann asked as Jason cut and served the pizza.

"Once the DNA and RNA are purified from our samples, the virus won't be infective. Paul can have anyone do the sequencing."

Ann chewed her bite of pizza until she could speak. "I think I love you."

Jason was stunned. He hadn't thought of their relationship in terms of love before, but the word fit. Comfortable with that, he still wasn't comfortable saying the L-word. "Well, ah, it isn't that great an idea."

Ann finished her pizza, dropped the paper plate in the trash, and wondered why guys were so afraid to commit. "Okay, be that way." She walked to the bedroom door, turned toward Jason, and unbuttoned her blouse. "You can sleep on the couch, under the table, or in bed with me. Which will it be?"

Jason nearly turned the table over scrambling to join her. At the door, she put her hand on his chest. "Not so fast, Romeo. Are we in love, or do you still think I was talking about your great idea?"

"Aahh . . ."

"Are we in love or do guys always think with the wrong head?"

With enough prodding and a few hints, even Jason could sometimes come up with the right answer. He put his arms around her and kissed her gently. "I've been in love with you for years."

St. Paul Campus
10:30 p.m., March 14

It was late, closing time at the Student Union. The few who saw
Ahmed descend the stairway thought nothing of it, although those
who were more observant noted that he glanced around nervously.
His confidence seemed to grow as he walked through the dimly lit
hallways and tunnels, from the basement of the Student Union,
under the street, through the administration building, and past the
lecture halls.

He kept to the shadows even though he knew only a few
students would still be in the labs, animal rooms, and maze of
hallways of the University of Minnesota veterinary school. He would
be home in Pakistan before anything was missed—but why take a
risk?

He entered the veterinary complex at the lecture halls on the
west and took a flight of stairs to the basement. The buildings of
the vet school were built on a slope. The basement, buried in the
hill, was the second floor of the Veterinary Teaching Hospital at the
other end of the building. He caught a whiff of formaldehyde a few
yards down the hallway. Through the open door of the anatomy lab,
he saw a clutch of desperate veterinary students gathered around
stainless-steel tables examining dog cadavers. *Must be a test tomorrow,*
he thought. He knew they'd ignore him.

The clang of steel slamming on steel startled him. His heart
racing, he pressed his back against the rough brick wall and checked
the hallway in each direction.

Empty.

He looked at his watch and relaxed. An intern would be doing late-night treatments in the wards. The sounds were cage doors slamming shut. No one in those rooms could see him.

He took a passage past an upright freezer sitting in the hallway and the open door of a teaching lab. A student in the lab, engrossed in her work, muttered to herself and swore as he walked by.

Ahmed recognized Margie, a senior veterinary student who never admitted to making a mistake. He didn't recognize the resemblance, but Margie's arrogance and attitude of entitlement mirrored his and that of his mother. That made him loath her.

His mother was from a liberal, politically connected family; his father, an army general and a martinet, came from a conservative military family. Ahmed carried the scars of the internecine warfare of his parents' marriage. Each had used him against the other, and he had returned the favor. Never exposed to unconditional love, he cared only for himself; used as a tool by his parents, he learned to manipulate others; caught between warring parties, his only principal became to get what he could.

The scholarship for graduate work in the US allowed him to put half the world between himself and his parents. He'd needed time to be away from their domineering influence, but American culture came as a shock. His arrogance masked a deep insecurity, and he'd walked a tightrope of social anxiety for five long years, afraid of looking foolish in public. Knowing that would be over was exhilarating. In a few hours, he would be on his way home, where he would no longer have to be polite to pushy women like Margie.

He took the second-floor walkway to the Vet Sciences building on Commonwealth Avenue as Margie tried to make sense of the petri dishes in front of her. She'd inoculated them the day before with an assigned unknown bacteria. Correct identification of all species of bacteria in the sample was a major part of the final grade in her course.

The bacterial samples she'd worked with as an intern at Cold Spring Harbor last summer were pure laboratory strains, and she'd developed bad habits in the lab. When Ann, the lab teaching assistant, reminded her that she had three different bacteria in her unknown and demonstrated the correct technique to separate them, Margie became huffy. If a laboratory that had won eight Nobel prizes in physiology and medicine praised her work, who was Ann to criticize her?

Had she paused to think, Margie would have realized that techniques adequate for culturing pure laboratory strains may be totally inadequate for working with mixed or contaminated bacterial samples. Instead, she ignored Ann's advice.

Tonight, for the fourth time she put a glass slide on the microscope stage, adjusted the focus, and saw tiny red rods scattered among small blue balls. Another in a string of impossible answers to her lab tests!

It was supposed to be a fun course, but life is hard when you ignore the advice of experts and cling to a conviction that you're right, despite evidence to the contrary. True, it works in politics, advertising, and marketing, but it sucks in science. Every test Margie ran produced contradictory results.

Margie was under pressure. A straight-A student since kindergarten, she had been a grade hound through high school, her undergraduate education, and for almost four years of vet school. She was so close to being a Doctor of Veterinary Medicine she could taste it, but now she faced a flunking grade and expulsion from vet school. Even were she readmitted to the veterinary program next year, getting into graduate school or an internship at a veterinary college would be difficult with a low grade in this stinking three-credit course.

Margie went over the edge. "Again! It doesn't make sense." She slammed her palm on the lab bench, tears welling in her eyes.

"Miserable fucking three-credit lab course." She sat on her lab stool and sobbed in frustration. Margie was in a raging hell of her own making as Ahmed entered the main hallway of the Vet Sciences building and headed for the elevator.

He took the elevator down two floors and walked west down a dark basement corridor. Others might walk hunched over in an unlit basement hallway. That wasn't his style, and style was important. He'd never worn the cutoffs and T-shirt that were the spring, summer, and fall uniform of grad students in the basic sciences. A patrician in his native land, in his five years at Minnesota he'd dressed better than most of the faculty. Lazy and snobbish, he valued appearance and status over ability and knowledge.

Grad students were expected to work like slaves. Ahmed had never been treated like that at home and hadn't submitted to it here. That didn't go over well with the faculty, and he bounced from one graduate advisor to another. As his government liberally funded his education and his research, the graduate school couldn't afford to expel him. Instead, the dean borrowed a page from the tactics of used car salesmen to coax graduate advisors to overlook his faults in return for supplemental funding for their projects. It remained a hard sell until Professor Nagabushana agreed to take him on.

Nagabushana was a short man, an East Indian with a dark complexion and a bushy, black mustache. Years ago he'd asked everyone to call him John or Naga as Americans seemed unable to wrap their lips around the syllables of his given name. He was sharp, but he often made his points crudely and aggressively, and he didn't know when to shut up when talking to university administrators. He often spoke too loudly for his own good, too.

Shortly after Naga took him on, Ahmed heard him talking with another professor. "Damn! Look at this letter." Naga had thrown a paper on his desk. "The dean of the graduate school has threatened to pull my right to have graduate students if another of my graduate students quits. My career will be ruined."

An hour later, Ahmed complained to Naga that he had too much work and threatened to quit. Naga was trapped. He had no recourse other than to do the work for Ahmed.

Naga hadn't taken the abuse silently. He'd railed against Ahmed and insulted him daily, but Ahmed knew he had leverage, and he used it. Naga despised sloth and sloppy work as only a man who'd worked hard all his life can, and Ahmed's air of entitlement had grated on him even before he'd forced Naga to do most of the work on his project. Ahmed was Pakistani, and Naga was Indian. That had made things worse.

Ahmed patted his airplane tickets to Pakistan in the breast pocket of his jacket as he walked down the dark hallway. In a few hours, Naga wouldn't be able to touch him.

Ahmed stopped at the door to a lab. He entered, turned on the lights, and checked the numbers on three upright freezers in the far corner, searching for the one in which Naga stored the samples from their studies. He could take his time. Anyone who happened to walk by wouldn't see him. He was screened from the door by outmoded or unused lab equipment piled on the long lab bench running the length of the room. The bright light from the long florescent tubes in the ceiling-mounted light fixtures made reading the numbers easy. The freezer identified, he pulled out his key.

It didn't fit the padlock on the latch welded to the freezer door. The padlock didn't look like the standard ones the university used, and it was so new the price sticker was still on it.

He dug through his book bag and brought out a small hacksaw. This would take longer than planned, but he had time. He was getting cramps in his hand and forearm by the time the saw broke through the last of the hardened steel of the padlock. The lock off, he found the samples from his studies and pulled them out. Naga would need these for future work. *Good luck with that*, he thought. Tonight, Ahmed was taking revenge for the insults and expletives Naga had thrown at him over the last two years.

As he pulled the last of his samples from the freezer, he noticed a new box of samples sitting next to his. He read the label on the box: *A. Hartman/J. Mitchell, BCV Calf Study # 3*. Ahmed examined the white cardboard box, his mouth hanging open.

These were the samples from the BCV study! That explained the new padlock. He opened the box. Six inches on a side and four inches tall, it was nearly empty. There were only ten small plastic vials in a box with slots for fifty.

He'd heard about the study and its startling results. After the story of Paul's instructions got around, even the janitors were talking about the virus, the FBI's involvement, and the conspiracy to keep it quiet.

Ahmed smiled. He'd picked up skills in manipulating people in the years of playing his parents against each other. Those skills gave him the courage to seize this opportunity. In his imagination, new possibilities sprouted like weeds in an empty lot. His hands held a potential weapon, a weapon of mass destruction. He let his mind wander lightly over the trouble spots of the world.

North Korea—no. That government had scientists of its own. They'd have no need to keep him around once he delivered the virus. He could end up a tastefully dressed corpse.

Pakistan? He didn't want to be anywhere near his parents, and the government already had nuclear weapons. They had no reason to work on something as chancy as biological weapons. Ahmed wasn't familiar with whatever unrest was present in South America, and sub-Saharan Africa was too poor to consider. There were so many pathogens rampant in the populations and wildlife already that one more was unlikely to impress a government.

He needed a client who would pay, a client without a cadre of virologists to question his expertise or do the work themselves. His client must not be on friendly terms with the U. S. Extradition was such a nasty word. His future compatriots should have money—or provide a home where living high could be done on the cheap.

Insurgents? Terrorists? He'd never had a modicum of sympathy for their causes, but he could be flexible. He could even play religious zealot if the pay was right, living was comfortable, and no one expected him to become a martyr. With terrorist and insurgent groups multiplying from Ethiopia to Somalia and north to Syria, he was certain he could parlay these samples into wealth and independence with one of them.

He shoved his plans for revenge aside and stuffed the vials from the box into his book bag. But what if Ann or Jason checked their samples before he could disappear? An empty box was too obvious. He smiled as he remembered that samples frozen at minus seventy quickly frost over when brought from the freezer, making it difficult to read the attached labels. Any vials of the right size might delay discovery. He replaced the stolen samples with vials from his study, examined the box critically, and congratulated himself. The box would pass a cursory inspection.

His bike chain and padlock were in his book bag. He put his padlock on the freezer, and made sure it was locked. Satisfied a casual observer wouldn't notice anything amiss with the freezer, he checked his watch. It was getting late; he'd have to hurry to pack and make his plane. Ahmed threw his book bag over his shoulder and hustled to the elevator.

Two floors above, Margie stomped out of the lab, tears blurring her vision. She dabbed at her eyes with a tissue and wiped her nose, silently cursing the teaching assistants in the lab. Her work had been praised at Cold Spring Harbor, one of the premier molecular labs in the world! It couldn't be her fault if she flunked a simple lab course in a fucking fly-over school!

She took the elevator down and stormed through the door as soon as it opened, slamming into a well-dressed teaching assistant equally impatient to get on the elevator.

The man glared at her. He shoved her out of his way, pushing her back into the elevator. "Watch where you're going, slut."

The elevator door closed, and Margie was trapped with the bastard. She lunged past him and hit the "door open" button. He shoved her against the elevator wall and aimed a finger at the "close door" button. Margie wasn't going to be a docile victim if this guy was thinking of sexual assault. She blocked his hand and forced him to turn toward her.

Margie had never even slapped a stranger before, but she'd never been this pissed off and had a jerk give her an excuse, either. "You miserable—" a knee there, "fucking—" swing with an elbow here, "male chauvinist—" a kick to the kneecap, "—pig," and her years of martial arts training had paid off. The elevator door was open. She stepped over the moaning figure on the floor and strutted down the hallway to the exit and the student parking lot, her tears forgotten.

Outside, Margie took a deep breath of the sharp Minnesota spring air and walked to her car in the moonlight. "God, it's a beautiful night to be alive," she told the empty parking lot.

Ahmed lay motionless for several minutes, blood spraying in a mist from his broken nose. He moved to a kneeling position and screamed from the pain in his knee and groin. Using the steel handrails in the elevator, he struggled to a standing position and punched the button for the second floor. Gasping in pain, he hobbled into the hallway when the elevator doors opened.

Walking was unbearable unless he kept his right knee rigid, and blood gushed from his nose. He remembered that Naga had a first-aid kit in his lab and shuffled down the hallway to get it.

The lab was a bloody mess by the time he finished bandaging his knee and stuffing cotton gauze in his nose. He took a perverse pride in having made more work for Naga as he limped down the hallway and tossed his keys under Naga's office door.

The walk back to his car was hell. He worried briefly about the bloody trail his shoes had left, but pain outweighed caution. When he reached his car, he found he couldn't use his right foot for the accelerator or brake pedal, and his swollen balls made movement of either leg painful when he sat. Gingerly, he put his right leg into the passenger side and used his left foot to drive.

He needed help and could think of only one safe place to seek it, but first he needed to track down some insurgent websites and begin the auction for his samples.

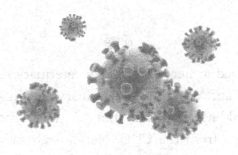

CHAPTER 3

St. Paul Campus
7:45 A.M., March 16

Graduate students and veterinary students were a cross-section of bright men and women, most in their mid-twenties. Some were mature and responsible, others not so much. Paul had posted a sign in his lab once, announcing that since no one's mother worked in the lab, the students should clean up after themselves. The email he'd just received from the dean suggested he might have to resurrect the sign.

Paul spotted Jason coming into the Vet Sciences building and beckoned to him to enter his office. He put his glasses on and reread the email as Jason entered. "Do you know anything about blood spilled in the hallways and elevator yesterday or last night?"

"No," Jason said. He hadn't collected any blood yesterday, and he didn't know of anyone who had.

"The dean got a complaint from the janitorial crew about blood spatters in the elevator and hallways. The janitor's union rep was hopping mad. His people don't have to clean up after lab accidents and spilled samples. Remind the other graduate students to clean up after themselves, would you?"

When Ann arrived at her office in the veterinary teaching hospital, she found Carla and Wendy, two veterinary students waiting for her. So was a tall, balding gentleman in a suit. He introduced himself as Dr. Al Gettelman from the CDC. Nervous about attention from a Federal agency, Ann put her briefcase down, unlocked her door, and invited him in.

"If you have time, I'd like to ask a few questions and collect throat swabs from you," Gettelman said.

Ann agreed and asked the students to wait as Gettelman took a clipboard and culturettes out of his briefcase and took a seat by her desk. The office door was still open. Carla and Wendy were leaning against the wall across the hallway from her door. They seemed to be examining their notes, but each had an ear cocked toward Ann's office door.

"Wait a second," Ann told Gettelman. She walked to her door. "I'll be busy for a few minutes," she told the women. "Why don't you go to the break room and come back in ten minutes?"

Ann closed her office door. "There will be enough chatter about your visit without students reporting on our meeting. Now, what was your question?"

Gettelman smiled and Ann thought he was making an effort to put her at ease. He asked her how she felt, whether she had symptoms of respiratory disease, and how much time she had spent with the Chinese student. Ann shrugged. "I am well. I have no signs of respiratory disease, and I met the student twice. Each meeting was brief, and I wasn't that close to him."

"What type of work was the student doing?"

"He assisted for two days in the feeding and observation of calves in a bovine coronavirus study."

Gettelman looked up from his clipboard with a jerk. "He was working with BCV?"

"With infected calves, yes. We're trying to determine if BCV can cause pneumonia in cattle."

Gettelman's smile disappeared. He tapped a finger on the clipboard, apparently lost in thought. "Have you been successful?"

"Not until the last study. The calves we infected on Monday had pneumonia by Thursday morning."

Gettelman stroked his chin. A possible case of SARS in a large population center was dangerous enough; he didn't need further complications. "Please describe the background of the virus and your results."

Ann leaned back in her chair. "Jason gave a relatively harmless BCV virus to day-old baby calves. He infected the first group, waited three days, collected feces from the calves, and gave it to the next group by stomach tube. After three days, calves in the first group barely got sick. Calves in the third group became so sick they had to be euthanized three days later to prevent suffering. Our challenge virus was collected from the feces of those calves."

Gettelman's eyebrows shot upward and he swore under his breath. "That's an impressive increase in virulence in nine days."

"Jason says it's a textbook case of increasing virulence by rapid passage in highly susceptible animals. The virulence of a pathogen is limited by how quickly it can spread to a new host. We provide that passage, and a rapidly mutating virus like BCV goes wild."

"Jason would be—"

"Dr. Jason Mitchell. Jason and I were in the same veterinary class at Michigan State. Paul Schmidt is his graduate advisor. Jason's something of a theoretical biologist; he's also studying the evolution of virulence in pathogens in the School of Public Health."

Gettelman leaned back in his chair. "Can you describe your most recent study?"

"We inoculated baby calves with BCV by blowing it in their nose or giving it by stomach tube. The calves were observed daily for a week. Joe worked with the calves for two days before he was hospitalized. Only the calves that were exposed to Joe and were given the virus by stomach tube developed a severe pneumonia." Ann glanced at a paper on her desk. "The pneumonia was fatal for sixty percent of those calves."

Puzzled, Gettelman looked through his list of names. "Who is Joe?"

"Zedong Xue. Don't hold me to that pronunciation, 'cause I know I butchered it. He asked us to call him Joe."

"Joe is the sick Chinese student?"

"Yes. Can you tell me how he's doing? Has a diagnosis been made?"

"I'm sorry, but others from our office are handling that end of the investigation," Gettelman lied. "Now, if I could collect the samples I need, I'll be done." He collected nasal and throat swabs from Ann and put the swabs in plastic sleeves for transport. "Your primary-care physician will call you with the results in a few days."

He shook hands with Ann, opened the door to leave, and turned back to her. "Could you direct me to . . ." Gettelman glanced at his notes, "to Dr. Mitchell's office?"

Ann returned from escorting Gettelman to Jason's office as Carla and Wendy arrived from the break room. She motioned them into her office and handed them a small three-ring binder. "These are inventory sheets for the samples collected during BCV calf studies two and three. We need to verify that the sample vials listed are actually in these freezers. Our freezers are old and compressors have failed. Two of the freezers we used crashed, and samples were shifted to other freezers, but the inventory wasn't updated."

The freezers failed in July, months before Ann's studies began, but it was the best excuse she could think of for verifying the inventory without mentioning the dean's directive.

Wendy, a woman slightly younger than Ann, paged quickly through the inventory sheets and asked, "What freezers are your samples in?"

"Room and freezer numbers are at the top of each sheet." Ann tried to keep the tone of her voice casual as she continued. "Wear scrubs, safety glasses, surgical face masks, and latex gloves. Change gloves and scrubs between freezers and be sure to shower when you're done for the day."

Carla, a tall blonde with a weathered face, was almost forty. A bright woman, she'd been bored with a dead-end job and returned to college as a non-traditional student. The administration thought that sounded better than "old." She and Wendy looked at each other with wide eyes. They'd never been told to take these precautions before.

Ann saw the look. "We can't risk a student becoming contaminated and dragging a hot BCV home to the family dairy," she added, trying to repair the damage.

Ann saw Carla give Wendy a quick look and silently mouth, "yeah, sure." Ann pretended she hadn't seen it and handed Carla a ring of keys. "Here are the keys to the padlocks I put on the freezers. If you have questions, you've got my cell phone number."

Carla asked why the freezers didn't have the standard university locks.

Ann hesitated. Every question she answered stoked the rumor mill. "Professor Schmidt asked me to put my own padlocks on the freezers. We've lost track of who has keys to the university's locks."

Wendy and Carla gave each other another look and Ann decided to cut the questions off or she'd be reading about her study in the

St. Paul Pioneer Press. "Give me a call if you have questions. I'll be in the tissue lab." She picked up a manila folder and took a step toward the door.

"Is it okay if we don't finish until Saturday?" Carla asked.

"Saturday is fine," Ann said. "I'll be in my office by nine Saturday morning if you need me."

Ann went to a first-floor lab in the old Diagnostic Laboratory. She put on a lab coat and surgical gloves and took a seat at a narrow counter attached to the wall. There, she sprayed her legs with insect repellent. The lab coat, gloves, and an exhaust fan were required by OSHA because she would be handling tissues in formalin, a known carcinogen. Bizarre as it seemed to the graduate students, tiny, biting flies would attack, even in March, if they didn't wear insect repellent. No one knew where they came from, but it made working in the lab miserable.

By late afternoon, Ann had almost completed selecting the pieces of tissue for technicians to slice and stain for microscopic examination. The insect repellent was wearing off and the flies were starting to bite when her graduate advisor, Bill Thompson, walked in.

Bill, twenty years Paul Schmidt's junior, was an associate professor of Population Medicine, specializing in the diseases and management of dairy cattle. Ann thought it made sense, somehow, that a guy who liked ice cream and rich desserts as much as Bill did would specialize in dairy cattle.

"Hi, Ann. Cutting in tissues?

"Ouch." Ann swatted at a fly on her leg. "I'm trying to finish the tissue samples from the last study. But these flies eat you alive. They must live in the wall." She swiveled around on her lab stool and sprayed insect repellent on her jeans again. "What's up?"

Bill stayed away from the lab bench. He knew where the flies congregated. "Thought I'd let you know that Joe is still in tough shape. From what I gather, he might have died if Paul hadn't called an ambulance for him." He glanced at the door and around the room to make sure they were alone. "This morning, a Dr. Gettelman from the CDC collected samples from Paul and me."

"He collected samples from Jason and me, too," Ann said.

"When I asked questions, Gettelman dodged around like a guy wearing dress shoes in a cow pasture, almost like Joe was positive for SARS."

"There was speculation in the hallways about that. Are we at risk?" Ann asked.

"Our exposure to Joe was limited, and it's been a week since we've been around him. Ten days is the extreme end of the incubation period for SARS. A couple more days and we'll be in the clear."

Ann relaxed, and Bill hooked a nearby lab stool with a toe and pulled it toward himself so he could sit near Ann but away from the bench. "The dean called to remind me that we need that inventory of samples; got to have the freezers locked and secure, too."

"I put the locks on yesterday morning, and I have a couple of students reconciling the inventory now."

"Good. Gettelman asked a pile of questions about your calf study and how much exposure the calves had to Joe. The dean, Gettelman, and some guy named Filburt of the FBI want those calf samples locked down until we have a handle on what that virus is."

"Did he say anything more about Joe?" Ann asked.

Bill shook his head. "If Joe has SARS, they may put off announcing it. They'll want to run confirmatory tests to be sure. Doctors, hospitals, and the Public Health department will be warned before they tell the public. Ouch!" Bill swatted at his leg and moved the stool a couple of feet farther from the bench. "They'll want to keep the public calm. They won't want some Chicken Little of a news announcer riling people up. A stampede out of the Twin Cities could spread SARS all over the country."

Ann paused, wondering how far she could push for answers. "We were out of money two weeks ago, and now I'm hiring students and Jason is ordering molecular kits for the lab work. Those kits cost a fortune. Where did the funding come from, and why is the FBI poking around?"

"The dean will find the money. He needs answers fast and wants to make sure we can account for every sample vial in case the FBI gets a wild hair up its butt. You weren't here when the FBI went nuts over anthrax over a decade ago. Those guys don't know squat about science, and neither does the university's legal staff. Iowa State destroyed a priceless collection of anthrax isolates, it's said, largely to get the FBI out of their hair. If this virus is a BCV-SARS hybrid, the FBI will classify it as a Select Agent."

"What are Select Agents?" Ann asked.

"Potential biological weapons. Anyone who has them in their freezers has to deal with a pile of security regulations, and USDA inspectors and the FBI stop by periodically to audit your records. If they list BCV as a Select Agent, BCV research in cattle will be nearly impossible. It could add a year to the work you're doing."

That bothered Ann. She'd heard of students who took six to eight years to complete their degree, and she didn't want to be one of them.

Bill stood and paced back and forth. "Nobody was fussy about security until the anthrax scare, but . . . goddamn it, the university's legal department is already going berserk over this. Every time somebody at the CDC or FBI blows their nose, the university's attorneys get stomach cramps and diarrhea. They call the university president, he calls the dean, and suddenly I'm up to my ears in legal shit."

"But why would they be worried—?"

"Look around." Glasses in his hand, he made a sweeping gesture. "We're so damned short of room and resources we've got freezers sitting in hallways. Students and employees, hell, even salespeople walk by them every day, and none of those yahoos has had a background check. Half of our graduate students are foreign. That really twisted the FBI's shorts in a knot for anthrax." He shoved his glasses into his pocket. "And if you think the students don't know what happened to your calves and Joe, you haven't listened to the chatter in the halls. The news couldn't have spread faster if it had been put on YouTube."

"I know," Ann said. "I'm trying not to feed the rumor mill, but everything I say seems to do just that. It might be better if I tell my student help what's going on."

"Yeah, I asked Gettelman about that. He said he'd get back to me, but he asked me to keep a lid on it for now. And we are not, under any circumstances, to mention SARS."

Ann tried to stifle a yawn. She'd been working non-stop since seven that morning. Bill looked at his watch. "It's late. Finish up here and go home. Get some sleep; you'll need it. Things will be interesting for the next couple of weeks."

Ann worked until six, finishing up lab work and bringing her notebooks up-to-date. Late-afternoon rush hour on Highway 36 in the Twin Cities was like sitting in an endless parking lot. Halfway home, she decided she couldn't face an empty apartment and took the turnoff to Little Canada and Jason's place.

Little Canada
Morning, March 17

Jason awoke first, snuggled up to Ann and let his fingers gently explore as he kissed her on the neck, trying to wake her up.

"Mmm, that feels good," she said. "It's nice to wake up with your arms around me." She pressed herself against him and felt a new growth. "Hmm, I see you weren't thinking of breakfast." She turned and kissed him. "With all this wood, you should be in forestry."

"We can give up breakfast today, can't we? I can think of better things to do before work."

They celebrated the arrival of morning and got in the shower together, "To conserve water and save time," Jason said. Ann kissed him and dropped one hand to his crotch. "I scrubbed this. Now, how about scrubbing my back?"

They left for the campus together. Her office was in the Veterinary Teaching Hospital, and Jason's lab was a short walk away and two floors down in the basement of the Vet Science Building.

Ann knew it was hard to have a romance in graduate school. The long hours and sustained concentration on their research had ended the marriages of three of her friends. She and Jason had come close to breaking up twice. It took Herculean focus to go, in only a few years, from an undergraduate's understanding of a science to being at the leading edge of what was known, from being an amateur to becoming a world-class expert in her discipline. She'd caught herself thinking of her research while she drank, played, and made love. There had been nights she was pretty sure Jason's mind had been elsewhere while they made love, too. At least they both understood what was going on, and they had more interests in common than most couples.

She had to admit it—she never would have begun her graduate program if she'd known the work and dedication it required, yet now she couldn't imagine doing anything else. Hands down, it was the most stimulating and rewarding thing she'd ever done. She hoped she and Jason could tough it out and stay together.

Ann supervised the two students as they went through the first freezer, finding vials, counting them, and reading the labels. It was slow work. The largest vials were the size of hotel shampoos; the smallest were a fifth that size, and frost rapidly obscured the labels when the vials were brought out of the freezers.

Carla and Wendy were down to the last freezer by noon. They expected to make short work of it as the inventory said there were only two boxes of fecal samples, one with ten vials and one with twenty.

The freezer was in an unused laboratory in the west end of the basement, a part of the building used primarily for storage of rarely used equipment. The only lab in regular use on the floor was Jason's. He'd been put there because his work included extracting viral DNA and RNA from feces for testing by PCR. The chemicals he used did the impossible: they made pig feces smell even worse than they did *au natural*. The west end of the basement became a lonely place.

Because the freezer might be difficult for Carla and Wendy to find, Ann took them to the basement lab, pointed the freezer out, handed the key to Wendy, and went back to her office. She'd barely gotten her computer booted when Wendy knocked on her office door. "The key didn't fit the padlock, and the padlock doesn't look like the others you used."

Pakistan, Saidu, Swat Valley
Afternoon, March 16

Twelve time zones east of Minnesota, Hamid had booted his computer. He'd connected with the Internet provided by the medical college of Saidu Sharif and downloaded a cryptic message forwarded by a friend in Egypt. It was a message Al-Mikhafi, his graduate advisor, would want to see immediately.

Hamid looked out the window at trees limbs swaying in the wind, the gray sky, and rain. He swore. It was the tail end of the rainy season and should have been a balmy spring day. He pulled the hood of his parka over his head, hoped it would protect him from the rain and sleet, and ran across the open plaza to the brick Chemistry Building. He cursed his luck. An inch of water covered the concrete plaza and his shoes were quickly soaked.

Wind blew rain in sheets through Saidu and lashed the pine trees on the rocky slopes above the city—if a large town with pastures and fields between the buildings qualified as a city. Even the bare branches of poplars and birch trees lining the streets near the medical college bent to the wind.

The steep mountains, forests, and waterfalls of the area were famous for their beauty, but Hamid was a city kid. He loved the colors and clamor of large markets, the variety of coffee houses that cities offered, and all night discussions about politics, religion, and the biological sciences. In this pimple on the dick of a sick camel, no one wanted to talk about anything but government contracts, the price of barley, and how smart their favorite goat was.

Hamid felt like puking when the conversation turned to their stinking goats.

For the last week, he'd had to smile and feign interest in the drivel that passed for conversation among these hicks. His graduate advisor and mentor Hassan Al-Mikhafi was visiting a friend in the college. Their stay required a certain delicacy, as the military and government functionaries who crowded this boil on the butt of civilization would not have approved. At least this message about a package would get him to Islamabad and civilization. They'd have to be discrete there, too, but after that it would be a nice dry flight back to Yemen, warmer weather, and safety.

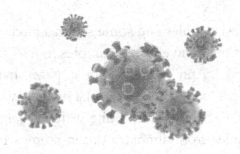

CHAPTER 4

A growing sense of unease gathered in the pit of Ann's stomach as she walked to the lab from her office. The unease became an ache when she saw the padlock on the freezer. All of her locks had been the same model, and this wasn't one of them. Her heart pounded as she double-checked to make sure it was the right freezer.

Carla pointed to the floor under the latch mechanism. "Dr. Hartman, look at this." She bent and scraped up a sample of fine black powder from the floor. "It feels like metal filings."

Ann examined the powder and rubbed it between her fingers. "Somebody used a hacksaw." She glanced quickly at the floor around the freezer and under the lab benches. "See if you can find my padlock around here. I have a phone call to make."

Ann stepped out of the lab and called Jason in his office. She needed his analytical, unemotional approach to problems.

He arrived five minutes later, shortly after Wendy found Ann's padlock under a lab bench.

Jason considered the reasons he would cut a padlock off a freezer. "Maybe someone with samples in the freezer needed them," he said.

"If I needed to test samples and some son of a bitch put a lock on my freezer, I'd cut it off. Who else has samples in it?"

"I've checked." Ann handed him a page, half covered with handwriting. "This looks like an informal inventory. It was in a folder taped to the side of the freezer." She watched Jason scan the list. "There are samples from almost a dozen studies run by people in four research groups."

Jason turned the page. "Some of these studies were done over ten years ago. Look," he pointed to the paper, "there must be three shelves of samples from Don Shroop's studies. He retired years ago. No wonder the department doesn't have enough freezer space. Nobody ever throws anything away."

"Maybe I should get a bolt cutter and return the favor," Ann said.

"No one is following up on Shroop's work, and Naga and Ahmed aren't doing any more lab work on their study," Jason pointed at two lines near the bottom of the page, "and these guys are writing papers on their work. Their lab work is done." Jason paused and looked at Ann. "None of these people would have needed their samples in the last two days."

Ann had reached the same conclusion. Her gut felt like a knot. "I better make another phone call."

She called Bill at his home. He told her to sit tight while he called the dean and campus security.

It took an hour to get someone from maintenance to arrive with a bolt-cutter and another fifteen minutes arguing with campus security. "Look," the campus cop said, "an Agent Filburt of the FBI talked to my supervisor and really lit a fire under him. No way am I going to let anybody touch that padlock again until we get someone from forensics to look at it."

"But that could take hours," Ann said.

"The freezer is working, right?" the cop asked.

Jason shrugged, "Yeah, but—"

"Then there isn't any reason you can't wait. I'll be damned if I'm going to catch hell 'cause you guys are in a hurry to get home."

An hour and a half later, a black SUV with Sheriff's Department license plates pulled up to the loading dock in the back of the Vet Sciences building. The front doors opened and two men in black jumpsuits and baseball caps climbed out of the car. They opened the rear hatch of the SUV and removed two metal cases of equipment. The passenger turned to the driver. "Tell me again, Jim, why the hell are we here on a Saturday afternoon?"

Jim took a deep breath and leaned against the SUV. "The same reason I gave you the last time you asked. A freezer has been tampered with, and it's a freezer that has the FBI's attention. You want to bitch, bitch to them. Tell your girlfriend you'll take her to a later movie."

They closed the hatch and climbed the concrete steps beside the loading dock. Jim tried the gray steel doors at the top of the steps and peered through the windows that made up the upper half of the doors. "Crap. The doors are locked, and nobody is here to open the place."

He set his equipment case down and banged on the doors.

His partner set his case down and resumed his favorite topic. "Some fricking grad student loses a key, cuts a lock off, and I spend another night sleeping alone. Why the hell they—"

"Goddamn it, Bob, quit your bitching. I'm not any happier than you are about this."

The campus cop opened the door and took them the few paces to the first-floor hallway and the elevator. Bob whined to the campus cop and Jim looked around the old elevator. His eye caught a brownish-red stain in a groove in the stainless steel plate behind the floor buttons, and below that, on the yellow wall of the elevator, was what looked like another partially cleaned bloodstain.

"Has anyone noted the blood here on the elevator walls and floor?" Jim asked.

"Blood?" the cop asked.

"Yeah, blood, here," Jim pointed to the floor buttons, "and here, and here," he pointed to spots on the elevator wall and grooves in the floor. "It looks like someone tried to clean it up."

"Nobody mentioned blood before," the cop said. "A student probably dropped a sample from one of the research animals."

"We'll find out." Jim put his equipment case down, opened it, took out swabs and vials, and collected samples of the stains. "Still think this is a stupid milk run, Bob?"

It took twenty minutes to verify that there were no blood stains between the elevator and the basement lab as they walked the hundred feet to the lab. There, they cut the lock off the freezer the way they wanted it done, dropped it in a sample bag, and labeled it.

An hour after he arrived, Jim allowed Ann and her students to open the freezer. Behind the freezer door, each of the six shelves of the minus-seventy-degrees Centigrade freezer had its own flimsy door made of white, insulating plastic. Ann put on gloves, safety glasses, and a facemask and opened the door. She checked the box labels, opened the boxes, counted the samples, and sighed with relief. "They all seem to be here." She checked a couple of vials from one of the boxes, brushing the frost off to read the labels before putting everything back in the freezer.

She turned to Carla and Wendy. "Finish your inventory, and bring that last page to my office when you're done."

"Do we still have to wear the safety glasses? Wendy asked. "They fog up and—"

"Wear them," Ann said. "No exceptions, and remember to shower when you're done."

Ann's team might have counted the vials in her boxes, checked the labels on one or two vials, as Ann had done, and called it good enough had it not been for the strange lock, the unusual safety procedures, and the blood in the elevator. They examined every label on the twenty vials in one box before returning it to the freezer and starting on the smaller box.

"Do we need to record every vial in the second box?" Wendy asked.

Carla hesitated. Students working at the veterinary college were accustomed to drudgery. Their jobs ranged from cleaning dog kennels to counting endless boxes of tiny vials. Today was different.

"What the hell. This is as close to excitement as I've been since my tenth anniversary," Carla said. "If I died in my sleep, my husband wouldn't notice it until he started looking for his breakfast. He can feed the kids tonight." She picked up her clipboard and pen. "It's my turn to record. Read 'em off."

Wendy picked up the first vial, "*P. multocida* vaccine challenge. Chicken 12A. Air sacks. J. Naga/A. Khan."

The two women looked at each other. Wendy put the vial back in the box and picked up the next vial. "'*P. multocida* vaccine challenge. Chicken 12A. Heart. J. Naga/A. Khan.' Holy shit."

She pulled out the next five samples, brushed off the frost that formed on the labels, and glanced at each. "'*P. multocida*,' '*P. multocida*,' and '*P. multocida*.'" She hastily replaced those samples and picked out a sample at the end of the row. "*P. multocida*."

She looked at Carla again. "Should we call her now or record all of the labels first?"

"Better have the full story before we call."

They recorded the identity of the samples in the box and circled the printed identity of each missing sample as assiduously as any homicide detective could have before they called Ann's cell phone.

Paul and Bill sat with Jason and Ann around a small table in Paul's office, trying to guess who could have cut Ann's padlock. She picked up her phone when it rang. The others in the room stopped speaking and watched her. They all suspected a phone call was bad news.

Carla told Ann about the samples. Suddenly pale, Ann looked at Bill and Paul. "Some of my samples are missing. The samples in the last box they checked are from one of Professor Naga's studies, one of those Ahmed worked on."

Everyone in the room knew Naga had spent most of Friday afternoon celebrating Ahmed's departure. Paul walked to his desk and called the dean while Bill called Agent Filburt of the FBI. The dean asked for a teleconference with Bill, Paul, and Professor Naga.

Ann looked at Jason as soon as she put her cell phone away. He nodded, and without a word they stood and headed to the basement lab. "This is one time I hope the students screwed up," Ann said, her voice quavering.

Jason avoided looking at her. "Those two are level-headed. I've never seen anything rattle either of them."

"Would Ahmed have a reason to steal the samples?" Ann asked.

"Beats me," Jason said. "He was pleasant when I talked to him, but he always seemed intense, on edge all the time."

"As though he had a chip on his shoulder, right?" Ann asked.

It took less than five minutes for Ann and Jason to walk to the lab, verify the sample box was Ann's, and the samples were Ahmed's. They returned to Paul's office for the teleconference.

Bill and Paul were staring at Paul's phone. Bill cleaned his glasses with a handkerchief as Paul leaned over the phone. His glasses were propped on his nose as he tried to read the small print under the buttons. "Damn it! You still there, John?" Paul asked. He looked up and saw Ann and Jason standing in the doorway. "Either of you know how to set up a three-way call? I've got John Naga on the line again, but I lose him every time I dial the dean."

Jason took the handset and a notepad with the dean's home phone number from Paul and punched a couple of buttons on the desktop phone. The dean answered on the first ring and Jason put the phone on speaker mode.

Paul told the dean who was in his office and on the line. "Hate to interrupt you at home, Bert, but it looks like some of the samples we talked about yesterday have been stolen. It looks like Professor Naga's graduate student may have switched them out with some of his samples."

"That's the Pakistani student who just finished up?" the dean asked.

"Yeah. Ahmed Khan. He left a little early—said he would write his thesis at home and send it to John electronically."

"The FBI has been called?"

"Bill notified Agent Filburt. The local forensics team has gone over the freezer and John's lab."

The dean sighed and the line was silent for a moment. "There isn't much we can do except cooperate with the Feds and provide background on the science. We'd better be damned sure we've covered our bases, though. Can you contact everyone else who has samples in that freezer first thing tomorrow? We have to verify that there isn't anything else missing or the samples didn't get put among someone else's samples. Tell them I'd like to have it in writing on my desk by 5:00 tomorrow evening.

"John, do you know what Ahmed's itinerary was?" the dean asked.

"What time is it?" Naga asked.

Paul looked at his watch. "A little after five thirty."

"Jesus! The lazy motherfucking son of a bitch should be half-way across the Mediterranean by now," Naga said.

"Shit," the dean said. "Paul, what would be the best way for him to transport BCV samples?"

"Line a cigarette pack with Styrofoam and slip the samples in it. The virus will remain infective for a week at room temperature in fecal samples."

"I'll call Al Gettelman and warn the university admin. The university lawyers will have heart failure. Keep me in the loop and I'll do what I can to cover you on that end."

The dean hung up. Naga stayed on the line. Paul paced behind his desk. "John, we don't know of any students who collected blood samples on Thursday afternoon. The blood the janitors found in the elevator and hallways might have been related to the theft of the samples. Did Ahmed have a problem with severe nosebleeds?"

"Not that I know of. The little prick didn't—"

Paul cut in. They didn't have time for Naga's tirades. "Is there a first-aid kit in your lab?"

"Every lab has to have one, even Sam's teaching lab. I got dinged on a QA audit last winter 'cause Ahmed—"

"So, we should check the first-aid kit in every lab that was open Thursday and Friday night. Did Ahmed still have keys to your lab on either of those nights?"

"I found his keys on the floor under my office door Friday morning. The stupid bastard couldn't even—"

Bill covered his mouth and laughed. Paul turned to him with a finger to his lips. "John, could you drop by your lab this evening and see if the first-aid kit has been used? It might help us determine when the samples were stolen."

Ann opened the door to the main student lab, a long room painted an institutional gray-green, and hit a set of switches to her right. Long fluorescent-tube light fixtures hanging from the ceiling in two rows flickered on over a double row of twenty black lab benches, each about six feet long. Jason checked the seal on a first-aid kit mounted near the door to the media kitchen as Ann did a quick walk past each of the benches. Everything was in order.

They walked to Paul's teaching lab used for a course on clinical bacteriology. The door was open and the lights on when they arrived.

Paul held a petri dish and its raised lid in one hand—a dexterous maneuver second-nature to microbiologists. He shook his head in exasperation as he examined the bacterial colonies, closed the lid on the dish, and turned the petri dish over to read the identification on the bottom.

Ann rapped on the doorframe. "Find anything?"

Paul looked up, looked back at the petri dish, and snorted. "Margie still hasn't gotten it through her head she has to streak for isolation. Looks like she left things in a mess."

He pointed to three pencil-like steel handles, each with a four-inch thin wire on one end, sitting next to a multi-colored stack of five petri dishes of different diagnostic media. All the dishes were upside down, sitting on their lids to prevent moisture that condensed on the lids from dropping onto the surface of the culture medium. "She's normally neat, almost fussy about cleaning up." He showed the petri dish to Ann. "All of her petri dishes are the same. Every one of the 'isolates' she's trying to identify is contaminated. She was probably mad as hell, stormed out, and left everything on the bench top."

"That would be Margie," Ann agreed. "Low frustration level, won't take advice, and never admits she's wrong."

Ann took the petri dish from Paul, flipped the lid ajar, and examined the bacterial colonies on the sheep-blood agar. They looked like tiny water droplets on the surface of the red jello-like agar. Some were white colonies a little larger than a period, while slightly larger colonies were gray and resembled tiny drops of mucous. To Ann's trained eye, irregularities in most of the colonies indicated they were mixtures of two or more species of bacteria. "What a mess."

Ann remembered trying to help Margie and being rebuffed. "Margie's a grade hound. I'll bet she was here at night, getting impossible answers on the tests she did and building up a head of steam. Probably blames me for her problems."

"Then, she could have seen something," Paul said. "Given where Ahmed and Margie usually parked, they both would have used the elevator Thursday night, but headed in opposite directions—Margie toward the student parking lot on the fairgrounds, Ahmed going up to the parking lot near the student union. I'll call the dean again. We can pull Margie out of class Monday if they want to question her."

He took the petri dish from Ann and put it upside down next to the others on the bench. "You guys find anything?"

"Nope. Sam's teaching lab was clean."

Paul headed for the door. "Good. Let's go to my office and wait for Naga."

Naga was locking his lab as the trio approached Paul's office. "Sorry to pull you out here this late. Find anything?" Paul asked.

He shook his head, no.

"You didn't find anything?" Paul asked again.

"No. I found everything. The goddamned lazy bastard left blood-stained cotton spread all over the fucking bench."

Ann and Jason each covered their mouth with a hand and turned to look at a poster about immunology taped to the wall. Jason's chest was shaking, and he leaned against the wall.

"Didn't you see it Friday?" Paul asked.

Naga put his hands on his hips in disgust. "No. Never went in the lab. I made a few phone calls, worked on a grant, and caught up on some reading in the morning. After that, I spent the afternoon . . . on a long lunch. I can't tell you how good it was to know that lazy ass was out of here. Working with that bastard was like having my nuts in a vise while the motherfucker smiled and twisted it tight."

Naga, his venting over, pursed his lips and thought a moment. "All that blood in the lab—do you think the arrogant prick hurt himself?" he asked, hopefully. "Son of a bitch left a trail of splattered blood all over. If it was from a nose bleed, it was worse than any I've ever seen."

Paul motioned with his head toward his office. "Time to call the dean again." As Paul ushered Naga into his office, he leaned toward his old friend and whispered, "If the dean asks any questions, just nod 'yes' or 'no.' I'll answer for you."

Jason put his hand on Ann's arm to delay her as the older men entered Paul's office. "Think Naga will help Ahmed find a job?"

The question was not without foundation. Naga had a reputation for bitching about his graduate students to anyone who'd listen and then working his tail off to make sure they got good jobs after graduating. Ann elbowed Jason in the ribs and walked into the office. Jason stayed in the hallway until he could keep a straight face.

The teleconference was short. Paul explained what they had found, and the dean asked them to lock the labs and get ready for security and the forensics team the next morning. Jason and Ann were going to draw straws to see who would talk to Margie on Monday morning, but Naga interrupted them.

"Margie—she's the tall woman, athletic, brown hair, always seems pissed off?" Naga asked. Dealing with American women had been a monstrous culture shock for him when he'd first come to the States thirty years earlier, and sometimes it seemed as though he still hadn't recovered. On a bad day, any female graduate student who looked him in the face was a femi-Nazi. This had earned him several trips to the dean's office, but he'd finally learned to keep his mouth shut on that.

"I wouldn't describe her quite like that," Ann said. "Maybe, 'self-assured, but easily frustrated' would be more accurate."

"Ahh, just . . . just a minute." Naga's brow furrowed; his lips pursed. He crossed his arms, looked at Paul and smiled. Naga's face was an open book to the other three. "There was blood in the elevator?" Naga asked.

Paul coughed and looked out the window to hide a smile. "Yup," he said.

Naga stood and gestured graciously toward the other three. "I'll talk to Margie Monday morning. You guys have already worked too hard on this."

Naga bid them goodnight and walked out of Paul's office with a spring in his step. Ann, Paul, and Jason looked at each other and giggled. Naga was a slave-driver for his graduate students, at least until he'd taken on Ahmed. It was about as common for tectonic plates to go surfing at the beach as it was for Naga to tell graduate students to take it easy.

"We'd better learn to get along with Margie," Paul said. "She'll have a fellowship in John's lab by Tuesday if she had anything to do with the blood Ahmed sprayed around."

Ann tried to picture Margie and Naga working together. "That'll be a pair to watch."

Paul's phone rang. The dean had news of Joe, and it was confidential. Paul covered the mouthpiece and looked at Jason and Ann. "Would you close the door as you leave, please?"

"Okay, I'm alone," Paul said.

"Joe almost died last night," the dean said.

Paul turned pale and sat. "You said 'almost,' didn't you?"

"Yeah, he survived. He's been delirious off and on since he was admitted—temperature spiked to 105 last night, his lungs were full of fluid, and even on oxygen he was cyanotic. He was breathing more easily and his temp was down to 102 this morning. They think he's through the worst of it. He won't be in any shape to work in the lab for several months. We'd send him home, but the doctors don't think he can take the stress of travel."

"What can I tell people here?"

"Only that he is recovering slowly. Work with the samples from those calves is to be done with every safety measure you can think of in place. As we discussed, any virus you isolate from the samples is to be treated as a BioSafety Level 3 human pathogen."

Paul picked up a pen and wrote, "BSL3," on a note pad.

The dean continued: "Any new studies with the virus must be approved by the Institutional BioSafety Committee. That committee is only supposed to consider the science. With the Feds involved, I . . . Be sure there's a signature line for me on the faculty review page. No further studies may be done with this virus without my approval."

An hour after leaving her office that evening, Ann was seated at Jason's kitchen table, trying to stay awake. She picked at her stir-fried tomato and beef on fried rice and tried to talk about the calves, Joe, and SARS, but her sentences trailed off unfinished, and her head drooped lower and lower. Her long hair was tied in a ponytail that kept it out of her food. She was asleep by nine o'clock, before she'd finished half of her dinner.

Jason carried her to bed, helped her undress, tucked her in, and crawled into bed beside her. As he draped an arm over her, she snuggled against him and pulled his arm tightly about her. She kissed Jason's hand. "What do you think will happen?"

He kissed her neck. "Shhh. Sleep. We'll talk about it tomorrow."

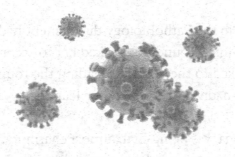

CHAPTER 5

North St. Paul
Morning, March 18

Ann did a long, languid stretch. Raised on a dairy farm, she was normally an early riser. This morning, however, she was warm and comfortable next to Jason and wanted to stay there. Jason was eager to start the lab work on the virus, but Ann knew that rushing complicated work led to mistakes. They had other things they could do that would be more satisfying.

They had been dating for three years. There had been some blow-ups, but she never felt more comfortable than when he put his arms around her. Ann snuggled closer to him. "Don't you think it's time you moved into my apartment? My roommate is graduating this spring, and in seven months you're going to be a daddy."

Pleased with how well that went, she decided to try it later in the week when Jason was awake.

St. Paul Campus
Morning, March 19

It was seven thirty, and Margie was suspicious. The most notorious male chauvinist in the PathoBiology department had interrupted her group on their clinical rounds and asked her to accompany him to his office. She'd looked to the clinician leading the rounds to insist that she stay, but he hadn't objected to her leaving. It was as though he expected this.

Professor Naga was being civil, almost charming, in a clumsy way. No one had ever seen that before, especially with female students.

Naga held the door of his office open for Margie. He was eager to hear the details of what happened to Ahmed. He bowed slightly and waved her into his office with his left hand.

"Please, Dr. Arndt, have a seat," Naga said as he closed the door behind him. Two filing cabinets and a floor-to-ceiling bookcase barely left room for Naga's desk and two chairs in the tiny office. Naga squeezed between a filing cabinet and the bookcase to sit behind his desk.

Margie was stunned. No student had heard Naga say please before, and she wouldn't be entitled to be called "doctor" for another two months. Warily, she did as Naga requested and sat rigidly in the chair across the desk from him.

Naga leaned back in his chair. "Professor Schmidt mentioned that you might have been working in his student lab, Thursday or Friday night."

Margie's knuckles turned white as she clutched the edge of her chair. *So that's what this was about,* she thought. *The arrogant bastard from the elevator must have filed a complaint, maybe even criminal charges.* Her lips were tight, and her jaws clenched as she admitted to being in the lab Thursday night.

"Did you see anyone in the basement or elevator?"

Margie's brow furrowed, and the corners of her lips turned down as she considered how much to admit. She wondered if she should have a lawyer.

Naga saw Margie's expression and realized she might fear that she was under investigation. He leaned forward in his chair and toyed with a pen on his desk. "Important and possibly dangerous isolates were stolen from a basement lab Thursday night. We believe the goddamned, arrogant, little . . . the thief, was injured in or near the elevator. Security and the FBI will want to talk to you, that is, if you saw anything out of the ordinary Thursday night."

Margie relaxed. Naga was reverting to form, and he wasn't pissed at her. They even had the same opinion of the jerk. "Yeah. When I tried to get off the elevator, a well-dressed guy, one of the foreign graduate students, shoved me back into it and called me a slut." Margie shrugged. "When he pushed me, I pushed back."

Naga eagerly leaned forward, arms on his desk. "There were blood splatters in the elevator. Did you hit him in the nose? Could he have been badly hurt?" Naga asked hopefully.

Naga looked like a kid who'd asked his mother if he could have a cookie.

"I gave him a knee in the balls, and—"

"Really? You really connected with his balls?" Naga smiled. This was beyond his expectations.

"Oh, yeah. Dropped his ass right in the elevator. I gave him an elbow in the nose and kicked him in his right knee on the way down." Margie leaned forward and rested an arm on Naga's desk. "We settled it amicably, I think." She batted her eyelashes and smiled, coyly. "At least, he didn't have anything more to say when I stepped over him and walked out."

Naga struck his desktop with a fist. "I knew you got the bastard. How fast did he drop when you hit him with your knee? Was there a crunch when you elbowed him in the nose? Did he bleed much? Do you think you tore ligaments in his knee?"

Margie was not immune to attention and flattery. She happily told Naga everything that happened and a few details she thought might have been true, now that she considered it. Maybe he had gasped and turned white when she hit him with her knee, and there could have been a little crunch when she broke his nose or a scream when she kicked his knee. Memory was such an uncertain thing.

"If you'd be interested, I have money for a graduate student next—"

A knock at the door cut him short.

The door opened and Paul entered Naga's office with a younger man. Paul's guest wore a charcoal-gray three-button suit. Only the two bottom buttons were buttoned, which seemed strange. Taut lines from the buttons to the back, a slight bulge on his hip, and a smaller bulge under his arm suggested concealed holsters. Concealment would explain buttoning the bottom button, but Naga wondered how much protection one man needed. *Maybe Filburt is from Texas*, he thought.

"Morning, Miss Arndt, Professor Naga," Paul said. "May I introduce Agent Filburt of the FBI."

Margie knew Filburt was not an academic. The faculty rarely wore ties unless they had a special meeting. The dean was the only person, other than lab supply salesmen, who routinely wore a coat and tie at the college.

With four people in the little office, there wasn't room for Naga to come around to the front of his desk. He stood and reached across the desk to shake hands with Agent Filburt. Margie had to lean back in her chair to avoid getting an arm in the nose.

"Agent Filburt would like to talk to Miss Arndt if she has time," Paul said. "You haven't discussed the events of Thursday night with her, have you Professor Naga?"

Naga could take a hint. "They were mentioned, but we haven't discussed it in detail, have we Miss Arndt?"

Margie shook her head and said nothing.

Paul escorted Filburt and Margie to a small conference room near the dean's office and went back to the Vet Sciences building. He thought of dropping by Naga's office, but decided there were some things he didn't want to know.

He went back to his office, where Ann and Jason joined him.

"Will Ahmed be arrested when he gets home?" Ann asked as she took a chair near Paul's desk.

Paul shook his head. "His father is a general and his maternal uncle is a powerful senator. If he has a direct flight, he's home free."

Paul put his feet on his desk, nearly toppling a pile of papers. "That's out of our hands. What we need to do is find out what happened to the virus to produce the respiratory lesions. Jason, will you have time to work on sequencing the virus's gene for the spike protein?"

Jason shrugged. "It will be tight. We have—"

"I'm afraid it will be tighter than you realize," Paul said. "All work will require a protocol approved by the Institutional Biosafety Committee and reviewed by the dean."

"What?" Jason was stunned. "We've never had to—"

Paul shook his head. "Don't waste your time complaining. It's not negotiable. This came from the dean. All the rules for work with BSL3 organisms apply to this project now, and the dean has final approval for any studies."

Jason wilted into his chair. "This will triple the time it takes to get anything done."

"Set up weekly meetings with Ann, Bill, and me to discuss your progress. Better copy the dean when you send the meeting invitations to Bill and me," Paul said.

"The dean?" Jason asked. These meetings would be rarefied air for Jason.

"Yes, the dean. I'd rather let him deal with the university's lawyers, the FBI, and the second-guessing and whining that will come from the president's office. Just watch. Some hotshot in the medical school will want to take over, and he won't know a damned thing about BCV or calves. Keep the dean informed and in our corner, and that's less likely to get traction."

Paul looked at a calendar on his desk. "We won't get the pathologist's report on the calf tissues until the end of the week. In the meantime, start reading everything you can lay your hands on about SARS."

He paused for a moment. "You'll be under pressure to take short cuts. Don't go that route." Paul took his feet off the desk and leaned forward in his chair. "Take the time to do this in a logical manner. No assumptions and no short cuts. I'll back you, and I know Bill and the dean will, too. Understand?"

Jason nodded. "Got it. Ann and I have done some brainstorming along these lines already."

"Good." Paul picked up a journal he'd been reading and dismissed Ann and Jason with a nod. As they left, Paul muttered to himself. "We'll let the hotshots take the short cuts. Serve 'em right."

Pakistani Consulate, Minneapolis
Morning, March 19

Several miles to the west of Paul's office, Consul-General Bilal Sharif was taking care of the messy details involving Ahmed's foray. Sharif cabled Islamabad with the news that Ahmed had been injured and allowed Ahmed to send his story to his father, General Khan. Sharif was not without resources of his own at the university, and he quietly made contacts and asked questions.

Gray-haired but still athletic-looking, Sharif stopped in front of a door and leaned on his cane. The crisp, white line of his French cuffs was a perfect half-inch from the sleeve of his Armani suit as he rapped on the door before he entered. It was a small, bare room, with only a bed, a nightstand, television, and an easy chair. There were no windows in the room, and it was swept periodically for electronic listening devices.

The old gentleman approached the bed. "How are you feeling this morning, Ahmed?"

Ahmed was sitting up in bed, watching the morning news. The remains of his breakfast cluttered a tray sitting on the nightstand. His nose was bandaged, and he moved carefully as he rolled to his side to reach the television remote. He turned the television off and turned to his visitor, careful to present the image of an injured patriot. "I'm feeling much better, Bilal. Did Omar get past security? Is the package on its way home?"

The young man's casual and familiar address was insulting to Sharif. Ever the diplomat, his expression remained impassive. "The package is safely on its way to Islamabad, but Fasihullah went in place of Omar. Fasi was scheduled to return home next week for his brother's wedding, and he looks so much like you we didn't think the TSA would interfere. No one raised an alarm before takeoff. He will change planes at Charles De Gaulle and then Cairo, all without further inspection."

"Good. Has my father—"

Consul Sharif raised an eyebrow slightly and interrupted. "Are you sure the thugs that attacked you were working for the American government? We have not detected activity by the FBI or Interpol to suggest they are looking for you, and your father expressed surprise that the US government had such inept agents." Consul Sharif leaned a little closer. "There were three, I believe you said, but you managed to escape."

"My father should give me as much credit as he gives the Bush administration," Ahmed spat. Acting indignant was his default strategy when caught in a lie. "I developed that mutant in my poultry vaccine project. Our people paid for it, and they deserve the benefit, no matter what the university claims."

"The university remains silent. They have made no claims."

"Do you expect them to admit what they've done?" Ahmed flipped the sheets to uncover his right knee. A large bruise covered the left side of the swollen knee and ice packs surrounded it. "Look at my knee! And my balls are the size of grapefruit."

Ahmed started to remove the sheets from his crotch, but Sharif held up a hand and averted his eyes. "No, don't bother. I believe you." *He does not know the meaning of 'modesty,'* the consul thought. "I was only transmitting your father's concern. He and your uncle approved your suggestion that one of our staff use your airline tickets and deliver your package. It's your father and uncle whom you will have to convince when you go home."

The old man leaned on his cane and appraised Ahmed carefully. He saw an arrogant fool playing a high-stakes game and making others carry all the risk. Sharif would feel better when Ahmed was on his way home.

"Fasi's airline ticket is for next week. Will you be able to travel by then?"

"I believe so. It depends on—"

There was a knock on the door. It opened and a man Ahmed's age entered, handed Sharif a note, and whispered in the consul's ear. "Sahib, from your relative at the university."

Sharif glanced at Ahmed. "Would you pardon me a moment?" He turned and read the note.

The consul suppressed a smile. Ahmed had been whipped by a girl, a veterinary student? Stealing the work of others? It all fit. If he couldn't tell the difference between one woman—one woman!—and three assassins, how could he be expected to tell what was his and what was not?

Sharif turned to Ahmed. "Dear boy, my apologies for the

GARY F. JONES 65

interruption. You have been through so much and comported yourself so . . . singularly. I'll make sure your father and the senator receive a complete report on the matter."

"Thank you, Bilal, I—"

"Now, to the business at hand. I talked to our physician again this morning. He thought you should be able to make the flight next week, provided you spend most of your time in bed and keep ice on, ah, on the swollen tissues." He nodded slightly to Ahmed. "Now, please excuse me. This note requires my immediate attention."

Outside the room, Sharif turned to Omar, a swarthy young man with a well-trimmed mustache and a powerful build, carefully hidden under a tailored dark suit—the same man who brought him the note. "Did you read this?"

Omar nodded.

This was another surprise. Sharif considered the implications. Omar knew he could be sent home in disgrace for reading the note, but he was brazenly honest about it. He would only do that if he had powerful connections Sharif was unaware of—connections he wanted Sharif to know about.

Sharif talked as they ambled toward his office. He looked down the hallway rather than at Omar as he spoke. "I would appreciate it if you do not discuss this with Ahmed. It will only cause him stress and possibly prolong his time with us. It would be best if he returns home as soon as possible. You should encourage him to stay in his room. He may, ah, possibly heal more quickly that way. His father will . . ." Sharif turned to Omar. The old man kept his expression bland, but his eyes were twinkling. "His father will be eager to speak to him."

Omar excused himself and Sharif paused, absently admiring a portrait of *The Woodland Maid* by Sir Thomas Lawrence. *Portrait painters had to lie*, he thought, *but a man never should. Our fool should have read Chesterfield*, Sharif thought, and shook his head sadly. *We scatter wisdom through our libraries that it may be ignored by our children.*

Sharif continued the walk to his office. Theft—the general would forgive Ahmed that. But letting a woman whip him? He'll roast the boy alive. He'd already nearly disowned him twice. Sharif smiled to himself. And the general and Ahmed's mother no longer lived together. There had been a fight in the family when Ahmed refused an appointment to the military academy, and last week one of the general's contraband shipments was intercepted. There were rumors that Ahmed's mother and uncle were behind it.

Sharif picked up his pace. His back was straighter and he carried his shoulders like the athlete he'd been forty years ago. He playfully swung his cane as he walked and wondered if the General knew of England's Henry II?[1] Sharif was sure the General remembered the story of *Shah Jahan*.[2] And Ahmed! Ahmed would not have been so cock-sure of himself if he'd known anything of the Imperial succession following Peter the Great or Ivan the Terrible.[3] Sharif thought that a great pity, and hoped Ahmed would live long enough to see the parallels.

---

1 Henry II (1154-1189) married Eleanor of Aquitaine. Eleanor and sons Richard (Richard the Lion Heart), Geoffrey, and John frequently fought against Henry, and in 1189, with Phillip Augustus of France, defeated him in battle. He died a few days later.

2 Shahabuddin Muhammad Shah Jahan (1592-1666), fifth Mughal Emperor of India and builder of the Taj Mahal, was overthrown and imprisoned by his son, Khurram, in 1658.

3 Tsar Peter the Great (1672-1725) had his only son tortured to death. Tsar Ivan IV (the Terrible, 1530-1584) murdered his only son. It's rumored they had issues.

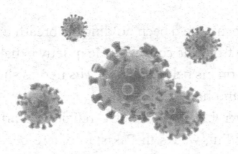

CHAPTER 6

A few hours earlier, Sharif had guessed that Ahmed was lying about the package, but the arrogant fool had connections. The consul decided that Fasihullah, a consular employee close to Ahmed's age and a dead ringer for him, would be safer if he knew little about the secret package he was carrying. He'd be less likely to be nervous and give himself away to the TSA.

Fasi had heard enough about the package for his pulse to quicken as he handed the TSA inspector Ahmed's passport and tickets. He knew that as Ahmed he wouldn't have diplomatic immunity, but he didn't feel it in his gut until the guard looked from him to Ahmed's passport photo and back again.

The TSA inspector smiled and wished him a safe trip.

With effort, Fasi kept his hands from shaking as he took off his shoes, put his belt, loose change, and luggage keys in a bin, and waited in line again. In his turn, he stepped up to the inspection area and held his arms away from his body. His sport coat, unbuttoned, hung wide open. The guard patted down his shirt, not his jacket. No one noticed the packet of cigarettes containing the stolen samples in the pocket of the sport coat.

Fasi didn't realize he'd been holding his breath until he picked up his carry-on bag from the conveyor. He quietly exhaled, collected his change, and put on his belt and shoes. His nerves shot, he stopped at one of the bars and had a drink.

He had never been particularly religious, and he didn't look forward to spending weeks in Pakistan where conservative Imams were gaining political power. He wouldn't dare be seen drinking alcohol at home; it would be political suicide. To brace himself for his homecoming and shake off memories of the TSA inspection, he freely sampled the mixed drinks offered on the Delta flights from Minneapolis to De Gaulle and De Gaulle to Egypt. His flight to Pakistan from the Cairo airport was delayed, so he parked his butt at the mahogany bar in Bill Bentley's Old English Pub in terminal one until the bright, white walls irritated his eyes. He realized he'd better eat dinner or he'd have to crawl onto his plane. He was in terminal one, and his flight home was to leave from terminal three, anyway.

He immediately felt better upon stumbling into the Hippo Bar and Grill in terminal three. There was more chrome, but the walls were dark, the off-red upholstered chairs were comfortable, and a soccer game was on the big TV screen nearest him. He had dinner, and continued sampling, working alphabetically through a Manhattan, an Old Fashioned, a Sidecar, and a Zombie. Topping off his previous intake like that might have killed him if the bartender hadn't taken pity on him and watered his drinks down.

A diplomat must be familiar with local practices, Fasi told himself, and drinking cocktails was practiced in every capital of Europe and the Western Hemisphere. When he boarded his final flight home Sunday evening, there were no cocktails available on Delta or at the Cairo airport that he hadn't tried, maybe twice. He was sure of it.

From Cairo to Islamabad, he guzzled coffee, which meant he spent a sleepless night at his father's home, a new four-story apartment complex in a gated compound just off the Kashmir Highway, close to the Shakar Parian National Park. Monday passed in a throbbing fog. He was groggy from jet lag and still hung over when Tuesday morning dawned and the morning sunlight scorched his eyes. Fasi groaned. The second day of what would be his three-day hangover was not appreciably better than the first.

Fasi considered writing something about hangovers in his diary for future reference, but it took more effort than he cared to muster as he leaned against a streetlight and waited for the taxi outside the wrought-iron gate to the compound. The day was hell already, and he still had to report to the Foreign Ministry and deliver Ahmed's package to the university.

The taxi took the circular drive and dropped Fasi off at the Foreign Ministry entrance. The glaring white of the modern façade of the building hurt his eyes. The staff was surprised to see him, and no one knew anything about the package. He called several numbers in the International Islamic University's Microbiology Department. Those had been strange conversations, a man with a thick tongue and throbbing head on one end and baffled secretaries on the other. No one seemed to know what was in the package or to whom it was to be delivered. Things didn't fall into place until Fasi received an email from Ahmed.

The message said that Ahmed was making arrangements for the package with a graduate student in the Biochemistry Department. The email instructed Fasi to go to the Biochemistry departmental office in an hour and ask for Hamid. "Tell Hamid you have the package from St. Paul, and he will show you where to take it."

Fasi arrived at the office in the Chemistry building and asked the receptionist for Hamid. The woman looked confused. "Hamid?" She scanned a list of names and office numbers. "His surname?"

"I do not know his family name," Fasi said. "He is a graduate student in the department."

She searched another list and turned to a secretary sitting at the next desk. "Mohammed, do you know of a graduate student named Hamid?"

As the secretary shrugged his shoulders and shook his head, a young man entered the reception area from the hallway and approached Fasi.

"Sahib Fasihullah, I am Hamid," the young man murmured. "Please follow me. The professor is waiting for you in his office. A thousand pardons for my tardiness. I hope you didn't have to wait long for me."

Hamid was about Fasi's age. Fasi was in no shape to walk rapidly, and Hamid was happy to stroll leisurely down the corridor to the elevator. "What are your duties at the consulate?" Hamid asked. "In the center of the country, do you monitor the US grain production?" Fasi enjoyed the attention. He had been at the bottom of the social ladder at the consulate, and being fawned over by Hamid was a pleasant change. "We are not supposed to talk about our duties," Fasi said. An answer that hinted at mystery sounded better than the dreary reality, and it troubled his brain less, too, as it seemed to spin and wobble in his head.

"Is you wife living in the US too?" Hamid asked as the elevator carried them up two floors.

"I'm not married."

"What is your social life like? Can you date American women? Are they as wild as we hear?"

The elevator door opened and Fasi tried to think of something that sounded better than admitting that his sex life was largely imaginary. His brain ached; he didn't want to think. "Satisfactory," he said as they walked down a hallway. *Let Hamid interpret that,* Fasi thought.

They stopped and Hamid opened the door to room 320. "This is the laboratory, sir."

Fasi entered the lab. The black bench tops were stacked with cardboard boxes, piles of ancient research reports, and old equipment. Unlike the hallway, the gritty floor looked dull, as though it hadn't been cleaned or waxed recently. The air smelled stale. A sign on the wall said something about asbestos, but Fasi couldn't focus well, the sign was faded, and two of the fluorescent bulbs in that area were flickering on and off. The strobe-light effect intensified Fasi's headache.

Fasi wondered whether the lab was being used, but he couldn't focus on what that meant. He waited as Hamid passed through the lab and into an office at the back. This was unusual, as access to an office through a laboratory had been recognized as dangerous by 1980 because of the opportunities for chemical contamination.

A tall, thin man emerged from the office and approached Fasi. Graying slightly at the temples and with a black, well-trimmed mustache with flecks of gray, he was the picture of a university professor. Unlike what Fasi remembered of other faculty, the man's name wasn't embroidered on his white lab coat, nor did he give Fasi his name when he shook hands with him. "I believe you have a package for me."

"Yes," Fasi said with a wince. He was not normally monosyllabic, but this was only the second day after his autodidactic cocktail seminar, and behind his eyes an ill-tempered imp was duplicating the cacophony of Islamabad's rush hour. Fasi pulled the Winston pack from his coat pocket and handed it to the man. "A receipt?" he asked.

The man looked at Fasi quizzically and speculated on where Ahmed found someone so naive.

Fasi took a deep breath and wondered how the professor could be so dense. "I will need a receipt for the package. For the department and Ahmed, you understand."

The man pulled the tape from the top of the pack and opened it enough to peek inside. The vials were smaller than he expected, but they were there. Satisfied with his examination, he noticed Fasi's shaky hands. He shrugged his shoulders. "This isn't that sort of package."

Fasi's face fell. His gut formed a knot. "Pardon me? What do you mean, not that sort of package?" He started to sweat. Part of it was due to lack of sleep and his hangover, but this trip had been highly irregular, from the appearance of Ahmed at the consulate in the wee hours of the morning, to his early trip home using Ahmed's passport. Now, he'd turned a package disguised as a pack of cigarettes over to a man without a name.

Fasi tried to sort out the politics, but he could only handle fragmented thoughts and keep his balance, too. Military Intelligence was recently rumored to be on friendly terms with scientists at the university. Members of the ruling party had seemed nervous and evasive in interviews with reporters, but given the history of military coups, Pakistan's politicians were always apprehensive about the armed forces. Fasi put a hand on the lab bench to stabilize himself.

Fasi realized that the consul general, a respected senior diplomat, had entrusted him with a mysterious package, and now he had neither the package nor a receipt. This could be the end of his foreign service career, or worse.

His bowels gurgled, as though to tell him they thought it would be worse.

He stood as straight and tall as he could. "I must have something, Sahib."

The man stared at him, unmoved.

Fasi felt himself swaying and put both hands on the bench behind him. "Please, sir. Anything. Can you give me a note with a date and 'Received' over your signature?" Fasi's knees buckled and he leaned against the bench. "Please, your Excellency?"

The man nodded, pulled out a notebook, and scribbled the statement Fasi had requested. "Would you like my student to co-sign?" the man asked.

Fasi nodded. A modicum of strength returned to his knees. The student stepped forward, looked at his professor's signature, looked at the professor, smiled, and signed the paper. The professor tore it from the pad, folded it once, and handed it to Fasi.

Fasi opened the note and tried to read it. His head was throbbing, and his hands felt clammy. With effort, he managed to keep his hands from shaking as he scanned the note. It was what he'd requested, nothing more. The signatures were scrawled, and he had trouble focusing. He couldn't read them, but they were signatures.

Fasi called a cab and sank into the back seat when it arrived. The cab took the bridge over the Nullah River and turned onto the four-lane Kashmir Highway. The city crowded against the access road on the north side of the highway; to the south were sprawling green spaces and parks. As they drove north-east, Fasi relaxed and closed his eyes. Six times he counted the change in road noise as the cab crossed rivers. He opened his eyes and sat up as the cab turned right onto Constitution Avenue. He looked for the fountains of the PSO Light and Visual Park on the corner, but they were still shut down for the winter. The cab pulled up to the Foreign Ministry building a block later.

After drinking a liter of water, Fasi tried to relax behind the desk in the office he'd been given for his time in Islamabad, but the chair was hard. At least he was better hydrated now, his head wasn't thundering, he was able to focus, and he only had to stay out of trouble for another few hours. He washed down Alka Seltzer with another liter of water and fruit juice before giving a verbal report to his superior, a man ten years his senior.

Fasi treated the older man carefully. The guy was famous for caution and the chip on his shoulder was the size of a babul tree. He'd advanced rapidly in his youth because of political connections and was demoted even faster after he demanded a bribe from a foreign company, unaware that his mentor owned it. He'd worked his tail off in the twenty years since, only to see younger men promoted above him.

At the end of his verbal report on agriculture, manufacturing, and politics in the American mid-west, Fasi told him about the package he'd transported to room 320. Almost as an afterthought, he handed him the receipt from the University.

News of the package and the receipt surprised the older man. A disguised package smuggled out of the US was likely to be important, the sort of thing to salvage or end a stagnant career. He told Fasi to wait while he checked with others about the package. Fasi napped for two hours before he was awakened by the older man's rap on the doorframe. He motioned Fasi to follow him. They walked to the elevator, Fasi a step behind. His superior didn't punch a button for the floor. He used a key.

As the elevator rose, Fasi tried to break the silence by asking if the army had suppressed the insurgents in South Waziristan. His superior looked at him and turned away without speaking. The elevator door opened on the sixth floor, a floor Fasi had never visited before.

The dark-green carpet felt plush and deep as they stepped off the elevator. The hallways were wide, the walls were light green with white trim; the indirect lighting was subdued. The few men they passed wore suits with braces, strolled leisurely, and spoke in hushed voices. The hallway ended in a circular area, at its center a fountain of dark green stone, a white arabesque decorating the rim. Only four doors opened on the space.

Except for the gentle spray and burble of the fountain, the

silence was so complete Fasi could hear his pulse. He sniffed the air tentatively. If power and wealth had a scent, it would be here, and Fasi wanted to remember it.

The air was fresh, nothing more.

His superior knocked on a door and ushered Fasi into a modest room. An army officer, a colonel, judging by the gold and green squares on his epaulettes, sat at the other end of an oblong conference table, reading the scrawled note Fasi had demanded at the university. Fasi's boss pulled out a chair at the end of the table nearest the door and motioned Fasi to sit.

Fasi heard the soft click of the door as his boss left the room.

The colonel looked at Fasi. "You gave the package to a man in the biochemistry building, a man with an office in room three twenty?"

"Yes, Sahib. The office was—"

"The University says that room is due to be renovated. It hasn't been used for two years."

Fasi started to speak, but the colonel held up a hand to silence him and studied the paper. After an interminable silence, he took a deep breath, lifted his head and stared at Fasi. He glanced at the bottom of the note again, held it up, and turned it toward Fasi. "Is this the receipt you accepted at the university?"

It was not a long table, and Fasi's vision had returned to normal. He was close enough to recognize the torn edge of the paper, with only the date, "Received," and the scrawls at the bottom.

A whisper of movement at his side drew Fasi's attention to his left. Out of the corner of his eye, he saw the polished brown shoe and khaki pant cuffs of a soldier standing behind him. A firm hand gripped his shoulder. Fasi struggled to maintain his composure and control his voice.

"Yes." Fasi tried to swallow, but fear made his mouth dry. The little saliva he could muster rolled around in his mouth like a marble.

His tongue stuck to his palate and seemed too big for his mouth. "I asked—"

The colonel cut him off with an abrupt wave of his hand. His eyes bored into Fasi's. "Tell me, what did Ali Baba look like? And how are . . ." The officer turned the paper around and examined the second signature again. ". . . his forty thieves?"

St. Paul
Evening, March 18

"Shit! Did you see that three-pointer?" a tall, bearded guy in his late twenties asked Jason "That son of a bitch has made four in a row, and I haven't seen anybody try to block him yet."

Jason was watching a basketball game with Gregg, a buddy and fellow grad student who lived down the hall from him. Both men were slouched on Jason's dumpy old couch, a bowl of popcorn between them. There was a muffled buzz. Gregg put his beer down, struggled out of the couch, and dug his vibrating cell phone out of his jeans. He looked at the caller ID. "Wife calling. I better go home and see what she wants. She's testy lately."

Jason raised his beer bottle to Gregg but kept his eyes on the TV and the basketball game. "Give her my regards. When is she due?"

"Another month. Thanks for the beer," Gregg said and let himself out.

Jason's cell rang a few minutes later. "Hey, Jason, Gregg. Did I leave a book at your place? Sue asked me to look at it before the game. It's a paperback, kind of small. I had it in my back pocket."

Jason glanced at the couch and an upside-down shipping crate that served as an end table. To Jason, like many bachelors, that constituted a search. "Nope. Not here."

Two hours later, Ann snuggled up to Jason on his couch. He

dropped his arm over her shoulder as she surveyed his living room. *What a pigsty*, she thought. She'd never seen dust bunnies as big as those that lurked behind a stack of books and empty pizza boxes in the corner.

"When is your lease up?" she asked.

"End of May. Why?"

"My roommate is graduating in May. You and I spend most of our time together. Why don't you move in with me? It'll be more convenient, and we'll save money. You *will* have to pick up after yourself, though."

Silence.

Ann waited for a response. "Don't go all romantic on me, now," she said, when the silence became unnerving. "I've finally gotten used to being ignored most of the time. I'd hate to have all that training go to waste."

"How much picking up?"

"You drop it, you pick it up within an hour or sleep on the couch. And we take turns doing the dishes. I'll take the even days. You'll move in on the first of June; we'll probably eat out that day, so you'll get a freebie."

"I've always liked freebies," he said and kissed her on the lips. "Will there be room for my furniture?"

"At the dump or on a bonfire?"

Jason considered the options. "That will make it easier to move." He stood and stretched. "Back in a minute," and headed to the bathroom.

While Jason was occupied, Ann stood and lifted the center cushion of the couch. "So that was the lump," she muttered as she picked up a paperback book lying under the cushion. She looked at the cover. "What on earth! *Pocket Guide to Baby Names?*" She looked in the direction Jason had disappeared and back at the book.

Ann dropped the book on the floor on her end of the couch when she heard the bathroom door open and Jason's footsteps approach.

She resumed her position cuddled next to him when he returned to the couch.

Jason put his arm around her and gave her a kiss. "I guess I could get used to picking stuff up."

Ann leaned against him. "How long have you known?"

"Known?"

"Yeah. Why didn't you tell me? It would have saved me a lot of worry."

Jason's brow furrowed. "Worry?"

"It happens all the time, but no girl likes to be uncertain how her man will take the news. I felt confident about you, but that's not the same as knowing." She kissed his cheek and snuggled closer to him.

"Knowing?" Jason's voice rose on the last syllable.

Ann ran a hand through his hair. "Yeah. I wasn't sure how you and Paul would take it. I don't want to give up my work on BCV, and with the questions now about human infection . . . well, you know how the faculty can fuss over everything."

"Everything. Yup, they sure can worry." Beads of sweat formed on Jason's brow.

"Did any of the names appeal to you?" Ann asked.

"Is it hot in here?" Jason asked. "Should I open a window?" He stood and went to the window without waiting for a reply.

"I'm okay, and it's still March. Kind of an expensive way to cool an apartment in St. Paul, isn't it?"

"Good point. Ah, would you . . ." Jason looked nervously around the apartment. Inscrutable conversations with women always ended badly for him. "Care for another beer?"

"I didn't have a first beer. You know I shouldn't . . ." Ann looked at him. "You don't know what we're talking about, do you?"

"Ahh," Jason swallowed, "not really."

Ann crossed her arms over her chest and sat as straight as she could on the couch. "Okay. Forget it."

Clueless but relaxed, Jason sat next to her. "So, back to my moving in. When—"

Ann stood and picked up her coat. "I said, forget it. You can shove your damned book up your ass. If it's not for me, who is it for?" She glared at him.

"What?"

"If you can't be honest now, you can fuck off, you two-timing bastard. I don't want to be in the same room with you." She put on her coat and stormed out the door.

"What, where did—" Jason stopped in mid-sentence when the door slammed behind Ann.

His phone rang as he opened the door.

"Hey, Jason, Gregg. Have you run across my book yet?"

Jason turned to look at his living room. "No." He hustled to the window and watched as Ann's car peeled out of the parking lot. "Where do you think you left it?"

"It was in my back pocket. If it fell out, it might be under the cushions of your couch."

Jason remembered that Ann mentioned a book. "What's the title?"

"*Naming the Baby*, or some shit like that. It's Sue's book, and she's throwing a fit about me losing it. Could you—"

"Baby? Naming a . . . a baby?"

"Yeah. Did you find—?"

Bits of his conversation with Ann flashed through Jason's mind. He pocketed his phone, grabbed his coat, and ran from the apartment.

Sliding through stop signs and skidding around corners in his twelve-year-old Camry, he arrived at Ann's apartment complex. He was talking into a box mounted at the entryway of her apartment building a minute later. "Please, Ann, please let me in. We need to talk. I can explain."

There was no reply. He pulled out his cell phone and touched

Ann's name on his contact list. His call rolled over into her phone messages every time he called.

He called Ann's roommate. She told him to blow himself.

He called Gregg and told him what had happened. "Can Sue call Ann and get me out of this?

"They're pretty close. I wonder if Ann told Sue she's pregnant— you are sure she's pregnant, aren't you?" Gregg asked, as he remembered an unpleasant episode of his own. "If you think you're in trouble now, talking about a pregnancy she doesn't have will make it exponentially worse. Been there, done that."

"I can't think of any other explanation."

"It would explain her temper." Gregg lowered his voice. "Living with Sue since she got pregnant is like living in a soap opera. You can't believe the mood swings."

Jason stepped away from the apartment house and looked up toward Ann's window. "Could you ask Sue now? It's cold out here."

"Okay, hang on."

Jason stamped his feet a couple of times to get feeling back in his toes and paced back and forth, phone to his ear. He looked past the parking lot to an undeveloped field. In the moonlight, skeletal trees stood in relief against the gray remnants of snow banks and pale drifts of dead grass. The scene was as depressing as his social life. He put his phone away, shoved his frozen hands in his coat pockets, and huddled in the entryway, his ears, toes, fingers, and hopes caught in Minnesota's glacial slide toward spring.

His phone rang as he lost feeling in his toes again. "Sue called her. It went to her voicemail, so Ann must have her phone turned off. Sue left a message, but she says you should be ashamed of yourself."

"Why?"

"Don't ask. You might as well get used to it. We're men. It's our job to apologize. Sue said she'll drop by Ann's office tomorrow morning."

"Thank her for me. Should I—"

"Don't even think of talking to Ann until after Sue leaves. It'll take Sue five minutes to explain what happened. Then they'll talk for thirty minutes about pregnancy, what selfish bastards men are, what they've heard about different obstetricians and pediatricians, morning sickness, and other stuff we don't want to know about."

"But she will talk to Ann early tomorrow, won't she?" Jason asked, as he stamped his feet again to get circulation in his toes.

"Oh, yeah, but it's going to take time. You and I would take three minutes to do it, but they'll settle in for a goddamned conference. They'll plan your life and mine and discuss how to fix our woefully deficient characters to make us passable daddy material."

"Should I go with Sue to—?"

"Good god, no! That's the last thing you should do. They will not seek, nor will they want, your input."

"Sounds like you've been through this before."

"Something pretty close. I cringe every time I think about it. If you ask me, women love this stuff, no matter what they say."

Jason walked to his car. "I owe you, buddy. I really appreciate this."

"Remember that when you move. I've got dibs on your television."

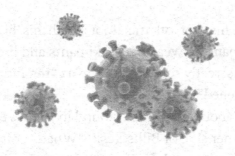

CHAPTER 7

St. Paul Campus
Morning, March 20

Professors ignore the social lives of their graduate students for the same reason graduate students pretend they don't know about faculty feuds: to avoid collateral damage. It usually works. Ann dropped by Paul's office and tearfully let him know it wasn't going to work this time.

Paul was disturbed. He took the second floor walkway to the Veterinary Teaching Hospital and walked into Bill Thompson's office at eight thirty. "Bill, we've got a problem."

Bill had been munching a cheese Danish. He put his hand to his mouth, chewed rapidly and swallowed. "Yeah, I know. Ann and Jason are the two best grad students I can think of to work on it, though. That was lucky."

"That's the problem. Ann came to my office this morning, crying and blubbering so badly I couldn't follow most of what she said. She made it clear that she will *not* work with Jason again. She doesn't even want to be in the same room with him."

Bill put his coffee cup down. "What? They were a couple before they moved here." He sat back in his chair, trying to make sense of the news. Bill was pudgy and a bit on the short side, so the movement almost brought his feet off the floor. With his brown hair, stocky build, and penchant for wearing khaki pants and brown shirts, some of the juniors discreetly referred to him as "the fudgesicle."

"What happened?"

"Something about a book Ann found in Jason's couch." Paul took a chair on the other side of Bill's desk. "Whatever it was, it really set her off. She's refused to take calls from him—she said she threw her cell phone in the toilet after he tried to call her five times last night."

Bill looked at his desk, his brows knit together. "Geez, that . . . that doesn't . . ." He looked up at Bill and rapped the eraser end of a pencil on his desk. "Ann's about as level-headed a student as I've had. What kind of book could do that?"

"No idea." His elbow on the chair's arm, Paul rested his chin in his hand as he thought. He leaned back in his chair, frowned, and looked at Bill. "I hope it wasn't something illegal, like kiddy porn."

Bill shook his head dismissively. "Nah, I can't see that. Jason's taste runs to well-developed women. I've seen him looking at what's around—hell, we all do in the summer—but I've never seen anything to suggest he was playing the field."

Paul noticed a clock on the wall as he mulled over Bill's comment. "Crap. I've got a lecture to give." As he stood, he put his hands on the arms of the chair and pushed himself off to give his arthritic knees a break. "I hope they get this straightened out." He put his hands on his hips in frustration. "It couldn't have happened at a worse time. I guess I'd better start thinking of someone to act as a liaison between them. I've never had a project like this. Every day is a new catastrophe."

Bill thought about women, or more accurately, his sister and his wife Betty. He absently sketched a cow's hoof with a pencil. He knew a lot about cows, and at least felt comfortable with them. "What you described is out of character for Ann. She's smart, rational, and normally emotionally stable." *She's like sis and Betty*, he thought, *except when* . . . "I wonder . . . do you think, well . . . could she be pregnant?"

Jason arrived at his lab in the basement. Windowless white walls measured just twelve feet per side. A black countertop, the lab bench, took up two walls. It was supported by gray cabinets that looked, except for their fiberglass construction, as though they belonged in a kitchen. Similar cabinets hung from the walls above the bench and a small microwave oven sat on the bench in a corner.

All work with the calf samples had to be done in the biosafety cabinet that covered the third wall. It was a narrow stainless steel table with both ends and back enclosed in stainless steel panels that merged with a hood four feet above the table. A glass panel hung from the hood, covering the front of the compartment to within six inches of the table. The opening provided enough room for Jason to insert his hands and forearms into the cabinet to work. Filter-sterilized air circulated within the hood to assure that neither the work nor the worker was contaminated.

Jason looked at tests set up the day before, entered the results in his lab notebook, and watched the clock. By nine thirty, he couldn't stand the suspense and called Sue. When she didn't answer, he called Gregg and asked if he'd heard anything.

"She's only been there twenty minutes. They're just getting warmed up. I'm guessing Ann started by telling Sue what a horse's ass you are. With a topic that fertile, it could be an hour before Sue has a chance to get a word in. Give 'em some time."

"That's easy for you to say, but I don't know what I'd do without Ann."

"Then I've got a book you can borrow in another month, and you have a shopping trip to make this weekend."

"Shopping?"

"It's called a ring. Women go nuts over them, show them to their parents, flash them at their friends. The way Ann exploded last night, you'd better get these details out of the way now so we don't have to go through this again."

"Thanks."

"Think nothing of it. I'd have kept my mouth shut and waited for you to get desperate again, but Ann and your television are the only things you've got that aren't junk. Hang on a sec. Sue's calling. I'll get back to you."

Jason pocketed his phone. He sat on a lab stool, crossed his arms, and waited as long as he could. The three minutes seemed like an hour. He stood and paced back and forth along the lab bench. He left his lab and was on the stairway to Ann's office when his phone rang.

"Jason, Gregg here. You're okay, but you'll have to do some groveling."

"What do you mean?

"Sue and Ann decided you should apologize for not telling Ann you didn't know what she was talking about."

Jason stopped on the stairs and leaned against the concrete wall. "That's ridiculous. I can't read her mind."

Slow learner, Gregg thought. "Do you want Ann back and your life on an even keel?"

"Sure, but damn—"

"Then shut up. Give Sue and Ann another five minutes and go to Ann's office. Apologize, tell her what she means to you and propose. Christ, man, do I have to tell you how to do everything? You do know what foreplay is, don't you?"

Jason went to the next landing on the stairs and suffered another five minutes of anguish before going to Ann's office. When Paul rapped on Ann's door an hour later, Ann and Jason were sitting close together. They said they were planning the next study for the virus.

The state of their hair and clothing suggested it was an intimate and active discussion.

Paul talked with them briefly and returned to Bill's office. The door was open and he walked in smiling to himself. "Bill, you know that concern I had this morning?'

"Yeah, if you mean Ann and Jason."

"It looks like they've solved it." Paul looked around to make sure no other ears were near. "I walked into Ann's office a little too soon after knocking. Jason was there, and they seemed to have a hard time keeping their hands off each other." He smiled and shook his head. "After all my years of teaching, for once I found that comforting."

Ann and Jason spent another hour talking before taking a leisurely walk to the student union for lunch. After the emotional rollercoaster of the last twenty-four hours, neither was able to settle down to work until mid-afternoon. Ann was yawning and threatening to fall asleep at her desk when her phone rang.

"Ann, this is Paul. Gettelman and Filburt want to meet with Bill and me at four. I'd like to meet with you, Bill, and Jason in about ten minutes. Can you make it?"

Ann blinked and shook her head. "Ahh, yeah, sure. What's on the agenda?"

"Bring your summary of the BCV calf studies we've completed."

"Okay. See you there." Ann hung up, rubbed her eyes, looked at her watch, shook her head, and tried to remember who the heck Filburt was.

Ten minutes later, Ann and Jason walked into Paul's office. They'd each brought cans of Diet Coke for caffeine. They sat together, leaning against each other and trying to keep their eyes open. It didn't register on either of them that Paul was wearing a white shirt and tie—a sign that a meeting with outside dignitaries was coming up.

Paul was searching his desk for his reading glasses. The search was such a regular part of his day that students joked about it. Piles of papers and scientific journals, stacked a foot high, teetered around the edges of the desk, penning a disorderly collection of loose papers in the center. Paul looked under and around several piles until he lifted an envelope covering the eyeglass case. He put his glasses on and pulled a manila folder from the middle of one of the piles, stabilizing the top of the stack with his other hand.

"I believe you have both met Dr. Gettelman of the CDC. He's bringing George Filburt of the FBI to talk to Bill and me about BCV, your last study, and the missing samples. Gettelman said he wanted to bring Filburt up to speed on the science, and Filburt wants as few people present as possible. He's already disturbed by the rumors going around."

Jason frowned. "He wants information about our studies, but he doesn't want to talk to Ann or me?"

Bill, also wearing a dress shirt and tie, walked through the door and took a chair. "Jason, you've hit on the reason why bureaucracies fumble around like a bear with a barrel stuck on its head. Bureaucrats put their trust in titles and ties. In science, that means they get their information from the people furthest removed from what happened and least likely to know why. We should feel honored that Filburt is willing to talk to anyone below assistant dean."

"So what do you want from us?" Jason asked.

Bill pulled a notebook out of his briefcase and put it on the table in front of him. "Paul and I need to review the study with you and Ann to make sure we understand everything. With the FBI involved and their history with investigations in science, you and Ann are better off staying out of this."

Ann was puzzled. "What do you mean?"

"Google Wen Ho Lee and you'll understand," Bill said.

Paul and Bill made copies of Ann's summaries and reviewed them with Jason and Ann. They'd nearly finished when Paul glanced at his watch and picked up his copy of Ann's summary. "Almost four. We'd better get going, Bill. It won't help if we make them wait."

They ran into Gettelman and Filburt in a hallway off the PathoBiology departmental office as they walked to the conference room. The conference room was barely large enough to hold an oval mahogany table and the ten steel and plastic swivel chairs around it. There were no windows in the room, but the cream-colored walls and overhead fluorescent lights made it feel airy and larger than it was.

Gettelman, in a sport coat, and Filburt, a trim man of about forty wearing a charcoal-gray suit, took chairs on the east side of the conference table; Paul and Bill took chairs across the table from them. Filburt pulled a leather notebook and pen from his briefcase.

"I've asked for this meeting," Gettelman said, "to let you know what Zedong Xue's lab results were and how that might bear on the results of your last study. I need your ideas and your help, and Agent Filburt needs background information on the virus."

Filburt had never trusted academics. They asked questions and ignored rules. He leaned forward in his chair and looked Bill, then Paul in the eyes. "But first, I must insist that no information about your most recent calf study or the missing samples be discussed outside of this group. Agreed?"

Paul slowly shook his head, and Bill frowned. "We can't agree to that," Bill said. "We have two very bright graduate students who ran the study, who know more about it than we do, and who will be testing the study samples. The testing and analysis of the data will be adversely affected if we can't discuss the study with them."

Filburt's face turned red, and he turned to Gettelman. Gettelman shrugged. "Professor Thompson's point is valid. It will only slow the work down, for them and for us, if . . ." Gettelman looked at his notes, ". . . if Ann and Jason aren't informed about Xue."

Filburt pursed his lips and drummed the fingers of his right hand on the table. Academics! "Okay, you can inform them, but they have to keep their mouths shut."

Paul nodded. "Do you want a confidentiality agreement?"

Gettelman looked at Filburt. "How much do you want in writing?"

Filburt shook his head. "I'd rather not have a damned thing in writing. If SARS is involved, it falls under the Select Agents Act. I'll start the paperwork to have them approved to handle Select Agents. The forms they sign for that will cover confidentiality."

"That's settled then," Gettelman said. He started to describe the PCR tests conducted on samples collected from Xue to detect any coronavirus similar to SARS.

Filburt held up a hand. "Wait a minute. What is PCR?"

Gettelman remembered how little Filburt knew about microbiology. "It's the acronym for the polymerase chain reaction. It allows us to target a specific stretch of DNA and multiply it thousands of times. An extra step is necessary, but specific strands of RNA, the nucleic acid that guides production of proteins, can also be multiplied by the test."

Gettelman, not blessed with a talent for condensing technical detail, droned on. He described finding two coronaviruses in the samples: the SARS virus and a previously unknown coronavirus. The unknown virus was by far the most numerous in the sample. Sequencing genes from the unknown virus proved it was a hybrid of BCV and SARS, as Jason had predicted. Gettelman put his notes down and looked at Paul and Bill. "We didn't find SARS or the hybrid virus in the samples from Ann or Jason."

Gettelman, Paul, and Bill discussed details of the calf study. Filburt tried to take notes but quickly gave up and sat with his arms folded across his chest. When the conversation between the other men ended, Filburt looked at Gettelman. "I have to explain this problem to a congressional committee, and the only thing I understood in this discussion was Jason's name. Why were he and Ann working on BCV?"

"BCV is a common cattle virus," Gettelman said.

Filburt nodded slowly. "If BCV is a common virus, why the hell are we worried about it now?"

Bill opened his mouth, thought a second, and nodded to Gettelman.

"We proved that RNA from the SARS virus was inserted into the BCV chromosome," Gettelman said. "That mutation created a new virus and changed its target from the gut to the respiratory tract. That's why the calves developed severe pneumonia."

"I thought genes were made of DNA," Filburt said.

"They are, in most life forms. A few viruses, like HIV, SARS, Ebola, and the common cold virus have genes made of RNA," Gettelman said.

"Okay, I got that." Filburt scribbled in his notebook and scanned his notes. "You said there was a mutation. Why did that happen?"

"If two RNA viruses infected one cell, the enzyme that makes RNA could have fallen off one chromosome, like a train jumping the rails, and dropped onto the chromosome of the other virus. The enzyme would have just kept going, producing a hybrid chromosome, which produced a hybrid virus. RNA viruses are also prone to frequent smaller mutations."

"Why?" Filburt asked.

Gettelman's expression didn't change, but he started to tap one foot. "The enzyme complex that makes RNA doesn't correct its mistakes."

"Why would you expect an enzyme to correct mistakes?" Filburt asked.

Gettelman put his clipboard down, uncrossed his legs, and

leaned toward Filburt. The foot that had been tapping stopped. That knee was now bouncing up and down. "Because the enzyme that replicates DNA does have a proofreading function. When it makes a mistake, it backs up and corrects it."

Filbert nodded. He was scribbling notes furiously, eyes focused on his note pad. "Why are we concerned about a biological weapon, if this is the sort of thing you expect?"

Paul recognized Gettelman's frustration and pretended to concentrate on his notes as he tried to control a smile. Gettelman remembered what talking to his four-year-old son was like. His knee went into overdrive. "We didn't expect BCV and SARS to ever be in the same cell. They were continents apart until Joe—"

Filburt looked at Paul and Bill. "Joe? That's the Chinese kid?"

Bill nodded and Gettelman continued. "We are worried about this as a weapon because the hybrid virus infected Joe and he nearly died. When animal viruses infect people, they tend to be either harmless or deadly, and when two viruses infect a host and one virus becomes predominant, chances are it is the most virulent one. This is an animal virus with genes from the SARS virus. It's likely to be nasty because it blew the SARS virus away when it came to reproducing itself in Joe."

Gettelman thought Filbert looked as though he might ask "why" again. "Talk to Jason if you want to know why animal viruses are so bad in people. He's more familiar with the evolution of virulence than I am. Just remember that influenza, HIV, Ebola, and SARS all originated in animals, and HIV, Ebola, and SARS are RNA viruses."

Although his expression remained neutral, Gettelman spoke slowly and deliberately. "What is critical is that we have identified a hybrid virus that infects people and cattle and causes a severe pneumonia in both."

Filburt's face showed his confusion. "So . . . let me get this straight. This is a cattle virus . . ."

Gettelman considered how difficult it was to condense a lifetime of study and research into a few sentences that a layman would understand. "It's an entirely new virus, a hybrid human-cattle virus, and it causes pneumonia. Think of AIDS. The HIV virus is a hybrid of two monkey viruses that infected a chimp and later a man."

Filburt dropped his notepad. "Christ! Is this virus transmitted by sex? Then how did Joe get . . . Are you saying the kid was banging the—"

Paul covered his laughter by pretending to cough, but his face turned red and his shoulders shook. He excused himself and stepped out of the room. Bill followed him.

"Good God, no!" Gettelman yelped. "I only used HIV as an example of another hybrid virus created the same way. Sex has nothing to do with this virus."

Paul and Bill returned to their seats as Filburt picked up his notepad and began writing again. "Okay, then why weren't other people infected by this hybrid virus? You said Jason, Ann, and student help were taking care of the calves?"

"All of them were repeatedly exposed to BCV," Paul said. "That immunized them to BCV, and we think it gave them a partial immunity to the hybrid. Their immune systems also weren't stressed out by travel, like Joe's was, and they followed our biosafety protocols. Joe broke safety protocols when he exposed the calves to SARS."

Filburt looked at his notes and chewed the top of his pen. "How bad an infection is this likely to be in people?"

Gettelman tried to count to ten, but by five he decided he'd already done his best. He glanced at Paul and almost imperceptibly nodded toward Filburt.

"We aren't sure," Paul said. "It's potentially deadly because it's related to SARS and, as Dr. Gettelman explained, it's also an animal virus that mutates frequently."

Bill changed the topic. "Any idea where that little skunk Ahmed or the missing samples are?"

Filburt pursed his lips and considered how much he could say. "We've learned he changed flights Friday morning. He took a Saturday flight to Paris, changed planes in Charles De Gaulle and Cairo and arrived in Islamabad on Sunday. Someone fitting his description traveled from the Pakistani Foreign Office to the International Islamic University on Tuesday morning, Monday night, our time. He returned to the Foreign Office complex but hasn't been seen since."

For the rest of the meeting, Paul and Bill filled in details of Ann and Jason's studies. Filburt asked a few more questions and took voluminous notes.

As the meeting wound down, Paul turned to Gettelman. "Questions will come up as we test the samples from the last study. Do we have permission to conduct further studies with the hybrid virus?"

Gettelman stopped putting his clipboard away. "Let's take that on a case-by-case basis."

"Do you have another lab animal model for the hybrid virus?" Paul asked.

Gettelman stood, picked up his briefcase, and pursed his lips. "You're right. We should talk about your next study soon."

The other men also stood to leave. Filburt looked from Paul to Gettelman. "You're going to let them do more studies? Here?"

"George, Paul reminded me that the calf is the only animal model available for testing this virus, and Ann and Jason are the only people in the world who have experience with it. The CDC doesn't even have buildings set up to hold calves. We can fund the studies and have them done quickly here, or we can delay them a year while we build a facility. Which would you rather do?"

Filburt shrugged. "Okay. Just asking."

Everyone picked up their notes and shook hands. Paul and Bill high-fived each other after Gettelman and Filburt left the room.

North St. Paul
Evening, March 20

Ann stayed at Jason's apartment that evening. Condensation on the vinyl-framed window in January and February had left water stains on the white wall opposite Jason's bed. Ann had ignored the worn, dark green carpet that cried out to be vacuumed. She wasn't going to become his housemaid, and it was more fun to cuddle next to him through the night.

She turned to him. "Who was Wen Ho Lee?"

"I don't remember the details," Jason said, "but the FBI investigated a nuclear espionage case a few years ago and messed up big time. They tried to pin it on a respected Chinese-American nuclear scientist and got it so wrong that the judge apologized to the scientist when the case went to court. He was cleared, but his career was ruined."

"Wow. Depressing." Ann thought of something more interesting. "Did you miss me?" She pulled the covers to her chin and snuggled against Jason. It was the first time she'd visited his apartment since their misunderstanding.

"How can you ask that after I washed the sheets, picked up my living room, vacuumed the floors, and scrubbed the countertops in the kitchen?" Jason asked. "I've never done that for anyone."

She kissed him and let a fingernail trail south from his chest. "That's easy to believe, at least that you've never done it for anyone else. But vacuumed, scrubbed? Really?" Ann traced her fingers north along the inside of his thigh.

Jason liked where this was going. "Ooh . . . ah, well, I wiped the countertops off with a clean sponge. God, I missed you." He wrapped her in his arms and kissed her gently, his kisses moving slowly down the side of her neck. "I don't want us to be apart again, I want to be there when junior comes along, and when the next one arrives, too."

Ann slipped her fingers through his curly hair. "Hmm. I guess you are glad to see me. But do I get a say in how many juniors there'll be?"

"If you'll marry me. Will you?" Jason asked again, and returned to kissing her.

"Maybe. If you're really, really, good in bed."

For once in his life, Jason got it right and let his actions speak for him.

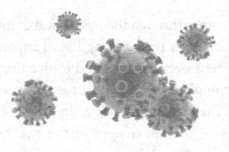

CHAPTER 8

Islamabad, Pakistan
March 21

The colonel pushed away from the desk, leaned back in his chair, and rubbed his eyes. It was late and he was tired. "Have you completed questioning Fasihullah?"

The master sergeant nodded. "He lost control of his bladder before I asked the first question. It was embarrassing. Fasi babbled everything he knew and guessed at more. I wouldn't believe a word he said once I strapped him on the water board. He would have said anything to make us stop. Most of my subjects would."

The colonel sighed. "That's usually how it is. How is he now?"

"He knows the penalty if he discusses what happened. There are no marks, and he'll recover his composure in a few days."

"Good." The colonel glanced toward the ceiling. "I hate doing this, but others expect it. Mark the information he gave voluntarily in the transcript. I want to know what's trustworthy."

"Yes, sir."

"And be kind to Fasi." The colonel gestured toward papers in a folder on his desk. "The report from Minneapolis indicates he didn't know what was in the package or who the recipient was."

"That was his story through the first round of interrogation." The sergeant shrugged. "After that, he implicated anyone I suggested."

The colonel bent over his desk and glanced through the report. "Did you show him pictures of the insurgents we suspect? Could he identify either of the men at the university?"

"The pictures he identified were of the two biochemists we've been trying to track. They left the university three years ago. Both frequented a mosque led by an imam close to the Taliban. We have reports putting them at a camp in Afghanistan, along the Northwest Frontier, and occasionally in Yemen."

"I see. File your report with the pictures. Clean Fasi up and send him home." The colonel collected the papers on his desk and put them back in the manila folder. He dismissed the sergeant with a nod.

The sergeant saluted and left. The colonel waited until his office door was closed before he picked up his phone and dialed. "Put me through to the general, please," he said. He relaxed and tilted back in his chair.

Pleasantries out of the way, the colonel approached his topic delicately. "I don't like this, sir. We are dependent on a source in Minnesota to tell us what was in the package, and—"

"Sharif is comfortable with the source," the general said. "That is enough for me."

"But sir, we are dependent on the university staff here to explain how the virus could be used. We have no proof our professors know anything about this virus. We don't even know if the Military Intelligence service is involved or who it might be aiding. It's like fighting from inside a tent—we can't see, we can't hear, and we don't know who is outside or what they're doing."

The general assured the colonel that all would be made clear when his son Ahmed returned. He admitted he'd been concerned about his son. The kid had spent too much time with his mother and her family; in the general's opinion, he'd grown up arrogant, lazy, and weak. Nothing in the reports from the university had contradicted that—until last week.

"This is the last report on Ahmed," the general said. "'Ahmed Kahn, at great personal risk, showed industry and initiative in recovering samples of a mutant bacterium . . .' And later the report says, 'He fought off several federal agents who tried to prevent him from recovering the property of the government of Pakistan. Ahmed presented himself at the consulate where he is recovering from grievous injuries sustained in the defense of Pakistan's rightful property.' This is a most welcome change in my son's attitude."

Neither man knew that Ahmed had written the report.

Pakistani Consulate, Minneapolis
March 23

Friday morning at the Pakistani Consulate, Ahmed tried out the shoes with lifts that Omar provided for him as he prepared for his trip. He would use Fasihullah's luggage and passport. He congratulated himself that the papers he carried describing his work and everything he'd heard about Ann and Jason's work would be carried in a diplomatic pouch.

There was no evidence the FBI was watching the consulate, but Sharif thought it best to exchange Fasi's ticket for a late-afternoon flight. If the FBI was watching, the car would be less conspicuous and more difficult to follow during rush-hour traffic.

A black Mercedes with diplomatic license plates carried Ahmed onto highway 35W at 4:00 p.m. It navigated the concrete canyon of sound barriers that protected miles of suburban homes from traffic noise until it came out on the open prairie north of Richfield. A Minnesota State Patrol car pulled up beside them and paced the Mercedes as it turned onto highway 62 and headed east toward the airport.

Ahmed watched the officer examine the Mercedes. His pulse quickened; his hands felt clammy. The patrol car fell behind, followed them for a mile, and turned off the highway.

"What . . . what was that about?" Ahmed asked the chauffer.

"Sahib, I was exceeding the speed limit, but that is common on this road. Perhaps it was our tinted glass. Glass this dark is not legal in Minnesota. When he dropped behind us he saw our diplomatic plates and left."

Ahmed relaxed. He hadn't been aware of how tightly wound his legs and shoulders were until then. Arriving at the airport, they drove along a low terminal for small commercial aircraft, then between the U-shaped three-story main terminal and two parking ramps that filled the center of the U. The road curved left up an incline at the base of the U and brought them to the check-in level of the Lindbergh terminal.

Ahmed found the first-class baggage check in the airy steel and glass gallery just inside the terminal. Fasi's diplomatic credentials insured the bags were not examined and Ahmed was waved through the international security checkpoint. He bought a cheap cell phone in the shopping mall connecting the terminal's concourses. From there, he passed under the full-size reproduction of *The Spirit of St. Louis* hanging from the ceiling and took moving walkways down the long gray hallways to terminal G. While he waited for his flight, he charged the battery of his new cell phone at one of the cubicles provided for computer and cell phone charging. *The Americans make this so easy*, Ahmed thought as he read the cell phone instructions from cover to cover—possibly the first male ever to do so.

The cell phone was charged by the time boarding was called for first-class passengers. Ahmed turned the phone off before he boarded and made himself comfortable in his cushy first-class seat.

He did some quick calculations and decided he could have a couple of cocktails and wine with dinner. It was a nine-hour flight, followed by a four-hour layover and a four-hour flight before he'd meet his new friends in Cairo. There wouldn't be anything on his breath by that time to tip off his new associates that he was not an observant Muslim.

His plane touched down in Amsterdam on Saturday. Ahmed was still sleepy, but it was ten in the morning in Amsterdam. He de-planed, visited the men's room, drowned his old cell phone in a sink, and dumped it in the trash. He checked on the gate and time his connecting flight was to board and found an Indonesian restaurant with a secluded table; heavy Dutch cuisine didn't appeal to him. Before ordering brunch, he drank several cups of black coffee to wake up.

He pulled out his laptop and browsed the internet, as instructed on the web site he found before going to the consulate. He'd been given instructions to find and decode the phone numbers he would need tomorrow. He visited several porn sites chosen at random before he went to the right one. He searched the site, navigated to the page he'd been told about, and found a string of numbers under a lurid picture. Ahmed pulled his computer closer to him and looked around to see if anyone else might have seen the pictures on the screen. He remembered he was in Amsterdam, not Minneapolis, and relaxed.

He wrote the numbers under the picture on a paper napkin. Being in no rush, he enlarged the picture, tilting his head to the left and right to examine it. Contortionists, he decided.

He was about to leave the site when he remembered he'd been told to visit more than one page, spending equal time at several of its offerings. Ahmed didn't mind. If this was espionage, he promised himself he'd practice often.

Next, he found "objurgatrix" on Wikipedia, found the word in the definition that corresponded to the first number he'd written, and from that determined the area code and phone number he was to call. He looked up two more arcane words before moving to other sites, including some of the porn sites he'd visited earlier—just to be careful, he told himself. He watched videos until the waiter arrived with his food.

It had been a long day, two days, really: it was the last day of his old life and the first day of his new life. *Now, it begins*, he thought and pulled out his new cell phone. No one, not the Americans, not his father, and certainly not his uncle or mother would be listening in on this conversation, or later be able to trace the connections he'd made.

His sense of security left him as he waited for his next flight. He questioned whether he could have slipped past American and Dutch security so easily. The longer he sat at the gate, the more he imagined that every man reading a paper or magazine was an agent surreptitiously watching him. He was jumpier than a mouse in a cattery by the time his flight was called. His heart pounding, he forced himself to hobble slowly up the Jetway to his plane when every nerve in his body demanded that he move as fast as his injured knee would allow.

His confidence slowly returned as the plane flew over Germany, Austria, and Italy, until somewhere over the Mediterranean he was able to sleep. Landing in Cairo, he was well rested and better able to keep his anxiety under control. He limped up the Jetway to the terminal and took a deep breath of warm Egyptian air. He felt relieved, free, and oddly at home. It was a matter of culture, not homeland. Here, he was comfortable and understood what society acknowledged as appropriate—socially, sexually, commercially, and academically. He felt he was relaxing for the first time after five years in the States. He wouldn't have to fret over how casual or formal he had to be with his professor, where he could find the foods and spices he was familiar with, how freely he could watch women without being rude, which ones he could approach, how and when.

He'd been a stranger in a strange land. No one had been at fault; Ahmed knew that intellectually, but it didn't lessen his resentment on a visceral level, or reduce his stress. His social anxiety was self-inflicted, but Ahmed wasn't given to reflection or self-criticism.

That was over now. He was in an Arab country and fifteen kilometers north of Cairo. He was home, or at least close enough to what would be his new home.

He caught himself: close enough, good enough, pretty good; damn! He'd been in Minnesota too long.

As his luggage was transferred for the last leg of his flight home, Ahmed carried his diplomatic pouch out of the terminal, into the Egyptian night and away from his old life. The car was waiting by the curb, as he'd been told. The front passenger-door window lowered. Ahmed looked at the driver—unsmiling, middle-aged, a day's growth of stubble. "Thursday?"

The driver nodded. "If you have the flight."

"Pan Am or TWA," Ahmed said, and with the code words, the driver unlocked the door. On entering the cab, Ahmed found a battered suitcase on the seat next to him.

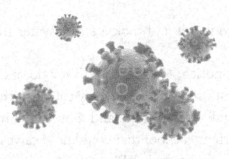

CHAPTER 9

St. Paul Campus
Morning, March 24

Ann and Jason met at her office to plan the next calf study, as Paul and Gettelman had requested. Ann watched Jason searching his pockets for a pen and wondered how anyone so bright could be so disorganized. She tossed him one of hers. "So, what are the questions we have to answer about the virus?"

The room felt comfortable with just the two of them. It would have been crowded if Jennifer, Ann's office-mate, had been there. The office was serviceable: fluorescent lights in the ceiling, pale yellow concrete block walls, and a tile floor the color of waxed dirt.

Jason slouched in his chair, legs spread out in front of him. "We have to find out if virus grown in tissue culture can cause disease as severe as the virus grown in calves, and we have to compare routes of infection—virus fed in the milk to virus blown up the nose."

Ann scribbled notes on a pad. "There was a third question."

Jason stretched and sat up in his chair. "How well does the virus spread, and how does it spread from calf to calf."

Ann remembered the long, rope-like strands of mucous that hung from the noses of the sickest calves in their last study and was glad she'd eaten a light lunch. Her stomach had been queasy recently. She fought an urge to vomit and took a sip of water from the bottle on her desk.

Jason didn't notice. He suggested they do one study to answer the first two questions. With over forty calves in the study, it would be the largest study they'd done and would require every isolation room in the veterinary school that could hold calves. "You've written our other protocols," he said. "Why don't I write this one?"

Ann looked at him cautiously. "Are you sure? Don't you have work in your lab that has to be done?"

"That's okay. This shouldn't take long. How hard can it be, ah, compared to molecular virology?" Jason stood and headed back to his office.

"I'll send you the template we're supposed to use," Ann called after him. She attached the protocol template to an email. "So he thinks if I wrote the other protocols, it can't be difficult, does he?" she whispered as she hit send. She thought of the minutiae in the protocol, Jason's temperament, and giggled.

Jason was sitting at his desk, glaring at his computer monitor when Ann walked in two hours later. "Why the hell do we have to use this protocol template? There's page after page of mind-numbing detail. It's insane."

Ann leaned over his shoulder, tousled his hair, and read a few lines on the screen. "That's how you make sure the study is done right. Screw it up and our careers will be over before they get started."

Jason turned and kissed her hand. "I'll have to work on this all weekend. There goes our shopping trip."

Ann put her hands on his shoulders, bent down, and kissed him on the cheek. "I don't care about a ring. We can't afford one anyway."

"I want a diamond on your finger so other guys don't think they can birddog you."

She left him to his work and dropped by again after finishing a report. Well before she reached his office, Ann heard him yelling at his computer. "What the fuck? Who cares what farm the calves will come from?"

Ann rolled her eyes and hurried to his office. Jason was giving his computer monitor the finger when she got to his door. "Quiet down! This is supposed to be confidential. I could hear you in the hall."

He got up from his desk and paced behind it. "Nobody else is in the building, anyway. It's the first nice day this month, and I'm stuck in here with the protocol from hell." He pointed at the computer screen. "Look at those damned questions! Who gives a rat's ass what size vial or what gauge needle we use to take blood samples?"

"That stuff is routine for . . ." Ann decided that now was not the time to tell him he was being a baby. "You need a break," she said. "I'll finish the protocol while you catch up on your lab work."

Jason agreed, sent Ann an electronic copy of what he'd completed, and stomped out of his office to his lab. Ann went to her office and finished the protocol in an hour. She slid a copy under Paul's door, put another in Bill's mailbox, and called Jason's lab. They drove to the Mall of America and hiked back and forth between jewelry stores until her feet ached and Jason admitted defeat. He couldn't afford any of the rings they liked. It didn't bother Ann; she was happy to spend time with Jason, basking in the glow she felt from what he'd said earlier.

Jason sat up in Ann's bed the next morning. He'd forgotten what really clean sheets felt like. He'd spent the night at Ann's apartment getting reacquainted with civilized behavior: picking up, putting things away, cleaning, and other customs foreign to bachelors.

Ann's roommate was away for the weekend, and it was the perfect opportunity to spend the night and prove he knew how to fold his clothes and what the drawers in a dresser were for. At the moment, he was lost in thought. "I wonder if I dare revise the protocol, now that we've given copies to Bill and Paul?"

"Hmm?" Naked, Ann was cuddled next to him, barely awake.

"Just thinking. We addressed two of our three questions in the protocol. We could answer all three if we expanded the study a little."

Ann yawned and snuggled closer to him.

Jason described his idea. "Think it would work?" he asked.

Ann sat up in bed. "No idea. Why?" She rubbed her eyes and yawned again.

He looked past Ann to the alarm clock on a table next to the bed. "Maybe I can call Paul and Bill at home."

"Are you trying to irritate them as much as you've irritated me? Nothing you can do this weekend will speed up the study."

"But I want to—"

Ann gently held Jason's chin in her hand. "Is talking all you guys do?" She kissed him as she ran her fingers down his thigh. "Can't you think of anything better to do with clean sheets on a Sunday morning?"

"Hunh?" The question caught him off guard, but the gentle stroke of her fingers focused his attention.

"Ever work with horses?" Ann asked.

"Only in vet school."

"Remember how we walked sweaty horses after exercise to cool them down?"

"Sort of."

She turned toward him, rolled onto her knees, and patted the sheets. "Scoot down, lay down flat."

Jason did as he was told.

"Now, have you heard the phrase, 'rode hard and put away wet'?" Ann threw a leg over his legs.

Jason shook his head.

"Well, it's time you learned, so pay attention."

Cairo
March 25

In Cairo, several hours before Jason and Ann woke, Ahmed examined his new passport. He wore a tattered suit with an economy class ticket to Djibouti in its breast pocket; he'd found them and the suitcase in the taxi from the airport last night. The driver had given him his instructions for today.

His tailored clothes were in a dumpster or on their way to Islamabad. He still wore his hand-made Italian shoes—there were some things he wouldn't give up, no matter what his new associates told him to do. He cringed when he saw himself in the cracked mirror over the ancient dresser in his room and tried not to think about the clothes he'd thrown away, the peeling wallpaper, the bare lightbulb in the ceiling or the musty smell of the mattress in this pigsty. He'd never been in a hotel that had only one lavatory per floor. He grabbed the battered suitcase his new friends had given him, hobbled down the steps to the dingy hotel lobby, and paid for the room with cash.

His gloomy driver returned to deliver him for his late-afternoon flight to Djibouti. His contact had chosen the flight because it boarded at a time when the airport was normally crowded and passengers were least likely to be closely scrutinized. They had to leave for the airport at noon because of Cairo's congested traffic. Except for domed mosques instead of cathedrals, the fifteen-kilometer drive to the airport was similar to what he'd seen in large cities in the US and Europe. Few American cities had highway medians with manicured shrubs and trees as attractive as those he passed. The early twentieth-century British commercial buildings soon gave way to modern high-rise apartments, hotels, and office buildings as they left the old city and headed toward the airport.

Ahmed was more aware of his surroundings at the airport than he'd been when he flew in the day before. Everything seemed to be stainless steel and glass. The black plastic seats with chromed metal supports in the waiting areas at the gates he thought of as International Airport Standard. Except for a few potted palms and passengers in Arab dress, he could have been in Minneapolis, Amsterdam, or London. *Well, maybe security isn't as tight here,* he thought as he boarded his plane.

It was a short flight to Djibouti. Ahmed was surprised to find it drizzling and in the mid-80s when they landed, but he reminded himself that even arid climates have wet seasons. He flagged a taxi and asked to be taken to the Hotel Horseed where he'd been told there was a room reserved for him.

The cabbie, a young black man in khaki pants rolled halfway to the knees, put Ahmed's bag in the trunk and held the rear door open for him. The taxi left the airport, turned onto the Boulevard du Général de Gaulle and headed northeast to the city. The boulevard took them past miles of blowing refuse, mud, and stinking hovels. People sat in the rain in front of their houses, flat-topped boxes of corrugated tin, plywood, cardboard, and canvas haphazardly slapped together. Doors and open spaces—unglazed windows, he assumed— were covered with blankets or sheets hung from ropes strung across the openings. Mud was everywhere; drainage didn't exist.

Now and then he caught a glimpse of an alley or maybe an old creek bed behind the shacks. It seemed to be filled with stagnant water, but rain on the cab's window interfered with his view. Ahmed rolled down the window for a better look. The acrid, all enveloping stench of raw sewage blasted up his nostrils. It was so strong in the humidity and heat that a foul taste coated his tongue.

"Idiot!" his cabbie yelled. "Don't ever open a window in this part of town."

Ahmed already had the window closed. He pulled out a handkerchief and spit, trying to get the odor and taste out of his mouth. *The stagnant streams are open sewers,* he thought.

The hovels gradually gave way to crumbling French colonial two-story buildings with arches and wrought-iron balconies. The roads in front of them had less trash lying about. Open stalls selling cooking pots and things he couldn't identify crowded around the buildings. Oversized black umbrellas covered some of the stalls.

A bit more than ten minutes after leaving the airport the cab turned off the boulevard and onto a clean street lined with trees and graceful French colonial buildings painted white, cream, tan or pale yellow, with touches of light blue or rust-colored trim. The cabbie pulled up a drive and stopped at a two-story entrance, covered with blue-glazed panels. The two white wings of the building were built in a style Ahmed thought of as Modern American Ugly. It gave him the impression of a hotel trying to look like a cheap motel.

"That will be 800 Djibouti Francs," the cabbie said. "Unless you want me to find a woman for you tonight. I know many girls, Ethiopians, Somali, Djibouti. Do anything you want. Very eager, very clean—almost virgins. Just got into town. Or I can bring you a boy or a big stud—all very clean, too."

Ahmed curled his lip in disgust. He'd heard about Djibouti's rampant prostitution and the concomitant AIDS and antibiotic-resistant STDs. "I don't have Djibouti Francs," he said. "There wasn't an ATM at the airport. Will you take US dollars?"

The cabbie pursed his lips, looked at the sky and pretended to calculate the fare at the current exchange rate. He picked a number that would fuck this tourist really good. "Okay. Twenty dollars American. Women or boys extra. What kind you want?"

Ahmed gave the cabbie a twenty, took his bag from the man, and walked into the hotel without answering. He checked into the hotel in an open-air lobby shaded by palms. Not as bad as he'd expected. Through a window he saw waves breaking on a sandy beach a few yards from the back of the hotel. *Gulf of Aden. Maybe things are looking up*, he thought. "How much per night is the room?" he asked the clerk.

"Six thousand Djibouti Francs. That's a little over thirty-six dollars, American," the clerk added as he handed Ahmed a brass key.

Ahmed did a double take. "Thirty-six dollars?"

The clerk nodded as he filed the form with the information Ahmed had supplied. "Breakfast can be served tomorrow for 550 Djibouti Francs extra. That would be a little over three dollars American."

Ahmed felt a sinking feeling in his stomach. "Then 800 Djibouti Francs would be," he did some rough calculations in his head. "Less than five dollars American." His fists clenched and his knee throbbed as he said it.

The clerk nodded. "About that. There is a produce market down the road and a restaurant. Return to the hotel by ten o'clock tonight or you will be locked out. The gates to the grounds are closed and locked at night to avoid theft."

"Too late for that," Ahmed muttered and picked up his bag.

The room was a disappointment. It was clean, but the walls were bare and the floor linoleum. The toilet was communal and lacked toilet paper. He tossed his bag on the bed, pulled the bottom sheet up enough to allow him to inspect the mattress. *Good*, he thought, *at least no signs of bed bugs*.

St. Paul
Morning, March 26

Consular Sharif looked through the official dispatches on his desk and answered one that needed a personal response. He delegated the handling of the other messages to the appropriate staff members and turned to several personal messages. The first was a thank-you note from General Khan, Ahmed's father, and another from Ahmed's mother and uncle.

The last message was a private note from a friend in Islamabad in answer to a question Sharif sent him by post. Sharif had not trusted the security of cables or email. Reflexively, he walked to the door of his office and made sure it was closed. Standing beside his desk, he looked to his left and right before he opened the letter. He caught himself doing it and felt foolish. This was his office. He knew it was secure, but an excess of caution had saved his career in the past.

He read the first paragraph. *I was right,* he thought. *Omar is in military intelligence!* Sharif wondered why he hadn't been informed of this through official channels—unless Omar was there to keep an eye on him. Perhaps a conservative imam had complained about his collection of European art. But why did Omar warn him?

Sharif paced back and forth in front of his desk, his hands and the letter clasped behind him. *Omar is subtle and intelligent,* he thought. *He should go far.* Sharif stopped and read further, nodding slightly as he did. He found the information he sought. Hassan, an old friend of Sharif's, was Omar's uncle, an uncle Omar was close to.

Sharif hadn't talked to Hassan in years. Decades ago, Sharif had extended simple courtesy to him when Hassan was in financial difficulty and snubbed by others. Sharif sat at his desk and pulled out his personal stationery.

St. Paul
Early Afternoon, March 26

Ann, Paul, Bill, and Jason sat around Bill's desk as Jason made the telephone connection to Filburt and Gettelman. Everyone said hello, and Ann described the proposed study.

"This is a very ambitious plan," Gettelman said. He'd seen too many complicated studies collapse. "Wouldn't it be easier to tackle the questions one at a time?"

Bill recognized Gettelman's underlying concern. "We've done several smaller studies similar to this," he said, "so Ann, Jason, and our staff are experienced in conducting these studies."

"But what difference does it make if calves can only be infected by the virus from feces delivered orally?" Gettelman asked.

Paul was about to answer when he looked at Jason. "Go ahead," he said.

"It's the difference between a major concern and a minor irritant. If only virus from calf feces can cause a serious infection, Ahmed and his associates won't be able to grow enough of the virus to be a threat to anyone. The calves he needs must be collected aseptically at birth by well-trained crews. They can't be allowed to nurse because milk from their mothers will have protective antibodies that could block the virus from growing. But without the maternal antibodies, the calves can't survive without expert veterinary care and special facilities. Those aren't available in the Middle East."

After a moment of silence, Gettelman said, "Do it. I'll call the dean and make sure you have isolation rooms and funds. But let me know when you start. I want to see this."

The protocol discussion completed, Ann and Jason were excused from the meeting. Paul brought up their other topic. "Al, Bill, and I would recommend that you approach the people at Ohio State or Oklahoma State about replicating our studies. They have scientists that are world class and have worked on BCV. If you start now, they'll complete their work shortly after we finish our study."

There was a prolonged silence on the line. Gettelman finally spoke. "To be honest, Paul, I've already made an appointment to talk to the lady at Ohio State."

Pakistani Consulate, Minneapolis
April 9

"Omar, please, come in." Sharif ushered the younger man into his office and closed the door. He guided Omar toward a settee near a wingback chair in front of a bay window. "Please, be seated," Sharif said, and pointed to the settee. Sharif made himself comfortable on the chair. "Have you heard anything of our former guest?"

A slight smile crossed Omar's lips. Sharif was less formal than customary. Omar guessed that Sharif had learned that he was in military intelligence, perhaps even learned why he was posted to the consulate. "Sahib, Ahmed did not go home, although Fasi's luggage arrived with Ahmed's belongings. The diplomatic pouch he was carrying has not surfaced, and rumor has it that Ahmed met friends in Cairo who supplied him with a new passport and new identity. It is believed that he and his package are in Djibouti."

"Djibouti!" Sharif exclaimed. "Many will be following his travels with interest. Was his father aware of the change in Ahmed's travel plans?"

Omar shrugged. "You will have to ask the General. I have only heard rumors."

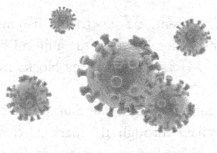

CHAPTER 10

Ta'izz, Highlands of Southern Yemen
April 13

The campus of the University of Ta'izz, founded in 1993, sat on a rise off the Sanaa road, a bit over a hundred yards from other buildings. Sparse shrubs and stunted trees clung to the steep and heavily eroded hills that formed the backdrop of the university. A tree-lined drive made a loop from the road to the university and back. The Life Sciences building was five stories of sand-colored concrete and glass, its entrance set in a four-story, crenelated sandstone arch that looked like the gate of a tenth century city. The outer walls and windows suggested an arched colonnade. The design of other buildings at the university, were variations on that theme.

Asphalt drives and parking lots separated the buildings. Except for the green grass, trees, and shrubs immediately around the buildings, unpaved spaces were covered with sand and fractured rock. Those areas resembled abandoned construction sites, a reminder that Yemen was the poorest of the Arab states.

Ahmed limped from his taxi up the steps of the Life Sciences building. The school wasn't well known, but he wanted to keep a low profile. He would be safe and comfortable here. He longed to shed his cheap clothes, have his knee repaired, and ditch the cane. To throw the CIA off his scent, his new friends had moved him through a series of inexpensive hotels across the gulf in Djibouti, all of them similar to the Hotel Horseed and many blocks from the expensive European hotels.

They'd flown him into Yemen at Sana'a, the capital. With little else to do, he walked through the narrow, crowded streets and broad plazas of the old walled city, famous for its red brick buildings and city walls decorated with whitewashed arches and geometric patterns. The arch of the thousand-year-old Bab-Al Yemen gate was made of gray stone flanked by rust-colored Greco-Roman columns. Atop the arch, sandstone framed a large rectangular panel of blue-gray stone and the upper third of the arch. The arch itself was over two stories high, and with the panel above it, the gate was slightly over three stories tall. The gate was impressive, but the four- and five-story ancient brick residences rising behind it were beautiful. Each was lent a graceful, almost lacey appearance by arched windows and whitewashed bands of brick latticework.

He'd almost felt out of place in the old city because of his clothes. A few men wore western clothing, but most wore the *thobe*, a long white robe, often with a Western suit coat or sport jacket worn over it. The men left their jackets unbuttoned to display their *jambias*, curved steel knives carried in the *azib*, an ornamented scabbard. The *jambia* and *azib* were worn on a belt, centered about where a Westerner would have worn the belt buckle.

The four-hour, 150-mile car trip from Sana'a to Tai'izz on the N1 highway wasn't as rough as he'd feared. His associates assured him they could provide a new identity and install him as a visiting Professor of Microbiology here at the University of Ta'izz. He would have prestige, income, medical benefits, and cover for his work with the hybrid virus, all in one package.

He walked through the revolving door and entered the air-conditioned five-story atrium. The rough granite walls and sandstone floors were shaded by potted palms. Burbling fountains at each end of the atrium lent a musical backdrop to the ambience of contemplation and rest.

He sat on a marble bench under a palm and watched students scurry past. Now and then, students deferred to men in suits. *Faculty,* Ahmed thought. *This is as it should be. In the States, the faculty dressed so casually, I couldn't tell professors from impoverished students.*

With a shudder, he recalled the first seminar he'd given at an important scientific conference in Chicago. He'd prepared a twelve-minute talk on his work with a *Salmonella* species during one of his periods between graduate advisors. *That was lucky,* he thought at the time. With minimal supervision from an advisor, he didn't have to please nit-picking faculty with his data, analysis, and conclusions before the meeting.

At the conference, an old man with a white beard stood as Ahmed ended his talk. Dressed in rumpled, nondescript clothes, the guy asked a couple of questions. Ahmed thought him a bum and barely listened to him. He answered the questions in a condescending tone, and walked off the stage, head held high, as quiet laughter swept the auditorium. He thought he'd put the old bastard in his place.

A friend asked him if he'd recognized the man. "Why should I care who the old fool was?" Ahmed asked. "I quashed his objections."

"Yeah. Sure you did. That was Richard Cornwall III."

Ahmed remembered the titters and giggles he'd heard as he walked off the stage. He turned white as he realized the audience had been laughing at him, not with him. Cornwall was the world's leading expert on Ahmed's topic. His questions had gently pointed out that Ahmed's data didn't make sense.

Ahmed hid in his hotel room through the afternoon meetings. He went to a bar and got drunk while his companions gathered for dinner and a night on the town. For the rest of the week, whenever he saw a graduate student or professor looking at him, he knew what they were thinking. The ones that pointed him out to their companions were the hardest to take.

Ahmed put the memory behind him, checked his watch, and took a business card from his wallet: Faculty of Biochemistry, Professor Hassan Al-Mikhafi, room 410. He was a few minutes late, but appointed times were elastic in Arab countries, he reminded himself. Best to spend a few minutes to review his story and decide how honest he would be with his new associates.

Secrets were the only constant in his life. First, he kept his own council with his parents to play them against each other. The facade of the agreeable graduate student in Minnesota followed, until he put the screws to Naga. Now he would be a studious professor to the university administration and an observant and devout Muslim to his other colleagues. In a Muslim country, at least he knew what the rules were for his new masquerades.

He glanced at his watch again. Ten minutes late. It was a relief to be shed of the American obsession with punctuality. He would never understand why powerful men allowed themselves to be tyrannized by the clock. Gingerly, he extended his right leg as he struggled to stand with his cane and good left leg. On his feet, he limped to the elevator and waited.

A few minutes later, he rapped on the open door of room 410. "May peace be upon you and may God's blessings be with you, Professor Al-Mikhafi."

The lean man behind the desk looked up. His trimmed mustache and black hair were flecked with gray. Ahmed was relieved to see that his benefactor wore a long-sleeved white dress shirt and tie under his white lab coat. At Ta'izz, Ahmed would be able to use appearances to judge to whom he should defer and politely nod agreement. That would be a considerable aid for an academic with a weak scientific background.

Al-Mikhafi smiled, stood, and came around his desk. "And may peace be with you. You must be Ahmed Khan."

As they shook hands, each put his left hand on the other's shoulder and they exchanged kisses on each cheek. Al-Mikhafi offered Ahmed a chair, closed his office door, and returned to the chair behind his desk. "We have talked on the phone many times. It is a pleasure to finally meet you in person. How was your trip?"

The men chatted about Ahmed's air travel, recent soccer games in Europe, alluded to the circuitous route from Cairo to Djibouti and thence to Yemen, and slowly approached the real topic. Ahmed eventually asked, "Did Fasi make his delivery in Islamabad?"

"All went as planned and the package is safely stored. It will be moved to a freezer in your laboratory as soon as you have settled in."

Ahmed and Al-Mikhafi talked for over an hour, covering Ahmed's official duties and salary in the Microbiology Department, his identity documents and new passport, housing, banking, safe roadside food vendors, and decent restaurants before Al-Mikhafi turned to Ahmed's other duties. "Have you learned more about the virus since our last conversation?"

Ahmed was prepared to cover his ignorance with supposition and guess work. "The virus is a mutant BCV that causes severe respiratory disease in cattle and is transmissible to man. It is believed to be a hybrid of BCV and the SARS virus, created accidentally when a Chinese graduate student with SARS took care of calves in a BCV study."

This was not the answer Al-Mikhafi wanted. He leaned back in his chair and put his fingertips together. His voice unconsciously took on the hard tones he used with dull students. "I gathered that from our previous conversations. Do you have any *new* information?"

"None since I left Minnesota. The virus is grown on a human

rectal tumor cell line commercially available as HRT-186. Cell culture conditions and requirements are standard."

Ahmed leaned forward. An offense might be his best defense. "You do have cell culture facilities in the Microbiology Department, don't you?"

"Certainly. The university has strong relationships with German and American universities. Our people are well trained, but we must be careful how we use them. Others must not know of this project."

Al-Mikhafi sat up straight and looked Ahmed in the eyes. "But getting back to your plans, how much work must be done before we will know if the virus can be used against the infidels?"

Ahmed, never comfortable around people with strong beliefs, leaned back in his chair to look relaxed and casual. He'd always been good at describing a future his listener wanted to hear, and Google had provided enough corroborative information to give him a veneer of expertise. "We will be able to grow vast amounts of the virus on HRT cells and disseminate the virus in infidel countries. Simple devices connected to air handling systems could create aerosols of the virus on airliners, trains, and in schools and movie theaters. Think of the terror it would inspire if we sprayed the virus into the air ducts of a large American or European elementary school."

Ahmed remembered he was talking to a jihadist and quickly added, *"Inshallah."*

A quick glance at Al-Mikhafi to verify he hadn't noticed the pause and Ahmed continued. "Fear for their children would cause schools to be closed and bring education to a halt. The virus could spread through the entire population, disrupting their economy and civil authority. SARS has a ten percent case fatality rate, three times higher than the Spanish flu of 1918. The hybrid might be more deadly. Used against cattle feedlots in the US, it will kill tens of thousands of steers, causing economic hardship and food shortages."

Ahmed sat up and, eyebrows raised, leaned toward Al-Mikhafi.

"The virus could even be a source of income if sold to certain friendly countries, or perhaps traded for nuclear weapons. This virus may make it possible to re-create the Caliphate, *inshallah*."

It helped that Al-Mikhafi was a biochemist and not a virologist, but he wasn't naïve. He looked sharply at Ahmed. "That is not what I asked. Have you done any work on the virus?"

"It is an infectious agent. It does the work for us," Ahmed said. "Once it begins to spread in Western populations, our work is over." Ahmed relaxed and sat back in his chair, confident he'd sounded knowledgeable and convincing.

Al-Mikhafi spoke slowly, without smiling. "That is a graduate student's answer, based on convenient assumptions. We don't know how lethal this virus is or how readily it spreads. There may be years of work to do before we can use it for jihad." He stood and paced behind his desk. He reminded himself that Ahmed had given up a comfortable life to join him, had already been injured fighting to secure the virus for the jihad, and was fresh out of graduate school. He was still a novice, more of a post-doc employee than an assistant professor. Al-Mikhafi realized he would have to act as an advisor and mentor until Ahmed had more experience.

Al-Mikhafi stopped, looked at Ahmed, and smiled. "There is another way, *inshallah*, we can use the virus to our advantage."

Ahmed was puzzled.

"No doubt the infidels are already looking for you and your package. The CIA must be nervous. They are imagining what we could do with the virus, and a few of them will be pressing to take action. Women and children will die when the Americans act from a distance, *inshallah*." Al-Mikhafi thought of the children he'd seen who had lost a foot, a leg, or an arm to land mines. *The dead were buried, but cripples? Cripples live among us in squalor and pain, a constant reminder of the righteousness of revenge.* "We will have ten new recruits for every peasant they kill and a hundred for every child they maim."

Al-Mikhafi spoke softly. "Rumors will launch warplanes, *inshallah*, and lies will destroy villages." Al-Mikhafi paused, looked at the floor and remembered pictures from other American wars. A naked girl running, screaming. Planes flew overhead, and the girl's back, coated with napalm, was burning her alive. He pictured an entire classroom of similar victims, their extended families recruited, and savored the idea.

St. Paul Campus
Afternoon, April 13

"I asked for this meeting," Gettelman began, "to bring all of us up-to-date. George, do you have any more information on where the virus may be or who has it now?"

Filburt looked around the table. "None that I am free to share," he said, *and none I'd ever share with academics and a kid who needs a haircut,* he thought. "It would help if you could tell me what danger the virus poses and what type of facilities terrorists would need to grow it."

Jason looked at Paul. Paul nodded his approval, and Jason proceeded. "Our last study indicates that only virus harvested from calves will cause severe or fatal disease in calves, and presumably in people. That limits how dangerous it will be in Ahmed's hands."

Filburt's brow furrowed and he chewed the end of his pen. He looked at Gettelman. Gettelman was nodding in agreement with Jason. Filburt sighed and put both hands on the table. "I hate to ask this, Al, but why? Why do you think Ahmed must grow it only in calves?"

Gettelman waved in the direction of Jason and Ann. "I watched them run their last study and saw the results. They know what they're talking about, George."

Filbert shook his head. "But why?"

Paul looked at Jason and gave him a subtle nod. "This virus mutates continuously," Jason said. "Grow the virus in tissue culture and you select for viral clones that grow best in tissue culture. That selection causes the virus to lose virulence. When we give the virus to calves, many different cell types are exposed to the virus, giving many different mutants a chance to thrive and mutate further. Think of it as enhancing diversity by letting it grow in nature as opposed to a tissue-culture zoo."

Filburt scribbled notes and nodded. "Okay, diversity is good for the virus, and you get diversity by collecting the virus from the back end of the calf. I can understand that, but is this theory or proven? Are you certain that the virus grown in tissue culture will not infect people?"

Jason shrugged. "No. Other than Joe, we have no proof that anyone has ever been infected with BCV or BCV-SARS. I'm basing my ideas on the mild diarrhea my crew developed when we started working with BCV, our results in calf studies, and theories on the evolution of virulence in pathogens."

Filburt leaned back in his chair and tossed his pen on the table. "So, what you have is an educated guess, right?"

Jason looked at Paul for help. The silence grew uncomfortable as Paul thought how best to proceed. "Correct. But Jason's history of educated guesses is excellent. He guessed that what produced the respiratory disease in the calves was a BCV-SARS hybrid virus, and he guessed that the mutation was in the gene for the spike protein. Dr. Gettelman's lab proved him correct."

Filburt scribbled more notes and looked at Paul. "Will this Ahmed character know that there might be a difference between calf-grown and tissue-culture grown virus?"

"Ahmed was not a curious student," Paul said. "He may give the virus to someone who has the curiosity and background to figure these things out, but I suspect an interest in evolutionary biology and the evolution of virulence is not common among fundamentalists."

"You mean terrorists?" Filburt asked.

Paul thought of the time he'd served on a local school board. "Whomever Ahmed is dealing with," he said. "Although I'd bet the statement holds true for fundamentalist sects of any religion. I think Ahmed and friends will check virology textbooks and use the traditional cell culture methods they find to grow BCV."

"Is there anything we could do to encourage that approach?" Gettelman asked.

Bill leaned forward and looked at Filburt and Gettelman. "Ahmed and friends will not have access to the calves they will need. We have to work hard to produce them and keep them alive, even with the university dairy herd right here on campus."

Gettelman took Bill's thoughts further. "Any lab work will require people with experience, sophisticated technical training and expensive equipment. In that area of the world, the universities, research centers, and research hospitals are under government control. Work with the virus will have to be done surreptitiously."

Filburt finished taking notes and looked around the room. "I think what you've given me is sufficient for now, except for . . ." Filburt looked at his papers. "Control measures. Would it be possible to make a vaccine to this virus?"

"A modified live vaccine to BCV is available for cattle now," Ann said. "We could—"

"Just a second. What's a modified live vaccine?" Filburt asked.

Paul answered. "It's a vaccine made with a live virus. The virus has been attenuated. It can infect the host, but it can no longer cause disease." Paul saw a puzzled look on Filburt's face. "The oral polio vaccine is an example of a modified live vaccine."

"Okay, how do you, ah . . ." Filburt looked at his notes. "How do you amputate the virus?"

"That's at-ten-u-ate," Ann said. "Growing the virus on tissue culture for forty to sixty generations usually does it. As Jason said, you end up with a virus that thrives in tissue culture but can produce only mild infections in people or animals."

"How long would that take?" Filburt asked.

Jason tapped the keys on a calculator. "Seven to ten months, if everything works on the first try. Double that to be realistic."

Filburt scribbled. "Okay," he reviewed a checklist of information he wanted to get during the meeting. "I'll pass this information up the line, and I suspect that someone will check back with you periodically as my colleagues learn more about Ahmed's . . . travels." He began to pack up his notes. "As before, do not discuss what we've talked about with anyone outside this group."

"What about the dean and researchers at other universities?" Paul asked.

Filburt paused. "I guess you have to be able to talk to the dean, but that's the only person. Dr. Gettelman is in charge of contacting other scientists."

As Filburt walked toward the door, Ann asked a question that threw him off his guard. "Did Ahmed make it back to Pakistan? Is the government there protecting him?"

Filburt turned to her. "Protect him? He never arrived in Pakistan, and his father signed the warrant for his arrest."

Gettelman left shortly after Filburt, but before he did, he handed a piece of paper to Paul. "She's expecting your call. I believe you've worked together on BCV before. You have my permission to provide anything she needs to replicate your studies."

Paul looked at the note. "Ohio State? Sure. I've worked with her many times."

Gettelman and Filburt left. Paul crossed his arms and leaned back in his chair. "Naga doesn't have anything good to say about Ahmed, but he hates his guts. Is there anyone at the U of M who would know Ahmed better? Someone whose opinion isn't colored by emotion?"

"What about your friend, the Pakistani grad student in poultry pathology?" Ann asked Jason. "Didn't he start here the same time as Ahmed?"

"His name is Harith Sabeeh," Jason said. "He arrived in this country with Ahmed and lives in my apartment building."

"Do you know him well?" Paul asked.

"I have lunch with him sometimes, and he comes over to watch sports on TV occasionally. I don't know if you'd call him a gamer, but he sure enjoys video games."

Paul was puzzled. "What's a gamer?"

The corners of Bill's mouth twitched, threatening to break into a grin. "People who take role-playing games, war games, and video games seriously. One of my boys wouldn't do anything else if we didn't limit his time online."

"Oh," Paul said. He'd never played a video game and his mental picture of a gamer was still foggy. "Jason, do you think you could have the guy over and ask him how much he thinks Ahmed might be able to figure out? You can't ask him directly, but you should be able to get an idea what he thought of Ahmed."

"I won't be running afoul of Filburt and his rules, will I?"

"Not if you let Harith do most of the talking."

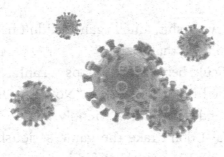

CHAPTER 11

St. Paul
Evening, April 16

Harith settled back on Jason's couch, a game controller in his hands. Harith's swarthy complexion, deep-set dark eyes, and black hair made Jason seem paler and his hair redder than it was. Both men were glued to Jason's forty-five-inch flat-screen TV. "Thanks for inviting me to game with you. Man, I wish my computer and television could interface like yours. This is awesome."

"Thank a friend of mine," Jason said. "The guy's a frickin' computer genius. He put in some kind of patch so we can play the game on the television. Uh-oh. Ooh, rats."

Jason desperately tried to hold up his end of their team. He furiously punched the buttons of his controller, but it was a losing proposition. A tiny paladin in armor, holding a sword before him, moved skittishly across the screen as Jason moved the controller. The paladin was moving through the ruins of a stone temple when it was blocked by another figure, this one a gold scorpion with the head and naked breasts of a woman. The scorpion woman leapt in front of the paladin. Jason punched a button on the handset and the paladin's sword swung wildly back and forth, missing the figure. The scorpion stung the paladin, which seemed to deflate and disappeared from the screen. "Aww, shit, killed again. I didn't have a chance. How . . . how'd that thing do that to me?"

"It wasn't difficult, believe me. Woops . . . ahh . . . damn," another paladin disappeared from the screen. "Now I'm dead, too." Harith looked at Jason and gave him a friendly elbow in the ribs. "You should be grateful I don't take the game seriously. Otherwise, I'd have to swirl you in your own toilet for getting my character killed."

"I thought it might help my game to have an experienced player show me the ropes."

"I tried, but damn, Jason. You really suck at this. Are you sure this isn't the first time you've played Diablo II?"

"Thanks. Anything that'll help build my confidence is appreciated." Jason tossed his controller to the side on the couch. "My nephew introduced me to it over spring break. Whipped my butt, too."

"He should be ashamed of himself. Tell him I said he shouldn't pick on his blind and feeble elders or Allah will zap his ass."

"I'll try to remember that."

"You're in the middle of your thesis project, like me. You don't have time to learn a game well enough to compete with high school boys. Wait until you've got your PhD and you're sitting around waiting for replies to your job applications. You'll have plenty of time to practice then."

"Yeah. You could be right about that. Care for a beer, or are you observant? I have diet soda, too."

"Okay. One beer should be alright. I try to be observant, but my friends keep placing temptation in my path and female vet students mistake me for some tall, dark, and handsome dude they heard about. It has made my life very complicated."

Jason went to his kitchen and brought back two cold cans of beer. He handed one to Harith and sat down with the other. "Want to play another game, or should I switch to Comedy Central?"

"Comedy Central. At least that won't cost me a character."

Jason put his beer down, clicked a couple of buttons on the remote, and Comedy Central came on. "Harith, how come you adjusted so well to life in Minnesota, but Ahmed always seemed to have a chip on his shoulder?"

Harith looked at Jason. This sudden change in topic suggested Jason hadn't invited him over just for the game. "Ooh, Jason. I've found that there are people who enjoy life as they find it and people who feel that they deserve better, whatever their circumstances. Sooner or later, those who believe they deserve better get serious about religion or politics and are never able to find happiness. I enjoy life as I find it."

"I didn't know Ahmed very well. What kind of a student was he?"

"Tsk, tsk, tsk." Harith shook his head, looked at Jason and smiled. "Jason, my friend, didn't they tell you to let me finish the beer before you pumped me for information?"

Jason feigned innocence. "What do you mean?"

"We are talking about Ahmed, right? The arrogant prick who stole your BCV samples, flew off to the Middle East, and disappeared?"

"Shit. I'm really not any good at this, am I?"

"Even worse than you are at Diablo. Don't ever volunteer for an intelligence agency. You aren't cut out for it." Harith took a long draught of beer before putting the can down on the empty peach crate Jason used as a coffee table. "Who asked you to do this? Paul? Even the FBI can't be that stupid."

"It was Paul."

"Good. You have restored my faith in your FBI. To answer your question, Ahmed had such, ah, I think you called it a 'chip on his shoulder.' He tried to study, but his anger and resentment got in the way, and he was not accustomed to work. Learning takes focus and work, and Ahmed couldn't get that through his head. If you let someone else do the work for you, then someone else learns the lessons."

Jason hesitated for a minute before deciding to come clean. "Ahmed isn't the sort of person to question normal procedures, is he?"

Harith thought for a moment. "What you are asking is, 'Will Ahmed assume that the usual course of action will work, or will he ask the necessary questions to get it right?'"

"That's it."

"Ahmed never loved biology the way you and I do. He will accept the assumptions we all make at the beginning of a project. Unlike us, he will not test them until it's obvious to everyone that it isn't working. At that point, he'll have no idea what went wrong. He'll revert to being an arrogant bastard and blame others for his mistakes."

"That's what I thought."

Harith laughed and tapped Jason on the shoulder with his fist. "Would Paul like me to write it out, so you get it straight?"

"Would you be willing to go to Paul with me and tell him yourself? I'd rather Paul knew what others have figured out."

"Oh, no!" Harith said. "I'm not going there. If I talk to Paul, the FBI will want to talk to me. I don't have time for that shit. I'll waste hours answering the same stupid questions, over and over, hours that I should spend working on my project, letting American women teach me about sex, and writing my thesis. Besides, I don't think the FBI will be as much fun to be around as you are." Harith took another swig of his beer. "Do you have any pretzels or chips?"

After dinner in his private apartment at the Consulate, Bilal Sharif logged into his computer and checked a Yahoo account opened under the user name 35BillESmith. Apart from an announcement that he had inherited a fortune in Nigeria, three ads for male enhancement, and exciting news about a wonderful bra that would change his social life, there was a note from his cousin's son, a young man with the username 82DarkandHandsome.

> *Dear Uncle BillE,*
>
> *Dad sends his best. The investment broker that stayed with you is not someone you should trust, but you knew that. He is unaware of a serious flaw in the business plan of the company he is touting. His competition is counting on his ignorance.*
>
> *Regards, D&H*

St. Paul Campus
April 17

Paul had news. "Our colleague at Ohio State called this morning. They tried to pass BCV-SARS on HRT cells to produce a seed stock for a vaccine. The virus lost all of the SARS RNA within four passes on HRT cells."

Bill, the only one at the small table in Paul's office who wasn't trained in molecular biology, looked quizzically from Jason to Ann. "So," Ann said, "as Jason thought, if Ahmed tries to grow the virus in tissue culture, it will become a normal and harmless BCV. He'll have trouble making calves sick, let alone people."

Jason grinned broadly. "And unless he tests his virus for the SARS RNA segment, he won't even know he's lost it."

"Everybody I know who does molecular work complains about how touchy RNA work is. Has Ahmed ever worked with the stuff?" Bill asked.

"He's a bacteriologist, and his project didn't include molecular biology," Jason said. "He's never had a reason to work with RNA."

"But he could get help and advice from other faculty members," Paul said.

Bill looked at Paul. "Has Gettelman heard about the Ohio results?"

"They were going to call him next. I should call him and let him know about Ahmed's limitations. Maybe Filburt could arrange . . ."

Paul stopped abruptly. "Ann and Jason, thank you for coming by on short notice. Bill and I have some things to discuss. Would you close the door on your way out?" and with a nod, he dismissed them.

When the door closed behind Jason, Paul turned to Bill. "I'll call Gettelman now. I trust Ann and Jason, but if information gets out, I don't want anyone suggesting they leaked it."

He put the phone on speaker mode and dialed Gettelman. "Al, Paul Schmidt here. I have news from Ohio State. They found that the BCV-SARS hybrid is unstable when passed on HRT cells. It loses the SARS insert rapidly."

"That's wonderful. Do you think Ahmed will think to test the virus if he grows it on HRT cells?"

"Unlikely, unless a virologist supervises him. Ahmed's never been the curious sort. The people that know him believe he will assume that what works for BCV will work for the hybrid."

Gettelman thought for a moment. "Hmm. Anything we can do to keep him on the wrong track?"

Bill whispered, "contract labs" to Paul.

"Bill just suggested we do what we can to keep Ahmed from working with contract labs that have cattle facilities. There are probably fewer than twenty labs in North America and Europe that Filburt would have to contact."

"Unlikely to work," Gettelman said. "Too great a chance Ahmed could find one greedy enough to ignore our requests."

"Can you contract with those companies to do other work that will fill their facilities? You could fund legitimate research and tie the lab facilities up for a year."

"We can do that for some labs. For the others we'll have an FDA official let them know we'll put them out of business if they even think of working with Ahmed. We can't do anything to the contract labs themselves, but the FDA can put the labs, their scientists, and all their corporate officers on a list of proscribed facilities and people. Their major customers, the big pharmaceutical companies, will cancel all work with them if they are on that list. They'll never work in biology again," Gettelman said. "It's a great idea, but I, ah, I should warn you, Filburt and his colleagues may have other plans."

"That sounds ominous," Bill said.

"I know of nothing planned yet. Just be aware of what might happen."

Bill and Paul looked at each other after Gettelman hung up. "Other plans?" Bill repeated. "I hope some damned fool isn't planning an invasion."

"Unless they know where Ahmed is working, they wouldn't know where to invade."

"When have they let that stop them?" Bill asked.

Pakistani Consulate, Minneapolis
April 19

Omar walked to his appointment. He appreciated the changes that had taken place at work. Without seeming to do anything out of the ordinary, Sharif had raised Omar's status at the consulate. Services and perks normally available only to senior staff were quietly placed at his disposal, and his uncle Hassan had received a handwritten letter from his old friend Bilal, a letter in which Omar was generously praised.

The old boy is cagey and smooth, Omar thought. *He gives offense to no one unless he's ordered to. He even treats representatives of unfriendly powers with impeccable manners.* Omar had decided to make him a model for his own deportment, even before he had learned of Sharif's connection to his uncle.

Green walls and carpeting set off the white-painted woodwork and almost gave Omar the illusion of spring as he stood before Sharif's secretary and gatekeeper. "I have a two-thirty appointment with His Excellency."

"Certainly, sir." The young man checked a list on his desk. "You may go right in."

Omar knocked on the door and entered. The polished maple floor, Persian rug, and antique furniture gave Sharif's office a formal but comfortable feeling. Sharif sat in a modern high-backed swivel chair behind a Louis XIV burl walnut desk. The desk had the elegantly simple lines of a library table, but with beautifully inlaid veneers no library could afford.

Sharif looked up and stood. "Come in, come in, dear boy. It was good of you to make time in your day to talk to an old man."

Omar was again guided to the settee in front of the bay window. Sharif took a wing-backed chair on the other side of a warm pool of sunlight from the window, pleased that Omar was providing intelligence to him, rather than about him. "How are your father and mother? I haven't talked to them in years."

"They are well, Sahib. My father sends his regards, and my uncle said he appreciated your kind note."

Sharif gave a dismissive wave of his hand. "It was nothing. It gave me great pleasure to write to him again. I should have done it long ago." Sharif leaned back in his chair. "How goes it with our former guest? Is he still in Djibouti?"

"He crossed the gulf to Yemen and is in the highlands near Ta'izz. He may have taken a position in Microbiology at the University of Ta'izz under an assumed name. Two biochemists, formerly of a university in Islamabad, are also at Ta'izz. They are believed to be the ones to whom Fasihullah gave our friend's package. We think they carried it to Ta'izz."

"I see," said Sharif. "Is this information being shared with the foreign office, or should I assume it is privileged?"

"I have not received official instructions. We know that the army is aware of the biochemists' role and their association with the university in Ta'izz, but they have not shared the information with my superiors or our elected officials."

"I will keep it confidential until I hear further from you. You may tell your superiors that I have a contact at the University of Minnesota who could be used to transmit information to the US authorities, should an extra-governmental channel be thought convenient and less likely to create problems with certain factions at home."

"I will let them know, sir. They sometimes disagree with you, but they have great faith in your integrity and judgment."

"Kind words are always appreciated." Sharif stood, signaling the end of the meeting. "Please let me know if there is anything we can do to make your stay in Minneapolis more pleasant."

He is a smooth old tiger, Omar thought. *Velvet and satin on the outside and steel on the inside.* Omar had heard of men who mistook Sharif's courtly manners for weakness. They no longer worked in the government, and one had nearly been tried for treason.

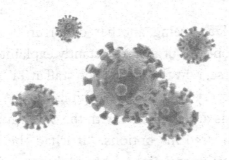

CHAPTER 12

University Hospital, Ta'izz
April 23

Damn! Cruciate repair, and quite possibly knee replacement in twenty years. Ahmed had suspected that was his problem, and the MRI had verified it.

"May the bitch who did this to me be kicked by donkeys and trampled by goats," he muttered. Rage didn't fix his problem. He concentrated on his options for the future as he put the brace back on his knee.

The surgery could be done in Yemen. The doctor in front of him was eager to try the procedure, as was the hospital, but Ahmed didn't feel like contributing to the training of either. The hospital building and equipment were impressive, from the large double arches of the entrance and the spacious waiting room, to the clean, white-walled exam room. He could have been in a European or American hospital, but buildings don't do surgery. People do, and he didn't trust the surgeon he was talking to. Ahmed had built his life on lies; trust in others came hard for him.

I could go to Saudi Arabia or Pakistan, he thought, *but the Saudis could toss me to the Americans on a whim if they identify me, and my father, my own father, ordered my arrest in Pakistan.*

Disappointed at seeing another opportunity slip through his fingers, the orthopedic surgeon reluctantly explained Ahmed's other options. "Of course, now that you are on staff at Ta'izz University, you may have the surgery done at any hospital in the Arabian Peninsula. The university has arrangements with the other gulf states."

Ahmed considered his options. "If I had the surgery in Saudi Arabia, could I return to Ta'izz for physical therapy?"

The surgeon was crestfallen. "Many have done that. You would have initial physical therapy at the Saudi hospital for a week or two, then transfer your records here. Our physical therapy department is small but experienced and competent."

The doctor had an idea. "I'd be happy to accompany you. I have vacation time coming and it would extend my training if I could assist in the surgery."

Ahmed frowned. He didn't want eager amateurs assisting in putting his knee back together, either. He was searching for a way to phrase his objection when the hospital administrator cut in.

"There is the Saudi German hospital in Jeddah. They are top flight, partially funded by the Saudi government and staffed with local and European specialists. Their work and care are superb."

Ahmed weighed the risks and decided the Saudis were unlikely to identify him. He turned to his orthopedist. "Would you contact someone on the staff at the Saudi German hospital and arrange an appointment for me?"

As he hobbled back to his car, Ahmed considered his next obstacle. How was he to convince Al-Mikhafi to let him take the time away from their work to have the repair?

Ahmed sat in Al-Mikhafi's office the following Monday. "You'd like a medical leave already?" Hassan Al-Mikhafi was incredulous. He'd begun to realize Ahmed felt entitled, but this bordered on the ridiculous. "You've barely unpacked. Can't you do this after we have developed our plans for the virus?"

"You said yourself it would be best to proceed slowly," Ahmed said. "My knowledge of virology is thin. I'll be at the hospital and then in physical therapy for a few weeks. That would give me time to do the reading to bring me up to speed on the coronavirus. It will also give you time to feel out the political and religious sympathies of laboratory technicians, find funding for a tech in my lab, and select one to enlist in our work." Ahmed smiled at Al-Mikhafi. "You could even spend time selecting an elementary school that we can donate lab supplies to."

Al-Mikhafi liked Ahmed's approach to education, and he knew Ahmed needed to brush up on virology. "We have leased an apartment in Djibouti. If you used it, you could leave a trail, perhaps use one of your old credit cards, or drop your old passport where it would be found and reported. That is where the Americans would start looking for you. We could use your time in the hospital to have lab supplies delivered to another address we will lease for you. By dribbling the information to them slowly, we will give them the impression you are working. Their apprehension will build until, *inshallah*, somewhere in their chain of command a man will lose his nerve. A fearful man sees phantoms behind every bush. Then the Americans will start the bombing."

Al-Mikhafi paused in thought. "But none of this will work unless they take the bait. We have to have something they can't miss, something that will be reported to them and seize their attention." Al-Mikhafi rubbed his brow and pursed his lips. He looked at Ahmed. "You will be that bait. The Saudi German hospital also does research. It has an extensive library. Take some virology texts and monographs with you to get your reading done. The nurses and orderlies will remember that. And when you are ready to be discharged, visit the research library and check out journals with research reports on SARS or monographs on biological warfare. The CIA may be checking at hospitals for that already."

Ahmed considered this. He had gone fishing once in Minnesota. He knew what happened to bait. This was not how he'd hoped this meeting would go. Al-Mikhafi had described a scenario that could be effective whether or not Ahmed survived. He was now a disposable commodity for both sides. Yet, he had to convince Al-Mikhafi that he was eager to do this or potentially lose his trust.

"I see," Ahmed said. He absently rubbed his knee as he thought. "I could also make phone calls on my last day in the hospital, calls with keywords they may be listening for or to numbers we suspect they monitor. I will have gone to Djibouti by the time they check the hospital. From Djibouti, I'll fly to Ta'izz to spend a secluded month in physical therapy."

Al-Mikhafi nodded. "We think alike. The surgeons probably are booked a month to two months ahead. Let me know when they schedule your surgery. In the meantime, I will have my people lease a building near a school or hospital in Djibouti. Then we will goad the Americans to react."

St. Paul Campus
April 30

A week later the dean sat in on a meeting. Gettelman spoke as he lifted a notebook out of his briefcase. "Sorry it's taken so long to get back to you. I've passed on your suggestions about blocking Ahmed's access to contract labs."

A secretary entered with a carafe of water and five glasses. Bill relaxed in his chair. "Thanks. I think it's the best option."

"I regret to say that your message was not well received. The people in national security prefer more active responses."

Academic amateurs, thought Filburt. He tapped a pencil and drummed his fingers as Bill and Gettelman spoke, occasionally casting sidelong glances toward Gettelman at mention of the military. He coughed lightly to get attention. *Time to get this meeting back on track.* "Our job is to provide them with information, not recommend options for them."

Paul frowned and looked at Bill and the dean. "Even if we find that there is little threat to people, here or over there?"

"If you have it," Filbert said, "then that is the information Al and I will forward to our superiors. But doing nothing is not a popular option in Washington since 9/11."

Gettelman leaned back and stared at the ceiling. He knew Filburt was right about Washington, but he agreed with Paul. "The data from Ohio State are a powerful argument for a careful and limited US or NATO response."

That settled, Paul brought up Jason's theory that people exposed to BCV might be partially immune to BCV-SARS. "Worth taking a look at," Gettelman said. "Send me blood samples from Jason, Ann, Joe, and a couple of other students. I'll have them tested in my lab."

Langley, Virginia
May 15

Five men in military uniform sat around a conference table in a windowless room. Agent Filburt, standing at the head of the table, came to the summary slides of his presentation. "So this is what we know:

"First, a cattle virus combined with the SARS virus, producing a hybrid virus that can infect humans. We assume it is deadly and has potential as a biological weapon.

"Secondly, Ahmed Khan stole samples of the virus. He was

injured in an altercation as he fled the university; he recuperated at
the Pakistani consulate in Minneapolis.

"The stolen samples were carried to Islamabad by a Pakistani
consulate employee and were turned over to people close to the
Taliban. The samples are presumed to be stored now at a university
or medical facility in Yemen.

"Ahmed Khan was given shelter and a new identity in Djibouti
by Ansar Allah insurgents suspected to be associated with Al-Qaeda.

"He may have traveled to Yemen. We expect him to join the staff
of a facility in which faculty members are working surreptitiously for
the Ansar Allah.

"The Pakistani government and army want Ahmed's ass. His
father personally signed the warrant for his arrest. Pakistan's Military
Intelligence may have assisted Ahmed initially. We do not know if
support from Military Intelligence continues."

Filburt closed his laptop on the podium next to the screen and turned
to his audience. "So that's it. A person working with the Ansar Allah
has a potential biological terror weapon. Any questions?"

Each man at the table paged through his printed copy of Filburt's
presentation.

"Why is the FBI hosting this meeting and not the CIA?" a Marine
colonel asked.

"I've been asked to assist the CIA because this began as a domestic
crime, and the experts on the virus are here in the US," Filburt said.
"For this project, I'm a liaison officer between the FBI and CIA. The
CIA station chief in Djibouti is in charge of the project and reports to
the CIA. The State Department is receiving weekly updates."

"Your summary gives the worst possible outcome, correct?"
someone from the back of the room asked.

"It is a worst-case scenario, but entirely possible," Filburt answered.

"The altercation at the university—what do we know about that?" the man closest to Filburt asked.

"He was kneed in the groin, elbowed in the nose, and kicked in the knee. No one knew there'd been a theft or fight until a couple of days after it happened. We have interviewed the young woman who had the disagreement with Ahmed. She suspects she broke his nose and may have caused serious damage to one of his knees. He may be walking with a cane or be in a hospital for orthopedic surgery. Your folder has a list of the hospitals we expect him to contact."

"A woman assaulted him?"

"Ahmed offended a feminist with martial arts training."

Someone said, *sotto voce*, "Rush Limbaugh's greatest fear." A ripple of laughter went through the room.

"What about phone calls, internet searches, and emails?" a younger officer asked.

"We are monitoring what we can. Key words and phrases we've used are listed on page four. Ahmed was in Djibouti, spent a few weeks in the highlands of southern Yemen, and returned to Djibouti. His cell phone transmissions now come from the African quarter of the city of Djibouti. Even the best of that area is worse than our slums. Much of the European section of the city was built in French colonial style between 1880 and the early 1900s. It's on an isthmus projecting into the Gulf of Tadjoura. Because of the beaches, there are several modern hotels in the European quarter. The central market and warehouses are between the African and European sections, as are primary schools, a mosque, and a religious school famous in the region. Population is about six hundred thousand."

"What NATO or US forces are in the country?"

"France has a large naval, air, and marine base in Djibouti. The

US has four thousand military and contract personnel at Camp Lemonnier, near the airport. Both the US and France have strong ties to the government of Djibouti. The Djibouti Armored Regiment is headquartered in the outskirts of the city."

"Languages?"

"Somali and Afar are the native tongues. Many speak French or Arabic. Most people who work in the tourist areas also speak English."

"Do we have agents in the area?"

"One. Others move in and out of the city frequently, as it's a major hub for sea and air travel. The agent on station is . . ." Filburt paused and considered how to make his point. This was a delicate issue. "The agent is unconventional, but he has an excellent working relationship with the French and an impressive record of success."

"Can we utilize the American troops in the area?"

"State and Defense want to keep their hands clean on this, and, frankly, the troops at Lemonnier are support personnel. They aren't combat troops or Green Beret. They may be of help with communications or equipment. Don't expect anything beyond that.

"Remember, our people may be faced with a large volume of highly infectious material in the middle of a large city. The government is friendly to the West, and the city is a tourist mecca. We don't want gung-ho guys with guns and explosives involved. Blowing this stuff up could create a deadly cloud of infectious virus. A gallon of industrial-strength bleach or disinfectant will be of more use than traditional weapons."

"So what the hell are we supposed to do?" a general asked.

"State said intervention by more than a few agents must be a last resort. We are in need of information and technical expertise now. A few senators have been apprised of the situation. There are high-profile senators who are often inclined to favor precipitous action, so please be careful how you phrase your responses to the questions you'll be asked."

Djibouti
May 16

Concrete and stone buildings lined the road. Canvas, cardboard, or plywood covered missing windows, doors, or parts of walls. Here and there a goat was tethered to a post or a house by twine. The street was littered with trash, and the stench from an open sewer behind the buildings nearly gagged Ahmed. He opened the door to a concrete block building that may have stood out in this neighborhood at one time, but that was a generation ago. Many of the blocks were crumbling now, and the door was weathered and warped.

Ahmed felt gall rising in his throat as the door creaked open. The interior of the building was one step removed from a goat shed. Mouse turds covered the windowsills. The layer of trash littering the floor was alive with vermin, including scorpions. Ahmed's skin crawled at the thought of sleeping here.

He turned on his heel and went back to his taxi. "Take me to the Sheraton."

"On the Boulevard de la Republique?"

"How many Sheraton hotels are there in Djibouti?"

"One. The one on the Boulevard, near the Hamoudi mosque."

"Then take me there, you moron."

In the back seat, Ahmed pulled out the new cell phone he had purchased on arrival in Djibouti and dialed Al-Mikhafi.

His voice was low but intense. "Al-Mikhafi, this is Ahmed. What camel-brained, sheep-molesting son of a stinking goat rented that apartment for me? It's a filthy shed. It is tiny and crawling with vermin. I can't live there or anywhere else without indoor plumbing and air conditioning. It's only May and it's ninety-three degrees here. It'll be close to one hundred tomorrow."

Al-Mikhafi's first impulse was to hang up and let Ahmed fend for himself, but he knew his people in Djibouti were accustomed to living crudely. "You may be independently wealthy, but our organization is not. Hire someone to clean it."

"That won't install plumbing or electricity, and I have no contacts here. You have someone clean that goat-shed and call me when it is ready. I'll spend a few hours every day there to make cell phone calls, but I'll be damned if I'll spend a night there. I'm staying at the Sheraton until I leave for Jeddah next week." Ahmed pocketed his cell phone and slammed a fist into the seat next to him.

Djibouti
Evening, May 16

E. Howard Frobisher, special liaison for agriculture at the US embassy in Djibouti, and his French counterpart walked to their table for what would appear to be a romantic dinner at the *Café de la Gare*. Their diplomatic cover was as transparent as the crystal goblets on the table. Ninety percent of Djibouti was a godforsaken rocky desert where starving goats and camels browsed on spiny acacia trees—if they were lucky to find that. The country had no commercial agriculture.

Howard walked behind the French diplomat. He loved the way her white dress draped and moved as she walked. At their table, the waiter pulled a chair out for *Mademoiselle* Juliet Gauthier and seated her as Howard seated himself. If the view from behind was lovely, the view from the front was gorgeous.

They ordered drinks and appetizers before getting to business. Juliet cocked her head slightly to one side. She enjoyed working with Howard. He was handsome, urbane, intelligent—and safe. "Howard, you made this appointment to discuss . . . how should I say it? Stolen goods? My superiors instructed me to assist you in gathering information. Until I receive instructions from Paris, you are on your own if you take action to retrieve or destroy the goods."

"I could not ask for more. Your help will be invaluable, as always. We suspect the thief is in Djibouti or Yemen and will be ordering supplies to grow the virus. We are unsure how dangerous the virus is. If it is deadly, he could create devastating problems simply by discarding the goods in the city market. Anything your people can do to help us find him will be appreciated."

Juliet smiled. "Won't our meeting like this warn the thief's friends that you are on the hunt?"

"Not if we make it look romantic. You do look fetching tonight."

"So you'll be spending the night with me?" Juliet smirked.

"If I may. Your husband is out of town; that will look good."

She nodded and looked at Howard, a smile twitched at the corners of her mouth. *Such a handsome man; such a waste*, she thought. "Maurice sends his regards. And your Stephen is not jealous?" She reached across the table and put a hand on his. "I should feel insulted if he isn't."

"Don't be. Stephen, ah, made sure I'd be looking forward to a quiet night's sleep tonight."

Juliet shook her head and giggled. "So, our religious friends don't suspect your tastes? They don't know that you and I will spend the night talking about business and what selfish beasts men are?"

St. Paul Campus
May 19

Bill leaned back in his chair at the conference table. "Seems kind of irregular, doesn't it? You're sure he'll be safe?"

Filburt nodded. "He'll spend some of his time in training and reviewing information transmitted to the East coast. Since Ahmed knows him on sight, someone will work with him on a disguise when he's overseas. He may be asked to grow a beard or dye his hair. He'll have company men next to him at all times."

They'll have to babysit him, Filburt thought, *or risk the kid blowing the entire mission.* Enlisting Jason to work with the CIA was about the craziest idea Filburt had ever heard—but he had his orders. Once the kid accepted the proposal, it would be someone else's problem.

Filburt saw that both Bill and Paul were still frowning. "Our people will be so tight to Jason he'll feel claustrophobic. We won't let—"

The conversation stopped as Jason walked in. Paul asked him to close the door and motioned him to a chair.

Filburt still didn't feel comfortable trusting a kid in cut-offs and a T-shirt, but orders . . . "Jason, you are unique. You are the only US citizen, other than Ann, who has a working knowledge of virology, knows Ahmed Khan by sight, and according to Dr. Gettelman's lab, is known to have an antibody titer to BCV-SARS. Paul tells me that Ann is pregnant."

Jason looked at Paul. Paul avoided his gaze. Filburt continued. "We have a proposal for you. It would involve working with a team on the East Coast and in the Middle East. When you travel overseas, the field staff assures me that risk will be managed and kept to a minimum."

Jason sat with his eyes wide and mouth open. He looked from Filburt to Paul and back to Filburt. Bill thought he looked like a pole-axed steer, except his tongue wasn't hanging out of his mouth.

Filburt only paused for a second before continuing. "Pay, as a veterinarian with graduate studies under your belt, would be several times your current graduate stipend and approximate the pay of a captain in the army. The job would delay your work here six months to a year, tops. Do you think you might be interested?"

Jason found his voice. "You want me to help catch Ahmed?"

"I said that some of your work would be on the East Coast, training and reviewing pictures and information we've gathered. We need someone who can explain the science to congressmen, to give them a realistic appraisal of the limitations of the virus as a weapon. That alone could limit the use of force and save the lives of innocent civilians. You may travel to the Middle East, but it will be as part of a team. We hope to keep your foreign travel limited and brief. Your job would be to evaluate what we find, help identify Ahmed, and advise the team leader on virology."

"Will I have to try to get information out of people during normal conversation?"

"That's unlikely. We have trained people who do that."

"Oh, good, 'cause Harith says I suck at it."

Filburt frowned. "Who is Harith?"

Jason cringed. *I can't keep my mouth shut, even when no one asks a question,* he thought. "He's a Pakistani student who tried to show me how to play Diablo II."

Filburt stared hard at Jason. "What else did you talk about?"

Jason tried to look innocent. "We talked about sports, preparing for our oral exams, Ahmed, and—"

"Stop right there," Filbert said. "Tell me everything you discussed with him relating to Ahmed. Do not omit anything."

Jason swallowed hard. "Harith knew Ahmed better than the rest of us, so I asked him how Ahmed is likely to tackle a project."

"Jesus Christ!" Filburt exploded. *This is what I get for working with academics and kids who wear cut-offs to work,* he thought. He stood, paced the length of the table, and finally pointed at Jason. "What in the name of heaven prompted you to do that?"

Jason turned white and glanced at Paul.

Paul stared at the table and wondered if he looked as uncomfortable as he felt as he raised a hand. "I . . . I asked him to do it. I thought—"

Filburt held up his hand. "Hold it. No need to go further." Filburt leaned over the table and slammed his hand on it as he looked at the other men. "But we must all agree, right now, there will be no more moonlighting. If you have an idea, you contact me if you're in the States or the CIA team leader if you're overseas. No exceptions. Got that?"

All three men nodded, their eyes downcast.

"I didn't hear that," Filburt said. "Bill, do you agree?"

Bill squirmed in his chair and looked at the table. "Yes."

"Jason, do you agree?"

Jason whispered, "Yes."

"Professor Schmidt?"

"Yes."

Filburt paced back and forth a few more times to get his temper under control. He reminded himself that they had to focus on the tasks ahead of them, not this latest folly. It felt like hours to the others sweating at the table by the time he sat down. Paul looked especially uncomfortable.

Filburt exhaled loudly and, with a dull thump, louder than he'd planned, brought both hands down on either side of the documents in front of him. "All right. Jason, after this meeting you and I will talk about your discussion with Harith. Right now, we still have a question. Would you consider taking this position?"

"How often can I come home to see Ann?" Jason asked. Quietly, he added, "She's five months pregnant."

"It's possible this will be over in a month, but we can't count on it. You can probably hitch a ride back by military transport once every couple of months, depending on what is going on." Filburt paused, looked at his notes and back at Jason. "Are you and Ann married?"

"Not yet."

Filburt wondered if it ever occurred to these eggheads that there were sound reasons for traditions. Paul and Bill, sitting quietly with downcast eyes, looked like chastened fourth graders to him. "My advice is to reject this position unless you are. The odds of something happening to you are miniscule, but you'll want to make sure any survivor payments and benefits go to Ann and the baby if something does happen. You might get an extra housing allowance, too, if you're married." Filburt leaned back in his chair, tossed his pen on the table, and rubbed his eyes. "So, is this something you might be interested in?"

"Do you need my answer now or can I talk this over with Ann?

"Kid, I'm not asking for a commitment now, and I wouldn't accept a 'yes' until you've talked to Ann. All I want now is a 'no' or a 'maybe.'" We'd like a definitive answer within four days, a week at the latest. I'm told things are in motion."

Jason said he might be interested and Filburt dismissed Paul and Bill. When Jason stood to leave, Filburt pulled out the chair next to him, caught Jason's eye and pointed to the chair. "Have a seat." He turned to the door. "Bill, would you close the door as you leave, please?"

Jason watched Bill close the door and reluctantly sat.

"Can you describe your conversation with Hamish—"

"His name is Harith Sabeeh."

"Okay, Harith. Describe your conversation with him."

"We played Diablo II, a video game, one evening. He told me I sucked at it, we had a beer, and I asked him why he gets along so well in the US and Ahmed always had a chip on his shoulder. Then I asked him how he thought Ahmed would—"

"Wait. Back up a minute. You said Harith had a beer. So, he isn't an observant Muslim?"

"He said he tries to be, but his friends keep putting temptation in his path and American women think he's tall, dark, and handsome."

Filburt remembered the intercepted email. His eyes opened wide. "He said American women called him 'dark and handsome'?"

Jason nodded, yes.

"Oh, for God's sake." Filburt drummed his fingers, paused, and held his head in his hands. *Of all the fucking luck,* he thought. *How the hell could this get worse?* He lifted his head and looked at Jason. "Okay. What else did you talk about?"

"What?"

"What else did you tell him?"

"I didn't tell him anything. I asked him how he thought Ahmed would approach a scientific problem."

"What scientific problem?"

"I wasn't specific," Jason said, defensively. "I wanted to know if Ahmed would do his work in a step-by-step process or if he'd make reasonable assumptions and try to take short cuts."

"And?"

"It took Harith twenty seconds to figure out what I was really after. He told me he thought Ahmed would make assumptions and skip steps. He offered to write his answer down for Paul. I asked him if he'd talk to Paul himself, but he said you guys would waste so much of his time it would cut into his social life."

"Your friend is sharp," Filburt said, and wondered if Harith was more than that.

Filburt dismissed Jason and asked him to close the door as he left. Alone and with the door closed, Filburt made a call. "Frank, I can be in your office in forty minutes. I have something I think you'll find interesting."

That evening, Jason wiped off his old table and put out two plates and place settings while Ann took dinner out of the microwave. "Here, let me get that for you," he said as he grabbed two pot-holders and took the covered casserole out of Ann's hands. "Sit down and make yourself comfortable." He got two glasses out of a cupboard. "Water or iced tea?"

"What's up?" Ann asked.

"What do you mean?" Jason said as he poured an iced tea for himself.

Ann giggled. "Make mine water, but Harith was right. You really suck at lying. Why are you so solicitous tonight?"

Jason took a seat next to her. He was unsmiling and serious. She looked in Jason's eyes and ran a hand through his hair. "Honey, normally, you don't come into the kitchen until dinner is on the table."

"I had a meeting with Paul, Bill, and Filburt this afternoon."

Worried, Ann put both hands in her lap but kept her eyes on Jason. "And?"

Jason tried to avoid her gaze. "Ah, Filburt says we have to get married, and soon."

Ann was stunned. "Since when has the FBI been worried about unmarried people making babies?"

"Since they decided they want me to work for them. I might have to travel to the Middle East for a couple of weeks," Jason said quietly.

"What?" Ann sat back in her chair, dinner forgotten.

"It makes sense. I'm the only American, other than you, who has experience working with the virus and would recognize Ahmed."

Ann bowed her head, one hand on her forehead. "No, that doesn't make any sense, Jason. You can't keep a poker face, you know nothing about espionage, and I'll bet Margie could deck you in a fight without dropping her books or breaking a sweat. You'll be helpless over there."

"He said I'll be mostly advisory, evaluating the information they collect and filling them in on virology. My income will be triple what my student stipend is now, and our co-payments for medical care will be cut in half. Filburt said they'll fly me home for a vacation with you every two months if what is happening allows it. It's possible I won't spend more than a month in the Middle East, and I'll have a couple of guards with me whenever I leave the embassy."

"Honey, I love you dearly, but you aren't cut out for that type of work. It'll take three guards working full time to keep you from saying the wrong thing in public. I can picture you spotting Ahmed, and yelling 'I see him, I see him.'"

Jason put his napkin on the table and took a moment to compose his answer. "I'm not demented or stupid, Ann. I'm just no good at lying. Somebody who knows something about this virus has to be there, and I'm the only one who has worked with it, other than you."

"But couldn't you consult by phone, or—"

"I've thought about this all afternoon. BCV-SARS isn't a threat if Ahmed is in charge. Even if he grows it in calves, and I don't think he can, a military response to destroy his facility is likely to backfire. The rest of the world will think the US blew up a farm or a school, killing innocent women and children. That would be more dangerous to the US and our kids than letting Ahmed spend the rest of his life playing virologist."

"How long will this assignment last?"

"It could be a year, but it might be as short as a month. Filburt said things seem to be moving fast."

Ann closed her eyes and thought what it would be like to live for a year without Jason and what might happen to him. At last she sighed and put her head in her hands. "Let me think this over. We can start planning a wedding, but it may be a couple of weeks before we can even arrange to be married by a judge. We'd better let our folks know now."

"Filburt suggested we could fly out to Reno or Las Vegas with a few friends and get married earlier. He wants me on board and married in a week."

"If that's the way it has to be, but Las Vegas for a wedding? Yuck!" Ann toyed with her food and looked at Jason. "I'll see what we can arrange here." She put her hand on Jason's. "I'm not saying 'yes' to your going to the Middle East. I have to think about that, but if you do go, promise me you'll be careful?"

"You and the baby are the most important things in my life, Ann." They stood and held each other. Jason bent and kissed her on the neck. "It took me a while to figure that out, but I know it now, honey. I'll do everything I can to get back to you in one piece."

The next morning, after breakfast and a discussion about their fragile finances, Jason called Filburt and said he would take the assignment.

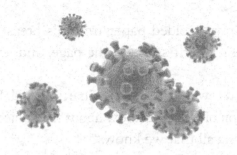

CHAPTER 13

Pakistani Consulate, Minneapolis
Afternoon, May 20

"Omar, so good of you to drop by," Sharif said. He stood to greet the young intelligence agent. "Please, have a seat. You indicated you wished to discuss a matter of importance. I believe it pertains to our former guest."

Omar made himself comfortable in a chair in front of Bilal's Louis XIV desk. *Only someone with a secretary and filing clerk at his beck and call could work at a desk like this,* Omar thought. Walnut, with inlays of cherry and oak and touches of gilt, it was more elegant writing table than desk. It was a desk at which to read, ponder, and sign documents.

Omar leaned back in his chair. "Sahib, the religious observances of our former guest are fickle, and his hubris is an affront to the humility and sincerity so pleasing to the Prophet, peace and blessings upon him. He is a precariously balanced boulder, as likely to crush friend as foe at the slightest touch. I've received intelligence to be passed, unofficially, to the Americans. You said you have a suitable conduit."

"Yes, a relative is a graduate student in the veterinary school and a friend of a scientist working on the bovine coronavirus project."

Omar withdrew a folded paper from his breast pocket and slid it across the desk. Sharif scanned the page, and, eyebrows arched, looked at Omar.

Omar nodded toward the page in Sharif's hand. "I believe it is an accurate reflection of what we know about the subject. I do not know if we are providing all that we know."

Sharif thought a moment and read the short message again. "You may tell your superiors this will be forwarded within twenty-four hours, and give them my thanks."

Early that evening, Sharif logged onto 35BillESmith@yahoo.com on his private computer. With rapid hunt-and-peck typing, he printed Omar's message into an email to 82DarkandHandsome.

> *My dear D&H,*
>
> *The package your friend seeks is in Yemen, and the person he seeks is in Djibouti, probably at one of the top three luxury hotels. His knee requires surgery. He is unlikely to trust surgeons in Djibouti or Yemen. He will probably seek a European-run Saudi hospital. He will need to set up residence in a city with a medical community for the physical therapy required.*
>
> *The city of Ta'izz has that and a scientific community for his work. The University of Ta'izz in the highlands of southern Yemen may become his permanent home. It is believed a biochemist at the university is holding the package for him.*
>
> *Discuss this with your friend, but remember that there are factions at home that might misunderstand your actions, should this become public knowledge.*
> *I remain, as always,*
> *Uncle BillE.*

Two hours later, Harith read BillESmith's message through twice. He shrugged his shoulders, deleted a few words, and printed the page. The clock on the computer said seven, *a good time to call Jason about watching the ball game tonight*, Harith thought.

Jason was alone for the evening and glad to have Harith's company. He answered the door almost before Harith finished knocking. "Harith, come in. How's it going?"

"Man, I need a study break. I read so many scientific reports, I feel like every time I tip my head, everything I learned about an esterase, a de-repressor, or an RNA hairpin loop will dribble out of an ear and I'll never recognize it again. I'm not interrupting you and Ann, am I?"

"Nah. Ann's studying for an exam at her apartment tonight. It's the last class she has to take. The Twins game just started. Grab a seat." Jason opened his refrigerator and called to Harith. "Beer or diet soda?"

"A diet soda for me." Harith made himself comfortable on Jason's decrepit couch. He examined the frayed upholstery, shook his head, and wondered how Ann tolerated it. "Is Ann going to let you move this old thing to her apartment?"

"Nope. She doesn't want me to bring anything from my apartment except my computer. All my furniture goes in the dumpster." Jason opened a bag of chips and poured it into a bowl sitting on the peach crate between the couch and television. "Do you want the couch?"

Harith shook his head vigorously. "No. Just thought I'd ask. Something like this in my apartment would ruin my social life. This thing is so disreputable-looking I'm surprised the Health Department let you bring it in."

On the screen, Pat Borders came to the plate for the Twins. It gave Jason an excuse to ignore Harith's comment. Harith waited to bring up the email until the first commercial break. "Have you heard about our friend, Ahmed?"

Jason turned from the bowl of chips to Harith with a jerk. "Ah, no. Have you?"

"He's in Djibouti city at one of the elegant Western hotels." Harith took a sip of soda, grabbed some chips, and looked at Jason.

"Ahh . . . Ahmed—?"

"Margie did a real job on his knee. I'm glad I'm not the one who has to grade her lab papers. Anyway, Ahmed's knee will require surgery, probably at a European-run hospital in Saudi Arabia. Some people think he will go to Yemen for recovery and physical therapy, probably to Ta'izz, which would make sense. The University of Ta'izz could supply his medical needs, the laboratories and trained technicians he needs for his work, and Ansar Allah insurgents have occasionally infiltrated the area. His package is already at the university."

Jason, mouth hanging open, stared at Harith.

"Jason, didn't your mother tell you to keep your mouth closed when you're chewing?"

Jason closed his mouth and swallowed. "How . . . why are you telling—?"

Harith handed him the page he'd printed. "I figured you wouldn't remember what I said, so you can have this to make sure you get your report right. Next time, you'll have to remember what I say."

Jason's mind was reeling. "Report?"

"Your report for the FBI and Paul," Harith said. "Just don't give them this paper or my name. Certain people at home could get nasty if they hear that I said too much while watching baseball. They might forgive me if it were a cricket match. I could always say I'd been talking in my sleep."

"Ah, you, ah, said something about 'next time?' " Jason asked.

Harith leaned back in the couch. "I love your big-screen TV, Jason. There's no telling how often I will forget myself and say things when I'm watching games with you. You'd better keep a notebook to write them down, without using my name, of course." Harith leaned

forward and looked closely at the screen. "Hey, look. Prieto is at bat."
He turned to Jason. "I thought they traded him last year."

Djibouti
May 22

A block off Avenue F d'Esperey in the European quarter of Djibouti,
Howard Frobisher took his seat across the table from Juliet Gauthier.
The covered patio within the Café de la Gare, comfortably shaded
from the midday sun by acacia trees and a tile roof, was nearly empty
because of the heat. "How do you manage to look so fresh and lovely
in this heat?" he asked, as he fanned himself with his Panama.

"Thank you, Howie. If I have you spend time with Maurice, do
you think you could teach him to drop compliments as beautifully
as you do?"

"I'd do anything for you, Juliet, but Stephen would become suspicious. He can be so unpleasant when he's like that. He'd be insufferable"

As he spoke, Howard surveyed the wall behind them and the
nearby tables. Satisfied that nothing appeared to have changed since
his last visit, he pulled out a cigarette pack and put it on the table.
As he did so, his thumb flipped a switch on the bottom of the pack
and it started to hum.

Juliet cocked an eyebrow. "Still using that? Really, you are in-
corrigibly suspicious, Howie. Is it still effective?"

He picked up her right hand, leaned across the table, and brushed
his lips against her fingertips. "The cost of success. Microphones
can be so small these days, but this pack takes care of those the
insurgents can get. Now, what do you have for me?"

"Your tourist has purchased round-trip plane tickets to Jeddah for
Wednesday, June third. He's planning on spending two weeks there."

Howard nodded. "A source indicated he required surgery and was likely to seek a European hospital in Saudi Arabia. Two weeks is more than needed for cruciate repair. Perhaps he is staying for the initial physical therapy."

Juliet continued. "He will print his boarding pass from his own computer, so we do not trust the address he gave the airlines. The apartment at that address isn't fit for animals. He stops there once a day, stays an hour, and scuttles back to the Sheraton's air conditioning and pool."

Howard sat back in his chair and fanned himself with his Panama again. "We were told the stolen package is in Yemen. Could it be at this apartment?"

"It would be worthless by now, if it was. The apartment has no electrical service and we haven't detected the vibrations a generator would produce; thus, no refrigeration. I believe you said the package has to be kept at minus fifty degrees centigrade, or colder, didn't you?"

"That's what our experts tell us. So you think the address is a dummy, a diversion, or could it be a mail drop?"

"That has puzzled us. It is too primitive to be a serious diversion, and we have not seen any mail delivered. We suspect they're rushing into something without planning, or they are blazingly incompetent."

Howard thought a moment. "Maybe they gave him a place to go every day to get him out of the hotel and make him visible. Perhaps they are trolling him, like bait?"

Juliet cocked her head to one side and ran a finger around the rim of the glass of ice water in front of her. "Why would they do that? Are they trying to get your attention? Or are they trying to incite you to do something?"

The waiter brought more cold water and the menus before Howard could answer. He opened his menu; the waiter hovered over his shoulder. "What looks good to you?"

"The salad with goat cheese, pecans and chopped dates is won-derful here."

"Hmm. The grilled sea bass with garlic butter appeals to me today."

"Wine?"

"You're the expert," Howard said.

"The Pouilly-Fuissé?" Juliet asked.

Howard found it on the wine list and almost gasped at the price.

"The Pouilly should be fresh on the palate, wonderful on a hot day." Juliet's eyes dancing, she grinned at Howard. "My superiors would make me pay for it, but surely you can put it on your tab for world peace?" She sighed dramatically. "If not, we could try a Pinot Grigio, Sauvignon Blanc, or Chenin Blanc. Those would go well with your fish."

Howard looked over the top of his glasses at her. "World peace, eh? It's an election year in the US. Not a good time to poke the accountants with sharp sticks."

They limited the conversation to further comments about the menu and wine list until the waiter left with their orders.

Howard shook his head as he watched the waiter disappear through a doorway. "Back to our friends intentions—we are as baffled by their actions as you are. Do you have anything else for me?"

Juliet leaned back in her chair. "The tourist's friends have rented a modest two-story commercial building next to an elementary school. The building is watched, and they have installed a cheap alarm system. There is an empty apartment on the second floor. Our cameras record traffic and who visits the building. There has been little activity, but at least this building has plumbing, sewer, and electrical service. It could be used for storage or possibly a crude laboratory."

"But there have been no visitors to the building?"

"Only one. I'll see that you get the daily logs and video from the cameras, and I'll call if anything turns up. I believe little will happen until your tourist returns from his trip."

Howard began to speak but stopped as the waiter arrived with their lunch and wine. As the waiter left them, Juliet leaned toward Howard and sniffed. "Ah, the aroma of your fish is mouthwatering. I'll have to try it next time." She glanced toward the waiter as he disappeared into the kitchen. "By the way, would you like to go on a field trip to the building?"

"I'd love to go anywhere with you, Juliet. Would anyone else accompany us?"

"*Non.* I can't take part in any action. You can take an associate, but this shouldn't be a convention, Howie." She grinned and leaned slightly toward him. "Think of it as peeking down their pants to see if there's anything interesting."

"You make the mundane sound so tempting. How could I refuse?"

"There is a building inspector I have worked with. You may accompany him on a routine inspection of the building. You can poke around, take pictures, and write them up on a few things. You should have fun just irritating the tourist and his friends."

"Does Djibouti have building codes?"

"Regrettably, only a few, and enforcement is lax except by the luxury hotels. We can claim that they are being enforced because their building is next to a school."

An hour later at the embassy, Howard sent a coded message to Washington. "WHAT IS REQUIRED TO GROW SEEDS? ADVISE SOON."

On Monday, Jason learned an unpleasant lesson about the promises of a sovereign, whether a monarch or a national government.

"But you said I'd have a couple of weeks of training and work on the East Coast," Jason said.

"The situation has changed," Filburt said, "but you'll get your training. It's just that it will begin in Djibouti. You can take your jeans, and pack some business casual—khakis, decent shoes, and shirts." Filburt paused. "You do have those, don't you?"

Filburt had trouble keeping a note of satisfaction from coloring his voice.

With a new passport and airline tickets in his shirt pocket and a book-bag packed with underwear and toiletries crammed under the seat in front of him, Jason scrunched into his seat. For the next nine hours, he absorbed a lesson on how to pack the largest number of people into the smallest aluminum cylinder, at the greatest level of discomfort consistent with getting the sardines to pay for the privilege. He was able to stretch his legs and walk around a little during a two-hour layover at Charles De Gaulle, but he didn't explore or wander far from his gate. The shape of the curved concrete walls of the concourse and few signs made him feel as though he was in the gullet of a giant worm. It wasn't a feeling conducive to exploring. He was tired and afraid he'd get lost and miss his flight to Cairo

In Djibouti, Filburt had briefed Howard about Jason during a teleconference. Howard assigned two people to meet Jason at the Djibouti airport, bring him to the embassy, and deliver him to Howard's office. Jason took a seat and Howard asked, "How's your French?"

"I took it for a couple of years in high school. I only remember a few words."

"That will help. We are going to accompany a local civil servant on an inspection of a warehouse currently leased by a front for the terrorists. You only have a couple of days to brush up on your French and learn a few words of Afar. At least learn the basics—be able to ask for help and the location of the men's room in French. You must learn a few phrases in Afar. You don't have to speak them, just recognize them." Howard handed Jason a paper. "Top of the list are, 'don't touch that,' and 'get out of here, now.'

"Your guides will take you to your quarters. If you have questions in the next few days, you can ask me or either of them." Howard dismissed Jason, but as Jason reached the door, Howard remembered another appointment he'd made for him.

"Jason, it is important that you blend in with European tourists in the area. I've made an appointment for you with the embassy hair stylist."

"What's wrong with my hair?"

"It would be perfect, if walking red haystacks were common locally. We don't want to make it easy for Ahmed to spot you or for his friends to describe you. Think of it as the first step in adopting your disguise."

Langley, Virginia
May 25

A few days after Jason's assignment to Djibouti, Filburt sat at his desk checking his Outlook calendar. He'd postponed talking to Gettelman as long as he could. He phoned Gettelman at his office in the CDC complex on the outskirts of Atlanta. "Al, how are things in Atlanta?" Filburt asked.

"Sprinkling right now. We've had showers moving through all day." Gettelman searched his memory. There was something he'd promised to do for Filburt and had forgotten to do it. "You asked about academic contacts I have in Arab countries?"

"Yeah. We believe the stolen samples are at the University of Ta'izz in Yemen. It would help if we could establish a relationship with someone there. The university's website shows it has a number of European and North American scholars on staff."

"Geez, University of Ta'izz, that rings a bell. Let's see . . . let me call you back. I have to check some files to make sure I've got the right guy."

Gettelman called back a few minutes later. "George, I think I have the contact you want. The guy's name is Dietrich van Kellen. He's a Dutch virologist who did a post-doc in my lab three years ago. He's a visiting fellow in the College of Life Sciences at Ta'izz—even has a graduate student."

Filburt swiveled back and forth in his chair. "How trustworthy is he? Do you know anything about his politics?"

"As I recall, he was a Social Democrat, pretty much a pacifist, and passionately against using microbiology for military purposes. Another student here used to goad him about biological warfare, just to watch Dietrich get hot. I damned near had to break up a fight once."

"Perfect. How would you like to take a trip to Yemen and feel him out for us? If he's agreeable, we can put him on the payroll."

"I'd like to see him again. There's an international virology meeting in Athens, Greece, in a couple of weeks. I could use it as a cover for being in the area. If you'd be willing to fund a travel grant for him, I could meet him there. I'll bet Jason would like to attend the meeting, too. It would give them a chance to meet."

"I suppose the budget for world peace can handle that, but you have to promise you'll keep tabs on Jason. He can't lie worth a crap. I shudder when I think of what he might say if somebody asks him what he's working on now."

"Ah, give the kid a break, George. He's young and an idealist. Speaking of the young and idealistic, if Dietrich works with us, it would help him if we could arrange support for a graduate student or post-doc for a couple of years at a US university. Think you could do that?"

"Maybe. I'll have to justify this to the budget committee," Filburt hedged. "How does it fit with intelligence operations?"

"The people who walk through labs every day and drop by to kibitz with each other are graduate students. A grad student might gather intel for money, but they are more likely to do it for a post-doc at a world-class research institute. That would allow them to compete for first-tier jobs anywhere in the world."

"How much money are we talking about?"

"Depends on the school," Gettelman said. "MIT, Harvard, and Stanford will be more expensive than a good state university or the CDC. The person we want will be a microbiologist, and funding a grant in pathogenic microbiology or molecular immunology is expensive at any school. For two years, the low end will range between two hundred to three hundred thousand dollars."

Filburt whistled. *Academics and money,* Filbert thought, *no common sense.*

Djibouti
10:00 a.m., May 27

Shopkeepers were beginning to hang their wares on the outside of their stands. A few women in yellow, green or red hijabs and men in jeans or khakis walked close to the buildings, as there was no sidewalk or curb. Traffic on the road was limited to a few Toyota pickup trucks and men on bicycles. Telephone poles, electricity and telephone wires, and the chubby, white minaret of the Hamoudi mosque, a few blocks away, were visible over the one- and two-story whitewashed shops and houses. The white and green Toyota van, with "Ville de Djibouti" and "Gabuuti" markings on the door, parked in front of a building next to the Noural-Imam Primary school.

Three sand-colored Roman arches formed the front of the two-story commercial building. The plaster was cracked and broken at the bottom of each pier supporting the arches and the concrete behind the plaster was crumbling at the edges. Wooden double doors, once painted green but now faded almost to gray, closed the arch on the far right. A window, covered on the inside with dark paper, enclosed the space under the arch on the far left. A bent and tattered marquee, the faded Arabic print illegible, hung over the middle arch. The shop door under the arch was ajar, and the light of a desk lamp was visible in the dark interior of the building.

Three men in khaki pants and white shirts, each carrying a clipboard, exited the van and stood before the building. A pudgy little man, whose belly hung over his belt just a little, walked briskly, chin up and back straight, in front of his compatriots. A few long strands of black hair crossed his head in a desperate comb-over, and "Ismail Mohammed" was stamped on the brass nameplate neatly pinned to his shirt pocket. His precisely groomed black moustache bristled indignantly as he examined the broken plaster and crumbling concrete under it. He tsk-tsked, scribbled on his clipboard, and peremptorily motioned the two behind him forward. Accustomed to being obeyed, he turned and walked to the door without looking to see if they complied.

He rapped on the open door, leaned forward, and pushed the door open further. "*Bonjour*," he called out as he stepped into the building, "*bonjour*." Without waiting for an answer, he turned to Jason and Howard and curtly motioned them in with his clipboard.

"You didn't tell me they were going to dye my hair, too," Jason whined. His hair, now brown, short enough to stay off his ears, and neatly combed fit nicely with his current masquerade as a civil servant.

"Dark brown fits in better and won't be remembered as well," Howard said. "It's a small price to pay to avoid attention. Hurry up, Ismail is waiting."

They stood in a hot, dim, dusty room, approximately thirty feet long and fifteen feet wide. The cracked and yellowed linoleum curled off the floor like a snake shedding its skin, revealing the bare concrete beneath it. The room was too big to be an office, yet the only furniture was a worn wooden desk, and behind it, a wooden chair missing one arm and two of the slats in its back. The only light in the room was a tarnished brass lamp sitting on the desk, its broken shade sitting akimbo at a seemingly impossible angle.

"*Salut*," inspector Ismail bellowed. He tapped a foot and put his fists on his hips as he peered into the gloom to examine the ceiling. The muffled thuds of cardboard boxes being kicked aside could be heard through an archway behind the desk. They were followed by a call that, to Jason's high school French, sounded like, "I'm coming."

A young man in dirty jeans and a T-shirt entered the room, rubbing his hands on his pants to remove the dust and dirt. As the man introduced himself in Afar, Ismail studiously ignored his extended right hand. In what sounded to Howard and Jason like a torrent of Afar invective, Inspector Ismail tore into the man, the building manager. Neither Howard nor Jason understood Afar, but Ismail's brusque and demanding tone made it clear he wasn't pleased with the condition of the building.

The manager shrugged and tried to placate the inspector, who brought out a flashlight and stalked about the room, muttering to himself as he examined the walls, floor, and ceiling, and busily scribbled on his clipboard. Jason and Howard went in different directions, taking pictures and making notes on their clipboards. Jason paid close attention to electrical outlets, air vents, and other evidence of air handling capability, and Howard looked closely for evidence of security equipment and surveillance cameras. When the inspector completed his examination of the first room, he moved into each succeeding room to repeat the charade.

Howard estimated the dimensions of each room and compared them to the blueprints on his clipboard. By the third room, he drew the floor plan he found, as the blueprints were outdated. The inspector and Howard moved into the last room on the first floor as Jason examined and photographed water stains on the wall and peeling paint on the rusty and corroded metal housing of the electrical box and the conduit leading to it.

The last room, at the back of the building, was apparently where the man had been unloading boxes from a van when they arrived. Boxes with English labels were carefully stacked against one wall. The inspector read a few labels and launched into another tirade that Howard couldn't understand. Howard used it as cover to photograph the boxes. When the manager looked to see what he was doing, Howard blunted his curiosity by fixing him with an icy glare and pointedly making more notes on his clipboard.

Jason joined them again as they moved to the second-floor apartment and the flat roof. They inspected, as before. Ismail pointed dramatically at cracks in the roof, glared at the manager, and wrote extensive notes on his clipboard. Jason and Howard returned to the air-conditioned van while the inspector ripped into the manager again.

"You'd better take a look at the pictures I took of the laboratory supplies while you were checking out the electrical service," Howard said. He handed his camera to Jason. "What do you make of it?"

"These are disposable plastic roller bottles for viral production," Jason said. He moved on to other pictures. "And these are bottles of tissue-culture medium, but the building doesn't have any refrigeration. The media will be worthless before they get this place in shape to use it."

"I'll check my notes against the blueprints again," Howard said.

"Even I could tell that the rooms we saw have no potential for a lab, and the measurements I took indicate there wasn't a hidden room. They must be planning on using the place as a warehouse or a diversion."

"I think you're right," Jason said. "I can't wait to ask Ismail what he told that guy. I've never seen anyone yell at somebody like that."

The driver's door opened and Inspector Ismail slid behind the wheel. He turned to Jason and motioned for silence as he pulled away from the curb. Four blocks later, he turned onto a side street and drove into a parking lot.

"What did you tell that guy?" Jason asked as Ismail pulled a wad of Djibouti francs from his shirt pocket.

"I told them the building wasn't fit to house the shit of dying camels. They must fix the roof or their electrical service will be cut off. They cannot store hazardous chemicals without a protective cabinet and permits, nor can they allow anyone to live in the second-floor apartment until they upgrade the building's electrical service," Ismail said as he counted out the francs and divided them into three piles. He handed one pile to Jason, one to Howard, who was sitting behind him, and pocketed the other.

"What's this?" Jason asked.

"The young man appreciated my advice and, with a little encouragement, insisted that I allow him to give us a token of his appreciation for our time and expertise and to assure us that it will not be necessary for me to file an official report. I believe in English you call it a bribe."

Howard tucked the money into his breast pocket and turned to Jason. "If Ismail hadn't asked for a bribe, the manager might have suspected we weren't civil servants."

At the embassy that afternoon, Howard invited Jason to his office.

The room was windowless, small, and utilitarian—light brown walls, brown vinyl flooring, a metal desk, two chairs, and a couple of filing cabinets. "What did you think of the building? Can they turn it into a virology lab?" Howard asked.

Jason shook his head. "Where do I start? A bacteriologist might be able to work there, with a little remodeling, but it would be easier to tear the building down and start over if they want to do viral work."

Howard sat back in his chair. "What equipment would they need to make it suitable?" he asked.

"They'll need to build an anteroom for gowning and three rooms to do the work in. The rooms must have sealed floors and walls that can be washed and disinfected, and modern air handling equipment that can HEPA filter the air. Air pressure in each of the rooms must be balanced so that air pressure is lowest in the rooms in which they handle the virus. After that, it's hard to know where to start—at least two hundred thousand dollars in sensitive, high-tech equipment. As is, that dump is too dusty and crude to even store that kind of equipment, let alone work with tissue cultures and a virus."

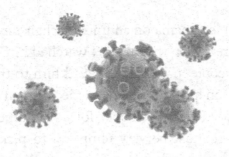

CHAPTER 14

Café de la Gare, Djibouti
June 4

Juliet and Howard arrived in separate cars just as most people at the restaurant were finishing lunch. They parked on different side streets off the broad Avenue d'Esperey, and met, as if by chance, near the restaurant's arched entrance. Howard doffed his hat, gestured to Juliet to precede him through the open wrought iron gates, and bowed slightly as she passed. They walked past the enclosed patio and continued to the welcome shade of the dining room.

Juliet's light gray suit and mid-calf skirt looked professional and didn't offend local sensibilities. The neckline of her blouse was more daring. Howard's white linen suit, pale blue shirt, and polished manners suggested a man of leisure, or a man accustomed to impressing the wives of others.

A waiter seated them at a corner table under a painting of men in long white pants playing tennis. The dark wood frame looked at home on the stucco-like texture of the white-plaster wall. The corner and a potted palm provided privacy, the leather-upholstered chairs comfort.

Juliet relaxed into her chair. "Your tourist hasn't learned to travel lightly."

Howard put his panama on an unused chair next to him and his fake pack of cigarettes on the table. "I watched him board the plane, and two of our people in Jeddah followed him to the Saudi German hospital. A nurse on his floor said he carried a small library with him. She's supposed to identify the books for us by tomorrow."

"Impressive! It must be very tempting to pick him up." Juliet looked at her menu.

"Not until we know we can . . ." Howard peered over his menu to make sure a waiter or other diners weren't approaching, "also pick up his package."

"How was the fish when we were last here? It looked wonderful."

"Excellent. I recommend it." Howard studied his menu. "Anything going on at the buildings his friends leased?"

Men, Juliet thought, *gay or straight, think of nothing but work.* "I don't know if I should answer that, Howie. You are being unusually cheap lately."

Howard looked over the top of his menu, again, this time at Juliet. "Hunh?"

"The banana Daiquiris by the pool at the Sheraton and the room service are divine."

Howard frowned and tried to think of how this related to their investigation. "What—"

Juliet chucked him under his chin. "Anyone watching us would think we are celibate. We haven't even been in the same bedroom for weeks. We could blow our cover."

Howard took her hand and delicately kissed her fingertips. "I promise our next meeting will be at the Sheraton. I didn't want to go there while our tourist was in residence. I'd like to keep our surveillance subtle."

"Our friends have moved more supplies into the building next to the school and requested an upgrade of the electrical service. They even dumped empty cardboard shipping containers for laboratory equipment and reagents in their dumpster. They put them on top of the trash and left the lid up." Juliet slid a manila envelope across the table to Howard. "Here are the pictures of the labels on the boxes, the building from the outside, and pictures that our people took inside the building."

Howard looked from the pictures to Juliet. "Amazing! Are you a magician?"

"When they requested expansion of the electrical service, Ismail told them an inspection wouldn't be necessary if they hired a competent electrician, like his brother-in-law. Our agent took the pictures when he worked up the estimate."

"Excellent." Howard put the envelope into his briefcase. "Our tourist's friends are very open."

Juliet sipped her lemonade. "Do you think it was an accident that the building they leased is next to a primary school?"

Howard glanced at the other tables and windows of the restaurant before speaking. "A trip wire or pressure sensitive plate? Officers go in, the whole block goes up, and we'd be blamed."

She nodded. "The children of many prominent people are enrolled in the school."

Jeddah, Saudi Arabia, Saudi German Hospital
June 5

Ahmed's hospital room had the pastel walls, counter and cabinets for medical supplies, sink, and dispenser of alcohol-based hand sanitizer that were nearly identical to those in private rooms he'd seen at the University of Minnesota hospital. So were his private lavatory and shower. The equipment, from hospital bed to vital sign monitoring devices, was made by the same companies that supplied hospital rooms in Western Europe and North America.

He could have been in any country, were it not for his view of the Red Sea, palm trees in the highway medians, and the thousand-foot high water spout of the King Fahd fountain. Not many Western cities had bright lights, traffic jams, and crowded stores at two o'clock in the morning either. Pain had awakened him in the middle of the night, and from one of the two windows in his room he'd been able to look down on Tahlia Street, a major fashion and shopping district. The lights and traffic had given it a carnival appearance. Jeddah seemed to come alive only at night, when the temperature dropped below eighty degrees.

It was the second day after his surgery. Ahmed groaned and fumbled for the control unit that held the television remote, controls for the hospital bed, and the nurse's call button. He pressed the call button, waited for a minute, and hit the button again. There was a faint crackle of static and a bored female voice came from the small speaker on the pale gray box. "Yes, sir. What do you need?"

"Can I have another dose of pain medication?"

"It would be better if you wait another hour. Then it will carry you through your afternoon session with the physical therapist."

Ahmed took his finger off the button and slapped the control unit down on his sheets. "Stupid bitch probably can't even tell time," he muttered. He remembered yesterday's session with the physical therapist and stifled a groan. He tried to move his right leg to see if a different position would feel more comfortable. He gasped in pain, let his leg slide back to its previous position, and stayed as still as he could as he waited for the damned nurse to bring him the pain pills.

The nurse's station for the sixth-floor joint surgery ward was on the other end of the hallway outside his room. An athletically built German physical therapist stopped there two hours later and reviewed Ahmed's chart. His blond hair, blue eyes, chiseled chin, and boyish grin guaranteed he was a favorite of the nurses. "How is my new patient doing?" he asked.

"Why don't you ask him?" a tall, Swedish nurse said. "He's been buzzing us every fifteen minutes to tell us his problems."

The therapist looked over the chart. "He has a low tolerance for pain, yes?"

"For dealing with it or spreading it around?" a younger nurse, sitting at a computer monitor, asked.

The therapist glanced at the nurse and hid a smile. "Have there been signs of inflammation or fever?"

"None," the younger nurse said.

The therapist sighed and handed the chart back to the tall nurse. "I gather he is not the stoic, athletic type." He turned and walked down the hallway to Ahmed's room.

The Swedish nurse accompanied him. She leaned close and whispered, "I hope he doesn't scream again when you help him bend his knee."

A few days later, Ahmed, his knee stabilized by a brace, limped down the hallway with the aid of a cane on one of his two daily walks. The physical therapist met him at the nurse's station. "You are doing much better today, Herr Professor Hadi," the therapist said. "Tomorrow we can adjust your brace to allow your knee more motion."

Ahmed nodded. "I was hoping I could make use of the hospital medical library for a few days." Ahmed grimaced as he thought of walking with even less support from the brace. "Walking is still slow for me. Could I use a wheelchair to visit the library?"

"If you think you need it, but it would be better for you to walk."

The Sheraton, Djibouti
June 12

Juliet sipped her banana daiquiri. She loved the warm feel of the sun on her skin. Lowering her sunglasses, she looked at Howard, lounging next to her by the pool. "Perhaps you and Stephen should have a drink with Maurice. He gave me an odd look when I told him I'd be meeting you here today." She smiled, stretched, and took another sip. "I believe he might be worried about us."

Howard looked at her and decided that if he ever had another affair with a woman, he couldn't do better than Juliet. In her mid-forties, she was intelligent, fashionable, beautiful, buxom, and toned. Today, lying next to him by the pool, she wore the stringiest of bikinis.

Howard paused as a sudden thought crossed his mind. "Good Lord! Stephen has acted a bit out of sorts lately, too. We'll have to nip this in the bud."

"Why? A little jealousy will do them both some good. They'll learn to pay proper attention to us." She sat up and grabbed her towel and drink. "Anyone who hasn't seen us by now is blind. Let's go back to the room and get out of the sun. I've got new pictures for you."

Howard glanced at his watch. "Jason should be there by now. He was impressed by Ismail and our little excursion."

"Jason?"

"Our virologist. He will be the one to look at your pictures. I asked him to drop by—thought you might want to meet him. If our tourist has friends nearby, they have probably been watching us here at the pool. They probably had difficulty taking their eyes off you."

Juliet smiled. "What is Jason like?"

"Young, agreeable, bright, and deeply principled, but chatty. He's never learned to dissemble, and you can read his face like a book. I imagine it's precisely what you'd want in a scientist."

Howard had ensured there would be no embarrassing gaffes when Jason came to his room. A marine from the embassy accompanied Jason. Dressed casually in shorts and colorful shirts, they crossed the hotel lobby, gym bags slung over their shoulders. Jason detoured toward a shop selling picture post cards, candy, and sodas, but his companion gently steered him back toward the elevators.

Once on an elevator, the marine blocked Jason's hand as he tried to push the button for the fifth floor. The marine silently shook his head and pushed button number seven.

"But Howard's—"

The Marine put a finger to his lips and shook his head.

They exited the elevator on the seventh floor and took the stairs down to the fifth. The Marine cracked the stairwell door open, verified the hallway to Howard's room was empty, and led Jason to the room. Key-card in one hand, pistol in the other, Jason's companion opened the door to Howard's room and cleared it before he allowed Jason to enter. Howard had splurged on an Executive Suite: plush carpets, two bedrooms, and a common room with a couch, wingback chair, and a table with four chairs. The outer walls in all the rooms were floor-to-ceiling gold-tinted windows with heavy drapes, now open. Silently, the marine pointed Jason toward the table and away from the windows before taking a post near the door—a post from which he could stop him if Jason tried to stand in front of the window.

When Juliet and Howard opened the door, Howard nodded to the marine and inclined his head toward Jason. The marine rolled his eyes toward the ceiling, smiled, and quietly left.

Juliet still wore her bikini, but had wrapped a towel around her waist. Jason scrambled to stand as Howard introduced him. When the drapes were closed and they were seated at the table, Juliet pawed through her overnight bag and removed a manila envelope. She slid a group of eight-by-ten-inch photos from the envelope onto the table.

"Ismail's 'brother-in-law' took these when he upgraded the electrical service," Juliet said. She fanned the pictures in the center of the table. "Our friends appear to have purchased used equipment. Not even the 'on' lights worked."

Jason examined the pictures. "The first picture is an old biosafety hood. The work area isn't useable. You can see scorching on the air vents." He picked up the second picture. "This one shows a trashed floor-mounted Beckman centrifuge." He held the picture closer to the light. "Looks like a broken spindle, and the tub the centrifuge head sits in has been torn up, probably when the spindle let go." He looked at Juliet and Howard. "This is nothing but scrap metal."

"Our friends are frugal." Howard looked at Juliet and frowned. "These amount to theatrical props. At some point they planned to let us see these, but probably not such a close look. I assume they don't know what crap they bought."

Juliet sat back in her chair. "A diversion or a trap?"

Jason found his eyes wandering to the contents of Juliet's bikini top so often he put a hand beside his face, pretending that his ersatz blinder helped him focus on the pictures.

Howard spread the pictures out to look at them closely. "You're positive these couldn't be repaired?" he asked Jason.

Carefully avoiding looking at Juliet, Jason glanced at Howard. "Junk. It would be cheaper to buy new equipment."

Juliet caught Howard's eye, winked, and nodded toward Jason, who had put his hand up as a blinder again. The skin around her eyes and forehead crinkled and a sly curl formed at the corners of her mouth. "What are we to make of it, Howard?" she asked.

Howard shrugged. He sat back in his chair, arms crossed before turning to Jason. "Juliet and I were concerned that they may have booby-trapped the building. A bomb could take out the school next door if we stage a raid. The US or NATO would be blamed. It would be a recruiting bonanza for our tourist's friends."

The room was quiet as the three mulled over that possibility. Jason sat up and leaned forward, and with elaborate care, focused on Juliet's chin when he turned to her. "Maybe we don't have to know what they are up to. Do your people know where the building manager lives and who he has helping him?"

"I'm sure we know that by now." Juliet smiled conspiratorially and leaned toward Jason. "What do you have in mind?" She put a hand on one of Jason's.

Very little of Juliet's ample breasts were not on view when she leaned forward, and Jason's gaze dropped when Juliet's warm hand touched his.

"Ah, I thought . . ." Jason swallowed hard and lifted his focus to Juliet's eyes. "Could . . ." Jason had difficulty concentrating. "Could, ah, could we have Inspector Ismail do another inspection?"

The corners of Juliet's mouth twitched as Jason's eyes roved again and a blush crept up his neck and settled in his cheeks.

Jason dragged his gaze back to Juliet's eyes, and his blush grew deeper. *Crap*, he thought. *I feel like a pizza delivery boy at a cougar convention*. He swallowed again, and with his free hand, he casually slid one of the photographs to the edge of the table, where it protruded over the edge and blocked anyone's view of his crotch. He'd been apart from Ann too long.

"But this time, can he close the place?" Jason asked. "Lock it up, condemn the building, and cut off the power and water? Better yet, arrest the manager, toss him in jail, and let him out on bail after he pays a big bribe?" Jason gestured, palms up, with both hands and shrugged. It gave him an excuse to extract his hand from under Juliet's. "It will look like another shake-down, so it shouldn't scare the others off. The police can pick them up later. Or should we wait, and let our friends invest more in the building before we move?"

Juliet and Howard looked at each other. "Another bribe!" Juliet said. A wicked smile crossed her face and her eyes danced. "Jason, you've been around Howard much too long. Ismail would love to have another go at them." She looked at Howard. "Clear it with Washington, if you need to, but I love it."

Their meeting over, Jason picked up his gym bag and held it in front of him as he stood. He excused himself and left the hotel room hurriedly. Juliet stifled a giggle as she watched him go.

"You were positively shameless," Howard said. "The poor boy will be blushing for a week."

She smiled and looked at Howard. "I know, but he was so innocent, and it was so easy."

Jeddah, German-Saudi Arabian Hospital
June 20

Ahmed checked out of the hospital, relaxed alone in the back of the airport shuttle, and took out his phone. It was time to drop a few hints to worry the CIA, but there was no reason to risk being arrested. He cast a quick glance at the distance from him to the driver and decided he could talk freely. He called the manager of the faux laboratory in Djibouti. "Ali, I can meet you at the laboratory in four hours. How is the, ah, the remodeling of the laboratory coming?"

"I'm in jail. The officer said my bail will be twelve thousand francs, and you'd better bring an extra ten thousand francs for his influential friends."

Ahmed looked at his phone and put it to his ear again. "Pardon? Ali, I believe we had some interference. Repeat what you said again, please."

In a corner of a crowded Djibouti jail cell, Ali repeated his request for bail. He listened for a response, tapped his phone, and listened again. "Ahmed, are you still there?"

"Yes. I thought you said you needed money for bail. What is going on? What happened?"

Ali yelled into his phone as a giant of a man offered to give him a back rub. "It's the building codes, the damned building codes. Don't do that. No, I won't . . . I don't do . . . Keep your hands off me." Other voices and the sounds of a scuffle were heard on the phone. "Ahmed, you didn't tell me about the codes. No! Get your hands . . . Ahmed, please, in the name of Allah . . . get me out of here."

The connection was broken. Ahmed looked at his phone, shaken, and called Al-Mikhafi. "Al-Mikhafi, Ahmed here. What happened in Djibouti?"

"Never call me at this number," Al-Mikhafi said, and the phone went dead.

A moment later, Ahmed's cell phone rang. It was Al-Mikhafi. "Sorry to be so abrupt, but we must be careful. You are on your way to Djibouti?"

"Yes. I called Ali to ask how the lab was coming and he said he is in jail and needs money for bail and bribes. What is going on?"

The line was silent for a moment. "Please repeat that, Ahmed."

Ahmed repeated Ali's request to an incredulous Al-Mikhafi. "In the name of all that is holy, what has happened? Why does he need bail?" Al-Mikhafi asked.

"Something about building codes."

"Djibouti has building codes?"

"Apparently. Is there someone in Djibouti who can make bail for Ali? He sounded desperate. Something nasty was going on in his cell."

"You and I must stay out of this. There is an attorney who has done work for us. I'll have him take care of it. When your plane lands in Djibouti, you must disappear earlier than we planned. I'll make arrangements to have you smuggled into Yemen tomorrow," and Al-Mikhafi hung up.

Ahmed's phone rang as he picked up his luggage at the Djibouti airport. "Ahmed, this is Al-Mikhafi. With Ali in jail, the authorities may be looking for you. We must get you out of Djibouti. Flights from Djibouti city are probably being watched. We will fly you out of Ali Sabieh tomorrow morning, *inshallah*."

Ahmed frowned. "Ali Sabieh?"

"It's a city southwest of Djibouti, ten kilometers north of the Ethiopian border. If the road is not washed out, it is a two-hour drive. Take a taxi to the downtown bus terminal and stand in the parking lot. Don't get on a bus. Friends are looking for a place for you to stay in Ali Sabieh tonight, and we are looking for a ride for you. Wait for a man who asks if you are on Flight two-ninety-eight A. That will be your ride. Follow his directions exactly, as the US has a small army base outside of Ali Sabieh and kidnapping for ransom is a thriving business in the area."

"Why would anyone kidnap me?" Ahmed asked. "I don't have money."

"How many front teeth are you missing? How many rotten teeth do you have?" Al-Mikhafi asked.

"None. Why?"

"Straight, white teeth mark you as rich or a westerner. People in Ali Sabieh can't afford a dentist. They don't know what orthodontia is. You'll be a target every time you open your mouth, so follow the directions your driver gives you." Al-Mikhafi hung up and wondered why his people wouldn't just do as they were told.

Ahmed used the last of his change to pay a kid to carry his bags to the taxi stand. The taxi took him across town to the bus terminal. Paying for the taxi took the last of Ahmed's small franc notes.

The terminal wasn't a building, but a collection of several kiosks and a couple of garages for maintenance work on the mini-buses providing service within the city and the slightly larger buses used for inter-city travel. Ahmed found a quiet place on the shady side of a garage, leaned against the wall to spare his right knee and leg, and examined every passing car and van as his potential ride.

Heat radiated from the blacktop surrounding him. The shade from an acacia tree on the edge of the street was laughably inadequate for half a block of open asphalt. Few other men braved the heat for long, and all were dressed in the local uniform of khakis, sandals, and a polo- or T-shirt. The rare women wore ankle-length, print dresses and the ever-present hijab. They were gone minutes after they arrived. Even in the early evening, temperatures were over one hundred degrees Fahrenheit. Sweating profusely, he loosened his tie, took his suit coat off, and silently cursed his dallying driver, Ali, Al-Mikhafi, his physical therapist, and whatever fates had created this parking lot. An hour later, he removed his tie and unbuttoned the front of his shirt. Exhausted, miserable, and thirsty, he didn't dare leave the parking lot in search of a drink. He couldn't leave his bags and he had no change or small bills to pay someone to watch them, and he might miss his ride. Ali's phone call provided Ahmed with all he needed to imagine what it would be like spend the night in a Djibouti jail.

What little fortitude and resolve Ahmed still possessed evaporated as he dehydrated. He stopped cursing his absent driver and silently pleaded for him to hurry. As the minutes rolled by, Ahmed began thinking of the driver as an angel of deliverance from the hellhole of the emptying parking lot.

Ahmed was sitting on the blacktop, an elbow on his left knee, fanning himself with a local newspaper when an older man in a dirty T-shirt and jeans approached him. His face was weathered and brown. He had two days growth of gray stubble, and his teeth were tinted green.

Hands on hips, the man stood over Ahmed and growled, "You on Flight two-nine-eight A?" in Arabic.

Ahmed struggled to his feet, using his cane to spare his right knee, still stiff from the surgery. "Yes. I've been waiting for you." Ahmed pointed to three suitcases beside him. "These are my bags. Where is your car?"

The man turned and started to walk off. "Follow me. My truck is around the corner."

"What about my bags?"

The man stopped, turned to face Ahmed, and shrugged. "That's okay. You can bring them. I should charge you extra for 'em, but I won't, this time."

Ahmed waited for the man to pick up his bags. The old guy didn't move. Ahmed grabbed a bag and asked plaintively, "Can you help me carry them?"

"I own my truck. I'm not anybody's servant. Grab your bags and follow me."

"What?"

"Follow me. Grab your bags or leave 'em here. You don't like that, you can stay here and keep your bags company tonight. I don't have time for this shit." The old man turned on his heel and resumed walking.

Ahmed put on his coat, grabbed a bag in each hand, and stuffed one bag under an arm. He gritted his teeth and made do without his cane. With the bags and his stiff knee, walking was more like a waddle. Ahmed gradually fell behind his driver as the bag under his arm repeatedly slipped out of his control and fell. The old guy didn't slow down or turn to see if Ahmed was following him. When he came to an intersection, he turned right and disappeared around the corner of a building.

Ahmed panicked as he watched the driver and his deliverance disappear. He ignored the pain in his right knee and tried to trot, but the bag under his arm slipped and fell again. This time the latch broke, the suitcase popped open, and clothes and toiletries spilled across the sidewalk. Ahmed only paused a second. Everything in the bag could be replaced. He turned, and with two bags, he trotted after the driver.

At the intersection, Ahmed rounded the building and stopped. His driver wasn't in sight. Pain shot through his leg every time he flexed his knee, and he felt weak and desperate. As he lowered his bags to the pavement, a horn honked, and a battered old snub-nosed Mercedes L-series truck carrying a load of goats halted on the street. The truck was red once, but the dirt and the sun had reduced it to an uneven rust color.

His driver leaned out the window. "Come on. Move your skinny ass. I don't have all day." The driver spat a long stream of greenish-brown liquid to the pavement. "Move!"

Ahmed grabbed his bags and hobbled across the intersection, dodging a mini-bus and a car as he did. Panting, he opened the passenger door. "Where can I put my bags?"

The driver glared at him and wondered what Ahmed would ask for next. He motioned to the back of the truck with his thumb.

Ahmed glanced in the back. There wasn't any bedding for the goats, and the floor was covered a half-inch deep in raisin-like goat turds. "Isn't there any room in the cab for my bags?"

"Sure, if you ride with the goats. Toss your bags in the back or in the cab. I don't care which, but move."

Exhausted, dehydrated, and desperate, Ahmed tossed his bags

in with the goats. He clambered into the old truck, trying not to use his right leg, and slammed the door. The driver spit another green stream to the pavement as a bus pulled up behind the truck and honked. As his driver edged the truck into the intersection and shifted into second gear, Ahmed looked in the rear-view mirror and saw the man's dilated pupils.

"You chew khat?" Ahmed asked the old guy.

"Been working since four this morning. Only way I can stay awake," he said, and he shifted into third gear.

Remembering what he'd heard about drivers on khat, a local stimulant with effects similar to amphetamines, Ahmed dropped his right hand beside his seat and felt for the seatbelt clasp. He felt damp, slippery metal, but no clasp. He turned to his right and peered between the side of the seat and the passenger door. The fingers of his right hand were covered with moist, brown goo, old manure of indeterminate origin. Ahmed made a face, wiped his fingers on his handkerchief, and felt around behind himself for a seatbelt buckle.

The driver spat out the window again and glanced at Ahmed. "What you looking for?"

"A seatbelt. Where is it?"

"Ah what?"

"A seatbelt."

"What's that?"

The age of the truck slowly dawned on Ahmed. "Do you have air conditioning?" he asked hopefully.

"Sure. I got everything. Window crank is on your right. Window in back of you slides open, too. I put that in special."

Ahmed sighed and pushed the window in the back of the cab to one side.

They drove out of the old city, past new sections of town, and gradually climbed toward Ali Sabieh and the highlands, four thousand feet above and southwest of Djibouti. The old truck ground along at twenty-five miles an hour, rolling over potholes and dodging boulders that had rolled down slopes onto the road. The eroded, washed-out, and gullied land they passed through was nearly barren. Only thickets of the thorny acacia trees and a few weeds provided some green in the landscape. The roar from the engine precluded talk, which was fine with Ahmed. After an hour, his back ached and his butt hurt from the jarring ride, and the pain in his right knee was worse than both put together.

Progress was slow but steady until they came to a section of road washed out by a flash flood. Only the roots of a big acacia tree on the bank above the road appeared to have prevented a mudslide. A rutted trail went off the road and around the washout. The driver stopped the truck and let it idle.

"Jump out and turn the hubs out for me," the old guy barked.

"What?" Ahmed asked.

"Get your lazy ass out of the damned cab and twist that center knob on each front wheel. We need four-wheel drive to get through this. Hop to it."

Ahmed opened the truck door and looked at the sea of mud below him and at his hand-made Italian shoes.

"Hurry up," the driver growled. "We need to get moving. We don't want to be close to that tree for too long, and there'll be bandits all over here at night."

Ahmed turned pale. His father had nearly disowned him when he got the bill for the shoes. "I can't do that in these shoes, and my knee—"

"Then take the damned shoes off. Listen, you rich little shit, if I have to do it, you can get out of my truck and catch the next bus. Get out and turn the hubs or get out and walk."

Ahmed looked again at the mud. The old guy reached over and shoved. This brought the mud closer, giving Ahmed a much better view of what cushioned the blow to his right knee when he landed.

He was on his knees in six inches of goopy clay. The heels of his hands slowly slid forward, lowering Ahmed gently face-first in the slop. He scrambled up, sputtering and wiping mud from his mouth and eyes.

The old guy glanced ahead at the muddy trail, turned, and spat another greenish-brown stream, this time at the stationary Ahmed. "Hurry up, and stay away from them trees."

Ahmed slipped and sloshed to the truck's front wheels and turned the hubs out. As he opened the passenger door and flicked mud off his hands to improve his grip to climb into the truck, the driver told him to stop. "I keep a clean cab. Take that muddy suit coat off before you get in."

They roared down the slope in four-wheel drive, through the washout, and ground slowly up the slope on the other side. Somehow, the old driver found solid ground under the mud and kept the truck moving through that washout and two more they encountered in the next forty kilometers.

"Why did you tell me to stay away from the trees?" Ahmed asked.

"You didn't see it?" the old man asked.

"See what?"

"The snake, kind of gray and brown laying on a rock. I saw one, probably a lot more in there. Acacia thickets around here crawl with black mambas. They got tempers."

Ahmed felt weak. He'd heard the black mamba was one of the most dangerous snakes in the world. "If I'd been bitten, you'd take me to a hospital, right?"

The old man kept driving. He didn't say anything.

"You'd take me—"

"Nah. Waste of time. You'd be dead before we could get to one. I saw one guy get nailed five times by a mamba so fast you could hardly see it. He died in twenty minutes."

Ahmed felt nauseous. He rode in silence and tried not to think about snakes.

The truck was doing better, up to thirty miles an hour, on a gentle upward slope when Ahmed felt a few drops of water on his left ear, rapidly followed by a yellow gusher.

"Aaaghh!" He shoved himself as far from the center of the truck as he could and looked questioningly at his driver.

"Yeah, that's why I never open that back window when I got a load of goats. One of them ewes always manages to pee right through the window. Close it, would you, before one of 'em pees on me, too."

Emotionally numb, Ahmed lacked even the energy to curse his driver. Dusk came and went. Ahmed took off his shirt and hung it on the side mirror on the passenger side, hoping it would dry out. They drove the rest of the way with the truck lights on, Ahmed naked from the waist up, waiting for his shirt to dry. The road was in better condition and nearly level for the last ten kilometers before Ali Sabieh. The driver, looking nervously to the knolls and few shrubs on the roadside, shifted into fourth gear and floored it.

At the outskirts of town, the driver pulled to the side of the road and stopped. He pointed to lights two hundred feet off the road. "That's where you're staying tonight. They'll drive you to the airport tomorrow. Hurry up, get your bags, and get moving. I gotta go."

Grimacing from the pain in his right knee, Ahmed climbed into the back of the truck for his luggage. He swore under his breath. The goats had opened one of the bags, and his clothes and three textbooks on virology were trod into the goat shit on the floor of the truck. Textbooks could be replaced. Ahmed carefully dropped his last intact suitcase onto the side of the road and lowered himself from the truck.

Ahmed limped in the dark toward the lights, suitcase in one hand and soiled shirt and coat in the other and tried not to think about snakes. He'd gone ten feet when the old man called from the truck. "Hey, what's the matter with you? Too cheap to give a guy a tip?"

Ahmed gave him the finger, turned, and stumbled forward through the dark. Soon he made out a cottage. Mosquitos buzzed around him. He waved his shirt at them, but there were too many and he was too tired. His neck, face, and torso were covered with mosquito bites, each slowly turning into a welt by the time he stood under the bare bulb in the cottage's covered porch. Standing in the center of a cloud of sated mosquitos, Ahmed knocked on the plain metal door.

A pot-bellied, middle-aged man, a few inches shorter than Ahmed, opened the door. Balding and sweaty, he stared silently at Ahmed. Ahmed dropped his suitcase and sighed. His mouth was so dry he could barely speak. "Flight two-ninety-eight A."

The man at the door opened it further and motioned Ahmed in with a jerk of his head. "You're late, what happened?"

He gave Ahmed a glass of water. Ahmed chugged the first one and motioned for a refill. As he downed the second glass, his host asked him again what had taken him so long.

Leaning against the wall, Ahmed stared silently at the ceiling. His contact was beginning to question Ahmed's sanity when Ahmed found the energy to speak. "Long story. Can I get . . . shower . . . clean bed?"

The man led him to a tiny bedroom with bare walls and showed him the bathroom across the hallway. Soap and clean towels were on his bed. "Wash up. I'll have a cold supper for you in a few minutes. Your ride to the airport tomorrow morning is at ten," the man said. He made a face, sniffed, and looked at Ahmed's filthy suitcase. "Get what you need out of that and stick it outside. It reeks." He turned and walked back to the kitchen.

Ahmed hobbled into the kitchen a few minutes later, dripping wet and wearing nothing but a towel. "How do I get hot water?" he asked.

"Hot water? Did you want tea?"

"No, for the shower. I couldn't get any hot water. The shower is freezing."

A man who stores his luggage in goat shit wants a hot shower, his host thought. He enlightened Ahmed. "Homes in Ali Sabieh have only cold-water showers. The new hotel by the airport has a bathroom with hot water, but that's for Europeans. I've never been in a house that had it."

Supper was cold roast goat and flat bread. Ahmed had little appetite. Shivering, he collapsed onto his bed. The mosquito bites itched and kept him awake all night. He fell asleep two hours before his host knocked on the door and told him it was time to get up.

Ahmed discovered he could hardly bend his knee when he tried to get out of bed. Pain and exhaustion blotted out all thought. He gritted his teeth, bent his knee, and held it together because there wasn't anything else he could do.

A small tan Renault sedan picked him up promptly at ten. The driver handed Ahmed his plane ticket and offered to carry his suitcase. He picked it up and immediately dropped it. He shook his hand to rid it of raisin-like dark gobs clinging to his fingers. "What is this? Your suitcase smells like . . . like goat shit, and . . ." the driver examined the suitcase, ". . . it's covered in goat shit."

"I'm too tired for this shit. Just carry the damned suitcase," Ahmed said.

The driver refused and they argued over how to clean the suitcase until his host intervened. He handed Ahmed a plastic trash bag. "Shut up, put the suitcase in this, and get out of here before somebody calls the authorities."

In the daylight, Ahmed could see he was on the edges of a sprawling city surrounded by mountains. Half a dozen modern two- and three-story buildings and a white minaret were visible in the distance. Traditional one-story whitewashed mudbrick buildings predominated. A few acacia trees in the distance were the only green Ahmed saw. Jumbled gray rock, bare dirt, and an unlimited supply of dust filled most of Ahmed's field of vision wherever he looked.

The airport was tiny: a single runway and a two-story air-control tower attached to a waiting room. The baggage check-in and exit to the planes was a single line cordoned off from the rest of the room by a frayed rope. The short, pudgy man who sold tickets also swept the floor, checked bags, delivered them to the plane, and sometimes took over the radio to land planes. His clipped mustache, polished shoes, and starched, white shirt testified to his fussiness about his appearance. He was equally fastidious about his work, lest the menial work he sometimes did denigrate his status in the eyes of passengers.

He was offended when Ahmed handed him the trash bag containing his suitcase. Ahmed was ordered to place his package on a dust-covered table near the door to the tarmac and wait until the head of security could examine it.

When the last of the other passengers were boarded, the little man put on latex gloves and attended to Ahmed's suitcase. "Good morning. I am head of security for the Ali-Sabieh International Airport." He waived dismissively at the trash bag. "Please open this . . . this package."

Ahmed looked at his dust and fly-speck-covered surroundings. *International airport?* he thought, but he didn't argue. He untied the twine holding the trash bag shut and pulled the bag down around the suitcase. The inspector staggered backwards as the odor hit him.

"In the name of Allah, close that thing," he yelled. "What are you carrying? Goat shit?"

Ahmed did as directed and explained that his suitcase had fallen into a pen of goats. The suitcase, wrapped in two more tightly sealed trash bags, was cleared after a severe lecture and a large bribe. At eleven thirty, Ahmed boarded a two-engine propeller driven plane and slowly bent his knee to get into his seat. He spread out across two seats and the aisle to give his knee a break when it was clear the plane would be nearly empty for the trip. He dosed fitfully, dreaming of snakes and goat shit. Hassan Al-Mikhafi arrived at the Ta'izz airport three hours later to pick him up.

It was easy for Al-Mikhafi to find Ahmed. There was a small crowd at the bus and taxi stands outside the terminal building, but no one stood near Ahmed. Al-Mikhafi took a sniff and gingerly put the plastic-wrapped suitcase in the trunk of the car. When he got into the driver's seat, he turned to Ahmed. "In the name of the Prophet, lower your window. You smell like goat shit."

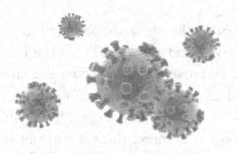

CHAPTER 15

Djibouti City Jail
Mid-afternoon, June 21

Attorney Abdullah Abdelmagid lifted his briefcase off a table at the police station. The envelope under it was smoothly scooped up by Inspector Ismail, who sat on the opposite side of the table. With the envelope under the table, the inspector gauged its thickness with his thumb and forefinger. "It was a pleasure to discuss Ali's problems with you, counselor. I'll see to his immediate release into your custody, but he will have to pay a fine for attempting to produce animal vaccines without a license." Ismail waited until Abdelmagid shook his hand and turned to go. "You do understand that if the fine is not paid promptly, you will be held responsible."

Abdelmagid whirled around. "What? Why will I be responsible?"

"Ali is being released into your custody; therefore, you are responsible. Good day, counselor," and Ismail closed the door.

Abdelmagid fumed in the hallway for a moment and made a mental note to get the money in advance from these clients in the future. He collected Ali, and they walked to the attorney's car.

"I still do not understand it. How did you end up in jail?" Abdelmagid asked his client as they got into the car.

Ali sat in the passenger seat and looked away from Abdelmagid as they pulled out of the station's parking lot. He didn't want to think about his arrest and night in jail. At last he sighed, "Building codes! They said I'd broken building codes and endangered children in the school and animal agriculture in Djibouti."

"Building codes and endangering animal agriculture?" Abdelmagid almost rear-ended the car in front of him. "Building codes are ignored, and Djibouti doesn't have ten francs worth of animal agriculture." Abdelmagid thought of the thick envelope stuffed with Djibouti francs and the impending fine. "I know a coffee shop where we can talk safely. We'll get a bite to eat, coffee, and you can tell me what happened."

Over coffee, Ali told Abdelmagid of the building next to the school, the laboratory reagents and supplies they stored in it, and of the first inspection and the bribes he'd paid. When nothing happened, he had upgraded the electrical service and scrounged discarded lab equipment from a hospital under renovation. A week later, Ismail and two gendarmes showed up for another inspection and ended it by arresting him.

Ali stopped his story there. He couldn't bear to talk about his night in jail.

"What is this charge of making animal vaccines?" Abdelmagid asked.

"Ismail said I was preparing to grow viruses. He told me the only reasons to do that were to make animal vaccines or grow a biological warfare agent. If it was a biological warfare agent, they would send me to The Hague to be hung, but if it was an animal vaccine, I'd only have to pay a small fine, *inshallah*."

Abdelmagid looked at his client, shook his head, and wondered where Al-Mikhafi found these idiots. He collected himself and asked the obvious question. "So you confessed to attempting to make animal vaccines without a permit?"

Ali silently nodded, yes.

The attorney closed his eyes, thought of his envelope again, and tried to think of a more productive line of questioning. He avoided asking Ali why he wanted to make the building appear to be a laboratory—the answer might create problems for a man technically an officer of the court. Instead, he asked, "Do you have surveillance cameras in your building?"

"Yes."

"If you have tapes from the cameras, can we review them at my office tomorrow?"

The following afternoon, Abdelmagid and Ali reviewed the surveillance tapes. After watching hours of footage, Abdelmagid was nearly asleep when Ismail, Jason, and Howard appeared on the screen. He watched the grainy film with growing apprehension until he came to a frame in which Howard looked directly at the camera and winked. Abdelmagid jerked around to stare at Ali.

"Are these the people that accompanied Ismail on his first inspection?"

"Yes. Ismail insisted I had to triple the normal bribe to pay all three of them."

Abdelmagid struggled for breath as though he'd been kicked in his chest. Recovering, he controlled his temper and spoke slowly, almost in a whisper. "Do you know who they are?"

"Ismail said they—"

Abdelmagid slammed a fist on his desk. "I don't give the maggots on a dead and rotting sheep who he said they were!" he bellowed, rising from his chair almost to a standing position. "The older man is the American CIA station chief in Djibouti. Even the little girls in the school by your building must know that."

Abdelmagid pointed to Jason and Howard on the monitor. "They bent you over, shoved your head in the mud, and beat you like a donkey, you fool, and you paid them to do it."

Langley, VirginiA,
June 22

Filburt took the podium and fiddled with his laptop until his presentation appeared on the screen behind him. He turned to his audience. "Mr. Vice President, I feel honored you could make time for us today, sir. Senator Walters, good to see you this morning," he said, nodding to a gray-haired man in front of him. He turned to several other faces new to his monthly coronavirus briefing. "Senator Nelsen, thank you for coming, and it's good to see you, too, Senator. "We are fortunate to have Dr. Jason Mitchell with us today. He is one of the few people who has worked with the BCV-SARS hybrid virus and is acquainted with Ahmed Khan. He has just returned from examining a facility where Ahmed and people connected to Ansar Allah were storing laboratory supplies." He turned to Jason, sitting in the front row, and motioned for him to stand.

Jason, in borrowed sport coat and tie, hair still dyed dark brown, briefly stood and nodded to the audience. Filburt continued, "Jason assisted in preparing today's presentation and is available to answer your questions."

Filburt moved quickly through his presentation, aware of the short attention span of senior legislators, men who had to get back to raising campaign contributions and schmoozing with well-heeled supporters. As before, he ended with a bullet-point summary slide for his audience, in case anyone had dozed off.

"In summary:

Two universities have proven that growing the virus in tissue culture rapidly destroys its ability to cause serious disease. We believe Ahmed is unaware of this.

The virus is dangerous only if grown in calves. Calves suitable for that are generally not available in the Middle East.

Ahmed and his Taliban-financed group have lost any support they may have had from Pakistan's Military Intelligence, which is periodically, but unofficially, providing us with intel through Dr. Mitchell and Dr. Ann Hartman, Jason's wife and research partner at the U of M.

We identified and investigated two facilities Ahmed's group was using in Djibouti, although we believe the stolen samples and the laboratory they will use are at the University of Ta'izz in southern Yemen."

Filburt closed the program and the screen went blank. "Are there any questions?" he asked.

A tall man, gray-haired and imperially slim, stood in the second row. His expression was both expectant and somber. "Have we destroyed their facilities in Djibouti, and if not, do you have a contingency plan to bomb them?"

Filburt shook his head. "No, Senator, we have not destroyed the facilities. One is in a crowded slum, the other is next to a well-known elementary school, and both appear to be decoys. They are unsuitable for doing any work with the virus or even storing sensitive equipment or reagents. Remember, Djibouti is a friendly country, a former French colony that still has strong ties to Europe. We don't want to create an enemy."

The senator frowned. "Have you identified other targets we could hit with drones or missiles?"

"We have not. The only potential target would be a laboratory at the University of Ta'izz, where it appears Ahmed is planning to expand the virus in tissue culture. That will render it harmless, so we don't want to interrupt his work. With any luck, he will burn through all of the samples he has before he discovers his mistake."

The senator, hands on hips, raised his voice. "So we are doing nothing?" The senator shook his head. "Am I to understand that you are sitting on your ass and letting these bastards grow the virus because people in ivory towers at a couple of universities think Ahmed is on the wrong track? Jesus!"

"With all due respect, Senator—"

The Senator's face became red and veins bulged in his neck and on his temples. The senator pointed a finger at Filburt. "Screw that. You are taking the word of a couple of eggheads who've never had anybody shoot at them, and you're doing it with the future of the free world, with capitalism and the American way of life in the balance. I say, bomb the crap out of the bastards. Bomb them, and do it now."

The Senator struck a pose he thought would look like righteous indignation and waited for an answer.

Filburt glanced at Jason. Jason timidly raised his hand, but Filburt waved him off with a subtle shake of his head. He wasn't going to put a politically naïve scientist in the ring against an old Washington pro on a rant. *Senator "9/11" Nuthatch*, Filburt thought. *Is the old goat so senile he thinks there are reporters here?*

Filburt shuffled a few papers before he answered the Senator. "I felt as you did, Senator, but the evidence that Ahmed is on the wrong track is overwhelming. The CDC reviewed studies done at the University of Minnesota and at Ohio State and had no reservations in accepting their conclusions. The scientists who are working with this virus believe that Ahmed Khan is incompetent and it is crucial to keep him alive and in charge of work on BCV-SARS."

The senator sat down and glared at Filburt. Filburt answered a few other questions posed with less emotion, and the meeting was over.

Jason called Ann, but didn't have time to visit Minnesota. He had to rush to catch his plane to Athens and the International Conference on Ruminant Enteroviruses. When he checked into the Acropolis Select Hotel on Falirou Boulevard, he discovered that Al Gettelman had reserved a suite for them. Al wasn't in yet, and jet lag was catching up with him. Too tired to enjoy the unaccustomed luxury, Jason went to bed.

Gettelman called the hotel operator as soon as he checked in. "Please connect me to Dr. Dietrich van Kellen, if he has checked in." Gettelman opened his suitcase as he held the phone, waiting for Dietrich to answer. The suite was spacious, clean, and modern—all for only one hundred forty dollars a night and close to central Athens. Filburt was getting off easy on this trip.

"I'm sorry, sir. Dr. van Kellen has not checked in yet," the receptionist answered.

Staff speaks excellent English, too. "Please ask him to call Dr. Al Gettelman in room five-forty-two when he gets in."

Dietrich called the room twenty minutes later. Al asked him to come up to the suite and knocked on Jason's door to rouse him. A few minutes later, Al ushered Dietrich, a tall, bearded man in his mid-thirties, into the suite. They exchanged pleasantries, Al handed Dietrich a local beer, and introduced him to Jason as Jason stumbled from his room. The three sat at a table by the window and got down to business.

Gettelman explain the problem. "Dietrich, I would have invited you to meet us for dinner, but it would be better if we aren't seen together in public. What I want to talk to you about is extremely sensitive."

"I gathered. You said someone at the University of Ta'izz is trying to make a biological weapon out of a BCV-SARS hybrid?"

Gettelman leaned back in his chair. "That's what we fear. Pakistani Military Intelligence may have protected the guy once, but they've gotten nervous about him and are quietly slipping us information on him."

"The guy has to be borderline unbalanced to make that crew nervous. You know how I feel about biological weapons. I'll do everything I can to help you, as long as it doesn't end in your people killing civilians with your drones."

"We've been able to rein in our hawks, so far. Knowing we have a person at Ta'izz will help us keep them in line." Gettelman rummaged through his briefcase and pulled out a manila envelope. He put it on the table and pulled three photographs from it. "This is the guy." Al pushed a picture of Ahmed toward Dietrich. "He recently earned a Ph.D. in bacteriology from the University of Minnesota and stole fecal samples collected from calves infected with the BCV-SARS hybrid. We've been told that he's working at the University of Ta'izz under an assumed name. He would have been hired within the last few months. We believe he recently had knee surgery at a hospital in Saudi Arabia."

Dietrich picked up the first picture and examined it. "Yes. He hasn't been around much, and he calls himself Ahmed Hadi now. His lab is on the first floor near the loading docks, but his office is on the third floor, down the hall from mine. He's been bugging my graduate student for advice." Dietrich put down the photo and thought for a moment. "If he's at Ta'izz and has a new identity, someone must be protecting him. The University is controlled by Yemen's ruling party. They wouldn't put up with an Ansar Allah sympathizer if they knew what he was up to."

Al nodded. "According to the Pakistanis, a biochemist from a university in Islamabad and now at Ta'izz is his mentor and connection to the Ansar Allah."

"That would be Hassan Al-Mikhafi. I would not have guessed.

He seemed always friendly and urbane, yes." Dietrich took a swig of beer. "Are you sure about him being involved with this?"

"Beyond any reasonable doubt," Gettelman said. "Pakistani Military Intelligence and the CIA both confirm Al-Mikhafi is the person in control. He's fooled a number of people in the past."

Dietrich drained his beer and absorbed the information. "How can I help you?"

"It would be a great help if you can let us know what is going on," Al said. "Jason can tell you more about the situation."

"We believe Ahmed is trying to expand the virus in tissue culture," Jason said. "We've shown that the virus rapidly loses virulence in tissue culture. Ahmed and friends aren't a threat, as long as they continue working with tissue culture. We will need to know if they change their approach. He could become a danger if he expands the virus in calves, the only animal host we know of."

Dietrich nodded. "Easy enough. Ahmed has us hold his hand for everything he does in the lab. It's my impression he has never done cell culture before."

"He hasn't," Jason said. "He's a bacteriologist and never much of a student."

"It might be a good idea if you felt out some of the graduate students," Al suggested. "Look for one with a distaste for funda-mentalist imams and the insurgents. We need a kid who will provide information on what Ahmed is up to, maybe even help sabotage a study, if that becomes necessary. We can promise a post-doc position at the CDC or a university of his choice in the US in return for his help."

"Hell," Dietrich said. "That ought to have them crawling out of the woodwork. My graduate student would jump at it."

Jason looked up at the mention of a post-doc. "I wouldn't mind getting in on that, either."

Al ignored him and directed his remarks to Dietrich. "Good. But be discreet. These people are academics but they play rough."

Gettelman showed Dietrich the other pictures, a photo of Ann's sample labels and one of a couple of short, thick white lines on a black background. "This is a stained agarose gel after electrophoresis of the PCR products of the coronavirus spike gene." Al used a pencil to point at one of the horizontal white lines. "The lane on the left is from BCV, the one in the middle is from the BCV-SARS hybrid." He pointed at the white line in the middle. It was a little closer to the top of the picture than the first. "As you can see, the BCV-SARS hybrid gene is about ninety base-pairs longer than that of the BCV parent virus."

Gettelman handed Dietrich a note. "Your contact information. It's an email address in Brussels that will automatically relay emails to me at the CDC. This address should look innocent if any of Ahmed's friends hack your email account. You can address the emails to 'Uncle Al.'"

St. Paul
Evening, July 2

Jason had badgered Gettelman until he agreed to let him visit Ann over the July Fourth weekend. When he opened the door to their apartment and tiptoed in, Ann was sitting at her computer, engrossed in revising a research report, her back to him. Jason carefully put his suitcase on the floor and quietly came up behind Ann.

He leaned forward, still out of her sight, and looked at the monitor. "Shouldn't that be a semi-colon in the third line?"

Ann jumped to her feet and whirled around. "Jason, you're home. God, don't scare me like that, not as far along as I am." She let him take her in his arms and kiss her.

Arms around his neck, she asked, "Why didn't you tell me you'd be home tonight?"

"I wasn't sure I could get away, and I didn't want to get your hopes up," he said, and kissed her again.

They held each other close while he told her about the meeting in Athens and the congressional committee meeting. "And in Djibouti, they hardly ever let me out of the embassy," he lied.

Ann was relieved but wasn't fooled. They devoted the next hour to becoming reacquainted, which was a lot more fun than talking about virology. They fell asleep as they lay together, Jason's hand on Ann's abdomen, feeling the baby move.

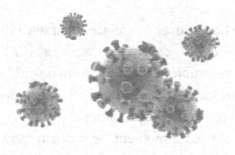

CHAPTER 16

Van Kellen Virology Lab, University of Ta'izz
July 7

To begin collecting information for Gettelman, Dietrich had his graduate student Mohammed Saiti help Ahmed in his lab. Mohammed was so skinny and short compared to Dietrich that Dietrich felt protective of him.

"Mohammed, how much time do you spend helping Professor Hadi?" Dietrich asked.

Mohammed leaned against a bookcase and paused to consider the question. Was this faculty politics? How cordial were the relations between Dietrich and Hadi? "Probably too much time, but it hasn't interfered with my classes or my own research yet," he said, and hoped that would satisfy Dietrich. Mohammed didn't want to get caught in a disagreement between two professors. A bright twenty-four-year-old, he'd learned to be cautious when working amongst a faculty riven with petty feuds.

"That is all right then," Dietrich said. "But I don't want you doing Hadi's work at the expense of your own. Is he still trying to grow BCV on HRT cells?"

"Yes, sir. But he's contaminating his cell cultures with bacteria and mold before he can even inoculate them with the virus. It would be easier if I did all of his cell culture work myself."

"Isn't he using antibiotics in his cell medium?"

"I've told him to, but his technique is so sloppy the antibiotics aren't enough to prevent contamination."

Mohammed paused a moment, wondering how much he dared to criticize one faculty member to another. The Western habit of speaking directly and candidly was foreign to faculty and students raised to respect age and social position.

He took a chance. "Hadi doesn't take instructions well from a graduate student. He didn't believe me when I told him he had to have a clean cell lab and a second lab to infect the cultures with a virus. If he ever gets that far, he's likely to contaminate all of his cell stocks with the first virus he uses."

Dietrich shook his head. "A clean cell lab is basic."

"Yes. Professor Hadi isn't at all like you," Mohammed said.

Dietrich cocked his head to the side. "How so?"

"Hadi is proud of his Ph.D. and veterinary degree. He asks me how to do things, then brags about his degrees and doesn't take my advice. It is very frustrating." Afraid he'd gone too far, Mohammed looked at the lab bench top to avoid Dietrich's gaze.

"Perhaps it would help if I paid Ahmed a visit." Dietrich had been looking for an excuse to look around Ahmed's lab.

Dietrich dropped by Ahmed's lab that afternoon and struck up a conversation. He gingerly turned the conversation to Ahmed's work and asked if he was making progress. Ahmed dodged the question and complained about his problems with contamination. He showed Dietrich two small rooms attached to his lab. Each room had a biosafety hood and the carbon dioxide incubators necessary for cell culture, and each was entered by an antechamber or air lock.

"Which room is your clean cell room and which one do you use for infecting cells?" Dietrich asked.

Ahmed paused, wondering whether to admit ignorance or lie. He pointed to the only room he was using. "This is my clean cell room."

Dietrich nodded. "Good. Be sure your people change lab coats when entering the clean room." As he walked over to peer through a window into the clean cell room, Dietrich noticed an upright minus seventy-degree freezer in a third room, between the other two. "You have your own minus seventy-degree freezer? I have to use one in the basement freezer room. Do you have special funding or a grant?"

"This was purchased with funding for a . . ." Ahmed racked his brain for a legitimate project. "For a camel vaccine study."

A slight rise in the tone of his voice on the word "study" suggested a question rather than a statement. "But I have to use the freezers in the basement for my other projects, like everyone else."

Dietrich walked Ahmed through the steps for culturing cells and identified a few problems—Ahmed hadn't stored his antibiotic solutions properly and had used outdated cell medium. With those corrections, the following week Ahmed was able to raise his cell cultures until they were nearly ready to be infected by the virus.

A couple of days before the healthy cells covered an entire side of a plastic flask, Dietrich walked into Ahmed's lab and asked him if he needed help purifying his virus to infect the cells.

The offer threw Ahmed into a panic. He paused and looked at the floor as he searched for a reason to reject Dietrich's offer and prevent him from seeing the purloined samples. "I can't ask you to do that, too," he said, carefully. "You've already spent so much time helping me. I'll be able to do it by following the protocol you gave me."

Dietrich watched to see if Ahmed made a trip to the basement freezer room during the rest of the day. He didn't. Visiting Ahmed's lab the next day, Dietrich noted that Ahmed was working a viral sample through the purification protocol. "How is the purification coming?" he asked. "We really have to get you a graduate student to do this lab work. You need time to read, plan studies, and write grant applications."

Ahmed hastily closed the notebook he was writing in and put it in a drawer. "I've asked for money for a graduate student, but I was turned down." Ahmed leaned against the lab bench behind him. "I'm a bacteriologist with an underfunded virology project. Even the university internal politics work against me. I'm not doing bacteriology, so I don't get support from the bacteriologists, and I'm an interloper to the virologists. Why should they help me siphon money from their funding pool?"

"Don't lose heart," Dietrich said. He put a hand on Ahmed's shoulder. "I'll see what I can do. I have an uncle, a wealthy philanthropist. I might be able to coax him into providing some money for you."

Ahmed's eyes lit up. "You could? That would be an enormous help, my friend."

Dietrich looked at a clock on the laboratory wall. "I'll go one better. Lunch is on me today. Let me give Mohammed instructions for this afternoon, and I'll drop by your office to pick you up. Okay?"

Ahmed agreed and went to his office whistling. Dietrich returned to his lab and asked Mohammed to come to his office. As he walked in, Dietrich motioned him to a chair and closed the door. "I'm taking Professor Hadi out for lunch. While we are out, check the container of medical waste in Hadi's dirty cell lab."

Mohammed nodded, and Dietrich continued. "There should be a small sample vial, maybe two milliliters. The label might still be on it and will indicate it held a fecal sample. If you find the empty vial, wear gloves, seal it in a sterile plastic bag and leave it on my desk under a piece of paper."

Dietrich turned to leave, but stopped at his office door as he thought of how his comments sounded to Mohammed. "If I'm going to help Ahmed, I need to know what he's working on, but I don't want to seem like I'm prying. Wash up and disinfect your hands afterwards, and put your lab coat in the laundry here. And don't mention this to anyone else. They might not understand that we're only trying to help. Keep it quiet, and you may have a shot at that post-doc I told you about."

"Of course. I understand," Mohammed lied.

He watched Dietrich walk to Ahmed's office and wondered if Dietrich really expected him to believe that crap. *These scientists make awful liars,* he thought, *but a post-doc at a US university, or even the CDC? That will make my career.*

Dietrich took Ahmed to the Leyali Al-Arab for their famous salads. It was a long lunch, and their return to their labs was delayed when Dietrich took a wrong turn in the old city. They'd gone only a short way before they were lost in a maze of narrow streets, barely wide enough for the car. Men wearing *futas* wrapped around their waists and western shirts walked past—but never with—women. The women, walking alone or in pairs, wore black neck-to-ankle *baltos,* their faces and heads covered by *abayas.* Pedestrians crowded around open-air shops where the road widened, bringing motor traffic to a slow creep. Bicyclists dodged pedestrians and whizzed past the barely moving cars, as though to rub it in. It took an hour to get back to a decent road.

Dietrich sat at his computer late that night and sent an email to his rich uncle Al in Brussels. "Identified an interesting freezer. Our friend needs another set of hands to be successful. I have a pair in mind if you have funding."

A few miles away, Al-Mikhafi sat at his PC in his apartment and sent a coded message to his source of funding. "My associate believes he has found extra funding for his lab. I am helping him develop a grant proposal for his benefactor, if there is one.

"Ahmed lacks much as a scientist. I do not know whether he is inept, too optimistic, or a liar, and I see no evidence of piety in him. This tale of funding from a philanthropist will be the last straw, if it does not materialize."

A few hours later, by the time it was morning in Atlanta, Gettelman read Dietrich's email and cringed. It sounded like a good idea, but he doubted whether Filburt would see it that way. He swallowed hard and did his best to write a persuasive introduction for Dietrich's idea. He reread what he'd written and forwarded Dietrich's email to Filburt at Langley. Filburt was on the phone to him an hour later.

"Al, I've gone along with you so far on this, but this latest idea . . . Goddamn it, Al, you've gone too far," Filburt yelled into the phone. "You can't be serious. You cannot expect me to ask my superiors and Congress to fund a lab tech for a henchman of Ansar Allah. I'd be drummed out of the FBI."

"George, I wouldn't suggest this if I didn't think it was the best idea I've heard. For the price of a plane ticket and a hotel room, Dietrich identified the lab and the freezer the samples are in. He's made himself Ahmed's best friend, and he's found a graduate student to put in the jerk's lab. Christ, what do you—"

Filburt put a hand to his brow. "Come on, Al. I want to keep my job long enough to have a pension. Look at it from my—"

"How much money do you guys spend on intelligence without getting anything like Dietrich's results? If we don't get all of those samples passed on HRT cells, we'll always wonder where the rest of them are and who might be working with them. Is that what you want?"

"Of course not, but—"

"Haven't you got some money in a fund that isn't being used? I thought your spooks always had slush funds stashed somewhere."

Filburt thought of the rumors he'd heard about the Djibouti bribes and some other funds. "Okay. Maybe there are a few small pots of money available, but none big enough to fund a graduate student, not like you were talking about before."

"Maybe we should fund it as a lab tech position," Al said. "That would cut the cost. I'll get back to you on that."

"Wait, don't . . . don't . . . damn."

Gettelman had hung up. Filburt slammed his handset back on the phone base. "I will not work with these goddamned academics again."

University of Ta'izz
July 21

Dietrich dropped by Ahmed's office and told him he'd talked his rich uncle into providing funding.

"How much time can Mohammad spend in my lab?" Ahmed asked.

"Half of every day. Will that work for you?"

Relief washed through Ahmed. "Can he start tomorrow?"

Mohammed started working on the clock for Ahmed the next day. As he was about to leave the lab for lunch, Ahmed called and asked him to drop by his office.

"Mohammed, how much do you know about bovine coronavirus?"

"I've worked with it a little. Dietrich did his thesis on it at Utrecht. I can ask him, if you have questions."

Ahmed frowned, but caught himself and put on a bland expression. A man as knowledgeable as Dietrich might discern too much. "No! You shouldn't do that," Ahmed said. "He . . . he has already done so much for me, I would hate to bother him further."

Yeah, sure, Mohammed thought. *What is it these guys are hiding from each other?*

"I picked up a number of recent papers on BCV, but I do not have time to read them." Ahmed handed Mohammed a six-inch deep pile of research reports. "Could you read them, pick out what might be relevant to my studies, and prepare a summary for me, typed, double-spaced? Boil all of them down to no more than two or three pages, total."

Mohammed struggled to avoid looking angry. He didn't see a way out of the extra work, but he knew that Ahmed watched porn on his computer and played beat the weasel over his lunch hour. "I can do that," Mohammed said. "But I will have to know what you're trying to accomplish in your BCV studies."

Ahmed was taken aback. He had to come up with more lies. "Yes, certainly. Of course, you will. I am trying to," Ahmed paused to sip from a cup of tea. He made a face and frowned at the cup. He smiled suddenly and put the cup down. "I must grow a challenge strain of BCV for a vaccination and challenge study."

"How much challenge virus will you need?" Mohammed asked.

"How much? Hmm," Ahmed put his hands in his lab coat and stared at the floor. "We will discuss that when you have completed the digest of the reports," he said. "You may go for today. I have work to attend to in my office."

Mohammed carried the stack of papers back to the office he

shared with another graduate student and dumped them on his desk. His office mate looked at him. "What's wrong?'

"Nothing," Mohammed lied. "But if I were you, I wouldn't shake hands with Professor Hadi in the afternoon."

Mohammed marched across the hallway to Dietrich's office. He rapped on the frame of the door. Dietrich was leaning back in his chair, his feet on the corner of his desk. He looked up from a recent issue of *Cell*. "Hi, Mo. What do you need?"

Mohammed cringed and checked behind himself to make sure no one was within earshot and closed the door. "Dietrich, please don't call me that. Someone else may hear you and we'll both be in trouble with the religious authorities. Abbreviating the Prophet's name is considered blasphemy. That carries a death sentence."

Dietrich's eyes grew wide; he took his feet off the desk and sat up. "I'm sorry. I didn't know. What do you need?"

Mohammed took a chair in front of Dietrich's desk. "I need to know what the hell is going on. Hadi just dumped a bunch of reading on me. He wants me to summarize a couple hundred pages of recent papers on BCV. 'Boil it down to two or three pages,' he said. He seems as determined to keep me from knowing what he's really doing as you were the other day."

Dietrich put his journal down. "Go on."

"You are each trying to hide something from the other, and I'm in the middle. I like you, and I think Hadi's a lazy jerk. I'll be glad to help you, especially if you can deliver on that post-doc, but I have to know what I'm really doing."

Dietrich nodded. He took a deep breath and sighed. "Fair enough. I'll tell you as much as it's safe for you to know. If you think you're in danger, come to me and I'll tell you everything I know. I probably haven't been told everything myself."

"Okay. That will be a start. You said I might be in danger?"

"There are faculty here who are involved in the Sa'dah insurrection. Ahmed is working with a faculty member in another department. Both of them have secret studies funded by Ansar Allah."

"Sa'dah's military wing? Shit," Mohammed said, and briefly buried his head in his hands. *I'm up to my butt in a Sunni-Shiite civil war,* he thought. "Might be in danger? We could have our throats slit just walking across campus. I thought Professor Hadi was trying to divert money from his grant to his pockets, or spending time with somebody's wife when he says he's in physical therapy."

"Nothing that innocent," Dietrich said. "You should also know that Ahmed stole the BCV samples he has. They aren't simple BCV. The virus is a hybrid, part BCV, part SARS virus."

"Ahh." Mohammed's eyebrows peaked, and he nodded. "So that's why you had me be so cautious with the empty vial."

"Be careful when you handle that stuff. For the reports Ahmed wants summarized, bring them to my office and we'll go through them together when Ahmed is at his physical therapy. I don't want him—or anyone else—to know that you've discussed them with me."

Mohammed agreed, and he and Dietrich reviewed the papers that afternoon. Dietrich put sticky notes on four papers. "The papers I've marked are papers you should go easy on," Dietrich said. "You can reasonably claim that they didn't seem to be pertinent to his studies."

Mohammed shrugged. "Sounds good, but wouldn't it be easier if you told me what you don't want him to know?"

Dietrich bowed his head. "You're right. I'm acting like those idiots who stamp everything 'confidential.'" He picked up the first paper he'd marked. "This paper identifies camels as being easily infected by BCV. We don't want Ahmed to know he has choices other than calves for his animal work. Tell him about the paper describing antibody levels to BCV they found in goats. The goat work is weak and will lead him astray. These other papers," Dietrich pulled three other papers he'd marked from the pile, "especially this Korean paper, suggest that growing BCV in tissue culture reduces its virulence. They don't say it plainly, but anyone who knows about growing challenge strains would latch onto it in a flash. Let's not tempt the fates by running it past Ahmed."

That evening, Dietrich sent another email to his uncle Al, suggesting Al put him in touch with the virologist he met in Athens. The young man would be interested in recent reports Dietrich had.

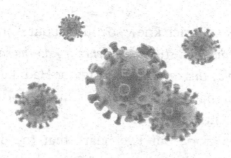

CHAPTER 17

University of Ta'izz
July 26

Dietrich and Mohammed looked at the notice on the bulletin board:

> *Wednesday, 28 July, Noon Seminar, Room 205*
> *Guest Speaker:*
> *Prof. J.D.P. Smyth, Department of PathoBiology,*
> *Royal (Dick) School of Veterinary Studies, University of*
> *Edinburgh, Scotland*
> *Advances in Ruminant Coronavirus Cell Attachment*
> *Report to The 21st International Conference on Ruminant*
> *Enteroviruses,*
> *Athens, Greece*

"I forgot he was visiting us after the conference," Dietrich said. "I should have known he'd repeat the seminar he gave in Athens."

"Is that a problem?" Mohammed asked quietly.

Dietrich glanced up and down the hallway. They were alone. "It depends whether our friend can drag himself away from his porn and keep his hands above his belt over the noon hour on Wednesday."

Mohammed choked back a laugh and looked sideways at Dietrich.

He hadn't realized Dietrich knew so much about Ahmed. *One professor might criticize another and still take offence if I do the same,* Mohammed thought. *Best to play this carefully.* "Professor Hadi has attended other departmental seminars. Is attendance required for the faculty? It is for graduate students."

"It isn't mandatory, but I've heard that the department chair questions faculty that don't show up," Dietrich said. "I can't think of a way to keep him away from the seminar." Dietrich looked absently at the announcement for a moment. "Have you given him your summary of the BCV papers?"

"I was going to give it to him this afternoon," Mohammed said.

Dietrich checked. They were still alone. "Hold on to your report until Wednesday, and give it to him as he's heading to the seminar. Maybe it will keep him occupied during Smyth's talk."

Thursday, Mohammed walked into Dietrich's office for their weekly lab meeting. "What did you think of the seminar?" Dietrich asked as Mohammed sat.

"Smyth's data proved that growing BCV in tissue culture reduces virulence. It was similar to the Korean paper you didn't want Professor Hadi to see."

"You noticed that, too, yes? Did Ahmed appear to catch on?"

"He didn't say anything about it or about the camel study."

"Oh God, the camel study." Dietrich smacked himself on the forehead. "It was as though Smyth had a checklist of things Ahmed needed to know. He'd have to be brain-dead not to catch on about the camels."

"He had his head buried in my summary for most of the lecture, and he didn't ask any questions after the talk."

That sounded promising to Dietrich. "Good. If Ahmed listened to the lecture at all, he should have peppered Smyth with questions.

Watch and listen for anything that indicates he learned something. We'll need a back-up plan if he decides to expand the virus in neonatal camels."

Mohammed nodded. "Okay, but can we spend some time today talking about my project?"

That evening, Dietrich sent another email to his uncle in Brussels. "Our friend sat in on a seminar on recent advances in his field. He is a slow learner. Can we meet to discuss options?"

Center for Disease Control, Atlanta, GEORGIA
July 26

Midafternoon, and Gettelman couldn't put it off any longer. He made the call to Agent Filburt. "Bad news, George," Gettelman said.

The line was silent for an uncomfortable period. "Are you still there, George?" Gettelman asked.

"How bad is it?" Filburt asked.

"Ahmed sat in on a seminar on the latest findings on BCV. So far, there isn't any indication he understands how he can use the new information. I don't know how long that will last."

"Great," Filburt snarled. "You're telling me that sitting on our hands and letting Ahmed putter away might not work?"

"That's the gist of it, but there's good news, too. We have a graduate student working in his lab."

"The one I stuck my neck on the block for?"

"Yeah," Gettelman said. "The kid knows what Ahmed is doing and has agreed to help us. We know everything that Ahmed plans to do in the lab because of that kid. Dietrich and the kid are working out options to block Ahmed if he catches on to the new information, so don't act like we've failed you."

"Yeah, but I'm toast if—"

"The money I asked for earlier is paying off better than any investment you've ever made."

Gettelman waited for a response. "Well, George? Hasn't it?"

Quietly, Filburt answered. "Yeah, it has. But if I have to stand up to Senator Nuthatch again—"

"Who?"

"Senator '9/11' Nuthatch. It's a code name I have for one of the war hawks in the senate. He has power and a short fuse, and I forced him to back down on this in front of other senators at our last security meeting. I'm going to be in deep shit if Ahmed finds a way to make a weapon out of this virus."

"We aren't at that point yet," Gettelman said.

"We'd better not get anywhere near it, Al," Filburt said, "because if we do, bombs will start dropping, drones will go hunting, and I won't be able to stop them."

"I understand, George, and we all appreciate your work." Gettelman paused. "I hate to ask you for help again, but Dietrich sent word that he wants to discuss the new developments on a secure line. Can you help with that?"

"That will be up to the CIA. The station chief in Djibouti is in charge of this. He's only a hundred and sixty miles away by air. He might visit Ta'izz to set up a teleconference in one of the safe rooms we have near the city."

Jason looked from a third floor window of a stone building near Ta'izz. Rare patches of green picked out by the late afternoon sun broke up the steep barren hills on the other side of the narrow valley. A sparse growth of brush and brown, dormant grass covered the valley floor. The only trees in sight were at the corner of the building he was in and near a stone house down the road. Even the corn on the slope behind the building looked stunted, the leaves brown and curled, when they drove up.

Jason remembered the green fields and forests of Minnesota and wondered if it ever rained in Yemen. "How does anybody make a living in this area?"

"It's the dry season. It'll look better after the fall rains." Howard pointed to the left side of the window. "You'll see more greenery on the edge of the valley if you crane your neck a bit and look towards Ta'izz."

In the distance, Jason could make out alternating bands of dull green and brownish-yellow that seemed to scale the steep hills. The pattern covered all of several hillsides except for the switchbacks of the road leading up to Ta'izz. A white castle on a mountain seemed to float above the city.

"You're looking at hundreds of narrow, rock-walled terraces below the city," Howard said. "Most are only wide enough for one or two rows of coffee plants. The term 'mocha' derived from the name of a port on the coast not far from here."

Jason turned from the window and helped Howard arrange the chairs. The room was above a restaurant that took up the first two floors. It was small, with barely enough space for a table, six chairs, and a counter along one wall. Both the outer and interior walls of the room were made of stone blocks, painted white where they formed arches over the windows. One window looked out over the valley. The other faced toward Ta'izz, a little over a mile away. The view from that window was obscured by a tree so close the leaves brushed against the window. Two bare bulbs in the ceiling augmented the light from the windows.

The aromas of garlic, fenugreek, cardamom, ginger, roast chicken, and lamb penetrated the stone walls, reminding Jason that he hadn't eaten. "Will we have dinner here?" he asked Howard.

"I took the liberty of ordering lamb saltah and chicken ogdat." Howard removed a telephone from a cabinet under the counter and put it in the center of the table. "It'll be an education for you, Jason. We'll be eating stew with nothing but our hands and flatbread used as spoons."

Jason pictured a stew of eyeballs or chicken heads. "Could I just get a chicken sandwich?"

Howard saw Jason's expression. "Don't worry. There shouldn't be anything to upset your Midwestern palette."

The driver who had picked them up at the airport entered the room with a tray of glasses and a pitcher of water. Dietrich and Mohammed followed right behind him. The driver took a position at the door while Dietrich introduced Mohammed. The phone rang, everyone sat at the table, and Howard put the phone on "speaker mode." Paul, Gettelman, and Filburt greeted them from Langley.

"I asked for this meeting," Dietrich said, "because Ahmed sat in on a seminar that should tip him off to a better way of growing his virus. He's not a very perceptive scientist. He may not have understood what he heard, but I thought you'd want to have options in place in case he does."

"What is Ahmed likely to do if he picks up on the new information?" Paul asked.

"If I were him, I'd expand the virus by passing it in neonatal camel calves." Dietrich leaned back in his chair and stretched. "It shouldn't lose virulence, and camels are susceptible to BCV."

Both Jason and Paul swore. "We never thought of camels," Paul said. "We only considered animal models available in the US."

"How much lead time will Ahmed need to pass the virus in a camel calf?" Gettelman asked.

Howard leaned closer to the phone in the center of the table. "This is Howard Frobisher, from Djibouti. Ta'izz is a center for camel racing. Healthy, pregnant camels are available in the area, if Ahmed has the money. He will have to keep quiet about what he plans to do to them, as the locals are quite fond of their camels. They even write poems about them."

Mohammed whispered something to Dietrich. "Better tell them," he said.

"This is Mohammed. The camel calving season is from November to May. A few calves might be earlier, but not many."

"That gives us three months to do something," Jason said. Tentative at first, he gained confidence as he spoke. "If Mohammed has access to Ahmed's freezer, I'd like to steal our samples back and replace them with dummy samples."

"Can you prepare new samples, with the correct labels?" Dietrich asked.

"Ann could prepare them in a couple of hours at the University of Minnesota dairy barn," Jason answered.

"We could send them overnight by air," Filburt said. "You don't care if they aren't refrigerated for the trip, do you?"

Mohammed was nervous. "This assumes I will have access to the freezer. The freezer is locked, and Professor Hadi could limit my access to it at any time."

"Back-up. We need a back-up plan," Filburt said.

Jason turned to Mohammed and asked, "What is the daily high temperature in Ta'izz, this time of year?"

"What was that, Jason?" Paul asked. "Can you get closer to the phone?"

"This is Mohammed. Jason asked me what the daytime temperature is in Ta'izz in August. Highs are generally between twenty-seven to thirty-two degrees Centigrade. Here in the highlands we don't get the extreme heat Djibouti gets."

"In Fahrenheit, that's . . ." Jason checked his pockets for a calculator.

"Eighty to ninety degrees Fahrenheit," Dietrich said. "Average daily high is eighty-six degrees."

"That's enough," Jason said. "If the freezer is unplugged for a few days and you tinker with the air conditioning controls for the rooms to let them heat up, the freezer's compressor is likely to blow when you plug it back in."

"Is Ahmed in his lab on weekends?" Gettelman asked. "Is his freezer alarmed?"

Mohammed rolled his eyes. "Ahmed only comes to his lab during the week. He's never there from Jummah until Monday morning."

"Jummah?" Jason asked.

"Friday afternoon prayers," Dietrich explained. "It's as close to a Sabbath, in the Judeo-Christian sense, as Islam has. Few people are in the labs on Saturday or Sunday."

Mohammed leaned closer to the phone. "What was the question about alarms?"

"Are there automatic alarms if a freezer gets too warm?"

"Only in the basement freezer room," Dietrich said. "Great idea, Jason."

"Good. Then we are in agreement on our first line of approach and our back-up," Gettelman said. "Paul, can you prepare and ship dummy fecal samples to Agent Filburt by next Monday?"

"Damn it," Filburt said. "Will somebody please tell me what the hell the back-up plan is?"

"Sorry," Jason said. "Mohammed can unplug the freezer on a Thursday and turn off the air conditioning in the lab for the weekend. Minus-seventy freezers can't take that kind of abuse. When he plugs the freezer back in on Monday, the compressor motor is likely to burn out. The samples will thaw and sit without refrigeration. It could be weeks before Ahmed sees that the freezer isn't working."

"And?" Filburt asked.

The group in Ta'izz heard Gettelman on the other end of the line. "George, BCV is sensitive to prolonged warm temperatures. The virus will be inactivated if it's at room temperature for more than a week."

The discussion ended shortly after that. The phone was put away and the driver brought plates and platters of ogdat and saltah. "That," Howard said pointing to a platter in front of Jason, "is the lamb saltah, a stew with chili peppers, tomatoes, fenugreek, and garlic."

"What about the other stuff?" Jason asked, and pointed to a platter with saffron-colored meat chunks in a bright red sauce.

Howard leaned toward it and sniffed. "That is a chicken ogdat, a stew with tomatoes, carrots, potatoes, and onions. It's a bit spicier than a saltah, but give it a try."

During the meal, Dietrich asked Howard, "In an emergency, how can I get in touch with someone fast?"

Howard rummaged through his briefcase. "Here," he said, handing Dietrich a satellite phone. "This can't be traced to the purchaser, and my number and the number of the manager of the restaurant here are number four and eight on the contact list." He handed the phone to Dietrich. "The other numbers are random from around the Middle East."

Dietrich looked at the contact list. "Your name is not on this."

"For safety, in case somebody else gets ahold of the phone. Nothing on the contact list will connect you to the CIA."

University of Ta'izz
August 10

Three days after the teleconference, Ahmed knocked on the doorframe of Professor Al-Mikhafi's open office door. "May peace be upon you and may God's blessings be with you."

Al-Mikhafi looked up. "And also with you, Ahmed. How is the knee recovering?"

"It is improving. It should be back to normal within a month, *inshallah*," Ahmed said.

Al-Mikhafi motioned him in. "Come in and have a seat. Close the door behind you, please."

Ahmed closed the door and took a chair in front of Al-Mikhafi's desk. "I've been thinking about Djibouti," Al-Mikhafi said. "We attempted to do too much with untrained people, and we didn't have time to supervise their work. We were made to look like fools. That was my fault. I was too eager to press ahead with a dummy laboratory to goad the infidels. I won't let that happen again, *inshallah*."

Ahmed nodded agreement. "Can we begin again to—"

Al-Mikhafi waived a dismissive hand. "It is too early. We must concentrate on your laboratory work and growth of the virus. One of my graduate students said the seminar on enteroviruses last Wednesday was extraordinarily informative. Did you get any new ideas from it?"

Ahmed couldn't remember anything about BCV mentioned in the seminar. He struggled to look relaxed and casual. "I am discussing some ideas with Mohammed, Professor van Kellen's graduate student, now," he said, breezily. "Van Kellen was able to come through with a small grant for me, and Mohammed is spending four hours a day working in my laboratory. He is a very bright student. We are reviewing the seminar and the many scientific reports on BCV and SARS that I brought with me from Jeddah."

Al-Mikhafi looked at him sharply and paused, thinking over what Ahmed had said. It sounded reasonable. "Excellent. Tell me, what from the seminar has prompted the most promising ideas?"

Ahmed gulped. "As with the decoy strategy, it is too early to pin our hopes on one line of thought from the seminar. We are looking at several. I don't want to raise expectations for an approach we may have to drop, or dismiss."

Al-Mikhafi sighed softly. Just once, he'd like to get a straight answer from Ahmed. "Can you prepare a short report for me by next Monday, outlining the plan you think is most promising and two back-up plans? A single page for each plan, and include a budget estimate and list of decision points for each."

"Decision points?"

"Yes," Al-Mikhafi said, and wondered why he had to explain this to Ahmed. "*Inshallah,* you will identify points at which you can make a decision on whether it pays to continue working on each approach. For example, if the RNA from SARS is lost by the virus when you use a procedure, or if the virus loses virulence in laboratory animals, you would drop the procedure."

Ahmed was nearly white. Al-Mikhafi glanced toward him, and his voice became conciliatory. "I don't expect exact dates or budget amounts, but give me a rough idea when you will be ready to stage a demonstration in Europe with your virus, perhaps in a movie theater or elementary school. That would get the infidels' attention, *inshallah.*"

Beads of sweat formed on Ahmed's brow. "Ah, Monday may be a little early. Can you give me more time, perhaps until next Friday . . . at least?"

Al-Mikhafi nodded. "For the final report. I'd like a list of your Plan A, B and C by next Monday, though." A few taps on his computer keyboard, and he looked at Ahmed again. "There. I've got it in my Outlook and made the same addition in yours." He looked at his watch. "Thank you for dropping by. I have to leave—a luncheon meeting with some of the people who are financing this. They are dangerous when irritated."

Ahmed picked up his briefcase and left the office, his mind racing, trying to forestall panic. *Mohammed, he must have some ideas,* Ahmed thought and walked rapidly to the lab. Mohammed wasn't there. He hurried to Mohammed's office, but it was empty. Cursing his bad luck and any gods he could think of, Ahmed sulked across the plaza to the student cafeteria. At least the food there, subsidized by the government, was inexpensive and the portions filling.

He wanted to be alone. The only meat he could afford was the goat saltah. He picked up his tray and found a small table in a corner, hidden from the other tables by ornamental plants. He put his tray on the table, dropped his briefcase beside his chair, and sat down. The more he thought of his meeting with Al-Mikhafi, the faster his appetite faded. Picking at his food and feeling sorry for himself, he overheard a group of graduate students take seats at a table behind him.

A tenor voice brought up the seminar. "What did you think about the data on the increase in virulence by passing BCV through neonates?"

A slightly deeper voice said, "Stunning. And he had data from some place called the Sand Hills in the US. Under natural conditions in a herd of cows, the virulence of the virus increased as it infected more calves. You don't often see lab data and epidemiological data fit that closely."

Ahmed could not believe his good fortune. He opened his briefcase, found a tablet and pen, and pushed his lunch out of the way. He scribbled for twenty minutes as the students talked about mutation rates, quasi-species, and other things he didn't quite understand, when a third voice, deeper than the others, chimed in. "Do you think the epidemiological data can be applied to camels?"

One of the tenors answered. "Maybe. They're susceptible and sometimes develop diarrhea in the neonates, just like cattle."

Camels! Ahmed thought. He'd already discovered there weren't suitable calves in the area, but camels? The area was crawling with them. He'd almost hit one on the road outside of Ta'izz.

He didn't have three ideas, but passage in neonatal camels sounded like a good one. One good idea and a mountain of bullshit would get him through the next couple of weeks. When it came to bullshit, he could supply as much as needed to bury Al-Mikhafi's concerns.

His appetite returned, and he dug into the remainder of his lunch. As he congratulated himself and chewed, he tried to remember if either the susceptibility of camels or the effect of multiple passages in neonatal animals was included in Mohammed's review. He couldn't remember seeing it, but the review was of the papers, not the seminar. That was probably why.

But the graduate students behind him had been so excited by the information they heard in the seminar that they talked about it over lunch, yet Mohammed never mentioned it to him. *That was odd*, Ahmed thought.

CHAPTER 18

St. Paul
Evening, August 13

Harith checked the email from BillESmith and called Jason's number. A recording asked him to leave a message before he remembered Jason was no longer in Minnesota. He scrolled through old emails until he found the one from Jason with Ann's number.

Ann picked up her phone and looked at the caller ID. Harith Sabeeh. Jason had mentioned something about Harith. She answered the phone. The conversation was short, almost cryptic. "Tell Jason," Harith said, "that the biochemist knows that an agent of the CIA was in Ta'izz for a meeting with someone at the University. He is suspicious of Jason's contact in Ta'izz. The contact should be careful. The biochemist is ruthless. He has had friendly conversations with people as he prepared to have them murdered."

This was not a message calculated to help Ann sleep. She called Gettelman at his home in Atlanta, rousted him out of bed, and transmitted Harith's message. It took Gettelman half an hour to calm her fears and assure her that Jason wasn't in danger. It was easier than admitting that he was worried, too.

❧

University of Ta'izz
Morning, August 14

Twelve time zones to the east at the University of Ta'izz, Ahmed handed Al-Mikhafi the list of options for future work with the BCV-SARS virus. Al-Mikhafi paced back and forth behind his desk as he scanned the paper, stopping occasionally and nodding approval. This was better than he'd hoped. He turned to Ahmed and smiled. "Good! These look very promising, Ahmed. I have underestimated you. Proceed as quickly as you can to work up the budgets."

Ahmed's face fell. He had no idea how to put a budget together, but he had no option but to promise to do so. As he stood to leave Al-Mikhafi's office, he took a shot at reducing the work. "I may not be able to work up budgets for all three proposals, but we will have the neonatal camel option in your hands by Friday morning, *inshallah.*"

His pulse quickened when he realized his slip. He hoped Al-Mikhafi wouldn't notice the "we," or ask who would help Ahmed.

Al-Mikhafi's expression didn't change. He'd been thinking of how this would relieve some of the pressure from his bankers. "Excellent. I'll let our liaison with the clerics know. But before you go, there is another matter we should discuss. How secure is your freezer?"

Ahmed stopped. It was a question he'd never considered. "The laboratory is locked, and the room is locked. The freezer is locked. For all of the locks but the door to the lab, only Mohammed and I have keys."

Al-Mikhafi wondered, again, about Ahmed's prodigious naiveté. "Are you sure of that?"

"I, ah, I have no way of making sure." Ahmed shrugged. "That is what the departmental secretary told me when he handed me the keys. Why do you ask?"

"Our friends tell me a CIA agent from Djibouti and a younger American were in Ta'izz to talk to a professor and a graduate student. The meeting was at a restaurant we suspect is a front for the CIA. The report couldn't be confirmed, and the source did not have the names of the men the CIA agents met."

Ahmed went pale. "Do you think—?"

Al-Mikhafi dismissed Ahmed's question with a wave of his hand. "We know little, but the university administration has been given a shipment of surveillance cameras. They were going to put them on buildings to record traffic around the university in case there is student unrest or infiltration by the insurgents. Our department was given several, but no one was sure what to do with them. Why don't we put one or two in your lab?"

"We can place one to cover the freezer and the other to cover the door to the room it is in," Ahmed said, "but I don't know how to set up surveillance cameras."

Al-Mikhafi closed his eyes and held his tongue. *How did this man get a Ph.D.?* he thought. "The maintenance department will do it for you. I'll have them check with you this week. You only need to show them where you want the cameras installed. Make sure the picture is transmitted to your office and the university security office on the first floor."

Ahmed left and Al-Mikhafi leaned back in his chair, clasped his hands over his stomach, and smiled. The irony was delicious. Ahmed would protect Ansar Allah's investment with surveillance cameras purchased to protect the government against the insurgents.

Mohammed found Ahmed waiting for him when he came to work the next morning. "You want me to work up a budget?" Mohammed asked. "How am I supposed to get prices for camels or camel feed? We don't even have a barn or pens to house them. Who can we hire to take care of them?"

Ahmed had no idea, and Mohammed's tone suggested he had better not press him too hard. "You can use this outline of a protocol," Ahmed said, as he handed him a single, handwritten page. "Determine the laboratory supplies you will need to screen a young camel for other viruses and inoculate it, collect the feces and nasal swabs, and prepare them to infect the next camel calf." He pointed to a bookshelf sagging under the weight of thick catalogues. "Use the lab supply catalogues for cost estimates and assume we will have to pass the virus in five or six camels, instead of the three I'm planning."

Congratulating himself on sounding authoritative, Ahmed graciously offered to do the hard work. "I'll take care of estimating the cost of the camels," he said. He thought about it in more specific terms and paused. "Does the university have a Department of Animal Science?"

"Not that I know of," Mohammed said.

Ahmed outlined the lab work he wanted Mohammed to complete. On his way back to his office, he thought of places to get information on camels. *What would a camel market look like?* He remembered used car lots in Minnesota, and tried to remember if he'd seen any camels tied by the side of the road with balloons or brightly colored flags. Then he thought of the insurgents. They were mostly illiterates, but they probably knew everyone with a camel within seventy kilometers. Al-Mikhafi could contact them.

University of Ta'izz
August 22

Ahmed stopped by Al-Mikhafi's office a week later. "Hassan, do you have any leads for a facility or camels?" he asked Al-Mikhafi.

"Ahmed, come in, and close the door," Al-Mikhafi said. With the door closed, he continued. "A colleague of ours in the countryside has an establishment near a mosque, fifty kilometers west of town. He sold most of his camels and was about to sell the buildings. There are two herdsmen at the facility who attend the same mosque and are loyal."

"Wonderful," Ahmed said. He leaned forward in his chair. "Can we drive out and examine the place to see if it will meet our needs?"

"I'm not sure. Can you draft a list of our minimum requirements by tomorrow?"

Ahmed stood. "Yes," he said, without enthusiasm. His hand on the door handle, he turned back to Al-Mikhafi. "May I ask Mohammed to help me work on this, and can I ask Dietrich how he conducted his BCV calf studies? He did his thesis on BCV at Utrecht."

Al-Mikhafi leaned back in his chair, his fingertips on his chin, as though in prayer. He wasn't comfortable telling Dietrich, an infidel, too much. "Be careful. If you discuss this with Dietrich, do not mention camels. Better yet, ask him if you could borrow a copy of his thesis. Then you will not need to tell him what you are looking for."

Ahmed nodded and smiled. "Of course. An excellent idea."

He went back to his office and sat down at his computer to list the facility requirements. He got as far as the title, "Facility Requirements," before he realized he had no idea what he would need. He put the title in bold type and centered it on the page.

It looked better, but he still didn't know what a pregnant camel needed or if he could purchase newborn camels. He didn't know the gestation period of camels, if he could safely move pregnant camels, what he could feed the calves, or whether camel milk would have antibodies against BCV. He didn't even know if there was a calving season for camels.

Ahmed tried to think of a rational approach. He paced back and forth in his office and looked at the clock. It was two thirty. Mohammed only worked for him in the mornings; by tomorrow morning, it would be too late. Ahmed would have to do the work himself—or ask Dietrich for help.

He'd never seen Dietrich talk to Al-Mikhafi. They were in different departments with offices on different floors. *If I talk to Dietrich, Al-Mikhafi will never know,* Ahmed thought, *provided I'm careful.* He called Dietrich and asked if he could drop by to discuss a problem.

"Sure." Dietrich said. "Just give me a few minutes to finish something."

"How about three o'clock?"

Dietrich agreed, hung up, and looked for a digital recorder, something small and discrete. He completed setting up the recorder only seconds before Ahmed knocked on his door. Dietrich motioned to a chair in front of his desk, and Ahmed closed the door as he entered. "How can I help you?" Dietrich asked.

"I have to determine what I will need in a facility to do BCV studies in neonatal camel calves, and I don't know anything about camels. How do I go about it?"

Dietrich, surprised and unable to control his facial expression, turned toward a bookshelf behind him and pretended to search for a text. He had never expected espionage to be this easy. Ahmed even made an appointment to divulge his plans. Dietrich swiveled back to face Ahmed when he'd overcome his shock. "Are you planning on building from scratch or modifying an existing facility?"

"We will rent an existing facility," Ahmed said.

"Was it built by someone who knew what they were doing or by somebody in research?" Dietrich asked.

"It was not built for research," Ahmed said. "They raised racing camels there."

Dietrich had heard about the love affair the locals had with their racing camels. He spoke slowly as he gathered his thoughts. "The people who built it knew more about camel husbandry than either of us ever will, yes? Let's concentrate on what we know you will need for your viral work and biosafety, and assume the guys who built the facility got the basic structure right for camels."

Ahmed's face lit up. "Of course. That is the answer I needed. You've helped me immeasurably." Ahmed stood to leave.

Dietrich mentally kicked himself. He hadn't meant to solve Ahmed's problem for him. Perhaps he could still come out ahead. "I'd be happy to review the first draft of your requirements if you'd like," he said. "Give me a call when you have it on paper."

"Would you? That is wonderful," Ahmed said. He excused himself and said he would return when the first draft was completed.

Dietrich watched him disappear down the hallway, closed the door to his office, and pulled out the satellite phone Howard had given him. If this wasn't important enough to use the phone, he wasn't sure what would be. He called the fourth number on the contact list.

A seductive female voice apologized in beautiful French for being unable to come to the phone and asked him to leave a message. Dietrich paused, looked at the phone, shrugged, and remembered that the contact list was set up to confound anyone attempting to investigate the bearer of the phone. "This is van Kellen. Our friends are moving to purchase a camel facility. We need to make plans, yes?"

His phone rang ten minutes later. "Dietrich, Howard here."

"Thanks for getting back to me. Our friends are preparing to grow the virus in camels. It will require time for them to get into production, but we should meet soon to discuss our options."

"We can't meet or call frequently, as each carries a risk. I'll contact the others and have your Uncle Al get back to you."

US Embassy, Djibouti
Afternoon, August 22

In his office at the embassy in Djibouti, Howard pocketed his satellite phone and turned to Jason. "Ever go hunting stateside?"

"You mean pheasant or deer hunting?" Jason asked.

"Yeah. Have you handled a rifle or pistol before?"

"Only a couple of times," Jason said. He didn't like where this conversation was headed. "Why?"

"Our friends in Ta'izz want to meet again." Howard stood and paced back and forth behind his desk. "The more often we meet, the greater the risk, and we've already picked up chatter on cell and satellite phones and on the internet that suggests you and I were noticed in Ta'izz at our last meeting. Someone on the street may have recognized me, or they may have been watching the restaurant. Either way, we can't chance meeting there again."

"Why do they want to meet?"

"Camels. Ahmed is looking for a facility to work on camels."

"We were afraid of that. How close is he to putting the virus into camels?" Jason asked.

"Apparently, he isn't close, yet. I'll call Langley and have them discuss this with Gettelman and the folks at the U of M. In the meantime, I'm taking you out to the marine target range at what they call Ammo Point, about fifteen miles southwest of the city." Howard opened a drawer in his desk and brought out a pistol. "This is an H&K P30S 9mm. It's empty and on safety. Leave it that way until Sergeant Williams shows you how to handle it." He handed the gun to Jason.

Jason looked at the gun and back at Howard. "Who is Sargent Williams?"

"The marine I'm going to introduce you to this evening. Put the

H&K in your briefcase," Howard said. "Drop by my office again in fifteen minutes. We'll eat on the way to the Point."

"Why don't they have the target range at the base?" Jason asked.

"The base is too small, it's too close to the commercial airport, and way too close to the French military airfield. Some of the men tell me they can feel the jet exhaust in their tents when the French fighters take off."

Howard introduced Jason to Sargent Williams that evening. After a lesson in safety, they went to a pistol range where Williams showed Jason how to verify the safety was on, how to put the clip in the gun's grip, and shoot. While Jason practiced, Howard and Williams walked far enough from the firing line so they could talk.

"What do you want me to teach him and how much time do I have?" Williams asked.

"You may only have a few days. Teach him to clean the gun and load it. I'll be happy if he can shoot well enough so the gun is more dangerous to a bad guy than it is to him."

Williams stroked his chin and looked at the dust around his boots before glancing back at Jason. He winced as he watched Jason shoot several rounds and remove the empty clip without putting the safety on. Jason absently pointed the gun in their direction as he slammed a full clip in the handle and turned down-range. He laid the gun on a shelf in front of himself—with the barrel pointed at his gut—while he blew his nose.

Williams's mouth was hanging open. Eyes wide, he turned to Howard. "Jesus Christ, Howard. That's a tall order, but I'll do my best."

"Thanks. That's all I can ask. You've got his ass four hours a day, every day until the meeting." Howard watched Jason picking up bullets he'd dropped while trying to load the clip. "Looks like you'll need every minute of it. Try not to let him kill himself."

University of Ta'izz
Afternoon, August 22

It was nearly five o'clock in Ta'izz when Ahmed brought his list of facility requirements to Dietrich for review. Dietrich quickly scanned the two-page document, noted the important things Howard should know, added a few words to a sentence and revised punctuation, and turned to Ahmed. "Add something about adequate electrical and water supply and a way to compost or disinfect the manure, and this should be what you need. I gather you plan to hold the inoculating dose of virus at the facility for only a few hours before you use it?"

"Yes. I plan to thaw the dose on the way to the facility and while I examine the camel calf. We will not attempt to purify the virus."

"What about potential bacterial pathogens in a crude fecal inoculum?" Dietrich asked.

"I'll put the calves on a cephalosporin antibiotic for the duration of the study."

"Good choice—broad safety range and very effective. Will you be bringing pregnant females to the facility or day-old calves?"

"We will buy calves the day they are born. I don't want to babysit pregnant females or have obstetrical problems," Ahmed said.

Dietrich asked if Ahmed had found a source of calves, how far they would have to transport them, how they would transport the calves and what roads would be used, what they would feed calves separated from their mothers, and how many calves he would inoculate at one time. Ahmed was pleased to prove to Dietrich that he had thought of everything, and with the recorder running, Dietrich learned the essential details of the study.

As Ahmed turned to leave, Dietrich added a warning. "If you have a virulent virus and there are many camels nearby, a slip or spill, or someone breaking into your facility and stealing samples could create an epidemic." Dietrich paused, saw a stunned expression on Ahmed's face, and quickly added, "In the local camel population."

Ahmed relaxed. "Of course, but that will not be a problem. The owner of the facility has his own militia, and we will be using his herdsmen and his guards. He took very good care of his camels, and there are no others nearby."

Dietrich felt his stomach churn, but kept his face impassive. "Then it sounds like you have covered everything you needed to. Be sure to write air-tight S.O.P.s for your staff so they don't drag the virus to places it isn't supposed to go, and specify what P.P.E. they have to wear."

Ahmed looked puzzled. "S.O.P. and P.P.E.? What are those?"

Dietrich tried not to look surprised; he couldn't imagine how Ahmed completed a Ph.D. at a veterinary college and not be familiar with those acronyms. "An S.O.P. is a description of Standard Operating Procedure. You'll need to write one for every procedure you will do at your facility. P.P.E. is Personal Protective Equipment. That would be coveralls, boots, gloves—that sort of thing. Be sure to list them in the S.O.P.s."

Ahmed arrived at Al-Mikhafi's office early the next morning, grinning like a high school student who thinks he has the world's best essay. He was waiting at the door when Al-Mikhafi arrived.

"Do you have a list of requirements?" Al-Mikhafi asked.

"Certainly," Ahmed said and handed him his list. "These are what we must have available. Whatever we settle on, we will have to remodel to provide isolation and biosafety, so I listed the minimum structural, plumbing, and electrical requirements we will need to go forward."

"Did Dietrich van Kellen assist you in this?" Al-Mikhafi asked.

"Of course not," Ahmed said. "That would be too risky."

"Good, good. Tell me, what do you know about van Kellen?"

Ahmed shrugged. "He worked with BCV at Utrecht, and I think he did a post-doc somewhere in the States. I don't know much, other than that. Why?"

"Some of our friends mentioned that he did his post-doc at the CDC. That is the group the CIA would turn to for assistance to defeat us. Our friends expressed concern about that. We are depending heavily on an infidel and a graduate student whose allegiance to jihad is unknown."

"But, I wouldn't have accomplished anything without their help," Ahmed said.

"I understand, but now that you no longer have to grow the virus in tissue culture, be careful how you make use of them in the future," Al-Mikhafi said. "We will take my car. The facility is less than an hour's drive if the traffic is light. I'm eager to have a facility the CIA can't visit at will."

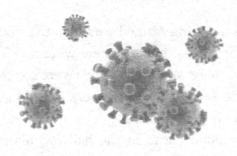

CHAPTER 19

University of Ta'izz
August 24

Thursday morning, Mohammed noticed that a water bath in Ahmed's lab had been moved. He knew Ahmed rarely worked in the lab himself and wondered who had moved it and why. When he stopped by Ahmed's office to ask about the day's lab work, there was a second monitor on Ahmed's desk.

Ahmed was seated at his desk, watching the new monitor. He hurriedly turned it off when Mohammed rapped on the doorframe and entered the office. Mohammed saw enough; there were two pictures—it was a split screen. Mohammed feigned disinterest in the new monitor as they discussed the lab work.

"Did you want the water bath to stay where it is?" Mohammed asked. "Or can I put it back where it was before? It's in the way where it is now."

Ahmed looked at Mohammed and tried to think of what he was talking about. "Water bath? I don't remem . . . oh, that water bath. A man from the Maintenance Department was working in the lab yesterday afternoon. It might have been in his way. Put it wherever you want it."

Mohammed nodded and left for the lab. There was something

new in the lab, something Ahmed was secretive about. Mohammed didn't know what it was, but he knew where to look for the first one, and he knew there were two, if they were connected to the new monitor. Chemical sensors? Nah, sensors would have an alarm or a red light, not a monitor. Cameras?

Mohammed stopped dead in the hallway, his gut in a knot. If Ahmed installed surveillance cameras, what was he worried about, and what else might he have installed?

Painted an institutional gray, the lab was long and narrow. Three tall windows framed one end of the room. A black lab bench, four feet wide, rested on a row of gray cabinets in the center of the room. It was nearly the length of the room, except for an aisle that bisected the bench in the middle of the room. Glass-fronted cabinets hung from the wall above a narrower black lab bench resting on cabinets on the other end of the room and on the walls flanking the door to the first-floor hallway. The wall opposite that door was bare except for doors to three smaller rooms.

Mohammed told himself not to panic but search. Afraid his search would look suspicious if Ahmed saw him, Mohammed picked up a small flask and an Eppendorf pipettor, a tool used for collecting or adding tiny but precise amounts of a liquid. It was similar in shape and size to a big felt-tipped marker. He knew Ahmed was so unfamiliar with his own laboratory procedures that he could disguise his search by carrying the flask and pipettor and walking from one piece of equipment to another as he looked around the lab.

The water bath normally sat near the door to the hallway. The top half of the door contained a large window. This close to the door, he was visible to anyone in the hallway. His gut churned and his mouth was dry; other professors or students wouldn't be fooled by the props he carried. He tried to look nonchalant as he examined the wall, cabinets, and ceiling above and around the water bath.

It seemed like forever to Mohammed, but it took him less than a minute to spot the camera mounted over the entry to the lab. It was pointed at the opposite wall and the door to the utility lab, the middle of the three doors on that wall. He thanked Allah that the maintenance men hadn't bothered to disguise the camera. He picked up his pipettor and flask, and entered the utility lab. Once inside, he closed the door, leaned against it, and breathed a sigh of relief. No one knowledgeable about laboratory procedures could see him now.

The only target of interest in the room was the minus seventy-degree freezer and the stolen samples it held. The gray and black freezer, slightly taller and deeper than a standard upright freezer for the home, took up a fifth of the floor space in the small room. His back to the freezer, Mohammed spotted the camera hung from the ceiling. He put the flask in the microwave and waited for thirty seconds, in case Ahmed was watching. He removed the flask, left the room, and got to work on the tasks Ahmed had assigned for the day. Knowing Ahmed might be watching was creepy.

Mohammed finished his work shortly before noon and hustled to Dietrich's office on the third floor. Everyone who glanced at him in the hallway fed his growing paranoia. If they smiled, he wondered why. If they didn't, he feared they might be spying on him. He knocked on Dietrich's door and, struggling to control his galloping panic, casually discussed his own project as he walked to Dietrich's desk, picked up a pad and pen, and wrote, "Surveillance cameras in Ahmed's lab. Appear to cover minus seventy freezer. Microphones in offices?"

Dietrich read the note, looked around his office, and took a deep breath. He tore the page Mohammed had written off the pad, put it in his shirt pocket, and wrote another note. "Unexpected. No more talking in the office."

As he wrote the note, he praised the work Mohammed had completed that week. "I looked at the gel electrophoresis you ran yesterday. I'm impressed. How about letting me buy you lunch? We can talk over your next steps."

Dietrich put a finger to his lips when they got in his car. If he couldn't trust his office, he didn't trust his car, either. He took Mohammed to an inexpensive restaurant on the edge of the campus. Tables toward the rear of the dining room were screened by plants. The short palms assured privacy but allowed them a view of other patrons.

"Good work, Mohammed," Dietrich said. "Al-Mikhafi must be behind this. Ahmed isn't that bright or suspicious.

"I'm getting spooked. They wouldn't put cameras in unless they suspected something, would they? If there are cameras, are there microphones? Where can we feel safe?"

Dietrich was torn. "I think I'm going to have to make another phone call. He scanned the dining room for anyone who might be close enough to hear him. "Watch out for big ears for me, will you?" he asked Mohammed, and pulled out the satellite phone Howard had given him.

The same seductive recording answered his call. "Dietrich, here. Our tourist has new cameras. He may have audio, too," he said. "Call, please."

He put the phone on the table next to his plate and turned to Mohammed. "I don't know if I'm getting rattled over nothing or whether we have a problem. Maybe my wife and kids should take a vacation and visit the folks at home. You and I should come up with a code word."

The color drained from Mohammed's face. "Code word? For what?"

"If things look bad, we need a word to indicate it's time to leave town. I'll ask Howard where to go and how to ask for help. He has operatives in town we haven't met and at least one safe house, probably more."

Mohammed was quiet. The knot had returned to his stomach. He looked at his meal and shoved his food around the plate.

"How about 'transposon' for the code word?" Dietrich asked. "It's technical, a non-scientist isn't going to know what it is or whether it's used correctly, and it's a word only a bacteriologist or agronomist would use. No chance either of us would use it accidentally."

Mohammed nodded, but what Dietrich said only increased his paranoia.

Dietrich put a hand on his shoulder. "Steady there, Mohammed. I'll get in touch with people tonight and have some answers for you tomorrow. I won't let anything happen to you."

They drove back to the campus. Howard returned Dietrich's call as they walked from the parking lot to the Life Sciences building. They were near a tree-shaded, secluded section of the parking lot. Dietrich answered his phone while Mohammed watched for passersby.

"Howard, Mohammed found two surveillance cameras in Ahmed's lab. They are covering the minus seventy-degree freezer. We assume Al-Mikhafi is behind it."

"You're probably correct. Another source warned us that Al-Mikhafi is suspicious of you."

"No! Do you think I—?"

"Your wife will take the kids with her when she flies home tomorrow for the funeral of her favorite uncle. Be sure you have a name for him. His death was completely unexpected. The tickets will be waiting for her at the KLM desk at the airport by noon."

"What do I tell people here?"

"Tell them what I told you. Terrible tragedy, but you couldn't stand the old bastard and begged off accompanying her—told her you were too far behind in your work. She didn't believe you, and now she's furious. You may have to fly home soon to make up with her. Getting you out of here for a week or two should allay Al-Mikhafi's concerns, too."

"I guess I can handle that. What about—"

"With your wife heading home, you will be a bachelor looking for dinner tomorrow night. Take Mohammed out for dinner. Don't draw attention to yourself by spending much or ordering drinks. Don't spend much time, and come to 325 South Twenty-second Avenue, apartment 4A. Be there by eight-thirty tomorrow night. I'll be there with Jason and one of my local operatives. You and Mohammed should meet him now so you know each other if it hits the fan."

Dietrich frowned. "Sorry, I have forgotten much of my American vernacular."

"The phrase is 'shit hits the fan.' It means if things go badly and you're in trouble."

"That reminds me, Mohammed and I came up with a code word to indicate it's time to leave town. It's 'transposon.' A virologist will rarely use the term. If you hear me or Mohammed use it, we need help fast."

"Are you comfortable handling firearms?" Howard asked.

"Four years in the Dutch army before I went to graduate school. I don't like weapons, but I'll carry one if you think I need it."

"I'll think about that. Most people are safer without them. Before I forget, we have a little box from Minnesota for you, one with ten little vials."

Djibouti
Afternoon, August 24

On the road to Ammo Point southwest of Djibouti, Howard put his phone away and concentrated on the traffic around him. They were driving through the slums between the airport and the city, a place where Howard kept his eyes on the road. It was depressing to see children playing next to the open sewers. "Hear that, Jason?"

"Yeah. Sounds like it's getting tense in Ta'izz."

"Not sure what to make of it. Al-Mikhafi might have heard something, or he might just be cautious. I don't want to pull Dietrich and Mohammed out if I don't have to, but I can't leave them if it's too risky." Howard thought for a while in silence. He had to brake and swerve to avoid a herd of goats straying onto the road. The goat herder shook his staff and shouted at the car.

"Watch out for goats if you ever have to drive here, Jason." Howard turned back into his lane and resumed normal speed. "It will cost Uncle Sam more to bail you out if you hit a goat than if you run over several of those kids in the slum."

A few miles past the airport, they turned onto a gravel road that led into parched countryside. The landscape was dirt, dust, and rocks except for a few acacia trees and brush growing where water had collected during the spring rains. On their left, three men mounted on camels seemed to be racing, their hands held out slightly to each side, holding the reins and urging their mounts on with an occasional lash with a whip like a riding crop. The long, lean legs of the camels covered ground rapidly, their riders bouncing along riding just behind each camel's hump.

Howard pointed at the camels. "Good racing camels go for hundreds of thousands of dollars. Faster than horses and with more stamina. They're supposed to be smarter, too."

Jason watched the camels run over and along the ridges of dirt and sand, occasionally dodging around a boulder. There wasn't anything green in sight. *My god, what a desolate landscape*, he thought. He knew this is what he would picture if he ever used the phrase "like hell" again.

"How are your lessons coming?" Howard asked.

"Maybe we should give the P30S to Dietrich. He sounds like he can handle guns better than me."

"It would be better if you each have something on you, but it's a last resort. I don't like giving guns to amateurs. They'd be safer keeping their eyes open for safe avenues of escape. Don't forget that."

"We have a meeting in Ta'izz tomorrow evening?" Jason asked.

"Yeah. We were spotted by an Ansar Allah sympathizer on our last trip. It could have been at the restaurant or the airport. We'll fly into a small airport sixty-two kilometers from Ta'izz and drive to a safe house in the city."

"You said it's an apartment?"

"No one lives in it, but we keep it stocked with furniture, clothes, and food. We'll be dropped off a couple of blocks away and walk to it. Remember to bring that little box in your briefcase."

Ta'izz
Evening, August 24

Dietrich drove down a gravel alley lined by whitewashed mudbrick walls. He came to a pair of wooden gates and pushed a button on his dashboard. The gates opened and Dietrich drove into a small courtyard behind the house he rented. A thirty-foot date palm midway between the house and the gate shaded the paved courtyard. The palm and a few potted plants near the house were the only visible vegetation. In front of the house, a wrought-iron gate lent a smaller courtyard a more formal feel.

The house, provided to visiting professors by the university, was a drab two-story building of brown mudbricks; the only color was around the arched windows and single door where the bricks were painted white. Dietrich took a deep breath before he entered the house and faced his wife. *"How can I tell her tha Ta'izz is no longer safe for the family, but I will be fine? And if the house was bugged, what then?*

His hands shook as he opened the back door and called, "I'm home." He told himself to *get a grip*.

"Where is everyone?" Dietrich called. He wandered through the living room and into the kitchen, where he dropped his briefcase on a chair. "Max, Julia, how was your day?"

Silence.

"Laura, I'm home." Dietrich's pulse was racing as he climbed the stairs and walked through the bedrooms. All were empty. He looked the bedrooms over closely. The family pictures were undisturbed on the walls. The small closet in the master bedroom was in order—his side was a jumble, Laura's was neat—and nothing on the dressers was out of place. The two smaller bedrooms of his children were no worse than they always looked. His heart pounded and he broke into a sweat.

He was on the stairway calling his wife on his cell phone when the front door opened slowly with a prolonged squeak. He could barely hear the faint sound of footsteps, as though someone was walking stealthily. He pressed himself against the wall of the stairway. There was nowhere to hide and the stairs would creak if he moved.

"Mommy, Daddy is home. His briefcase is on his chair in the kitchen."

"Tell him to come help me with the groceries."

Dietrich gathered Max in his arms as he went to help Laura with her packages. At the curb, where the taxi had deposited the family, he put Max down and embraced Laura. Tears were welling in his eyes when he relaxed his hold of her.

"Honey, what's wrong?" she asked.

He picked a sack of groceries up in each arm. "Let's get the kids and groceries inside. I'll tell you in back, in the courtyard."

Groceries put away, Laura and Dietrich walked into the courtyard. Dietrich told her about the cameras, his fear that their apartment might be bugged, and Howard's plan for her and the kids to fly home tomorrow. Little else was said while they held each other for several minutes. Dietrich helped Laura pack for the kids that evening and called to have a taxi take them to the airport the next morning.

Al-Dhala
August 25

Howard and Jason flew to Al-Dhala, Yemen, in a small, two-engine propeller plane the next afternoon. A driver in a dusty, nondescript Land Rover picked them up for the rugged drive to Ta'izz. It was less than forty miles, but they were miles driven in four-wheel drive through a moonscape of steep brown hills strewn with jagged rocks and boulders. *It's like looking at earth a billion years ago,* Jason thought. *How can people survive here? Who in hell would want to?* They bounced over ruts and potholes, and the Land Rover swerved from side to side, often coming close to the edge of cliffs as their driver dodged fallen rocks in the road. The windows of the Land Rover were covered in dust so thick that Jason could hardly see out of the vehicle. His back ached, his butt was numb, and his attitude was in bad shape by the time they pulled onto a paved road a few miles east of Ta'izz. "How the hell can we get out of Dodge fast if we have to return on that road?" Jason griped.

"We took it because no one would expect a couple of Americans to take that route. Al-Dhala is one of the poorest areas in Yemen. We can be picked up at any of three small airstrips around Ta'izz if we have to move fast."

The green around Ta'izz was a welcome change from the dust, dirt, and poverty along the road from Al-Dhala. Without warning, they pulled to a stop in the middle of a block. "Time to get out. We're here," Howard said. He stepped out of the car, crossed a narrow median planted with scrubby trees, and headed toward a man standing by a car parked at the curb with the hood up.

Jason scrambled out of the passenger seat. "Where are we?"

Howard nodded almost imperceptibly to the man standing by the car, and walked past him. The man turned to look down the sidewalk, in the opposite direction.

Concrete, two- to four-story apartment buildings lined the street. Offices, restaurants, and small stores with names written in Arabic characters across their windows filled the first floors. The buildings were separated by narrow driveways that led to parking lots behind the apartments.

The sidewalks were not crowded, but there were enough pedestrians that Howard and Jason didn't stand out. "We're a couple of blocks from the meeting place," Howard said. "I'll lay a trail in the wrong direction, if something happens. You cross the street at the corner ahead of us, continue to the next corner, and turn right. The third building on your right, apartment 4-A is where you're to go."

They were at the corner when they heard shouting behind them. Howard shoved Jason straight ahead, into the street. "Don't run. Don't look back," he said and was gone.

Jason did as he was told. Visions of bearded men in robes, waving scimitars and chasing after him, scrolled across his mind. *Don't look back, don't run,* Jason thought. *That's a hell of a lot easier to say than do.* He breathed easier as he came to the next corner and turned right. At the third building he turned into the entrance and found a door marked 4-A.

He knocked on the door. There was no answer. He knocked again, louder, but again there was no answer. He tried the doorknob. It turned easily, and the door opened slightly. Jason took a deep breath, pushed the door open fully, and walked through the doorway. He closed the door, resting against it and breathing heavily. He stood in a dimly lit foyer and strained to peer into the darkened room beyond.

He tried to remember if Howard said whether there would be others here when he arrived. His mind was a blank. As he tiptoed toward the next room, he quietly called out, "Is anyone here? Anyone? For the teleconference?"

He stood in the entrance to a room, probably meant to be a living room. Blinds over the windows were closed. He took another step into the dimly-lit room.

A shadow on his left moved and plowed into him. He lost his balance. His head slammed into the wall on his right. He tried to defend himself, but his right hand was already pinned behind his back in a hammerlock, and he felt the cold, steel barrel of a pistol shoved against his neck. Bad breath and garlic assaulted his nose.

The sight on the barrel gouged a chunk of skin from below his ear. Blood trickled toward his collar as pain radiated from his twisted shoulder.

The gun jabbed deeper into his neck, and a whispered voice demanded, "Who da fuck 'er you, and wha you doin' heah?"

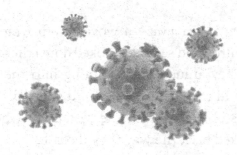

CHAPTER 20

Ta'izz
Afternoon, August 26

When Howard separated from Jason, he turned to see the man who'd been working on the car fighting with two thugs. He walked across the street at a right angle to Jason's route when he was sure one of the toughs was watching him.

He continued walking slowly for a block to give the goons time to get closer to him and lose interest in Jason. He crossed to the other side of the street to make it easier for them to see him and continued moving away from Jason's route. He walked another block. Assuming even Jason would have had time to be out of sight, he ducked down a narrow alley.

The alley's shadows seemed opaque after the brilliant sunlight of the street. He moved slowly until his eyes adjusted to the dim light. Sand and fetid, muddy patches filled depressions where the original brick pavement had settled. Reeking garbage cans were stacked behind every store. Old newspapers, scattered by the wind, littered the alley. Howard put a handkerchief to his nose and followed the alley to the back door of a restaurant. There, he crouched behind a small dumpster and watched the alley until his pursuers stopped at its entrance.

The two men, in *ma'awaz*—a woven cloth wrapped around the waist—dirty T-shirts, and sandals, looked down the street and peered into the alley. They argued, one pointing into the alley, the other down the street. In the shadows, Howard snorted, "Amateurs," and holstered his pistol. He entered the restaurant when his pursuers gave up and walked back the way they'd come.

Howard tipped his hat to the surprised staff as he walked through the kitchen, exited at the front of the establishment, and doubled back toward the site of the meeting. His caution increased as he neared the safe house. He stood in the shade, took off his Panama, and paused at both of the last two street corners before the apartment to make sure he wasn't being followed.

He had worked up a sweat losing the thugs, and the cool evening breeze felt good on his bare head. Satisfied at the last corner that he wasn't being followed, he hurriedly walked to the apartment. He tried not to think of ways Jason could have gotten into trouble, as that would splinter his attention and lead to mistakes. Knowing Jason, it was difficult not to worry.

At the apartment, he quietly opened door 4-A and turned on the lights.

"Jason, my boy," Howard said. "I see you've met Benji. Benji, put the gun away and shake hands with Jason, our new associate in this frightful mess."

"But, he din't know the password," Benji growled, without letting Jason go.

"Do you know it?" Howard asked.

Benji glared at Howard. "No." He released Jason, turned him around, and brushed the dust off Jason's shirt. "You din't tell me what it was."

"That's because we don't have one for this meeting. Shake hands with Jason, now, and go keep an eye on the street, would you please?"

Benji did as he was told and left the apartment. "Benji is a good sort, but a terrific stickler for detail," Howard said, and removed a card table from a closet. "I'll have to remember to provide sufficient details for him in the future."

Howard set the table in the middle of the room, retrieved a speakerphone and cords, and prepared the phone for the tele-conference. The blare of the speakerphone's dial tone briefly filled the room.

Jason, still shaking, glared at Howard. "I could, could have been killed. Did you know that crazy bastard was here?"

"Of course. Guarding the apartment is Benji's job. Sorry I didn't mention him, but we were in a bit of a hurry back there." Howard pointed to the kitchen. "Pull some frozen dinners from the fridge and pop them into the microwave, would you please?" Howard brought two folding chairs from the closet and set them up at the table. "The fare is limited tonight, but I couldn't risk going back to the restaurant again."

They ate in silence, Jason delicately dabbing with a handkerchief at blood seeping from the gouge below his ear. There was a knock at the door after dinner as they cleared the table. Jason hurried to set up more folding chairs as Howard ushered Mohammed and Dietrich into the apartment. Mohammed was subdued, Dietrich nervous.

"Good," Howard said. "You're ten minutes early. We'll have time to talk before calling our friends in Langley."

Dietrich sighed. "I need to talk to someone. It's either you or a therapist." He turned to Mohammed. "Do you want to start?"

Mohammed, still disturbed by the cameras, shook his head and kept his eyes on the card table in front of him.

Concerned about his student, Dietrich explained, "Mohammed is taking this pretty hard. He's the one who found the cameras and realized what they were focused on. He checked the labs his friends work in. None of them have surveillance cameras."

Howard saw Mohammed's drawn face and gently asked him

about the laboratory, the freezer room, and the cameras. Given the information, he leaned back in his chair and absently looked at the ceiling. "Are the lights in the laboratory left on at night?"

Mohammed and Dietrich both said, "No." They looked at each other, and Dietrich continued. "Hallway lights are always left on. People turn the lights off in their labs when they leave in the evening. I don't know if Ahmed has changed that for his lab."

Howard drummed a pencil on the card table. The tabletop rattled with every tap of the pencil, irritating everyone but Howard. "We can aim the camera in the larger lab in a different direction. The lab with the freezer will be a problem. In a small room, the camera will pick us up no matter where we point it."

Mohammed nodded. "The freezer takes up a lot of space in that room."

Howard stopped his drumming. "We could hang a small black screen in front of that camera. Get the screen close to the camera, and a foot square would be enough."

"When would you put the screen in place?" Dietrich asked.

"Seconds before we do the work. We'll tape the screen to the ceiling, if the ceiling is within reach. A small step stool should allow that."

"Can we locate the camera in the small room in the dark, or with minimal light?" Howard asked Mohammed.

"Sure, if you're familiar with the layout."

"That will be our biggest hurdle. Everything else is window dressing."

There was palpable relaxation around the table. Dietrich asked, "What else did you have in mind?"

"I still like Jason's idea of the burned-out compressor. It would give everyone cover if we do it right." Howard glanced at a clock on the wall behind Jason. "Time to place our call."

Filburt answered at Langley, where he sat with Gettelman and Paul Schmidt. Howard brought them up-to-date and told them how he planned to switch the samples.

"How close to having a camel facility are our friends?" Gettelman asked.

"They've found a facility fifty kilometers west of Ta'izz. We suspect they'll have to do extensive remodeling for biosafety before they can use it. Construction will take at least a month. Our first warning that they are ready may be Ahmed asking Mohammed to prepare samples for the trip to the facility."

Sitting in Atlanta, Filburt hit the mute button and turned to Gettelman. "I don't like this, Al. Too damned much is unknown."

"We should be safe if they do this quickly," Gettelman said.

Filburt tapped the mute button. "Howard, this is George Filburt. When will you switch the samples?"

Howard looked at Mohammed and Dietrich. "Tomorrow night."

Mohammed, Dietrich, and Jason gaped at Howard. Each had the wide eyes, blank stare, and partly open mouth Howard associated with panic. "I should have consulted my colleagues before I spoke," Howard said. "This came as a surprise to them, and they're all giving an impression of Wile E. Coyote watching a piano falling toward his head. We will do the work, but Mohammed and Dietrich will have to get us into the lab."

"Who is 'we'?" Filburt asked.

"Jason and me, or only me, if Jason doesn't feel up to it."

The four at the table in Ta'izz heard a muffled conversation on the line. "You'll have to speak up, George," Howard said. "We can't hear you."

"Sorry," Filburt said. "We were conferring on whether Jason should be put at risk like this. He's an amateur, a scientist, and a student. It's not easy to do a project with anybody in even one of those categories, and Jason is all three. Al and Paul feel an obligation to watch out for him, and Howard, I don't want you getting yourself killed, now that I've memorized your phone number."

"Your concern is appreciated, but Jason knows more about the samples than anyone here except Mohammed." Howard looked at Mohammed. The kid's face was white. *No point in considering it*, Howard thought. "Mohammed may already be under suspicion, and I don't wish to put him in jeopardy."

A little of his normal color returned to Mohammed's face. Howard saw Dietrich's face relax, too.

"Dietrich here. Jason's never been in our lab. Won't that be a problem?"

"Tomorrow is Friday," Howard said. "The university will empty out in mid-afternoon as people go to Jummah. Can he and I visit the lab then? We could wait in Dietrich's office until we are ready."

Dietrich formed a mental picture and frowned. "You said you'd have a screen. How are you going to bring it in during the day?"

"Briefcases. The screen will be small." Howard smiled. "Don't you guys have salesmen interrupting your work? Pharmaceutical detail people, that sort of person?"

He's got that right, Dietrich thought.

"You and Mohammed shouldn't be there when we raid the lab," Howard said, "but you said the freezer and the room it's in are locked. If Mohammed would give his keys to Benji, he'll make copies for us. Benji can return your keys before you leave this evening."

"What if the lights are on in the lab all night?" Mohammed asked.

"It will only be an issue in the small room," Howard said. "But we'll know that tonight. Dietrich can check. All he has to do is find an excuse to walk past Ahmed's lab, or drive by if the lab has windows."

"Sounds like you're ready. What about a back-up?" Filburt asked.

"Jason's idea of helping the freezer crash is an intriguing approach," Howard said. "It will provide a reason for the BCV-SARS to be inactive. With a mechanical reason, Al-Mikhafi won't have a reason to look for conspirators, if we are successful, and it will be a back-up in case we miss anything."

"If you unplug the freezer tomorrow night," Dietrich said, "Mohammed can wait until the following weekend to adjust the lab's air conditioning. By then, the contents of the freezer will have thawed. The combination of a hot room and warm contents should fry the compressor when the freezer is plugged back in."

"Won't Ahmed notice a warm freezer if he gets something from it?" Jason asked.

"Ahmed only processes the virus samples, and now there is no reason to do that again," Mohammed said. "The freezer runs quietly, so a casual look in the room won't detect anything wrong."

"Looks like we have our bases covered," Howard said. He leaned closer to the phone. "Al, I'll call you Saturday from Djibouti with my report. That's it for tonight, guys. Thanks for joining us."

Howard turned to Jason. "You have the box of samples from Minnesota with you?"

"It's in my briefcase."

"That's it, then. Nice to see you again, Mohammed. Dietrich, when you call me about the lab lights, you only need to say 'bright' or 'dark' for a message. I can figure it out. Benji will see you to your car."

It was dark and the streetlights were on when Dietrich and Mohammed left the apartment, Benji walking several feet ahead of them. He led them to their car, pointed at it, and took a place in the shadows where he could cover the driveway to the street. Neither Dietrich nor Mohammed talked much on the way back to the university.

He dropped Mohammed at his apartment and took a route home that passed the university and the Life Sciences building. Near the top of a knoll, he slowed. In the distance, he saw lights on in two labs in the Life Sciences building. Neither was close to Ahmed's lab. Dietrich double-checked to make sure he had the right building and labs in sight, and drove home.

As Dietrich drove home, Howard showed Jason to the bedrooms. "Do you snore?" he asked. Jason said he didn't, and tossed his briefcase onto the top bunk. "There's a second bedroom, but if I hear a noise in the night, I want to know where you are before I take the safety off," Howard said. "The dresser over there," Howard pointed to a nondescript old dresser, "has fresh socks and underwear of various sizes in the top drawer. Bathrobes are in the closet, towels and toiletries in the shower room."

Howard went back to the card table to place another call when Jason went to shower. He wanted to use a landline for the call, and he didn't want Jason to overhear the conversation. He dialed an unlisted number at a home in Sana'a, capital of Yemen.

"John, this is Howard, from Djibouti. How is embassy duty treating you?"

"It's keeping me busy. I assume this call is about the project in Ta'izz?"

"Yes. I'm in Ta'izz tonight, and a couple of thugs were waiting on the street for us. I've been in Ta'izz twice recently, and we think I was recognized both times. I wasn't on the street for long, either time, and visited opposite sides of the city. Would you run a security check on our communications?"

"I'll put someone on it tomorrow. I've never thought of our fundamentalist friends as techies. Maybe we've underestimated them."

"Thanks. I'd appreciate that. I'll do the same on my end. I'll be working with an untrained colleague this week. Would you have someone monitor my satellite phone Friday night and Saturday? The word 'transposon' is the cue for help. I'm sending more information to you through Langley."

"Do you want a team standing by?"

"I'd appreciate it. I've got a radio beacon in my satellite phone to guide them in if we need help."

Howard hung up and checked his phone mail. The message from Dietrich was short: "Dark."

Howard undressed and went to bed. "Awake, Jason?"

"Yeah. Just thinking about tomorrow. What if Ahmed is there and recognizes me?"

"You underestimate how well your new haircut and dye job change your appearance, and I have a theatrical makeup kit in the car. Our driver will bring it around tomorrow morning. Ann wouldn't recognize you by the time I'm done."

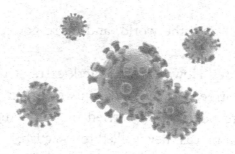

CHAPTER 21

Ta'izz
Morning, August 27

Jason woke early and rummaged through the freezer for breakfast. He'd finished eating and was tidying up when Howard came out of the shower wrapped in a towel. Howard looked at a wall clock and said they had to get moving.

"I thought you said we weren't going to the university until mid-afternoon?"

"We aren't, but we have a lot to do before then."

"Makeup?" Jason asked.

"That we do just before we go to the university. We have to get dark suits, heavy black plastic or cloth with a matte finish, and a couple of bags on wheels."

"What kind of bags?" Jason asked.

"Ever see salespeople for laboratory supply companies at the U?"

"Every day."

"Remember what they looked like, what they were dragging?"

"Hunh?"

Aren't scientists supposed to be observant? Howard thought, and walked past Jason to the bedroom. "They wore dark suits and were dragging bags and briefcases on wheels, right? Well, it's the same at universities all over the world, and we're going to look like lab supply salesmen."

Two hours later, Howard paid a clerk extra at the Dalma Men's Store on Doha Street to have the adjustments to their new suits completed before noon. Jason carried the shopping bags with the shoes, shirts, and ties as they walked to the curb.

Their car pulled up, and they piled in. "Why did you insist on neckties that have to be tied?" Jason asked. "I've always used the clip-ons that are already tied."

Howard reminded himself that Jason was still in his twenties. "Jason, a man must have standards. I would rather fart loudly in church than wear a pre-tied necktie, and I will not be seen in the company of a man wearing one."

Jason's makeup took an hour—cotton was stuffed in his cheeks and lower lip, his hair was dyed brown again to color the red roots, a realistic-looking mustache was glued to his upper lip, and putty altered the shape of his nose. Howard put Jason in front of a mirror. Jason looked at himself, moved closer to the mirror, and viewed himself from each side. He was impressed.

The driver picked them up at one o'clock in order to arrive at the Life Sciences building after the start of Friday afternoon prayers. He dropped them off at a side entrance of the nearly deserted building. They avoided the central atrium by using that entrance and went directly to Dietrich's office, dragging their bags and briefcases behind them as salespeople did all over the world.

Dietrich did a double-take when Jason walked into his office. "Jason?" He turned to Howard. "If he was not with you, I would not have recognized him," he whispered.

Howard nodded, and put a finger to his lips to remind him that they hadn't checked the office for microphones. He pulled a black box from his brief case, adjusted a dial, and swept the office for electronic listening devices. "Seems clear," he said, and brought out his faux pack of cigarettes and turned it on. "We can talk safely now. I didn't find any bugs, and this pack," Howard pointed to the cigarette pack humming on the desk, "will make it difficult for anything I missed to record what we say."

"That's a relief," Dietrich said. "I've been going nuts since Mohammed told me about the cameras."

The group sat around Dietrich's desk. "Do you know who monitors the cameras?" Howard asked.

"Mohammed said there's a new monitor in Ahmed's office, and I saw one in the security office near the main entrance to the building. Ahmed's lab shows up on both. I don't think there are any others."

"What are the university security people like?" Howard asked.

"Generally lazy. Most of them get their jobs through family or political connections."

"Not unusual," Howard said. "I gathered that might be the case from what Mohammed said about the placement of the cameras. We can probably turn the lights on in the freezer room and cover the camera without inciting suspicion. Do the guards patrol the hallways?"

Dietrich tried to remember if he'd seen guards during the day. It wasn't something he normally paid attention to. "Not during the day, that I remember. I've seen them come through after hours when I've stayed late. I don't know if they have a regular schedule or do it randomly."

Howard nodded. "If things go smoothly, we'll be out of here before the building closes for the evening. Tell Mohammed to go home early and spend the evening with friends. We want him to have a good alibi. You should go out to dinner. Make sure the restaurant staff remembers you—over tip, send something back to the kitchen, whatever it takes. Go home, call Laura, and fly back to Holland tomorrow—claim you had to make the trip to save your marriage."

Dietrich explained that Mohammed had gone to the mosque for

prayers and led the way to Ahmed's lab. He tried to act nonchalant, but glanced nervously into every room that had an open door or a large window in a door. They didn't encounter anyone in the hallway, but Dietrich nearly became airborne when Jason's briefcase fell with a clatter off the suitcase on wheels. Dietrich stopped and leaned against the wall, breathing rapidly.

Howard and Jason stopped beside him. "Are you okay?" Jason asked after he picked up his briefcase.

Dietrich nodded. "Give me a second, and I will be alright, but Jesus, Jason," Dietrich whispered, "don't scare me like that again."

They stopped at a door that opened into a laboratory. Dietrich nodded to the lab, visible through a large window in the upper half of the door. "This is it. First camera is on the ceiling, a few feet inside the door. The second camera is in the room behind the middle door, straight ahead."

Howard and Jason peered at angles through the windows to examine as much of the lab as possible before they opened the door. The lights in the lab were on, although the lab was well lit by afternoon sunlight streaming through the windows at the end of the lab.

"Mohammed said Al-Mikhafi came to Ahmed's lab this morning," Dietrich said. "He demanded that the lights be left on day and night. He called Ahmed an idiot for having to be told to do it. Ahmed was seething and took it out on Mohammed."

Howard nodded and unpacked a collapsible step stool attached to his suitcase. "Jason and I will take care of things from here. Go back to your office or strike up a conversation with someone in their office to give yourself an alibi if something goes wrong."

Dietrich didn't need further encouragement to leave. As he hustled back to his office, Howard entered the lab, climbed on his stool, and turned the first camera to aim at the end of the lab opposite the windows. Satisfied it was no longer a threat, he waved Jason in and they moved a few feet along the wall to avoid being visible to any passerby in the hallway.

"Quick," Howard whispered. "Scan the walls and ceiling for anything else that looks like a camera."

Nervous, Jason compulsively examined each square of ceiling tile in detail.

"Let's go," Howard said before Jason finished examining even a small section of the ceiling. "This room is clear." He opened his briefcase and pulled out the piece of black plastic and adhesive. "Ahead, center door. Don't come in until I say 'clear.'"

On the far wall of the lab, Howard opened the center door a crack and looked into the room to spot the camera before he flipped the light switch off. A lab bench was on the wall opposite the freezer, directly under the camera. Howard hopped onto the bench and examined the camera in the dim light from the door. "This camera is only a few feet from the freezer," Howard whispered. "The lens looks like a fish-eye. It would have to be, to focus on anything but a bit of the freezer door. I'll cover it with the screen."

Howard stripped a foot of tape off a roll of clear strapping tape and stuck the black plastic to the ceiling a few inches from the lens and hopped off the bench. "Clear."

Jason opened his briefcase and removed a flashlight. Howard held the flashlight as Jason unlocked the freezer with Mohammed's key. Frosty air poured down from the freezer and spread across the floor when they opened the outer door. They faced six white horizontal doors, one for each shelf of the freezer. Hoarfrost began to coat the doors. Jason opened the second shelf from the bottom, as Mohammed had instructed. The shelf was empty except for a small white plastic box.

"Ahmed made this easy for us," Howard whispered.

Jason nodded and pulled out the box of replacement samples from his briefcase. As he did, they heard footsteps, sounds of a man bumping into something, and an oath in Arabic.

"Close the freezer," Howard whispered. He turned off the flashlight. They ducked behind the far side of the freezer as the door opened a foot, and a hand came around the doorjamb and the light was switched on. The door squeaked as it opened wider, and they heard a man mutter something under his breath. A moment later, the door closed and they heard footsteps fading into the distance.

Howard glanced at the ceiling. His screen was still in place. He pulled out a pistol, readied himself, and pivoted from behind the freezer. The room was empty. "Back to work. We have to hurry. If that's a guard, he'll go back to check the monitor. All he'll see is our black screen. He may come back."

Jason was sitting on his butt at the side of the freezer. He dropped the stolen samples from their box into a plastic bag in his brief case and carefully replaced them with the replacement vials from his box. He did a quick count of the vials dumped into his case. "Shit. I have ten replacement samples, and there were only nine samples in the box. Ahmed used one already."

"So what?"

"Ahmed's probably kept track of which sample he used. I'll have to reconcile the samples here with a list of samples to figure out which one he used."

"Screw it. The guard could be back any second. Let's hope Mohammed can correct the sample number before Ahmed notices the error."

They moved out of the room. As Jason crouched behind a lab bench, Howard returned to the room and pulled the screen from the ceiling. A small amount of tape stuck to the ceiling.

"In case he comes back," Howard said, "we'll circle around the far end of the lab bench and stay low until we're on the far wall."

They scuttled like crabs behind the center lab bench, out of sight of observers in the hallway and the camera they had repositioned, until they came to the end of the bench under the windows. Howard tapped Jason on the shoulder. "We can go over the bench and along the wall to the doors," he whispered.

As Jason reached the door, he heard muffled swearing and footsteps approaching. Eyes wide, Jason looked at Howard and pointed to spaces under the lab bench where lab stools were pushed under the bench. The bench was built like a desk at those points, with an open space for the knees and legs of the lab techs. Jason hid under the bench behind a stool and Howard crawled under the bench on the other side, his P30L out and the safety off.

The guard came in, swearing in Arabic. He looked at the camera, briefly scanned the lab, stalked angrily to the freezer room door, and did the same for that room. Jason froze, his heart thundered in his chest as the guard retreated from the room, cursing all the way. Jason remained in his cubbyhole, shaking, until Howard came around and motioned for him to get out. "Clear, I think," he said, "but let's wait here for half an hour. This guy was an unpleasant surprise. I thought the guards would be napping."

They waited, huddled low on either side of the exit to the lab, and watched each twitch of the second hand on a clock mounted high on the wall of the lab as it measured out thirty minutes. "It's going to be too late to walk out the main entrance," Howard said. "We'll have to go out the way we came in."

He took out his phone and told his driver to park at a spot at the side of the building, screened by a clump of palm trees. He collapsed the handle on his case and turned to Jason. "Quieter and faster to carry them."

Howard slowly opened the lab door a crack and listened.

Silence.

He closed the door and turned to Jason. "Quiet now. At least our guard is loud. If he stumbles on us, we'll brazen it out. Let me do the talking. I'll tell him we are technicians called to fix the cameras, and we're leaving, now that the job is done."

"We forgot the plug," Jason whispered.

"What?"

"I forgot to unplug the freezer," Jason said.

Howard looked back at the freezer room and shrugged. "Too late. Forget it. We've got the samples—not safe to push our luck."

Jason and Howard made it to the side exit without encountering the guard. To Jason, it seemed like the longest hundred feet he'd ever walked.

At the exit, Howard checked his watch and stopped Jason from going through the door. "At this hour, they may have turned on alarms on the side doors. If an alarm goes, we head to the car as fast as we can." He made sure Jason knew where the car was before they each took a deep breath and bolted through the door.

A loud, quavering buzz sounded as soon as the door opened. They ran down a few steps and across a small plaza, trying to stay in the afternoon shadows as they covered the eighty feet to the clump of palm trees and the car. Jason heard a shout from the building they'd left as they rounded the clump of trees and sprinted the last twenty feet to the car. They piled into the back seat; the car accelerated slowly and drove quietly to the street.

The car delivered them to their apartment. Jason put the bag of samples in a microwave-safe plastic bag. He sealed the bag and microwaved the samples on high until the plastic vials melted. Jason recognized a whiff of cooked feces, but the bags kept most of the odor contained.

They dumped the microwaved samples in the trash and heated

frozen dinners in the microwave. Traces of the odor from the samples clung to the room and microwave.

Jason became talkative, a veritable raconteur, as he always did when stress was lifted. Safe after their evening's raid, he launched into a learned lecture on the noxious gasses produced by anaerobic bacteria in feces. "A fecal sample can contain three to thirty trillion bacteria per ounce," he began.

Physicians, veterinarians, and microbiologists often seem unaware of the effect their shoptalk has on laymen during meals. Jason appeared to be winding down and Howard began to show interest in his food until Jason said, "I nearly forgot the clostridials. Those suckers . . ."

Howard groaned, pushed his dinner toward Jason, and left the room to take a shower. Jason ate his dinner, most of Howard's, and spent a fruitless ten minutes rummaging through the freezer looking for a dessert.

Howard woke Jason at four-thirty the next morning and called for the Land Rover. They packed their gear and set out for Al-Dhala, stopping at a roadside stand at the edge of the old city. Little more than three walls, a couple of chairs, and a hot plate, the stand sold *muddabaq*, a doubled pancake filled with roasted eggs, tomatoes, and herbs. Hard-boiled eggs were purchased from urchins at the side of the road. Howard and Jason stayed partially hidden in the dusty Land Rover and let their driver dicker for the meals.

Howard filled Jason in while they waited. "Our communications must have been hacked for our friends to identify me on both our trips to Ta'izz. I expect an incident on our trip to Al-Dhala."

Jason looked at him wide-eyed. "You expect problems on the way to Al-Dhala?"

"People are monitoring my satellite phone. To get help, call me from your phone and repeat 'transposon' until someone cuts in." He asked for Jason's phone, fussed with it for a second, and handed it back. "Your GPS coordinates will be broadcast to the extraction team."

Jason's hand shook as he put the phone away. "What . . . what kind of trouble do you expect?"

"We'll know it when we're in it."

Jason's face looked green, and he clutched his stomach. "Don't worry," Howard said. "It doesn't do any good, and our driver knows every bend in the road to Al-Dhala."

The driver returned with the eggs and muddabaq. Howard ate, and Jason picked at his breakfast as they left the city, drove through the suburbs and green parks of Ta'izz, and descended into drier country. The high green plateau around the city gave way to jagged hills and ridges with patches of green interspersed between parched, bare soil. The closer they approached Al-Dhala, the fewer the green areas were and the hotter and drier the air became. Stony pastures along the road were gradually replaced by barren jumbles of rock. Stunted and twisted bushes and weeds struggled for life where water from infrequent rains collected between boulders.

The road deteriorated with the scenery. The Land Rover was in four-wheel drive shortly after they left the suburbs. By the halfway point, the engine groaned as the car plunged from deep rut to pothole and swerved back and forth across the road to avoid fallen rocks and gaping holes. The trip seemed endless. Jason ignored his aching back and butt and watched the roadside for a gun barrel, a face, or a *shora* and *egal*, the scarf and headband worn by the locals. Howard watched the other side of the road.

The landscape became ever more craggy and desolate until it looked as though nature had created a landfill of broken hopes and crushed life. The tension eased as they topped a rise and saw the Al-

Dhala airstrip four miles away. Jason saw a white dot on the distant tarmac. "Hey, look. Our plane."

"Screw the plane," Howard said. "Keep your eyes on the hills."

A half-dozen potholes and two hundred yards farther, Jason saw a rag or piece of paper sticking above a rock on the slope above the road. The car approached it until Jason could identify the snatch of white as a cloth. His mouth went dry, and his pulse raced. "Look!" he yelled as the car slowed to make a hair-pin turn and he could at last make out the black head band, the egal, of a white shora as it moved between two rocks topping a jagged mound eighty yards away.

Howard turned to him. "What do—?"

Jason saw a head rise under the cloth as the side of the road ahead of them erupted in flame, dust, and flying rocks. His world went silent as the shock wave smashed into his ears. Stones broke the windshield as the blast flung the car into the air and off the road. Jason was alternately slammed into his seat, the door, and against his seat belt as the car cartwheeled down the slope, away from the blast and the insurgents. His world spun until the Land Rover, with a mighty crunch of crumpling steel and shattering glass, slammed into a pile of car-sized boulders.

The IED would have demolished the car and killed all of them had the insurgents detonated it a few seconds later. The tops of the boulders that stopped the car were peppered by automatic rifle fire from the rocks above the road. The slope of the hill and edge of the road hid the car and its occupants from the attackers, and the broken and jumbled granite the car had bounced over slowed their advance.

Howard and Jason hung upside down by their seat belts in the wreck. Both were groggy and disoriented, but Howard prodded Jason into movement. Howard released himself from his seat belt and helped Jason out of his. He kicked out what remained of the window on his side, the side away from the rock, and crawled out of the car, pulling Jason after him.

In the front seat, blood pooled under the driver. Jason went to help him, but stopped when he saw the open gash across the driver's neck. Bright red blood from the carotid arteries drained across the glistening white of the trachea where it had been sliced open. The guy was dead.

The smell of gasoline, the sound of voices, and rifle fire were all the incentive Jason and Howard needed to ignore their pain and move. Jason in the lead, they crawled under and between the boulders that stopped the car and emerged in a gap in the rocks ten yards away.

"Keep down and quiet, stay in the shade and under rocks. Follow this gully as far as you can," Howard said. "I'm going back."

Before Jason could ask why, Howard turned and crawled toward the car, favoring his right hand and arm. Jason found himself in shade at the bottom of a tortuous slot, varying from two to five feet wide and bordered by rocks four to ten feet tall. He moved forward slowly on all fours through tall, sparse undergrowth. Crawling with his left shoulder against the rock at first, he stood to a crouch when he found himself in thistles. Repeatedly, he turned to check for Howard or pursuers. He stopped when he came to a bend in the slot, returned to his hands and knees, and waited for Howard.

The rifle fire slowed or the sound was blocked by the rocks. Louder shots, shots that echoed through the little gully, came from the direction of the car. Jason's gut ached and he broke into a sweat. He wondered if Howard had been shot or if their pursuers were coming down the gulley. Jason pulled the P30S from his pocket, ignored the stings, and crawled into a patch of three-foot tall thistles to lie down and watch for Howard.

He saw movement in the gully and a second later heard the "whump" of pooled gasoline igniting. Howard, limping and crouching low, made his way toward him. Like Jason, he stayed in the shadows close to the left side of the gully. His progress was slow; Jason saw blood dripping from his right hand.

Two shadows materialized behind Howard and moved slowly toward him. Jason saw the ends of rifle barrels poke over the rim of the gully. A ragged cloth appeared at the top of the rocks above Howard. It moved toward the edge of the rock until Jason could see a deeply tanned nose and forehead.

Howard lay in tall brush, hugging the rocks. He looked toward Jason and started to move. Under overhanging thistles, Jason held his palm out toward Howard. Howard turned, saw the shadows, and froze. They each waited, motionless as the shadows moved past them and down the gully.

When the shadows were no longer visible, Jason counted slowly to three hundred and chanced a look down the rim of the gully. It was clear. He turned to Howard and motioned him forward.

Howard was gasping when he caught up to Jason. "Stick to . . . rocks . . . covers trail. Move."

Jason put the safety on, pocketed his pistol, and moved forward. Something on the Land Rover, probably a tire, exploded as they rounded a twisted sapling. Unsure of the source of the noise, Jason froze. Howard tapped him on the butt to get his attention and pointed to a dark area behind low brush and weeds. It was a cavity, a shallow cave in the rocks. They made for it and scrambled in. Howard laid back and caught his breath.

"What did you do back there?" Jason whispered.

Howard's chest heaved with every breath. It was a while before he could answer. "Shot . . . gas tank . . . drained . . . started fire. It'll cover us . . . keep 'em from searching car. May not see we escaped."

Panting, Howard pulled out his satellite phone, selected a contact, and handed the phone to Jason. "Call," he said.

Jason took the phone from Howard's hand. The hand was cold

and the phone wet with blood. His call rolled over to phone mail. "Transposon . . . transposon . . . transposon," he repeated.

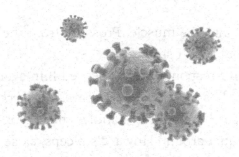

CHAPTER 22

Near Al-Dhala
Afternoon, August 28

Out of Jason's sight, four insurgent gunmen prowled over the boulders and jagged rocks, looking for the occupants of the burning car. They found the narrow gully in the rocks, but preferred to examine from above by walking along its western edge, the better to avoid ambush. Jason and Howard's trail was hidden by the shadow of the gully wall. Jason repeated the word "transposon" quietly every fifteen seconds for a couple of minutes before he closed the phone and checked on Howard. Blood was running down Howard's arm and pooling where his hand rested on sand and rock. His lips looked pale.

"You're losing blood," Jason whispered. "How's your arm?"

Weak and in pain, Howard turned his right arm so Jason could see the gash. "Took . . . took piece of glass . . . when car rolled."

Jason gently moved Howard's shirtsleeve out of the way and blotted blood from the cut with a clean handkerchief. The cut was deep and quickly filled with blood again. As the blood welled up, Jason noted that the center of the pool in the cut pulsed. Jason realized it had to be coming from the brachial artery.

He saw Howard was still conscious. "It's pulsing but not spraying," Jason told him. "You must have cut an artery clear through, and the end pulled back into the muscle. Pressure from the muscle reduced the blood flow but didn't stop it."

Howard didn't respond. Jason checked him again—his forehead was cool and his lips pale and dry. *Hypovolemic shock*, Jason thought. He packed the cut with a clean handkerchief, took off his belt and applied a tourniquet around Howard's biceps, close to the shoulder.

Jason carefully looked up and down the gully for moving shadows. Seeing none, he moved Howard from a sitting to a lying position as best he could in the cramped cave and tried to elevate his feet.

Black smoke, muffled crackles, pops, and the distant bang of another tire blowing came from the burning Land Rover. As he listened, Jason heard voices and gunfire. Some of the voices seemed to be celebrating, others sounded argumentative. Jason hunkered down behind the weeds and brush at the mouth of the cave and watched in the direction of the burning car.

In the cramped quarters, he could only see four feet directly in front of the cave and less than fifteen feet up and down the gully in either direction. Remembering the satellite phones, Howard's and his own, he pulled them from his pocket and turned them off. He wasn't sure how to put them on vibrate, and he couldn't afford to have either phone ring if he could still hear voices.

After an eternity, but only fifteen minutes by his watch, he turned his phone on, went to "outgoing calls," and repeated his last call. He was rolled over to phone mail again, and waited for the tone to leave his message. Almost in a whisper, he said, "Transposon . . . transpo—"

A shadow fell across the crevice near the cave. Jason turned off the phone and held his breath. The shadow moved toward him. He pressed himself as far back into the cave as he could and held his breath. He thought of the P30S in his pocket, but left it where it was. A gunshot would bring all of their pursuers down on top of him.

The shadow didn't hesitate. It moved to the cave and passed it at a slow, steady pace. Jason's left leg began to cramp. The muscle became a hard knot and a hot ball of pain formed in his calf. He gritted his teeth and straightened the leg as much as he could within the confines of the cave, flexing and extending his ankle and rubbing his calf to relieve the pain. The pain and cramping continued until the shadow returned. Jason froze, gasping from the pain. Sweat beaded on his forehead and ran into his eyes as the shadow passed the cave without pausing.

Minutes later, he again heard the murmur of voices from the direction of the burning Land Rover. There was less emotion evident this time. Jason silently implored the gunmen to move as the fire in his left leg continued.

A few more shots were fired, and the voices faded. Jason peeked out of the cave. Seeing nothing, he crawled from the cave, stood in a crouch, and walked back and forth until the cramp resolved.

He returned to the cave to check Howard's arm and release the tourniquet for a minute. Howard was still unconscious, and he felt colder. Jason took off his shirt and covered Howard's chest with it. The shirt was thin and accomplished little.

Jason thought of the phone's GPS signal. He turned his phone on and scrolled through menus until he found the ring control. He put it on vibrate and set the phone under the weeds at the mouth of the cave. With Howard's phone, he repeated the "transposon" call every ten minutes until the battery died.

Howard came to and asked for water, but they hadn't brought any. He slipped into delirium and began to babble. Jason tried to comfort him, if only to keep him quiet in case the voices came back.

At the mention of water, Jason realized how thirsty he was. His mouth was dry; his tongue stuck to his cheeks and teeth. Speaking was difficult. He gave up repeating "transposon" on his phone.

Four hours after the IED exploded, Jason heard the *whoopa-whoopa-whoopa* of a chopper flying low over their cave. He grabbed his shirt from Howard, crawled from the cave, and scanned the sliver of sky visible from the bottom of the little gully. Keeping low so the rocks would screen him from anyone except those directly above, he waved his shirt. A minute later he heard boots running over the rocks above him, calling his name.

Jason stood. His head seemed to sprout from the rocky crevice, almost under the boots of a startled marine. "Dr. Jason Mitchell?" the marine asked.

"Yes, sir. Howard Frobisher is in the cave. He's injured, lost a lot of blood."

The marine spoke into a small radio strapped to his forearm. "I got 'em. One injured."

Jason led the marine to the cave as two other marines appeared and stood guard over them. The marine slung his rifle over his shoulder and helped Jason move Howard out of the cave. One of the marines above them lifted Howard out of the crevice as the other marine helped Jason out. With a marine carrying Howard on his shoulder, the group moved rapidly across the rocks, past the smoldering Land Rover, and up the slope to the helicopter. They were airborne within four minutes of leaving the gully.

A medic inserted a needle in Howard's left arm and started an IV drip of fluids and platelets shortly after lift-off. Someone shoved a plastic bottle in Jason's hand. He drank a half-liter of water in an unbroken series of gulps and started on another half-liter before he tried to talk. The marines weren't very talkative, and Jason remembered he was working in intelligence. He wasn't supposed to talk, either.

The flight to the French airbase in Djibouti and its hospital took two hours. The copter landed at the hospital and Jason followed Howard to the emergency room. Howard regained consciousness after two units of blood, but he was still weak.

"What . . . what are you doing here?" he asked Jason.

"Making sure you're all right."

"Thanks." Still groggy, Howard struggled to organize his thoughts. "Get report in. Ask ambassador's secretary . . . make secure connection . . . Langley. Give verbal report." Howard paused to gather strength. "Draft written report . . . include stuff . . . forgot to tell 'em."

Jason did as he was told. He staggered to bed just before midnight in his room in the embassy compound.

Dietrich flew home to Holland while Jason was on the road. The university asked Mohammed and others a few questions about the people seen fleeing the Life Sciences building the night before, but everyone had been at prayers. Mohammed's alibi was solid. Nothing was missing in any of the labs or offices, which suggested the affair was similar to an earlier theft of ethyl alcohol from one of the labs, or a couple of scientific supply reps accidentally leaving through the wrong door after the building closed. Nothing connected it to Ahmed's lab, and neither Al-Mikhafi nor Ahmed questioned the integrity of their samples.

Ahmed dropped by his laboratory the following Tuesday. "Mohammed, have you completed running the gels on BCV? I won't be able to tell my, ah, my . . . vaccine from the parent BCV until we have that information."

Dipshit, Mohammed thought. *You couldn't tell the two viruses apart without a printed label.* He kept his eyes on the clutter of glassware in front of him and moved some of it around to pretend he was working. "Ran the gels yesterday. Here are the pictures." Mohammed handed three five-by-seven pictures to Ahmed.

Ahmed looked at the pictures. He frowned, squinted at them, and nodded. "Yes, yes. Excellent work." He showed one of the pictures to Mohammed and pointed at a column of small white horizontal lines. "Is this lane the BCV sample or the mutant, ah, the vaccine mutant?"

Mohammed looked at the picture, took it from Ahmed and turned it right-side up. "It's neither. It's the DNA ladder." *Doesn't know top from bottom or what a DNA size standard is! Could a dead camel be dumber?* Mohammed thought.

"Oh, of course, yes. Good work. Carry on." Ahmed turned to leave the lab.

"I'll repeat running the gels tomorrow to verify we have it right, but what do you want me to do after that?"

"I'll . . . I'll have to think about it. Check with me Friday morning." Ahmed looked at his watch. "I have to get out to the camel facility. They can't get anything done without me," he said, and left hurriedly.

Camel facility, right, Mohammed thought.

Ahmed didn't make it to the facility. Al-Mikhafi called him to his office after lunch. "How is your work on the facility going?" Al-Mikhafi asked.

"Speedily. Everything is going well, but they won't lift a hammer without me there to interpret the blueprints for them."

"And the laboratory work?"

"Mohammed is doing well. We can differentiate the BCV and the hybrid mutant by gel electrophoresis now."

Al-Mikhafi raised his eyebrows and leaned forward. "Did he use an RNA or DNA gel? What endonucleases did he use to digest them?"

"I, ah, I," he cleared his throat. "I . . . I think it would be better if Mohammed explained it. It would be good for his ego. He's been depressed without Dietr . . . Professor van Kellen to provide guidance on his project." Ahmed mopped sweat off his forehead with a handkerchief.

Al-Mikhafi nodded. "Very thoughtful of you. What will you have Mohammed work on next?"

Why this inquisition? Ahmed thought. He felt like a target at a rifle range. "I have spent so much time at the camel facility that I haven't been able to organize my ideas. I was planning to go over that with Mohammed on Friday." Ahmed's pulse was pounding. He cast about for a way to change the topic. "Do we know anything more about the alarms that went off last Friday?"

Al-Mikhafi shrugged. "Very little. Nothing is missing, nothing broken. Probably a student leaving late who forgot about the alarms on the side doors and was too embarrassed to wait for the guards. Was there anything picked up by the surveillance cameras in your lab?"

Ahmed hadn't looked, but he didn't dare admit it to Al-Mikhafi. "Nothing." He tried a safer topic. "Do you know when Dietr . . . Professor van Kellen will return from Holland?"

Ahmed saw Al-Mikhafi look at him sharply. It lasted barely a second, a flicker of suspicion. "It's just that I worry about Mohammed. He seems lost without van Kellen's guidance," he added.

Howard's sources also reported that the insurgents and Al-Mikhafi didn't seem to be worried or suspicious about the alarms the night of their raid on the lab. Dietrich returned to Ta'izz and gave the university administration the story about a disagreement with his wife. He said she wanted the children in Dutch schools and refused to leave Holland, but he would work another three months at the university to oversee completion of Mohammed's project and oral exam.

A few days after Dietrich returned, he took Mohammed out for lunch again. They found a quiet table, away from other diners and close to a clattering fan. They discussed Mohammed's research for the first several minutes. He was surprised when Dietrich told him that he had accomplished enough in the lab. It was time for him to gather his data, write his thesis, and set a date for his written and oral exams.

"But I still have so much to do!" Mohammed objected.

Dietrich laughed. "The old saying is still true. Good graduate students never believe they have done enough. They always want to do one more study. Mediocre graduate students drive their advisors crazy asking, 'Am I done yet?'"

Mohammed looked around to verify no one was close enough to eavesdrop. "What about the tenth sample? It was processed for inoculating tissue culture. The cameras make it too dangerous for me to touch it now, and I never know when Ahmed might walk in." Mohammed looked around again to verify they were still alone. "He drops by to brag about how brilliantly he's running the remodeling. He's picked a damned inconvenient time to get excited about his work."

Dietrich spoke softly. "We pressed our luck as far as it was safe. Jason and Howard know about the cameras. They haven't suggested we try anything. For now, we just provide information."

Ahmed arrived at the camel facility unannounced. Midday, and nobody seemed to be around. He walked through the partly gutted building, slipping between the metal framing members for the walls between isolation pens.

The metal framing had been Ahmed's choice; the metal members were pre-measured, pre-drilled, fit together easily, and wouldn't soak up contaminated liquids. He'd done his homework. Stone interior walls took too much time, mud brick couldn't be washed properly, and wood wasn't available. And with the prefabricated metal studs, he didn't have to worry about the local jerks screwing up measurements.

The contractor had wanted to build in stone; he could buy it from his uncle and hire more of his relatives to do the building. He'd been whining to Al-Mikhafi since construction started. That morning, Al-Mikhafi had chewed Ahmed out for an hour about cost overruns due to the cost of the metal framing. At least that was what the contractor claimed was the reason.

That's why Ahmed was at the facility an hour earlier than normal. Al-Mikhafi had shoved the latest bills in his face and almost thrown him out of his office. Ahmed felt like his balls were on a chopping block and he wanted to know why.

He rounded the corner of an intact outer wall and saw the building crew carrying prayer rugs and headed toward the mosque, a few hundred feet away. He ducked back behind the wall. *Crap,* he thought. *If I don't join them they'll talk about my lack of piety.* He peeked around the wall again. Nothing suggested that they'd seen him.

This could be my chance. He backed away from the wall and walked to the lab at the front of the building. The contractor was using it as an office. He searched through the contractor's papers for five minutes. Nothing about the cost of the metal frames. Not a damned thing. Frustrated, Ahmed stood in the middle of the lab, hands on his hips. Through a window he saw the contractor's pickup truck.

Maybe, Ahmed thought. He slipped out of the building and hustled to the pickup, now and then looking over his shoulder to see if any of the men had returned. A plastic and metal writing desk was mounted between the front seats, a key in the lock at its front.

Ahmed smiled, his eyebrows arched. *Best place to start looking.* He was soon comparing the contractor's bills with the invoices for the metal framing. He ducked out of the truck and checked to be sure he was still alone. His smile broadened and he chuckled. *Time to set up a meeting with this bastard. I've got that donkey fucker by the balls, now,* he thought, and took the papers back to his car.

Ahmed discovered that a braggart working undercover leads a frustrating—or short—life. He was desperate to crow to someone, but he could only brag about a few of the things he'd accomplished—and none of what he'd found out. That doubled his frustration. For the next couple of weeks he spent an hour every morning telling Mohammed how helpless the construction crew was without him and another hour in the afternoon at the camel facility lecturing the crew on how lucky they were to have his guidance. His few conversations with the contractor were hushed, short, and a hell of a lot more direct.

Four box stalls were converted to rooms with sealed walls, ceilings, and floors. What had been an open walkway along the stalls became an enclosed clean hallway that could be rigorously disinfected. Entrance and exit showers were installed, and the office and a tack room were remodeled to be a limited laboratory and freezer room.

Ahmed's mood swung from pessimistic to excitedly optimistic as the project moved from preliminary drawings toward completion. Al-Mikhafi was also excited. Every invoice and bill that hit his desk pushed his mental stimulation to new heights. The project was over budget, and he repeatedly had to request more money from his sources in the Ansar Allah.

Cost overruns reached three times Ahmed's original estimate for the project two months after Jason switched the samples, and new invoices continued flowing like a river. Al-Mikhafi dithered for two days over whether he dared ask the people who ran his piggy bank for more. Remembering that Ahmed couldn't load a gun, but the people at his bank didn't even go to the restroom without an AK-47, simplified his decision. He called Ahmed to his office.

"How is the camel facility coming?" he asked.

"Better than we ever expected. I have done so well supervising the work that it is almost completed. Only the dirty hallway and the air handling and balancing system are left to be finished. Then we will install the lab equipment—the minus seventy-degree freezer, the centrifuges, the—"

"Are the dirty hallway and air handling systems absolutely necessary? Aren't the freezers and centrifuges here adequate?" Al-Mikhafi stood and paced behind his desk. "Can't you infect camel calves and collect feces without HEPA-filtered air? Feces are still shit, even if a camel coughs on it." He put his hands on his desk and leaned over it toward Ahmed. The move had always intimidated Ahmed before. "Our friends have neither bottomless pockets nor scientific educations. They do have guns and tempers. You can't build this facility as though the Saudi oil fields were financing you."

"But we need the dirty hallway and air-handling systems for biosecurity and biosafety."

Al-Mikhafi shook his head. "Ahmed, I did some reading. BCV is an enveloped virus. Desiccation and sunlight kill it. We are in Arabia. Can't we depend on heat and sunlight?"

Ahmed knew that being right is never a substitute for being in charge. "As you wish. I'll have the contractors complete the clean hallway and the lab and drop the rest. Passage of the virus in camels can start next week if we can purchase neonatal camel calves."

St. Paul
October 13

In the late afternoon, Harith gave up revising his thesis and took a break to look at his emails. Most of them were advertisements or blogs on topics he had no interest in, kindly forwarded to him by friends with too much time on their hands. On the third page of the emails was one from uncle BillESmith. Harith opened it, afraid it was the one he'd been expecting.

> *Dear D&H,*
> *The carpenters are finished and we have moved into the new*
> *apartment. The baby is due any day. Will be very busy when*
> *it arrives.*
> *Best,*
> *BillESmith*

Harith called Ann. The phone rang five times, and he was about to hang up when he remembered that Ann moved slowly now. She was almost due herself. She answered on the sixth ring. After her assurance that she was doing well, just clumsy, slow, and eager to have the pregnancy over, Harith gave her the news that the camel facility was completed and Ahmed was looking for neonatal camels. "You should probably let your contact know right away."

"Crap," Ann said. "I was hoping Jason would come home soon. I miss him so much, Harith." She started to cry.

Harith tried to think of something to say. He couldn't come up with anything better than, "Sorry, Ann. He might make it back before . . ."

Ann thanked him, sniffed a little, and said she'd better let him go and call Gettelman. She reached Gettelman at his home and gave him the message. "Al, could you . . ." she stifled a sob and waited until she had her voice under control again. "Could you talk Filburt into letting Jason come home for a few days?"

"I can ask," Gettelman said slowly, "but I can't . . . wait. Camels won't begin calving for several weeks, and Filburt has to update the committee soon. I'll suggest Jason be here to help with questions."

Thousands of miles away, Dietrich was telling Howard about the camel facility by phone—the embassy had installed new safeguards against hacking in their phone system. Harith's call to Ann reached Langley before Gettelman's or Howard's. Ann's phone was tapped.

Gettelman called Filburt with the news and asked if he'd need help with the committee, since a sample had been missed in the raid on the lab. Filburt remembered a senator he'd pissed off at a previous meeting. *The old bastard might be close to senile*, Filburt thought, *but he never forgets an insult.*

Jason was on a flight to the US five hours later.

"Your original report indicated you destroyed nine of the ten samples, and now you think the tenth might still be a threat?" Gettelman asked.

"That's the gist of it," Jason said. "Ahmed purified the tenth sample so he could use it to inoculate tissue cultures. He didn't use it because of the switch to camel calves. I saw vials on another shelf in the freezer that night. They were consistent with Mohammed's description of the processed tenth sample."

Filburt and Gettelman looked at each other.

Filburt pursed his lips, tapped a pencil on the notebook in front of him, and thought of Senator Nuthatch. "Where does that leave us?"

"We can't be sure," Jason admitted. "It wouldn't be unusual to lose ninety to ninety-nine percent of the virus during purification, and Ahmed is inept in the virology lab. He could have lost it all. If he did, or if he leaves it in the lab and only uses the fecal samples we switched to inoculate the camels, the tenth sample will be nothing but a bad memory."

"And if they use it on the first camel calf?" Gettelman asked.

"One percent of a billion is still ten million viral particles. That should be enough to infect a calf."

"What happens then?" Filburt asked.

"We don't know how the hybrid virus will affect camels," Jason said. "The calf might develop pneumonia or it might become an asymptomatic carrier."

"What's that?" Filburt asked.

"The calf might be infected and contagious but not get sick. If the safety protocols aren't followed, the animal caretakers could become sick."

"What's the bottom line?" Filbert asked.

"Ahmed has a chance at success. If he infects a camel, he could collect enough virus to infect dozens of camels and then thousands of people."

The room was silent for several minutes.

Filburt crossed his arms over his chest. "Help me out here. What do I suggest to the committee? My butt is exposed, and there are a couple of senators itching to tear me a new one."

"Ask Mohammed to cook the tenth sample now, if he can, or wait until Ahmed starts bragging that his camel facility is completed. He'll have to take the sample to the facility lab. We could try to get it while he's on the road or steal it from the lab when he gets it there."

"Any other options?" Gettelman asked.

Jason thought a moment and looked at his notes. "Ahmed is lazy. He'll have Mohammed collect samples from the camels, carry them back to the university and do all the lab work. Someone could work with Mohammed to inactivate the samples on the way back to the university."

Jason stopped for a moment. "Or you could pick up the phone and tell the government of Yemen about Ahmed and Al-Mikhafi. That would be the simplest way, wouldn't it?"

"We've done that for other issues, but the information always leaked to the wrong people," Filburt said.

The committee meeting was held the next day. Filburt massaged the egos of the senators and the vice president and gave them Jason's summary. The committee members fidgeted in their seats, reviewed the printout each had in front of him, and whispered to each other until Senator Nuthatch stood.

The senator's face was red. Veins stood out in his neck and forehead. "We represent the most powerful nation in the world. This is the most unacceptable course of action ever proposed to us. It is cowardly, it is vacillating, and it is un-American. For the love of God, why not blow up the camel facility now?"

The senator threw his copy of the presentation on the table and sat. Heads around the room nodded and murmurs of approval circulated through the committee.

Jason thought that bizarre. The senator was attacking a plan that hadn't even been proposed yet. He stood and stepped to a microphone near the podium. Filburt subtly shook his head and motioned for him to sit. Jason ignored him.

Jason took the microphone. "I didn't speak at earlier meetings because I didn't feel I had enough experience. I've been infected with BCV, exposed to SARS, chased by armed guards, shot at, hunted by the insurgents, and nearly blown to hell by an IED. The agent with me almost bled out while we hid in a cave. As the closest thing to an expert there is on this virus, I've earned the right to speak."

Jason looked around the room, daring anyone to object. "To answer your question, Senator, Arabs love their camels, and there is a mosque less than two hundred feet from the camel facility. Al-Mikhafi would love it if we took military action. Hit the facility and kill baby camels or hit the mosque and you will create a new generation of enemies for the United States. Hit the lab and vaporize stocks of the virus while people are in the mosque and we could be the ones to start an epidemic in Yemen."

Jason gave the committee the same advice he'd given Filburt and Gettelman the night before. "You should remember," he added, "that the mutant we are discussing was created by nature, not by man, and nature will create it, or something like it, again.

"Natural biological threats like this will emerge frequently in the future. Around the world, people are destroying natural habitat, moving into areas close to wildlife, and eating bush meat. Diseases carried by wild animals, such as Ebola, Marburg virus, SARS, and West Nile virus, are often more virulent when they infect people than they were in the original host. Any of those diseases can become potential pandemics if they begin to spread from person to person. The public health organizations of the world have been remarkably successful in preventing that from happening. Those are the first lines of your defense, and they have worked magnificently so far. Remember that the next time you cut the budgets again for the CDC, state public health organizations, and biomedical and agricultural research."

Jason returned to his seat without taking questions. Senator Nuthatch slammed his hand on the table and stormed out of the room.

The discussion was rancorous, and the meeting was postponed twenty-four hours while Langley polled its agents to see if they had a dependable contact in the Yemen military. During the break, Gettelman walked across the lobby of Jason's hotel and saw him checking out.

"You're leaving?"

"Going home to Ann. She's due any day, and I've done everything I could. You and Filburt have more experience in these meetings than me."

"You're underrating yourself, Jason. Go home to Ann. Spend a couple of days with her, and I'll give you a call. We still need you in Yemen."

Jason promised to think about it, checked out, and took a cab to the airport.

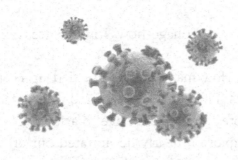

CHAPTER 23

North St. Paul
Evening, October 15

Jason quietly let himself into his apartment and looked for Ann. He heard a flush from the bathroom as he tiptoed past it. The doorway to the spare bedroom, now transformed into a nursery, was open. Jason poked his head in and turned on the lights.

When he heard the faucet gush in the bathroom, he turned off the light, scampered to the end of the hallway, and hid in their bedroom, sitting where he could watch the full length of the hallway. There, he fumbled for his cell phone and waited.

As the bathroom door opened, Jason tapped his cell phone and Ann's phone rang. She walked to the kitchen where she'd left her cell.

"Ann, how are you feeling tonight?" Jason asked.

"Tired. I'm ready for this pregnancy to be over. Even having people scramble to open doors or carry groceries isn't worth it anymore. When are you coming home?"

"Soon, honey. Very soon. There isn't much more I can do here. When did you paint the spare bedroom?"

"Two weeks ago. I couldn't focus on my work anymore. Greg and Harith helped me move the crib and dresser in. Sue said I could use her . . . How do you know I painted the room?"

"Honey, I'm in espionage now. Intelligence, remember? I know these things."

"Yeah, sure. How many agents are tied up keeping you out of trouble now? Last I heard it was two, and they called for back-up."

That hit a sore spot. "You'll have to ask the CIA station chief in Djibouti. The explosion nearly decapitated our driver, and I had to dig a glass shard out of Howard's arm, pack his wound, and make sure the bad guys didn't find us." Jason looked closely at the bed. "I really would have appreciated fresh sheets that night."

"Fresh sheets? Jason, what are you talking about?"

"I see you changed the sheets today. That'll feel good."

"Jason," Ann waddled as fast as she could to their bedroom. "Where are you?"

They caught up on departmental gossip the next morning, as well as on how their projects were doing and what else they needed before the baby arrived. Jason luxuriated in domesticity—something he'd taken for granted before, but found he loved now. Breakfast with Ann, coming home to his own apartment, leftover beef stew, and fresh sheets combined to make a life he didn't want to leave again.

North St. Paul
October 18

Jason answered the phone and recognized Gettelman's voice. Al asked if Jason could meet with him in the Vet Sciences conference room. When Jason seemed reluctant, Gettelman said he and Filburt could drop by Jason's apartment.

"Come on, Al. That's playing dirty," Jason said. "Ann is due any day. I don't want to put her under that kind of stress." He agreed to meet them in the departmental conference room.

"So what is this about?" Jason asked as they sat around the table.

Filburt nodded to Gettelman. "You agreed to think about working on the project again after a couple of days at home," Gettelman said. "I was hoping you'd be bored with domestic life by now. We think things are getting ready to happen in Ta'izz. Mohammed sent word that Ahmed plans to use the sample of purified virus on the first camel. I believe you have some ideas on how we should proceed if that happens."

Jason looked at the polished tabletop and avoided eye contact. The room was silent.

"Howard said to tell you that you're missed," Filburt added. "He said this would be a piece of cake compared to what you went through the last time you raided Ahmed's lab. We need you to finish this project."

Jason crossed his arms over his chest and kept his eyes on the table.

Filburt continued. "Spend a week in Yemen. If you can't get the job done in a visit to the lab, set up a system that Mohammed and Howard can run, and you can come home permanently."

"This time we thought ahead. We've put together a couple of sample cases," Gettelman said. "The cases are identical to the ones salespeople from molecular biology supply companies have, complete with samples, brochures, and your new business cards."

Jason looked at them and put his hands on the table, palms up. "Why do you need me?" he asked.

Filburt shrugged. "We need you and Howard to visit Ahmed's lab again. You'll pretend to be salesmen for your cover. Howard doesn't know any more than I do about virology and molecular biology. It'll be clear he's an imposter if anybody at the university asks a question. Like last time, Howard will cover your butt in case . . . you know, in case there's a hiccup in the plan."

Jason briefly glared at Filburt.

"If you do this," Gettelman said, "we have a much better chance of keeping Senator 9/11, his drones, and his missiles out of the mix. Fewer locals die; fewer kids grow up hating Americans; your kids and mine grow up in a safer world."

Jason's shoulders slumped. He put his elbows on the table and rested his head in his hands.

Filburt got up and paced back and forth behind the table, shoes squeaking on the floor. After a minute he stopped and turned to Jason. "Shit, kid. We need you. You know that isn't easy for me to admit. I never thought I'd need an academic in cutoffs and a T-shirt, but it's true."

Jason sat back in his chair and looked at Filburt. "When do I have to go?"

Filburt rocked back and forth on his heels and avoided Jason's gaze. "Soon."

Gettelman sat back in his chair. "Take your time. Have dinner with Ann tonight. I'll pick you up tomorrow at noon. We'll have a barber freshen up the dye-job and give you a fresh haircut en route to the airport. A military transport will be waiting for you there. It has a communications system that will allow you and Howard to discuss the plan and go over your ideas. He'll meet you at the airport in Djibouti and fly with you to Ta'izz."

Jason received a special message an hour after takeoff: Ann was in labor. Things went rapidly, and a corporal brought Jason a message from the cockpit as they approached the coast of France. Ann and their daughter were healthy and sleeping peacefully. Jason wept as relief and elation overcame him. He leaned against the window next to his seat and tried to see the wing through the darkness. In the distance, a brilliant needle of pale blue and gold from the east pierced the purple blackness of the night. The needle grew longer, wider and brighter as they flew east and the dawn hastened toward them. *Am I flying to a sunrise for the baby, Ann and me, or toward dawn and disaster?*

Djibouti French Military Airport
Noon, October 20

Under a clear sky and a blasting sun, Jason stepped out of the cool transport into a furnace. The small terminal shimmered in the heat seventy yards from the plane. Heat from the tarmac rolled over him in waves while the sun baked him from above. He descended the steps from the transport, the handrail too hot to touch. Sweat rolled off his forehead and into his eyes, soaked through the back of his shirt, and ran down his belly and into his crotch as he lugged his suitcase and briefcase to the terminal. The heat seemed to double their weight. Ninety-one degrees and sixty-five percent humidity in a country where it almost never rains. *Go figure*, Jason thought.

His sweat-soaked briefs bunched up as he walked. He felt like an idiot when he stopped and alternately stretched one leg and then the other, trying to get comfortable. Cool air enfolded him as he stepped through the door of the terminal. He walked a few feet, put his bags down, and shoved a hand down the front of his pants to get the knot out of his shorts.

Howard threw his left arm around Jason's shoulder. "Jason, how was your flight? Congratulations are in order, I understand." Howard gave Jason a hug as they walked. "Welcome back, kid. Try to smile.

I've seen corpses that looked happier than you do. Ann and the baby are doing well, I understand?"

"Going home and leaving after a couple of days was almost harder on her than if I'd stayed here. Before we got married, I . . . I promised her I'd be with her when she delivered." Jason's voice quavered a little.

Howard started to say something, but thought better of it.

They walked down a hallway marked *"Personnel autorisé seulement"* and entered a small conference room with an oval-shaped dark wood table and chairs. Jason looked at the bare and featureless cream-colored walls. They looked as bleak as he felt. With his left hand, Howard pulled out a chair at the head of the table and sat.

Left hand, Jason noted. *Howard's right handed, but he hugged me with his left arm, too.* Jason collapsed into a chair next to him, and Howard handed him a menu. "Would you care for lunch? A salad, a sandwich, lemonade, iced-tea, a beer?"

"How is your right arm doing?" Jason asked.

"Couldn't be better." A waiter seemed to materialize from nowhere and they ordered. Howard watched the waiter close the door as he left. "We have a flight to Ta'izz in an hour. I packed for you."

"A military plane? Won't that draw attention?"

"Not military. My associates have a small airline. It rents planes to European and American corporate interests around the Middle East. If I beg, I can use one for company business occasionally. Since trips by salespeople and executives are common on this line, we shouldn't draw any notice."

"You said we are going to be salesmen again. That didn't go well last time."

"Nonsense! We were 90% successful, and this time we only have to filch one ten-mL tube. That's only about a third of an ounce. We'll visit Mohammed in the lab tomorrow morning, supposedly to discuss RNA purification. You are conversant in RNA purification kits?"

"Spin columns or enzyme purification kits? Most are too

expensive for academic budgets, but I've used a few and know how and why they work."

"Excellent! I don't have to understand it, as long as you can convince a biochemist or molecular biologist that you do." Howard relaxed and sat back in his chair. "I feel better about this operation already."

Jason noticed that Howard gestured primarily with his left hand. "So I'm the one who will have to talk our way out of trouble if something happens?" Jason felt his gut getting tense as the waiter returned with sandwiches and lemonade.

Howard was silent until the waiter left and the door was closed. "Don't worry. I'll have something to back you up."

"How well do you shoot with your left hand?"

Howard looked Jason in the eyes. "My right arm is a little stiff. It won't interfere with our work, or I would have arranged for someone else to accompany you."

Jason took him at his word. There wasn't much else he could do. Jason wolfed down his stale egg salad sandwich and hoped it had at least been kept cold while the lettuce wilted.

Their plane landed at a small airport on the outskirts of Ta'izz. A driver loaded their luggage in a white Ford Explorer with four-wheel drive and drove them out of the airport and gradually uphill toward the city.

The scenery was greener than Jason recalled—September and October were relatively wet months for the area. As before, the old citadel and white limestone governor's palace, built on a rocky prominence projecting from the mountain, seemed to float over Ta'izz. Traffic was light and within thirty minutes the car pulled up to the gray four-story Al-Andalus Royal Sana'a Hotel on Ta'izz Street in the center of the city.

"This is a long way from the university, isn't it? Jason asked.

"True, but succeed or fail, we won't be coming back here. There are four-lane highways near the hotel that skirt the university, and this hotel is a favorite of business travelers. It fits with our story."

Howard stepped out of their car, waved a bellhop toward the rear of the Escort, and led Jason into the hotel. The lobby was large, with elegant lines but in need of remodeling, if not outright restoration. *Stale sandwich at the base,* Jason thought. *What did I expect for rooms? Billions in the defense budget unaccounted for, but they aren't being spent on us.* Jason followed Howard and let him check them into their suite.

Like the lobby, their rooms were outdated. They reminded him of pictures he'd seen of his parents' honeymoon suite. They'd been on a skimpy budget when they married in 1985 and the hotel they stayed in was a bit worn. Like those pictures, the suite Jason and Howard had might have been elegant in 1970, but the drapes, furniture, carpeting, and bathroom fixtures hadn't been updated since.

Jason tossed his suitcase on his bed and thought about what Howard had said of their work tomorrow morning. Howard met him in the sitting room that connected the two bedrooms.

"It sounded as though you think we'll be under surveillance." Jason asked. "What are the odds we'll run into Ahmed?"

"Just being cautious. We'll be in Ahmed's lab late in the morning. Mohammed says Ahmed could drop by, but he thinks it unlikely. Mohammed says Ahmed has a hobby that he works on in his office over the noon hour."

"What?" The color drained from Jason's face. "Our necks could depend on Ahmed's interest in a hobby?"

"Mohammed says Ahmed is absolutely devoted to it. Not to, ah, beat a dead horse, but the only things he allows to interfere with his hobby are meetings the faculty is required to attend."

Jason looked closely at Howard. He could have sworn he saw the trace of a smile flicker across his face. "Ahmed never struck me as a hobbyist," Jason said. "What kind of hobby is it?'

"Mohammed wasn't, ah, absolutely clear on that," Howard said, and seemed to be studying the ceiling. "Frankly, I hadn't thought our friend the hobbyist type, either."

Hotel Al-Andalus Royal
Morning, October 21

Jason felt like he'd slept in a museum, or at least on a mattress from one. They had breakfast in their suite to avoid being seen again in public. Between breakfast and eleven-thirty, when their driver was due to arrive, they rehearsed Jason's part in the raid, applied Jason's makeup, and dressed in dark suits and ties. With nothing left to do but worry, Jason paced back and forth across the sitting room until the driver called. The car was at the hotel.

As the driver negotiated late-morning traffic, Howard handed Jason a tiny pebble. "Put this in one of your shoes."

"What for?" Jason asked.

"While we are in the Life Sciences building and the lab, you should slouch and limp, just a little. The slouch and limp shouldn't be pronounced—we don't want you to draw attention to yourself— but a slouch and subtle limp will do almost as much as makeup to hide your identity if we run into Ahmed."

Dragging their sample cases, they stopped at the guard's office in the atrium of the Life Sciences building and explained they were visiting Professor van Kellen and Mohammed Saiti. The guard called Dietrich, verified that they were expected and told them how to reach Dietrich's office.

They walked through the marble and polished granite atrium to the elevators. Howard seemed cool and urbane. Jason tried to look casual but nervously scanned the atrium and hallways for Ahmed. In the elevator, Howard pushed the button for the third floor and leaned close to Jason. "Smile. Salesmen, whores, and politicians always smile. It works wonders for their business."

In Dietrich's office, Howard quickly swept the room for electronic listening devices. Finding none, he put his faux cigarette pack on the desk, and switched it on. Dietrich called Mohammed to confirm the lab was clear and he was ready for them.

"What should I do if we meet Al-Mikhafi or Ahmed in the hallway or the lab?" Dietrich asked.

"Our names are Eric Kessler and William Wulf. Introduce us," Howard said, "and ask if they are interested in kits for RNA purification. If we have to, Jason is prepared to show them a variety of kits and discuss the strong points of each."

Jason glared at Howard. Dietrich nodded and led them back to the elevators and the labs on the first floor. They passed a number of people in the hallways, but they didn't meet Ahmed or Al-Mikhafi. Jason's right hand was twitching slightly as they stopped in front of Ahmed's lab and Dietrich opened the door.

Dietrich walked into the lab and stopped abruptly, hesitated a second, but continued forward. "Professor Al-Mikhafi, Professor Hadi, allow me to introduce sales reps for GWR International. Mohammed and I are trying to find a better way to purify the small interfering RNA he is working on, and we asked them to stop by to show us the kits they have available." Dietrich turned to Howard and Jason. "I'm sorry, gentlemen, I've forgotten your names."

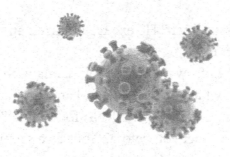

CHAPTER 24

University of Ta'izz
Noon, October 21

Ahmed and Al-Mikhafi, wearing white lab coats, were standing in the middle of the laboratory, talking to Mohammed. A fourth man, also wearing a lab coat, was behind Al-Mikhafi, leaning against a lab bench. He was roughly Ahmed's age. Bearded and muscular, dirt was ground into his hands and under his fingernails. He wore work boots rather than dress shoes and his lab coat seemed uncomfortably tight across the shoulders and at his armpits.

Mohammed seemed rooted to the floor. His eyes were wide, his complexion pale.

Howard stepped forward and shook hands with Al-Mikhafi. "I'm William Wulf," Howard said. He turned to Jason, "and my associate, Eric Kessler. We dropped by to discuss Professor van Kellen's problems with RNA purification, but if you need to purify RNA, we would be happy to include you in the discussion or drop by your offices later."

"I'm in proteomics," Al-Mikhafi said. He looked at his watch. "I have previous obligations, but my associate, Professor Ahmed Hadi, is working with RNA viruses. I'm sure he's interested." He turned to Ahmed. "You can fill me in on the latest in RNA purification when

we discuss our issue later." He excused himself and left the lab with
the fourth man in tow.

Ahmed stepped forward and shook hands with Howard. "I'd be
very interested in what you have to say. I am passing an RNA virus in
camels and will have to purify the RNA for testing." He shook hands
with Jason. "Have I met you before? Your face seems familiar."

Jason shook his head. He spoke in tones deeper than he normally
did and hoped the cotton Howard had stuffed in his cheeks would alter
his voice. "I don't believe so, but I meet many people in laboratories
and at meetings. Were you at the International Conference on
Ruminant Enteroviruses in Athens?"

"No, I wasn't able to attend," Ahmed said. He continued to stare
at Jason.

Jason felt his right hand twitching again. *Get a grip. Talk about
the science and what you know. Switch his attention to the damned samples,*
Jason thought. He put his sample case on the lab bench next to him
and opened it. "You are both familiar with the principles behind spin
columns. You add a small amount of your cell sample to a sealed tube
containing a silica membrane and a few drops of a chaotropic buffer.
The buffer lyses the . . ."

Jason continued for ten minutes holding forth on spin columns,
exclusion columns, and enzymatic nucleotide purification as he
slowly regained his composure. Ahmed, arms crossed over his lab
coat, listened closely. Mohammed leaned against the lab bench next
to Jason. His complexion returned to normal as he listened.

Howard and Dietrich stood behind Ahmed. Dietrich listened, at
times nodding in agreement. Howard alternately glanced at the door
to the hallway and made subtle hand signals to Jason, trying to get
him to finish his talk.

Jason was talking about laboratory procedures, a subject he
loved. He didn't notice Howard's attempts to shut him up until he'd
completed his comparison of the various kits, and then he didn't

seem to understand what Howard was trying to signal. Jason turned to Ahmed and did what graduate students are trained to do after delivering lectures.

"Do you have any questions?" he asked.

Howard put his hands over his face and swore under his breath. He turned red when Dietrich raised his hand. "Then, Ja . . . just to be clear, the enzymatic kits are more expensive, but they recover more of the RNA, they require the addition of fewer reagents, and they don't require use of hazardous chemicals. Is that right, Eric?"

Howard tried to smile, but only contorted his face into a rictus-like grimace. Pretending to answer Dietrich's question, he leaned over to whisper in his ear. "Jesus Christ, Dietrich, for god's sake, shut up. We need to get Jason the hell out of here before Ahmed recognizes him."

Ahmed asked a few questions and continued to stare at Jason's face. Jason answered the questions at length as Howard made ever more desperate hand signals. Ahmed shifted his eyes to the floor and listened to Jason's last answer.

"It is rare to find a salesman with your grasp of our problems. Forgive me for bringing this up again, but even your voice seems familiar. Are you sure we haven't met before?" Ahmed cocked his head to one side and looked at Jason quizzically. "Did you ever attend the University of Minnesota?"

Howard turned pale and his left hand felt for his pistol. "I'm sorry, but we have another appointment we must get to." He looked at his watch and glared at Jason. "Eric, give Ahmed your business card, and perhaps you can continue this conversation later."

Jason froze for a moment. He didn't think he had any business cards. "Perhaps you'd be interested in these brochures," he said. "Our contact information is stamped on the front." As he pulled a few brochures out of the sample case, he saw a little packet of business cards. He handed one to Ahmed and one to Mohammed. Ahmed responded by handing his business card to Jason and Howard.

Howard could no longer bear to watch. He turned around and kept his eyes on the door to the hallway. Dietrich caught Jason's eye and drew a finger across his neck. This time Jason understood. "Please feel free to contact us with any further questions, Professor Hadi," he said. "Mohammed, I'll leave these sample columns for you to try, but we must be going."

Howard said their good-byes and moved to hustle Jason out of the lab. They were at the door when Ahmed caught up with them.

"Again, I'm sorry to detain you," Ahmed said.

Jason turned around, his heart pounding in his ears.

"I noticed you forgot to give Prof. van Kellen your business card," Ahmed whispered. "He might feel slighted."

"Oh, sorry," Jason said. "Please express my regrets to the professor," and he handed Ahmed a couple of extra cards.

Ahmed nodded, smiled, wished them well, and handed one of the cards to a very pale Dietrich.

Howard waived good-bye and pushed Jason through the door. He called their driver as they walked through the atrium and waved to a guard at the security office.

"Aren't we—" Jason whispered.

"Not another word. Not another motherfucking, goddamned syllable," Howard said under his breath, as they walked down a few steps and got into their car. "Take us to the apartment," he barked to the driver.

He turned to Jason. "Didn't you notice how tight the lab coat was and the bulge under the arm of that thug that followed Al-Mikhafi around? The guy had a gun, and not a small one. Dietrich said he'd never seen the man before, so Al-Mikhafi was doing something special today, possibly grilling or threatening Mohammed. I don't know what the hell it was, but we should have gotten you out of there as fast as possible. Instead, you gave a fucking dissertation, and then . . . and then you asked for questions. Aauugh!" Howard looked away from Jason and hit the armrest of the door with his fist. "Jesus Christ, don't ever do that to me again."

"I'm sorry. I didn't understand your signals. I was scared, so I stayed in my comfort zone—talking science."

Howard glared at him for a second, set his jaw, and turned away. The rest of the trip to the safe house was silent.

Howard and Jason microwaved a couple of frozen dinners and ate in their apartment. The immediate danger passed, Howard apologized for losing his temper and admitted that Dietrich's question and slip of the tongue had almost given him a heart attack. They agreed that in the future, if Howard scratched his right ear, Jason was to complete whatever he was up to and be ready to leave in a hurry. If Howard held a finger up and rotated it, Jason was supposed to stop everything and follow Howard's lead.

Howard felt a little easier after checking the messages at his Djibouti office. A message from Dietrich explained that the thug following Al-Mikhafi around the lab was one of Ahmed's bankers, checking up on his investment. Mohammed said that Ahmed had enthusiastically praised Jason's presentation and told him that he'd sent an email to GWR International praising Eric Kessler and asking where he was from.

Dietrich and Mohammed met with Howard and Jason at the safe house later that night. Dietrich apologized for getting caught up in Jason's talk, and Howard explained the hand signals. Mohammed was still rattled. "I was waiting in the lab for you guys, the doors opened and Hadi and Al-Mikhafi walked in with that goon. I was almost paralyzed."

"You looked a bit piqued," Howard said. "But that's over. Tonight, we need to plan our next steps. Now that Al-Mikhafi and Ahmed have reason to associate Jason and me with Mohammed, another attempt to get at the virus sample at the university might put you in danger. We'll wait for them to move it to their camel facility."

Howard reminded them that Mohammed had said that most camels gave birth between November and May. A few of the breeders might have day-old camel calves available in late October or early November. From intercepted telephone transmissions, his agents had identified two of these breeders, had plotted the most likely routes they would use to move the calves to Ahmed's facility, and located suitable places for an ambush.

"Killing a calf will only delay Ahmed a few weeks and cause Al-Mikhafi to increase his security," Dietrich said.

"We aren't planning on killing the calf. We want to delay the delivery to rattle Ahmed. Ahmed is likely to have Mohammed thaw the virus when he thinks the calf is on its way. Jason tells me that delaying the inoculation by 24 hours will reduce the number of viable virus particles by 100 to 1,000-fold, and upsetting his plans by a day could prod Ahmed into making mistakes."

"Good points," Dietrich said, "but they still leave much to chance. How will we know how the calf responds?"

"Ahmed doesn't like to work," Howard said. "He will probably have Mohammed do the daily examinations and sample collections. There are other resources that you don't need to know about, at least not yet."

That caught Jason's attention. He waited until the meeting was over and he and Howard were alone. "What didn't you want to tell Mohammed and Dietrich tonight?"

Howard continued to put chairs and a card table away. "Technically, Ahmed is on our payroll, and so is his contractor. The only difference is that Ahmed hasn't a clue and the contractor is grateful."

"What?" Mouth open, Jason stared at Howard.

Howard moved on to putting things away in the small kitchen. "The contractor got greedy. Ahmed found out and taught him what real greed was like. Poor devil has had to make payments to Ahmed and swallow the cost of a surveillance system installed at the facility. The contractor's allegiance to the jihad was faltering, and he jumped at it when my agents gave him a chance to get his money back and screw Ahmed. We offered to pay all of Ahmed's bribes, provided the surveillance system at no cost, and had our technician install it."

"A surveillance system? You mean cameras?"

"In all the principal rooms at the facility. It has sound, too, but Ahmed doesn't know that. He only gets the video. We get video and audio, and this time, we control the system."

University of Ta'izz
Morning, October 28

Ahmed walked into his lab with a spring in his step, a smile on his face, and a twinkle in his eyes. "Mohammed, we have a calf." He rubbed his hands together in anticipation. "It will be delivered early this afternoon. Can you pack the samples? I'll take them to the camel facility right after lunch and inoculate the calf."

"Do you want me to add dry ice to the pack?"

"No, no. If we put them on wet ice it will give them a chance to thaw slowly as I drive out." Ahmed walked back and forth along a lab bench, inspecting equipment sitting on the bench and fiddling with control dials, too worked up to stop moving or do anything constructive.

"I've waited so long for this. Man, I am so excited. And tonight, to celebrate, I am having dinner with a young lady." He paused and looked at Mohammed. "She is French, a widow, and very liberated." He waggled his eyebrows like Groucho Marx and leered. "I've been celibate too damned long."

So you won't be flogging the dolphin over lunch? Mohammed thought. "Should I pack a single vial or all the samples?"

Ahmed continued to pace, now with his head down and his hands clasped behind his back, almost as though he was trying to look like Groucho. "Pack the semi-purified virus I worked on and two of the fecal samples. I'll give the calf the semi-purified virus and one fecal sample today and the other fecal sample tomorrow. We don't have enough samples to work out a minimum dose." He stopped, smiled, and looked at Mohammed. "We only need to make sure this calf gets enough."

Ahmed headed out of the lab, stopped at the lab door, and turned to Mohammed. "Call me when the samples are ready to go."

Mohammed waited until Ahmed was on the elevator to his office on the third floor before he bolted from the lab and took the stairs two at a time to Dietrich's office. The door was open. Panting, Mohammed knocked on the doorframe and leaned into the office. He and Dietrich had agreed on a code, in case they were overheard or someone had bugged Dietrich's office.

"Dietrich, the game is afoot. Moriarty will be at work shortly after lunch." Mohammed didn't add that he would quit if Dietrich ever asked him to say anything that stupid again.

Dietrich looked up from his reading. "Got it. This is earlier than anticipated. Thanks."

He picked up his phone, called Howard, and left a cryptic message. "The game is afoot. I must cancel Moriarty's one-o'clock meeting this afternoon." Dietrich was sure the imams weren't Sherlock Holmes fans.

Back in the lab, packaging the samples in a Styrofoam cooler didn't take Mohammed long. There were no government rules for packaging, documentation, and transport of viable microbes in Yemen, as there were in developed countries.

Instead of calling, Mohammed carried the package to Ahmed's office. Mohammed never called during the noon hour if he could visit Ahmed's office. Interrupting Ahmed's porn break and embarrassing him was too much fun. On one of his surprise visits he'd gotten a chance to see what Ahmed was watching. He always hoped to get lucky again, although usually he only got to hear the cheesy soundtrack and theatrical moans.

He was disappointed today. Ahmed was reading up on coronavirus animal studies when Mohammed walked in. "Here you go. Vials packed on ice packs."

Ahmed thanked him and went back to his reading.

Howard called his agents immediately after receiving Dietrich's message. Each had selected a section of road where an accident could be arranged. They didn't want anything serious—something more than a fender-bender but less than serious injuries.

Shortly after nine o'clock in the morning, Howard received word of unusual activity at one of the camel breeding establishments. Handlers had separated a day-old calf from its mother and a pale green pickup truck with tall panels enclosing the back had arrived. The agent told Howard where the accident would take place and described where Howard should be for his part in it.

Howard rolled out a map of Ta'izz and its outskirts on the dining room table at the apartment and studied the stretch of road where the accident would occur. Jason looked on as Howard explained the plans. "My agent will follow the truck until it approaches a section of road under repair. He will pass the truck and be directly in front of it through the construction zone." Howard pointed to a straight section of four-lane limited-access highway on the map. "Traffic will be limited to two lanes because of the repairs. Passing isn't allowed in the construction zone, so a couple of cars will be able to slow traffic to thirty miles per hour."

Howard smiled at Jason. "Traffic will be tied up. That's when my man will hit the brakes and be rear-ended by the truck. The car will be carrying pipes sticking out of the trunk. The trunk has been reinforced so the pipes can't be pushed into the car's back seat. The pipes will puncture the truck's radiator, or at least it will look like they do. I'll guarantee a tire will blow out and the radiator will leak."

"The local drivers are nuts. How can you assume the truck won't pass on one side or the other or be sure these idiots will slow down?"

"Because my second associate will be driving a few cars ahead of our first car and I'm damned good with my rifle." Howard nodded toward a metal and plastic case Jason had been wondering about.

Howard drew a line on the map parallel to the road. "There's a low ridge topped by brush or a hedge about one hundred fifty yards from the road. The rifle is a Colt LE6940, similar to an AR-15. I'll use .223 pistol cartridges. They're accurate at that range, and the rifle and bullets are quiet."

Jason's face showed his confusion. "Quiet bullets?"

"Pistol rounds are subsonic. You can't use a silencer with rifle rounds and the bullets break the sound barrier. That would cause a small sonic boom that the drivers would hear."

That was more information on guns than Jason was interested in. He was more concerned about the Yemeni drivers. "These drivers are still nuts."

"If anybody pulls out to pass, at least one of them will have a flat tire, too." Howard nodded toward his rifle case again. "It could take hours to straighten out the traffic and the rest will go as planned."

Howard looked at his watch. "We'd best change clothes and get moving. I want to be in place at least a half-hour before our target shows up."

Jason and Howard were in light camo jackets and ops camo pants, peering from bushes overlooking the highway an hour later. Howard was lying on the ground, Jason kneeling beside him. Below and one hundred fifty yards ahead of them, light traffic whizzed through the two-lane construction zone as though it were a NASCAR track. Howard put a short two-legged support on the rifle barrel, mounted the scope on the rifle, and rested the rifle on the ground in front of him, the barrel protruding slightly from under an acacia hedge. He chose a section of highway and sighted in through his scope after estimating the distance with a pair of binoculars and the wind by checking a strip of bright cloth his agents had tied to a fence near the highway. "Now we wait," he told Jason. "Let me know, very quietly, if you see a pale green pickup with a camel calf in the back or if anyone is coming up behind us."

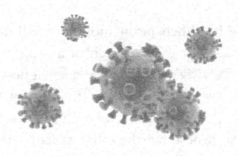

CHAPTER 25

A green pickup rolled down the highway toward Howard and Jason. By chance, the car tailing the pickup was a similar shade of faded green. The air was still and the day becoming uncomfortably warm and humid. The rainy season was approaching.

Sweat ran down Howard's face and got in his eyes. He stretched his right arm and moved his shoulder to ease the stiffness in the arm. Jason waived a hand at mosquitos buzzing about his ears and leaned forward through the brush. Moments later, the green car passed the green pickup and entered the construction zone. Jason tapped Howard on the shoulder and whispered that the camel truck was approaching the target zone and slowing down.

Howard took a deep breath and sighted on the truck's grill. Looking through the scope, he put the fourth mark to the right of the crosshairs and one dash up on the center of the grill to allow for the truck's speed and the drop of the bullet shooting at a downward angle. He slowly put pressure on the trigger as Jason leaned further into the bushes to improve his view and whispered, "Oops."

The left lens housing of Jason's binoculars had pushed a small

branch to one side. When Jason moved to follow the truck, the
branch snapped back. It wasn't much of a snap, but the snapping
branch hit a smaller twig and dislodged a small nest of wasps.

Jason looked down in time to see the nest hit the hard-packed
dirt at the base of the brush, a few inches to Howard's right.

It was not a large nest, but the inhabitants made up in zeal what
they lacked in number. Howard heard Jason's whisper, but he was
concentrating on the pickup. The "oops" didn't register until two
wasps got under the collar of his shirt and several attacked his hands,
while another crawled into his left ear. By then Jason was gyrating
wildly and slapping at wasps attacking his arms and face.

Howard did what he could to maintain his aim on the truck, but
the furious buzzing and stabbing pain of the stings shredded his
concentration. Seeing a green fender and tire in his scope, he shot
the left front tire of his associate's car. The tire blew; the car lurched
into oncoming traffic and struck a full sized van. The van skidded
sideways into the pickup's lane, forcing it into the lane under repair.
The pickup blew a tire on a spike of exposed rebar and wobbled into
the shallow ditch on the right. The driver and camel were shaken,
not stirred, and suffered only slight bruises.

On the highway, brakes squealed, glass shattered, and sheet
metal crinkled in slow motion as trucks, buses, and vans traveling
in both directions tossed compact cars back and forth in a game of
automotive dodge ball. Jason and Howard didn't stay to admire their
handiwork, but ran as fast as they could toward Howard's Santa Fe.

A shepherd watching his sheep nibble at the few green sprouts
and thorny shrubs available noticed Jason and Howard running,
jumping, and waving their arms wildly. He saw Howard's rifle and
shook his head. With the insurgency gaining strength in the area,
even lunatics were carrying firearms.

Safely in the Santa Fe, Howard peered between swollen eyelids at Jason. "Oops?"

Howard's face and eyelids were so swollen Jason wondered how he could see. Jason averted his eyes and hung his head. "I'm sorry. I didn't see—"

Howard held his hand up. "Later," he said, and forced himself to concentrate on their mission. "We still have a job to do. We have time to get to Ahmed's facility before the calf arrives."

Howard stopped at a store to get ice. With time to spare, they cold-packed their stings in the parked vehicle until Howard could see well enough to drive. He skirted the edge of Ta'izz and drove through the countryside to a spot beside a pile of boulders clustered around a weathered sandstone monolith, roughly thirty feet tall, fifty feet long, and fifteen feet wide.

It was noon, and there would be no shade on the west side of the monolith where they were parked. They opened their doors to catch what breeze there was, took bottles of water out of a cooler in the back seat, and continued to cold-pack their swollen wounds. Ice pack pressed to his ear, Howard opened a laptop and tapped on the keys until he could see the interior of the lab at the camel facility. He turned on the audio and flipped through the feed from the other cameras. Nothing stirred or made a sound in the building.

"We are a hundred yards behind Ahmed's facility and on the edge of an old race course they used for training. Get your binoculars and follow me."

Howard closed his laptop, put it in its case, and slung it over his shoulder. Together, Jason and Howard climbed to the top of the monolith, staying in shadows below the crest until they reached a ledge about four feet below the crest. Howard took his binoculars from their case, and crawled up the slope to the crest on his stomach. Jason did the same. Fifty yards in front of them was a chain link fence. The fence surrounded a complex of two buildings and a guard shack. The building closest to them was a metal shed, roughly forty feet long and thirty feet wide. Ten yards beyond that was a long, white building, about one hundred fifty feet long and forty feet wide. What looked like air handling equipment sat on the roof at the far end of the building.

The long building was set at an angle to them, allowing a view of one side and the rear. A concrete pad ran the width of the rear of the building, with a loading dock in front of a set of double doors on the right.

"My sources say the long building is the barn," Howard said. "The short building is open on the east. It has a pen for a few milking goats and a hut for milking equipment in half the building. Feed for the goats takes up the rest."

"What about feed for the camel calf?" Jason asked.

"That's what the milking goats are for."

Jason examined the length of the barn with his binoculars. "Looks like they've closed off doors and windows on the side of the barn, except for one door and a couple of windows on the far end."

"The lab is on the far end," Howard said. "If you follow the gravel road from the loading dock on the west end of the barn to the lab and the fence farthest from us, you'll see the guard shack. It's staffed at all times. With nothing but bugs and the goat's caretakers to watch, the guards have gotten complacent and sloppy."

Jason focused his binoculars on the guard shack and the gate, two hundred yards from where he lay. A rutted private road continued a hundred yards past a mosque to a gravel road running north and south to a village a hundred yards down the road. A blacktop road was a half-mile to the south.

"Do the guards have monitors? Do they get the feed from the cameras?" Jason asked.

"They can see the feed from the lab and the clean hallway."

Howard pointed to the gate in the cyclone fence nearest them.

The gate blocked a path leading from the rear of the barn toward the old racetrack.

"Focus on the gate near us, directly behind the shed. It was used to bring the camels to this practice track, but no one uses it now. It's locked and alarmed electronically, or at least Ahmed thinks it is."

Jason glanced at Howard, pointed the binoculars at the gate, and focused.

"There's a camera aimed at the gate. The contractor disabled it a week ago and no one seems to have noticed. An alarm was installed on the gate by Ahmed's contractor. At my suggestion, the alarm was set to be hypersensitive. It went off at all hours, day and night. It took the contractor several return trips to 'fix' the problem. He disconnected the alarm and the lock when he disabled the camera. Ahmed and the guards were so happy to have peace and quiet that they didn't test it."

"And the militia?" Jason asked.

"Al-Mikhafi spent too much money on the barn. My sources said the private militia that's supposed to guard the place had to be reduced. There's only one guard on duty at a time, and by this time of day he's usually sleeping in the guard shack. The militia on call lives in the town about three hundred yards past the facility's driveway. That was cut back to only a couple of people on reserve at a time. It will take three to five minutes for them to get here, if Ahmed sounds an alarm and they are ready to go. My people tell me they haven't had any practice drills, so they're likely to be slow."

Jason thought he hadn't had any practice drills, either. "What's the plan?" he asked.

"You will have to do this. You know what the dangerous sample looks like and how it can be destroyed. The facility is empty now—no camels, no people, except the sleeping guard in the shack and an animal caretaker sleeping in the feed shed. You'll have to work your way down to the gate and get into the facility before the camel

arrives. You should have thirty minutes to an hour before Ahmed
arrives. Find a place to hide near the lab, preferably inside. I'll keep
watch on the feed from the surveillance cameras and tell you when
Ahmed brings the samples and when no one is in the lab."

"How?"

"Radio. I've got two headsets." Howard pulled a head set and
battery case out of the computer case and handed it to Jason. "Put
it on, but keep the volume down. You don't want Ahmed to hear
anything if I call at the wrong time."

Ta'izz
1:15 P.M., October 28

Ahmed had to stay close to the speed limit in the city, but his foot
became heavy and he ignored the limit once he was on the highway.
Humming a tune, tapping out the rhythm on the dashboard and
steering wheel, Ahmed was pumped.

He took chances driving down the slope of the foothills, passing
cars, dodging trucks, and swerving around the few donkey carts
on the roads. He rounded a blind corner and saw a line of camels
leisurely crossing the road. Ahmed slammed on his breaks; his
car skidded sideways and almost left the road. Just before he slid
broadside into the camels, Ahmed took his foot off the brakes and
turned the steering wheel to the left. The car fishtailed safely past the
last camel in line.

Ahmed pulled off the road, shaking. He stayed there until his
heart rate returned to normal and he could control his hands. His
driving was conservative the rest of the way to the camel facility.

On a desolate stretch of highway with only a small mosque, dried
brush, and sand in sight, he turned onto a dirt road. He bounced over
the road for a hundred yards, a rooster tail of dust rising behind his

car—a measure of how parched the soil was, not an indication of speed. He stopped at a guard shack at the gate of the chain link fence. The guard was asleep, a lone fly buzzing around his head.

Ahmed honked his horn; the guard roused himself, recognized Ahmed and opened the gate. Ahmed drove another forty feet, now on gravel, and parked at the door of the newly remodeled lab. He carried the cooler into the lab and unloaded the samples. Each was in a clear plastic tube the size of a marking pen. He tipped them slightly one way and another. They weren't thawed yet, so he put the wire rack holding the samples on a lab bench and waited for them to thaw. The calf had not yet arrived.

Ahmed walked through the facility, making sure all was in readiness. When he'd checked everything twice, he paced back and forth, periodically checking the samples to see if they were thawed. It took the samples most of an hour to thaw.

He placed the wire rack with the samples in the refrigerator, checked his watch, and calculated he would have over an hour to get ready for his date if the truck arrived soon.

Howard waited until Ahmed came out of the lab and scanned the road for the truck. "Ahmed's here. He's outside now, seems to be watching the road. Where are you?"

"I'm in a broom closet, in a hallway just off the lab. Should be safe—I can't picture Ahmed doing any cleaning up."

"What is your plan?"

"He will keep the sample refrigerated until—"

"Yeah," Howard said. "I saw him carry a cooler into the lab."

"Tell me when Ahmed is busy outside of the lab. I don't want to chance him walking in on me."

"I'll let you know when the camel gets here. That should keep him busy for a few minutes."

"Okay. I'll grab the sample then. I'll dump it in one of his jugs of disinfectant and make up a dummy sample in the same tube."

By three o'clock, Ahmed had worked up a sweat, pacing back and forth in front of the lab. He entered the air-conditioned lab and called the truck driver. "Where in the name of all that is holy have you gone with my camel?"

"Just getting out of a massive traffic pile-up," the driver said. He described how he'd been forced off the road and his tire blew. That was repaired and the police and tow trucks had finally cleared some of the road. He would be late, but he would deliver the camel calf that afternoon.

Ahmed called the driver again at four o'clock. "Where are you?" he screamed into the phone.

"I've made it around Ta'izz and I'm going as fast as I safely can. There are crazy people on the roads today."

When Ahmed pressed him to drive faster, the driver accused Ahmed of sexually molesting lame donkeys in public.

At four fifteen, Howard radioed Jason that the animal caretaker was leaving the facility. Ninety minutes later, he radioed Jason again. "A pale green pickup is approaching the guard shack. Looks like our camel is finally here."

"Where is Ahmed?"

"He's opening the door by the loading dock at the other end of the facility."

"Time for me to move. Let me know if you see him coming toward the lab."

While Howard and Ahmed watched the driver back the truck up to the loading dock, Jason slipped out of the broom closet. He took a wire rack of samples out of the refrigerator and set it on the lab bench. There were ten samples, but none of them looked as they had when he and Ann had taken them and put them in their freezer. Each was now mixed with liquid in a fifteen-mL plastic centrifuge tube with a blue plastic screw-on cap.

One by one, Jason picked up the samples and tried to read Mohammed's labels. Mohammed's handwriting was even worse than Ann's. On the eighth sample he examined, the handwriting was different and the date on the sample was July 17. All the other samples had been mixed with the liquid buffer and dated that morning, October 28. Jason set the July sample aside and put the rest back in the refrigerator.

Jason began opening the cabinet doors beneath the lab bench. Most of the cabinets were empty. He worked down the row of cabinets until he came to a sink set in the laboratory counter. Under it, he found a gallon of household bleach and a gallon of chlorhexidine, a blue disinfectant. He grabbed the gallon jug of bleach and tried to read the label. It was in Arabic. He opened the jug, sniffed, and set the jug in the sink.

"Where is Ahmed now?" Jason asked.

"I think they are putting the calf into the isolation room. Wait a sec—yeah. They are all in the isolation room now."

Jason unscrewed the caps on the jug of bleach and the test tube and dumped the sample into the jug. He gave the jug a swirl, rinsed the sample vial with straight bleach, and dumped the rinse back into the jug of bleach.

"What are they doing now?" he asked Howard.

"Ahmed completed his exam of the camel and started an argument with the driver. They just left the isolation room. I can't see them now."

Jason tried to move faster. The timing was going to be close. He rinsed the sample vial with water and filled it again with water. He was looking in cabinets again when Howard called.

"The pickup is leaving. Ahmed has left the loading dock, headed toward you. You've got maybe two minutes."

Jason nodded, then remembered Howard couldn't see him if he was watching the camera feed from the hallway Ahmed was in. "Understood."

In the next cabinet he opened, Jason found a fifty-pound bag of a commercial milk replacer used to feed calves if milk wasn't available. He took a pinch and dumped it into the sample vial, screwed the cap on, and replaced it in the refrigerator. As he headed toward his exit door, he heard Ahmed's hand make contact with the lab door. Only the door separated him from Ahmed and Jason had a fraction of a second to act. He stepped behind the door as it swung open.

Ahmed swept into the lab and marched to the refrigerator. He didn't see Jason slip out around the door as it swung shut. Something odd about the noise of the door closing, possibly Jason's footsteps, made Ahmed turn and look at the door, but Jason was already out of the lab and moving down the hallway.

Jason trotted down the hallway, slowing only to check the doors of animal rooms. He found a door that wasn't locked and stepped into the room. With his back to the room, he carefully closed the door before turning around. A neonatal camel, all legs and appetite, nuzzled his chest, looking for a teat to suckle.

With the caretaker gone, Ahmed had to feed and inoculate the calf himself. He looked at the clock. It was five after six. He decided not to change clothes or shower as required by his S.O.P. He put on Tyveks, plastic coveralls, over his street clothes. He knew Tyveks weren't waterproof, but they repelled water. That was close enough for him tonight.

He put on boots, latex gloves, goggles, and a clear faceplate, but the goggles and faceplate became fogged with the slightest exertion. *Shit. I don't have time for these. I'm the director here. I set the rules,* he thought, and tossed the goggles and faceplate and put on a surgical mask. He decided that would be good enough. He would just be careful not to splash anything on his face. Satisfied with his abbreviated precautions, he hustled off to feed the calf.

Ahmed had managed to get a degree in veterinary medicine in Pakistan and complete a Ph.D. program in veterinary microbiology in the US without ever feeding a calf, bovine, or camel. Ahmed knew his staff lacked even a high-school education. If those ignorant jerks could feed a baby camel, he reasoned, it would be simple for a man with advanced degrees. There were only three steps to complete: warm goat milk in the microwave, stick a nipple in the stupid camel's mouth, and wait.

Ahmed warmed up two liters of goat's milk and put it in a large bottle with a camel-sized nipple, an inch wide and four inches long. He marched down the clean hallway to the isolation room.

Howard radioed Jason. "What the hell are you doing in the camel room? Ahmed is coming down the hallway to feed the calf. Get out through the other door."

The camel calf was ravenous. It was turning his shirt into a sodden mess as it tried to suckle. Jason pushed the calf away and kept moving as he answered Howard. "I'm leaving, if I can get this beast out of my way."

The calf tried again for some nourishment. "Ouch! Damn you." Jason slapped the calf lightly on the nose and gained enough time to scramble through the door to the dirty hallway. He swung the door shut, but the calf was trying to get its head through. The calf heard Ahmed opening the other door and trotted to that door as Ahmed entered. The calf, beside herself with hunger, assaulted Ahmed and gave Jason a moment of peace to close and latch the door.

"I'm in the dirty hallway. Which way to the exit?" Jason radioed Howard in a whisper.

"Go to your right, down the hallway, follow the hallway around a corner and take the only door to your left. That'll put you outside."

"Thanks."

"What was the 'ouch' I heard just before Ahmed came in?"

"Damned calf quit sucking on my shirt and grabbed my ear. Hurt like hell. Okay, found the door. I'm out."

Howard watched Jason slip through the back gate a couple of minutes later.

Lambs and calves reach as high as they can for their mother's teats, 'cause that's where those things are in nature. A female camel has long legs, and their calves have similar legs and very long necks.

Ahmed tried holding the nipple bottle where it was convenient for Ahmed—waist high. The calf sucked on his shirt and chewed on his left nipple. Ahmed gave a yelp, shoved the calf's head away from him, and tried to interest the calf in sucking lower. The calf obstinately refused to adjust her ancient instincts, and went for his ear.

Ahmed thought of the time and his date, and held the bottle shoulder-high, where the calf was attempting to suckle. That worked for several pulls on the rubber teat. Ahmed thought he was home free, but the calf got the nipple bent at an angle that shut off the flow of milk. The calf followed instinct and butted the nipple bottle. A camel cow would have interpreted the butt as gentle and adjusted appropriately, but Ahmed and the nipple bottle were less forgiving. Ahmed yelled at the calf. The nipple pulled off the bottle; the milk gushed out, ran down Ahmed's arm and soaked through his coveralls. It soaked through his shirt, onto his new silk tie, and drained off the tie down his pants.

Enraged, Ahmed batted the calf in the head with his fist, a mistake a ten-year-old farm kid would never make. Ruminants and their relatives may not have big brains, but even their babies have world-class skulls. Ahmed swore, dropped the nipple bottle, and held his throbbing hand between his knees. If the calf thought of anything other than her empty stomach, it would have been something like "slow learner."

Jason sprinted from the back gate to Howard's car. Howard wasn't there. He crawled part way up the rocky mound, saw Howard looking at his lap, and called softly to him.

Instead of coming down, Howard motioned him to come up. Jason crawled next to Howard a minute later. Panting, Jason said, "Let's get the fuck out of here."

Howard shook his head and laughed. "Un-unh. You've got to see this. I'm recording Ahmed feeding the calf."

Ahmed picked up the empty nipple bottle and stomped out of the isolation room through the wrong door, contaminating the clean hallway. He marched back to the lab, pulled a frozen bottle of goat milk from the freezer, and put it in the microwave to thaw. While he waited, he soaked his rapidly swelling hand in cold water.

On the next bottle, the calf gave Ahmed a master course in how to feed her properly. Her student was stubborn and prone to tantrums. A determined teacher, she had Ahmed trained within an hour. But just when things were going well, Ahmed got sloppy. She soaked him with warm milk again, and, still hungry, chased him around the room until he escaped through the door.

Ahmed's clothes, from his pants to his socks, were soaked through with goat's milk. His pants and shirt clung to him. His shoes squished as he walked. In the ninety-degree heat, he was getting a little ripe even for the calf to maintain a good appetite. He swore as he walked down the hallway to the lab, where he warmed up two hundred milliliters of goat's milk.

Ahmed looked at the notebook and saw he was supposed to reserve two of the tubes to give the calf another dose tomorrow morning. He had thawed all the tubes. Knowing the sample virus wasn't stable after thawing and might not be effective tomorrow, he dumped all of the viral samples into the milk.

He made a mental note to send Mohammed out tomorrow morning with two more vials of samples. He put the nipple on the bottle and stomped back to the isolation room, the squish of his milk-logged socks providing a counterpoint to the slap of the wet shoes on the floor.

On the way, he remembered how the calf had pulled the nipple off the bottle—twice. He realized he'd put all of his prepared samples in this bottle. Lose it, and he'd have to drive back to the university, thaw and dilute more samples, and return. He cringed as he calculated the lost time. "Spill this, and it will be two more hours shot to inoculate the little bitch," he muttered.

This time, Ahmed carefully did everything as the calf had taught him. The calf drank all but a few ounces of the milk and virus mixture. Satiated and apparently in a celebratory mood, the calf decided to share. She spit the remainder of the milk back in Ahmed's face.

Startled, Ahmed wiped the milk off his face, sprayed a paper towel with isopropyl alcohol, wiped off his face, and decided that would be clean enough. He completed the day's study records and put the folder on a high shelf he was sure the calf couldn't reach.

Back in the lab, he wearily took off his coveralls, stuffed them in a trash barrel in the dirty hallway, and walked back to the showers.

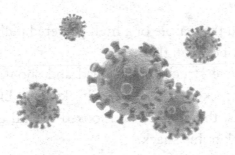

CHAPTER 26

In the guard shack, two flies were drawn to a drop of mucous hanging from the nostrils of the guard. They landed near it and began to feed, tickling his nose. The guard awoke. He sneezed, wiped his nose on his sleeve, and looked at the time. His replacement for the night shift was late.

He stretched and stepped out of the shack, scanning the drive and road for headlights. There were no cars in sight. He cursed and turned to walk toward the lab.

Howard and Jason stood on the crest of the monolith, outlined by the setting sun. Howard picked up his computer and they walked and crawled down to the ledge. On the ledge, their heads and shoulders were still visible over the crest.

The guard saw both Howard and Jason standing on the rock. No one was supposed to be on the old practice track. Confused, he pulled out a pair of binoculars and looked again. Two clean shaven men in western dress. The guard ducked into the guard shack, grabbed his rifle, and fired three shots at them.

The first bullet hit the rocky crest, blowing chunks of rock and gravel at Howard and Jason. An instant later, they heard the report of the first shot and the warble of a high-powered bullet as the second bullet cut the air between them.

Both men were struck in the head and shoulders as the next shell turned the rock into shrapnel. Shocked and bleeding from the shower of stones, they turned and looked behind them. The guard was hustling back to his shack.

"The car, fast," Howard yelled, and he hopped from the ledge to a boulder and then to another, descending as rapidly as he could. Jason was seconds behind him.

They scrambled into the Santa Fe. Howard started the car, slammed it into four-wheel drive, and drove south on a rutted track leading to the paved road. The trail was barely visible in the failing light, and the ruts and holes made it dangerous to do over twenty-five miles an hour.

Jason peered out of the windshield, trying to see their previous tracks, which was difficult because he was being jounced about in the car. "Can you . . . turn the lights . . . on?" he asked.

Even with his seat belt on and holding onto the steering wheel with both hands, Howard was also being thrown about. "The . . . guard will call . . . the militia. Headlights . . . off-road, will . . . be a goddamned beacon for them. We'll . . . be on the road shortly and can make . . . better time."

A pair of headlights crossed their path and raced north twenty yards ahead of them. "There's the . . . road. Ta'izz is . . . south . . . and east, the village . . . militia to . . . north," Howard said as they bounced over a pair of deep ruts. "When we . . . get on the road, open . . . the box sitting behind your seat. It . . . has smaller boxes . . . in it. Be ready to hand me . . . hand four or five, and have that . . . many ready for yourself."

A moment later, they drove onto the road and turned south toward Ta'izz. Howard opened the console between them and handed Jason a pocketknife to open the box behind him. The Santa

Fe accelerated through the dark as Jason cut the tape, opened the box and put smaller boxes, each weighing two or three pounds, on the console between them.

Jason glanced behind them. "Headlights coming onto the road from the direction of the town." He watched the headlights for a moment. "They're gaining on us."

Howard turned on the headlights, floored the accelerator, and lowered his window.

"If you've got the boxes up here, sit down and buckle up," Howard said. "Roll down your window and do as I do. Toss the boxes up and to the rear."

Howard picked up one of the boxes, held it out of the car window, and threw it up and toward the center of the road. A moment later he threw another and Jason tossed his first.

Jason turned to watch the headlights following them. They still seemed to be drawing closer. Muzzle flashes appeared above the left headlight and something thudded on the roof of the SUV. Seconds later, the back window of the Santa Fe shattered.

"They're shooting at us. What were the boxes for?" Jason asked.

"Watch them," Howard said. "If they continue to gain on us, toss a few more boxes out."

Jason turned and watched. The headlights wobbled, lurched left, then right before leaving the road and coming to a stop.

"Looks like they're in the ditch, stopped. What's in the boxes?"

"A very old and time-tested device," Howard said. "Caltrops. They go back to Alexander the Great, I believe. Take a look."

Jason pulled the top off one of the small boxes still in his lap. Too dark to see, he reached gingerly into the box and felt dozens of sharp points. He pulled one out and held it to the light. It looked like an oversized game piece for the kid's game of Jacks, but the ends of each prong were sharp, rather than rounded.

"Neat. An all-purpose tire shredder."

The facility guard had not kept Ahmed in the loop. Unaware that Howard and Jason had been spotted and chased, Ahmed put his stinking street clothes in a plastic bag and put on a clean pair of surgical scrubs for the drive back to his apartment.

He slowed down a bit while he pulled his cell phone out, called his date, and apologized. He would be two hours late. While he explained his delay, a white Santa Fe streaked past him, its broken rear window caught briefly in his headlights. "Damned rich kids," he muttered, and increased his speed to one hundred and ten kilometers per hour.

At his apartment, Ahmed showered, changed, and drove to an upscale apartment complex to pick up his date. He buzzed her apartment and announced his arrival. She made him wait ten minutes before she met him at the door. Although she was French, her clothing was an attractive mix of European and local styles. Her almost transparent golden silk hijab allowed careful observers to see that her dark blue, mid-length dress had a daring neckline.

Ahmed looked only at his watch. "We will have to hurry or lose our table. Was the elevator working?" he asked as he walked her to his car.

She looked confused. "There are no problems with the elevator. Why do you ask?"

He opened the door to his car for her. "Then what took you so long?"

Her mouth dropped open. She glared at him but said nothing.

As they drove, Ahmed told her how expensive his car was, how young he was to be a full professor, and how lucky the university was to have him.

She didn't respond. Didn't even look at him.

He moved on to a monologue about his many accomplishments

in the medical sciences and his substantial income. By the time he parked the car at the restaurant, his review of all he had to offer a woman had improved Ahmed's mood; it did not appear to have affected hers.

He ate most of the *buraik*, an appetizer of puff pastries stuffed with minced meat, and she didn't care for the *shorbat addas* (lentil soup) he ordered for them, without consulting her. He didn't ask her preference when he ordered them both *hanid*, spiced lamb with banana leaves, and *fasaulia*, a dish of beans, tomatoes, onions, garlic, and hot peppers.

She answered direct questions, but her answers became ever shorter as the night wore on. After a long description of one of his imaginary triumphs, Ahmed asked her if she thought he had handled the situation well.

She didn't answer.

He talked about himself and stared at her chest through most of the meal. He tried to hold her hand as they waited for the valet to bring Ahmed's car, but she switched the little black bag she carried to the hand next to him.

Ahmed had spent more on the dinner than he could easily afford. Convinced that he deserved compensation in return, he parked in a dark corner of the parking lot behind her apartment complex. With no small talk or subtlety, he put an arm around her shoulders, and launched himself at her.

She scrambled out of the car. "Fuck off, you pig," she hissed in French, and walked quickly toward her apartment building.

He caught up with her, grabbed her arm, and forced her to turn toward him. He didn't know what hit him when she whipped around and used the small clutch she carried, a clutch with a role of ten rial coins in it, to clobber him in the eye. She followed up with a knee to Ahmed's crotch, but he blocked it with his thigh.

That was enough for Ahmed. He retreated to his car as the young lady ran to the light and the apartment entrance.

Howard and Jason were over the Gulf of Aden in a small plane beginning the descent to the French military airport next to Camp Lemonnier in Djibouti when Ahmed arrived back at his apartment, alone.

Ta'izz
October 29

Jason and Howard both slept late. They had brunch together and were in Howard's office at the US embassy writing their report by one thirty in the afternoon. The rough draft completed, Howard called the military airport as Jason stood and stretched.

Howard held the phone away from his face. "There's a military flight to the States you can catch if you hurry. It leaves at four thirty. I can give you a ride to Lemonnier and get you a connecting flight to St. Paul while you're outbound."

Jason nodded, and Howard told the airport to hold a seat for him.

The camel calf was in marvelous health, although Ahmed kept running from his office to the men's room. He had diarrhea, possibly from the BCV spit in his face. He sent Mohammed out to collect his samples and was crushed to learn that the insufferable beast was the picture of health. He assuaged his disappointment by chewing out Mohammed for an imagined safety infraction.

Ahmed called the camel facility in the afternoon, hoping to hear the calf had at least developed diarrhea. The wretched beast remained perversely healthy.

Ta'izz
October 31

Ahmed's gut was under control, but the camel calf was still healthy. Mohammed collected samples the following day, escorted by a graduate student from Al-Mikhafi's lab. The other student helped Mohammed again the next day, and on their return from the camel facility, Dietrich called Mohammed to his office.

Dietrich's door, as usual, was open. Mohammed knocked on the doorframe. Dietrich asked him to close the door and take a seat.

"Professor Ahmed apparently has secured additional funding," Dietrich said. "It comes through Dr. Al-Mikhafi's lab. You can concentrate on writing your thesis full time now."

"I won't be working for Ahmed?" Mohammed asked. A slow smile spread across his face.

"Correct. From what I understand, Dr. Al-Mikhafi has taken control of the keys to the minus-seventy freezer in Professor Ahmed's lab and will be responsible for the samples you've collected."

Mohammed frowned. Why was Dietrich being so careful to use academic titles? He leaned closer to Dietrich, and whispered, "Doesn't Al-Mikhafi trust me?"

Dietrich shook his head. He did not whisper "No. I suspect there is concern about Professor Ahmed's lack of experience in virology." Dietrich put a finger to his lips. "This is your chance to finish your thesis early. Get to it, and I'll see if we can move your thesis defense up."

"Could—"

Dietrich shook his head vigorously and put his finger to his lips again. "Go back to your office and start writing. You can leave my door open." Dietrich motioned with his hands, shooing him out.

He's afraid his office is bugged, Mohammed thought and left the office without finishing his question.

That evening Dietrich sent an email to his uncle Al in Brussels. He pulled his car over on the way home and called Howard. He told him that the camel calf was healthy and Ahmed had been unable to detect any virus in the samples that had been collected.

"So our worries are over?" Howard asked.

"I think so, but ask Jason. Al-Mikhafi brought another graduate student into the lab, a kid with experience in virology. I suspect he's making arrangements to have the samples tested again. They may still come up with the hybrid virus, but they'll only find it by growing it in cell culture. Do that and it will be harmless."

In the following week, video and audio feeds from the facility, picked up by Howard's agents, showed that the camel calf was in wonderful health. The caretakers loved their darling calf, and she loved anyone who would bring another bottle of goat's milk.

The caretaker called Al-Mikhafi several days later and asked if he could sell the calf to his brother, who had a string of racing camels. Al-Mikhafi was desperate to find ways to recoup some of the cost of Ahmed's experiments before he had to talk to his gun-loving bankers. He held out for the best price he could get for the calf.

Ahmed listened to Al-Mikhafi and turned white. He gripped the arms of his chair. "How did you hear this?"

Al-Mikhafi paced behind his desk. "My contact met me here and we discussed what happened. He asked me if he could use my office. I let him, but I left a cellphone on my desk to record his side of the conversation." Al-Mikhafi stopped his pacing and looked at Ahmed. "These guys are furious about the money we spent. They're going to make an example of you."

"What about you?"

"They didn't mention my name, but I'll attend a science symposium in Poland and take my time coming back. Give them time to cool off." He sat at his desk and leaned forward. "I'd suggest you get out of the Middle-East for a couple of years. They may be watching your apartment now. If they are, they could be watching the airport and major roads, too."

Shaken, Ahmed left the university and drove to his apartment. He parked a block away in an alley, sat in a coffee shop across from his apartment building, and watched the street. A Toyota pickup with two men in it was parked fifty feet from the entrance to his apartment. From where they sat, they had a clear view of the apartment's entrance. Ahmed sipped his coffee and had another cup. The men didn't move.

Ahmed left the coffee shop by the back door and walked down the alley to his car. He couldn't use the airport—it would be watched. He'd have to be careful about main roads—Al-Mikhafi had said they'd watch those, too. About the only contacts he had in the countryside were the camel breeders he'd called. The list was still in his briefcase, next to him in the car. *It's the start of a plan,* he thought.

He used the ATM at a hotel that catered to Europeans and emptied his bank accounts. On his way out of town, he stopped at a store and bought two cases of bottled water.

St. Paul
Evening, October 31

Jason let himself into his apartment and looked for Ann. He heard the shower going as he tiptoed past the bathroom. Jason moved on down the hall and poked his head into the nursery. A nightlight was sufficient to see Samantha Ann, sleeping peacefully. He moved to pick her up and decided not to. *Ann might have worked a long time to get her to sleep,* he thought. Like many men his age, Jason was timid about picking up babies. He stood at the crib admiring his daughter until Ann put a hand on his shoulder.

They talked for hours, Jason eager to know how Ann and Samantha were doing, Ann desperate to talk to an adult. "When do you have to go back?" she asked.

He kissed her. "Never. It's over. All the samples we know of have been destroyed. The camel calf didn't get sick."

North Of Ta'izz
November 1

Ahmed looked for a place with a little shade but no trees to lure small mammals and the snakes that ate them. He'd been careful about snakes and getting close to snake habitat ever since his encounter with the black mamba in Djibouti. Yemen didn't have mambas, but it had cobras, adders, and vipers.

He spotted a shady place beneath a high rocky cliff. The trail ran through the shadow cast by the rock, so Ahmed didn't have to fight with his camel to get to it. He'd traded his car early that morning for a map of trails and back roads between Ta'izz and Ibb, a camel, and all the tack necessary to ride it. The man swore this camel was the best choice; it was calm, it was well trained, and it had been raised near Ibb. It would find Ibb in a blinding sandstorm.

Ahmed lost whatever faith in humanity he might have had within the first hour of riding the beast. It complained loudly whenever Ahmed tried to urge it forward any faster than a leisurely walk. It ignored his reining until Ahmed pulled hard on the reins. The only thing good about it was that it stuck to the trail he was on with no guidance from him.

Ahmed reined the camel to a stop. He looked around—rocks, sand, dirt, and a few straggly shrubs of some sort about fifty feet away. Good. No snakes.

"Koosh, koosh," Ahmed said loudly, and waited for the camel to lower itself to the ground so he could get off and give his butt a rest.

The camel ignored him. He sighed, reached below him to a case of water bottles strapped to the camel, and wrenched one free. He guzzled the bottle and tossed it away.

"Koosh, damn you, Koosh," he muttered. The camel slowly dropped to the ground.

Ahmed dismounted and walked back and forth beside the beast, trying to get feeling in his numb backside. He stretched, rubbed his butt with both hands, and opened a pack in back of the saddle. He sorted through packages of food wrapped in paper and removed a piece of flat bread folded over a slice of spiced grilled chicken. He wondered if it was still safe to eat, but hunger overcame concern.

It was mid-afternoon, and he guessed he was still thirty miles from Ibb, a city of 160,000. From there he would take a bus to Hodeidah and its airport. After that, he'd wing it. He'd take whatever plane he could get to a city north of the Mediterranean or in the Northwest Frontier of Pakistan. He had no idea what he'd do after that, but at least he'd be alive.

It would be tomorrow afternoon before he'd get to Ibb. He turned to the camel and put one foot in the stirrup. The beast stood before he could swing his other leg over the hump. He tumbled onto his back, glad his foot hadn't been tangled in the stirrup. He managed to hold onto the reins, so at least the camel hadn't wandered off. He scrambled to his feet and screamed "Koosh, koosh, koosh," at the puzzled animal.

The camel started walking along the trail. Ahmed tried to hold it in place, but the camel was bigger and a lot stronger than he was.

He stumbled along beside it, up hills and down, unable to bring it to a halt and not daring to let it go. All of his water was strapped to its side.

After an hour, he gave up trying to stop the camel. It quit shying away from him when he gave up pulling on the reins. He tried yelling "koosh" occasionally, to no effect. By dusk he and the camel walked together, Ahmed talking quietly to himself. He could see the lights of Al Qadi off to his right, but he was still too close to Ta'izz to feel safe entering a town.

By nightfall, he was hungry and thirsty, his feet were aching and blistered, his legs were sore, and he was exhausted. In the moonlight, the camel was leading him. He could barely see the trail by the faint light of a quarter moon. It wasn't long before he twisted his ankle on a rock in the trail. He stumbled and tugged on the reins. The camel stopped.

He gritted his teeth and whispered "koosh." The camel laid down. Relieved, Ahmed hobbled to the saddle, forced himself to stand on his bad ankle while he put the other foot in the stirrup, then swung the leg with the sprained ankle over the hump. This time the camel didn't stand, even after he was seated.

What was the order to rise? he thought. He couldn't focus. Nothing came to mind. He tried a clicking sound out of the side of his mouth, but the camel paid no attention. *Damn, what was that word?* He tried, "hut," and the camel's rear end rose.

Ahmed rode all night, dosing off occasionally and waking abruptly whenever he started to lean left, right, or backward. At dawn he woke to find the camel was grazing in a patch of grass by the trail. It obeyed Ahmed's commands, he dismounted, and raided his food pack again. The camel lowered itself to its knees, stretched out its neck in the sand, and dozed off. Exhausted himself, Ahmed sprawled on his side to give his butt a rest and the two of them slept for a couple of hours before starting again. By mid-morning he heard the sounds of traffic in the distance.

They crested a rise and Ahmed saw a town, Al Mishraq according to his map. He rode into the town and stopped at a little market where he traded his western clothing for the clothes off a local's back. At the edge of town he bathed his feet with bottled water, dried them, and put on a pair of sandals. Dead tired and bone sore, at least he was confident no one looking for Professor Hadi would give a lame man in a worn *ma'awaz* and threadbare, dirty T-shirt a second glance.

He rode into Ibb, asked a local where the bus station was, and found it without trouble.

St. Paul
November 20

Harith called while Jason was sitting in the living room, reading the morning paper. Jason answered Ann's cellphone.

"Jason, my friend! When did you blow into town?"

"I've been home close to a month. By the way, thanks. Ann told me you and Greg did a lot to help her."

"It wasn't much. Do you have a tablet nearby?"

"Hunh?"

"Jason, have you forgotten? I call you whenever I have an urge to watch sports on your big screen television, and I tell you things I'm not supposed to know."

Jason swore under his breath as he hunted for a pen and pad. He'd hoped the cloak-and-dagger nonsense was over. "I have a pen; go ahead."

"Have you heard about our friends Ahmed and Al-Mikhafi?"

"No. What happened?"

"When the camel Ahmed inoculated didn't get sick, Al-Mikhafi sent the remaining fecal samples from Minnesota and the samples they'd collected from Ahmed's camels to an outside lab. They tested the samples and found only BCV—no evidence of a hybrid virus. The insurgents didn't take that well. It was clear even to those guys that Ahmed didn't know what he was doing. They put out a fatwa on Ahmed and beat the crap out of Al-Mikhafi."

"Like having the mob for a banker," Jason said.

"Yeah. Ahmed heard about the fatwa and somehow beat it out of the country. We think he went by camel or bus."

"How did he handle the lack of air-conditioning and room service?"

"He must have learned to rough it. The only word we have of him since he left Ta'izz is an unsubstantiated rumor that he's in a village in the Northwest Frontier. That's like living in the countryside of Yemen, but with frostbite as an extra."

"What about Al-Mikhafi?"

"He hasn't been heard from since he got out of the hospital. He's alive, but I'll bet his jihadi zeal has faded."

Northwest Frontier, Pakistan
November 30

A cold wind whipped around a stone hut on a mountainside in the Kandia tehsil, a highland district between the Indus and Kondia rivers, north of Swat in the Northwest Frontier. The lead-colored sky meant there would be snow or sleet in the wind soon. Ahmed shivered as he drove half a dozen goats up the slope and into the hut. Inside, he tied shut the leather flap that served as a door and packed dried grass around the edges to keep the wind out. In the dark hut, he fumbled to find and light a rusty kerosene lamp. The lamp and body heat from the goats would help him stay warm tonight. He rested on his knees in the goat's side of his home and called one of the goats to him. He picked up an old metal pail in the dim light of the lamp and started milking her. It wasn't much, but it would be dinner.